THE SMACK

THE SMACK

RICHARD LANGE

MULHOLLAND
BOOKS

HODDER

First published in Great Britain in 2017 by Mulholland Books
An imprint of Hodder & Stoughton
An Hachette UK company

1

A CIP catalogue record for this title is available from the British Library

Trade Paperback ISBN 978 1 444 79004 7
eBook ISBN 978 1 444 79005 4

Printed and bound by CPI Group (UK) Ltd, Croydon CR0 4YY

Hodder & Stoughton policy is to use papers that are natural, renewable
and recyclable products and made from wood grown in sustainable forests.
The logging and manufacturing processes are expected to conform to the
environmental regulations of the country of origin.

Hodder & Stoughton Ltd
Carmelite House
50 Victoria Embankment
London EC4Y 0DZ

www.hodder.co.uk

For Kim Turner:

I've so many things to tell you,
or, rather, only one,
but that one huge as the ocean,
as deep and infinite as the sea.

—La Bohème, Act IV

Here's a dollar, mama
Made it in the rain
Here's a dollar, mama
Made it in the rain
It's a hard old dollar
Made it just the same

—Mance Lipscomb, "Rocks and Gravel
Makes a Solid Road"

THE SMACK

1

Rowan Petty considered his options. He could watch the Packer game in his room or downstairs in one of the hotel's bars. The casino even had a small, somnolent sports book where they'd be showing it on five TVs. Today was Thanksgiving, though, so he felt like a change of scenery. He was going a little stir-crazy after spending the past week holed up in a mini suite, working a phone while staring out the floor-to-ceiling windows at what was left of the Reno strip and the snow-dusted hills beyond. It'd be nice to take a walk and eat somewhere besides the hotel's coffee shop.

"Mrs. Carson? How are you today? Good, good. Great to hear. My name's Bill Miller, and I'm vice president of the growth and income division of Golden Triangle Mining Company. I believe you spoke with my associate Mr. Bludsoe yesterday. You did? Wonderful. Now, Mr. Bludsoe indicated that you were interested in more information about the exciting full-partnership shares we're currently offering, and if you have two minutes, I can tell you all about them. Great! Here's the deal: our engineers recently discovered a massive deposit of high-grade ore in one of our mines in Peru, and, as a result, we're giving a select group of investors a limited-time opportunity to join one of the fastest-growing and most successful mining ventures in the world. How's that sound?"

It was all bullshit, of course. There was no mother lode, no mine, nothing but a slick website and some expensive stationery. The bottom rung of the scam was a crew of homeless meth heads and alkies in Miami who cold-called hundreds of numbers a day in search of rubes gullible enough or lonely enough to sit through the initial pitch. The names of these suckers were passed on to Petty, whose job it was to reel them in, touting a 25 percent tax-free return on any investment while at the same time trying to extract as much personal information as possible: bank accounts, credit cards, Social Security numbers. Anyone still on the hook after this he kicked up to Avi, who closed the deals and sent Petty 10 percent of whatever he took off the marks.

Petty wasn't happy about being so low on the totem pole. In fact it was downright humiliating, especially since it was he who'd shown Avi the ropes on a setup exactly like this one, back when the dude was still peddling steaks door-to-door and worrying about his next pimple. Petty was twenty-five then, living in New Jersey. He'd been getting by on his wits since he was fifteen and was bringing in enough from various schemes to give his wife and little girl everything they needed along with some of the extravagances that separated man from beast.

A friend of a friend brought Avi in one day and asked Petty to help the kid out. Petty talked to Avi, and he seemed to be with it, so he took him under his wing, taught him what was what, and let him wet his beak on a silver scam he was running at the time. Good karma, he figured.

Flash-forward to now, fifteen years later. Petty gets hung up in Sacramento, working a real estate hustle that busts. He heads to Reno to try to recoup his losses at the poker tables, but his car breaks down as he hits the city limits—a thousand bucks, the mechanic says, to get it running again. So a rough patch. He scrolls through his contacts, sees Avi's name, and decides to give him a call to see what sort of action he's got going and to check if there might be room for him. And what does the punk say? "You can man a phone, tell the tale, but that's the best I can do."

Telling the tale? The same goddamn job Petty had given him when he took him on way back when? A slap in the face, but at the same time, Petty understood. The law of the jungle was the law of the jungle: nobody gives a fuck about a loser. He punched another number into the phone, cleared his throat, and launched into his spiel again.

"Mrs. Fedor? Happy Thanksgiving. How are you this afternoon?"

He barely made it through his introduction before Mr. Fedor got on the line and told him he must be a real asshole, trying to pull something like this on a holiday. Petty cut the guy off mid-rant and moved on to the next number on his list. Before he could enter it, his personal phone—not the burner he was using to do business with—rang.

The call was from Don O'Keefe, Dandy Don, who'd been a friend of Petty's father. The last Petty heard, Don had dropped way down in class after doing some time. Petty thought about letting the call go to voice mail, but his curiosity got the better of him.

"Hello?" he said.

"Rowan?"

"Don."

"I hear you're in Reno."

"Yeah?"

"Yeah. And guess what? I am, too. I live here now."

"Huh."

Don picked up on Petty's caginess. "Okay, okay," he said. "You want to know who's been talking. It's like this: I called Avi about a line I have on something, and he said he had all he could handle right now, but you might be interested."

Petty got up off the bed and went to the window. A heavy, gray afternoon was growing grayer, and down below, on the wet sidewalk, a solitary figure, hunched against the cold, marched to his fate with grim purposefulness. Petty touched a finger to the glass and stared at the print it left behind. Avi didn't do favors, so siccing Don on him had to be a joke. Petty couldn't hang up on the old man, however. After his dad ran off, Don kept an eye on Rowan and his mom, slipping them a hundred bucks now and then, dropping off groceries, and making sure the gas and electricity got paid. Petty owed him a modicum of respect for that, so he played along.

"My plate's full, too," he said. "But I can spare a minute."

"Let's meet somewhere."

"Can't you tell me about it over the phone?"

"It'll be better in person. I'll buy you a drink and lay it all out."

The barely concealed desperation in Don's voice both saddened and repulsed Petty.

"Today?" he said.

"Why not?" Don said. "I'm staying with my daughter, and I could use a break from her kids. They scream everything they say. Is that some new thing off TV?"

"I don't know," Petty said.

"Anyway, we're eating at seven, so how about four thirty?"

Petty was staying at the Sands Regency Casino Hotel. It sat two blocks west of Virginia Street, where Reno's other downtown casinos were clustered. With rates half that of the places on Virginia, the Sands appealed to retirees, traveling salesmen, penny-slot addicts, and other low rollers who appreciated its clean if slightly worn rooms and the homey, unfussy disposition of its staff. The casino catered to a local crowd, beckoning them with cheap drinks and five-dollar blackjack dealt on faded felts. Dining options included a 1950s-themed coffee shop serving twenty-four-hour breakfast specials, a piss–elegant "Italian steakhouse," and a $10.99 "Carolina Seafood Buffet" on Fridays.

Petty had flopped at worse places—he'd been jumping from cheap hotel to cheap hotel ever since the bank had foreclosed on his Phoenix condo six months ago—but something about being stranded at the Sands at this particular moment in time weighed heavily on him, and he found himself slinking around the place with the humiliated air of deposed royalty. He'd recently turned forty, and this fact caromed inside his head when he stared at the cigarette burn on his room's garish polyester bedspread, ate a dollar hot dog for dinner, washed his underwear in the sink, and got hung up on by widows from Des Moines.

If the slump was temporary, fine. He'd been down before. What haunted him was the possibility that there was more to this lull than there'd been to the others, that he'd finally used up all his luck. Because in the end, you were only given so many chances. And while everybody took an occasional tumble, the cracks healed more slowly as you got older, allowing what little charm you had left to seep right out of you.

Don O'Keefe, for example. Ten years ago, an operator par excellence. At the top of his game, money rolling in from half a dozen different hustles. And now? What the fuck? Things started going downhill for him after his wife died. He'd loved her with all his heart, and the loss made him sloppy. He filled the hole she left with booze, filled the lonely hours with gambling, and eventually got popped in Seattle for a stupid rock-in-a-box scam and served eight months in the King County jail. Dandy Don, who'd never drawn even an overnighter before. He hadn't bounced back after that, had been out six months now and couldn't get anything going. Seventy years old and living on scraps, whatever the hotshots let fall. Former associates whispered behind their hands about him. If they saw him on the street, they crossed to the other side. None of them wanted to look into his eyes. None of them wanted to catch what he had.

Petty raised his first drink of the afternoon to the poor bastard. Because he himself was down to his last five grand, and if this was it, the end of all good things, he wanted someone somewhere to toast *him* someday, remembering him at his best.

He was sitting in the Jackpot Saloon, his favorite of the Sands's three bars, tended to by a skinny old cowgirl with an ugly smile. She wore her hair in a bright red bouffant to compensate and sported the kind of makeup job department store cosmetics clerks gave women in order to sell them a ton of shit they didn't need. She and Petty had become friendly during his stay. She called him Rowan, he called her darlin', and he hoped she had something at home that made her happy, a cat or a favorite TV show.

He'd showered and shaved after getting off the phone with Don, dried his hair, and slapped on some Armani cologne, ninety bucks a bottle. A pair of nice jeans, a dress shirt, his leather coat. He didn't go for pinkie rings and gold rope like the guidos did, preferring to let his watch and shoes do the talking. The Submariner he wore these days was a knockoff, and his Bruno Maglis were showing their age, but both were plenty good enough for Reno. He'd been watching his drinking since going to work for Avi, trying to take the gig seriously, so his first sip of Black Label was a treat. He swished it in his mouth before letting it slide down his throat. Happy fucking Thanksgiving!

"You gonna get some turkey this evening?" the cowgirl asked him.

"Honestly, I never liked turkey much," he replied. "It's tradition and all, I understand that, but I'd rather have a steak."

"You're like my daddy," the cowgirl said. "He used to tell us, 'You know why the pilgrims ate turkey? Because they didn't have KFC.'"

"Sounds like a funny guy."

"For a mean drunk. You ever hear of turducken?"

"That's what—a turkey stuffed inside a duck stuffed inside a chicken?"

The cowgirl laughed and smiled her jagged smile. "Other way around. A chicken inside a duck inside a turkey."

"Oh, right," Petty said. "That'd work a lot better."

He turned in his seat to survey the casino. Because of the holiday it was more crowded than it would normally be at 3:00 p.m. The players at the blackjack table directly in front of him hooted and hollered over the dealer busting, but they were a bunch of suckers. It was a five-dollar single-deck game, which sounded good, because your odds against the house were always better with a single deck than with a shoe, right? Wrong. Not when the payout for a blackjack at the single-deck table was 6:5 instead of the standard 3:2. That changed everything.

9

A basic-strategy player at a twenty-five-dollar 3:2 table being dealt out of an eight-deck shoe could expect to lose $11.20 over the course of eighty hands. At a 6:5 single-deck table, he'd lose twenty-nine dollars.

Over the past few years casinos everywhere had quietly been switching their single-deck tables to this version of the game, and even though the changed payout was printed right there on the felt, Joe Schmoe, in town for a weekend blowout, still sat down and handed over his hard-earned cash, subscribing to the old dictum that single-deck was where it was at.

Petty had nothing against a sharper taking off a mark, but this swindle was so blatant it depressed him. There was nothing slick about it, nothing skillful. It took no balls. The gaming-industry bean counters were simply exploiting the casual gambler's tendency to cling to the common wisdom rather than run the numbers himself. Petty couldn't decide who pissed him off more, the corporate nickel-and-dimers or the cinches at the tables who allowed themselves to be fleeced this way.

His head ached thinking about it. He'd been breathing nothing but the recycled air of the hotel for the past week, and the smutty funk of cigarette smoke, desperation, and disappointment had settled into his bones like a cancer. Hoping to preserve the tiny spark of holiday cheer he'd managed to muster, he downed his Scotch and hurried for the exit.

2

THE COLD GOOSED PETTY AS SOON AS HE STEPPED OUTSIDE. He winced and fumbled for the zipper of his coat. Even with his collar turned up and his hands fisted deep in his pockets, he shivered. He didn't have clothes for this weather, had planned to be somewhere warmer by now.

The feathery snow that had begun to fall brightened the dirty slush left over from the day before. Delicate flakes mounded on the dented cars and muddy trucks in the Sands parking lot and clung to Petty's eyelashes. He hated snow, hated ice. The antipathy stemmed from a fear of slipping, almost a phobia. The mere possibility of losing his footing made him feel like his skin was too tight. He wasn't so much worried about getting hurt if he fell as he was afraid of looking ridiculous on the way down. He couldn't bear to be laughed at. He set off up 4th toward Virginia, carefully placing each step.

A car crawled past with its headlights already on. Night was still two hours away, but it seemed later. Clouds obscured the sun, the snow damped the sound, and the steel-gray ponderousness of a premature winter dusk intensified the melancholy carnival come-on of the casino neon up ahead.

The street was lined with run-down motels, most of which were boarded up. Those that continued to limp along rented rooms by both the month and the hour, casting a wide net. A tall, thin black chick in a pink down trench coat and crazy high heels stood in the driveway of the Rancho Sierra Motor Hotel. She pretended to be engrossed in her phone but raised her eyes and smiled whenever a car whooshed by. She was twenty-one, twenty-two, with great lips and great teeth and a long blond wig that made her look famous. Petty smiled back at her when she stepped out to block his way.

"How are you, baby?" she cooed.

"Doing great," he said. "How are you?"

"Cold," she said. "Want to warm me up?" She opened her coat to flash him the stars-and-stripes halter top and denim short shorts she was wearing underneath. In this weather. You had to admire that kind of fortitude.

"It's tempting," Petty said.

"So go on and give in. Treat yourself for Turkey Day."

"How about I treat you instead? Let me buy you a drink."

"Why you want to waste all that time? I got a room here. We can cozy up right this minute."

"I'm old-school," Petty said. "I like to flirt first."

"Flirt?" the whore repeated, making a "What the fuck you talkin' about?" face. "You do understand I'm workin', don't you?"

"Sure," Petty said. "But I also know Nevada law says you get a coffee break."

"Ha!" the whore said. "Listen at you. I like you, Old

School." She punched a number into her phone and turned away to speak quietly to whoever answered.

Petty waited, shifting back and forth from foot to foot. He had a soft spot for hookers. Not the dope fiends or the spooky man haters but the ones who had their shit together and treated hooking as a business. He'd met some smart whores over the years, some truly sharp ladies.

"I'll call you," the whore said into the phone. The person on the other end kept talking, and the whore shouted, "When you gonna figure out I ain't listenin'?" and ended the call.

"I don't want to get you in trouble," Petty said.

"Please," the whore said. "Don't nobody own this bad bitch." She slipped her arm through Petty's and pulled him close. "You got sexy eyes, you know that?"

"Not as sexy as yours," Petty said. "Now, mind the ice here."

As much as he disliked snow, he had to admit that the feathery tumble of the flakes coming down was a pretty sight. He watched them fall through the dregs of daylight as he and the whore walked toward the casinos and wondered if it was true that every one was unique or if that was just more of the stupid shit they sold you when you were a kid.

The whore went by Tinafey. "Like that white lady on TV, but all one word," she said. Petty didn't ask her real name, had no reason to. They sat at a table in a lounge at the Silver Legacy, where a guy at a piano sang a Beatles song, then something by Neil Diamond. Tinafey ordered Kahlua and coffee.

"I'll have the same," Petty told the waitress.

"Where you from?" Tinafey asked him.

"You mean originally?"

"Sure."

"I was born in Detroit, but we moved around," Petty said.

He always told whores the truth. They could spot a lie a mile off. "My dad was a gambler, and my mom was a gambler's wife."

"Poor thing," Tinafey said.

"We followed my dad's luck. A couple years here, a couple years there. Chicago, Vegas, Atlantic City. He ran a back-room casino in Philly for a while."

"Did you like movin' around or hate it?"

"Would it have mattered? I was a kid. Nobody cared what I thought. Dad eventually dumped us in Florida and took off with a Mary Kay saleswoman. Must have been the pink Cadillac."

"And how'd you turn out?"

"Growing up like that?" Petty said. He shrugged and swept a bit of cigarette ash off the table.

"So you're a rambler and a gambler, too, huh?" Tinafey said.

"I had a place in Phoenix, but I'm between cities now."

"That's okay. The world needs ramblers and gamblers."

"What about you?" Petty said. "Where are you from?"

"I'm from Memphis," Tinafey said.

"I hear it in your voice."

"Yeah, but I been all over. I even went to Mexico, to Cabo San Lucas."

"How was that?"

"Baby, it was like a dream, the ocean and the desert come together like that. I laid in the sun, drank margaritas, and fell asleep every night listenin' to the waves, happy just smellin' the air. I told my friend I was with, I said, 'Girl, I could be poor here, I swear to God.' You wouldn't need nothin' but a hammock, some rice and beans, and all that beauty."

She smiled, thinking of it, and Petty saw her real face for the first time, the one you fall in love with. He smiled, too.

"You gonna take me to Cabo San Lucas?" Tinafey asked him, spoofing her wistfulness.

"Grab your purse and let's go," he said.

"A boy down there asked me if I was a model, and he wasn't jokin'."

The waitress delivered their drinks. They had whipped cream on them, like hot chocolate. Tinafey scooped hers up and ate it separately, then played around with Petty, licking the spoon. He got her talking about her customers. Whores always had good stories about their johns and all the kinds of freaky they were. Tinafey leaned in close and spoke quietly. She had class, didn't want the whole lounge to hear about the Zucchini Man, who liked her to use a squash on him at the same time he was doing her, or the old guy who paid her twenty-five bucks for used condoms. Petty's favorite was the dude who got on all fours underneath a special blanket he brought with him. He told Tinafey he turned into a kitten when he was like that, and he'd crawl around and mew for a while before she stuck her feet under the blanket so he could lick them with his little kitten tongue.

"It tickled," Tinafey said, "but he got mad if you laughed."

Petty checked his watch and saw he had fifteen minutes to get to his meeting with Don. He took a hundred out of his wallet and slid it across the table.

"I've got to run," he said.

Tinafey feigned surprise. "I thought this was foreplay."

"This was two friends having a drink," Petty said. "If we ever get to foreplay, you'll know it."

Tinafey picked up the money and tucked it into her sequined clutch. "When you decide you want somethin' more, you know where I'll be," she said.

Petty stood and slipped on his coat.

"You have a happy Thanksgiving," he said to Tinafey.

"You, too," she replied, already on her phone.

The piano player, a skeleton in an ill-fitting tux, tinkled out a sweet rendition of James Taylor's "Fire and Rain." He probably hated having to sing it night after night, did it on autopilot while wondering how many smokes were left in his pack, but it was one of Petty's mom's favorites, something he remembered her humming while she washed dishes, so he dropped a five in the guy's jar on his way out.

The cavernous second-floor sports book at Club Cal Neva resembled a homeless shelter, filled as it was this afternoon with bums on the lam from the cold outside. Shaggy, bedraggled men wrapped in greasy parkas slouched on the chairs and couches that faced the wall of big-screen TVs, the plastic grocery bags and filthy backpacks containing their possessions stowed at their feet. Most pretended to watch television, but a few dozed, slack-jawed and snoring, in violation of the casino's no-sleeping rule. The security guards let them be, giving everyone a break for once, the holiday and all.

A must of unwashed bodies and mildewed clothing wrinkled Petty's nose when he stepped off the escalator that brought him up from the casino. He surveyed the human flotsam left high and dry in the room and wished Don had picked somewhere else to meet. Being so close to so much ruinous luck and so many bad choices made him nervous, especially with his own ship racing toward the rocks.

Don waved from his seat at the big square bar at the center of everything and gestured to an empty chair beside him as if to say, "Look what I got you." It had been fifteen years since Petty had last seen him. He'd let his hair go gray—he used to dye it black—and wattles of loose skin dangled under his chin.

"If I'd known you were dressing up, I'd have put on a suit," he said, fingering the collar of his Tommy Bahama Hawaiian shirt. He was wearing baggy khakis with it, and grandpa tennis shoes that had Velcro straps instead of laces. Not so dandy anymore. "I keep it casual these days," he said by way of apology.

"Whatever works," Petty said.

Don chuckled through their handshake, saying, "That's right, that's right." He'd missed a spot shaving, too, left a patch of white stubble on his chin, but Petty cut him some slack. Old folks slow down, he reminded himself. It was natural.

"Scotch, right? Rocks?" Don said.

"You remember," Petty said.

"Everything," Don said. He waved the bartender over and put in the order.

"How's Reno?" Petty said. "You like it here?"

Don shrugged. "It's where I am, where I ended up," he said. "My options were limited."

"I heard about Myra."

"I'm sure you did. There's nothing people love more than passing on a sad story about somebody else and acting like they give a shit. But the bottom line is, it wrecked me. I'm still a wreck, and I'm not ashamed to say it. We were married forty-two years. We raised three kids. She was the only thing I gave a damn about. The kids, but that's different. I struck oil when I found her. I hit pay dirt."

His eyes shone, and his voice went hoarse. The bartender delivered the drinks and melted away.

"To Myra," Petty said, raising his glass.

"Give me a break," Don said. "You barely knew her."

"Yeah, but cheers to *anybody* who put up with *you* for that fucking long," Petty said.

Don clinked Petty's glass and said, "And to your old man, too."

"Nah, fuck him," Petty said.

"He did his best."

"That's everybody's excuse."

The two men sat in silence, pretending to watch the pregame show on one of the TVs, until Don finally said, "Anyfuckingway, what about you? You and Carrie split up, right? And you kept Samantha?"

Petty hid his frown behind his glass. So people were talking about him, too.

"That's pretty much it," he said. "Carrie took off with Hug McCarthy twelve years ago, and I haven't seen her since."

"Hug McCarthy?" Don said. "He's a bad penny. What was she thinking?"

"You'd have to ask her," Petty said. "I dragged Sam around with me for a while but ended up sending her to live with my mom. It was better for school and everything. She's going to college in L.A. now."

Don moaned. "I remember her in diapers," he said.

Petty was irritated at the old man for making him think about the past. Enough small talk; time to get to it.

"What did you want to discuss?" he said.

Don glanced at the bartender, at a passing waitress, at a derelict ordering a dollar Bud Light. "Let's move somewhere more private," he said, as if everybody in the place were eavesdropping on them.

They relocated to a booth at the edge of the room, as far from the crowd gathered around the bar as they could get. Petty waited with gritted teeth while Don spent five minutes trying to shim the wobbly table with a cardboard coaster. When the old man finally had it to his liking, he straightened his stupid shirt, took a sip of his drink, and leaned in to speak quietly.

"This is the big one," he said.

"All right," Petty replied.

"Avi'll be sorry he didn't listen when I brought it to him."

"He's a busy man."

Don snorted. "Don't give me that," he said. "I don't know how you swallow it from that prick."

"I'm not swallowing anything," Petty said. "I'm helping him out temporarily."

"That's not what he says. He says you came crawling to him, begging for some action. He says you're desperate."

"Oh, yeah?"

"'I've got all I can handle right now,' he said, 'but Rowan's desperate for a score. Why don't you take it to him?'"

Petty kept his face blank, acted like it wasn't anything, but inside he was knotted up. Fuck Avi. And fuck Don. A year ago he'd have been on his way out the door by now, and even in a slump there was a limit to how much shit he was willing to stand for.

His voice sounded angrier than he wanted it to when he said, "I'm not desperate, Don. Things are slow right now, but I'm not fucking desperate. So don't think you can pull some rinky-dink something on me because I'll grasp at straws."

"Whoa, whoa, whoa," Don said. "This is legit, I swear."

"All I'm saying is, I've been grifting long enough to know that guys like you—like me, okay?—are cannibals who wouldn't think twice about gnawing one of their own down to the bone if they got hungry enough, and for all I know you might be that hungry."

"I'll sketch it out for you," Don said. "If it sounds like something you can do something with, we'll talk further. If not, hey—we shake hands and part friends."

Petty picked up his drink and swirled the ice in the glass. "You've got three minutes," he said.

Don leaned in even closer. "You know I did a little time recently, right? I'm sure word went around about that, too. Well, while I was inside, I met this kid, your typical fuckup, your typical junkie, in again as soon as he got out, one of those, but we became friendly. Okay, not *friendly*, but you're in there, you're bored, so we used to shoot the breeze sometimes, swap stories.

"Now, this kid didn't have the brains God gave a fucking billy goat. I mean, he was constitutionally incapable of keeping his mouth shut about shit he should've been keeping his mouth shut about. Ninety-nine percent of it was jibber-jabber, useless, him bragging about all the badasses he knew on the outside and all the jobs he'd supposedly pulled. But one day one of his stories caught my attention. No. More than that. It got my heart going. It made my palms itch. So I set about reeling him in. I gave him stamps, made deposits to his canteen, and gradually I dragged the details out of him. And what I got—well, let's just say that if you took what he told me and were willing to do a little legwork, you might be looking at the score of your life."

Petty sat back with a sad smile. "Seriously, Don?" he said. "Off a junkie's jailhouse ramble?"

"The kid was useless. I stated that right off," Don said. "But if he was even halfway on the level regarding this thing, it'd definitely be worth looking into."

"What thing?" Petty said. "What's the deal?"

"Just like that?" Don said.

"Why'd you bring me here if you're not gonna tell me?"

"I...well, I..." The old man was flustered. Dandy Don, the smoothest talker Petty had ever met, tripped up in the middle of a pitch. Unmasked. *Man,* Petty thought. *We're all going down.*

"Okay, all right, sure," Don said, regaining his composure. "I'll tell you. Why not? The whole thing starts in Afghanistan, with a soldier stationed at Bagram Airfield, the main base over there. This soldier is in charge of paying Afghan trucking companies for deliveries they make to other bases, supplies and shit, and the payments are all made in cash, dollars, because cash is all the towelheads trust. What eventually happens—and I don't know what sort of idiots we've got running things there, because a blind man could see this coming from a mile off—what eventually happens is, this soldier cuts a deal with the trucking companies where he pays them for deliveries that never happen, and the companies kick back a percentage of these payments to him.

"He then passes the money along to another soldier at the base, a guy whose job is packing containers with gear for shipment back to the U.S. This second guy hides the cash in the containers, slaps a special military seal on the boxes so they won't be inspected by customs, and sends them to an army base in North Carolina. A soldier there retrieves the money from the containers and sends it to another guy, and this guy—get this—stows the money in a safe in his apartment, the plan being they'll divvy the take when everybody gets back from overseas."

His story finished, Don sat back and grinned.

"So what's your play?" Petty said.

"Well, obviously, someone needs to get into that safe," Don said.

"Someone."

"You!"

Petty shook his head. He sipped his drink and said, "Not that I believe a word of this, but how much money are we talking about?"

"If you don't believe what I've told you so far, you're definitely not gonna believe this."

"Try me."

"Two million."

"Two million dollars?"

"So my buddy said."

"Your buddy the junkie. And where did you say he got his information?"

"His brother was the soldier in North Carolina, the one in charge of getting the money off the base. He got lit one night and laid the whole thing out for my pal. Diarrhea of the mouth runs in the family, apparently."

A commotion erupted near the betting windows, two bums going at it over a D cell battery. "Gimme that, motherfucker," the big bum screamed, then punched the little bum in the face. The little bum dropped to the floor, and the big bum raised his boot to stomp him, but a security guard stepped in to wrestle him away. A second guard yanked the little bum to his feet and walked him to the escalator while a smart-ass at the bar applauded.

Petty watched the ruckus while thinking about two million dollars sitting in a safe in some stooge's apartment somewhere, thinking how insane that sounded. And he couldn't help it; he started thinking of ways to get hold of it.

"The safe complicates things," he said to Don. "It means you can't just break in while the guy's out and make off with the cash."

"Right," Don said. "So?"

"So you'd have to do it while the guy's there," Petty said. "You'd have to get him to let you in, then you'd have to persuade him to give you the combination. And that means a gun."

"That'd work."

Two million dollars. The kind of score Petty had always dreamed about. Abracadabra, and all his problems solved in an instant and forever. But the reality of the situation was something else.

"The thing is," he said to Don, "I'm pretty sure this junkie was yanking your crank."

"But what if he wasn't?" Don said.

"Then we come to number two: that's not my line. Robbery, rough stuff. I *talk* chumps out of their money."

"You're a smart guy," Don said. "You'll figure something out. Hell, you wouldn't even have to grab all of it for it to be a great score. Getting your hands on just some would make you a happy man."

True enough, but Petty still couldn't see himself drawing a gun on some dude and putting on enough of a badass act to convince him he'd pull the trigger if he didn't get what he wanted. He wasn't that desperate.

"You know what?" he said. "I'm gonna pass."

"Take some time to think about it," Don said.

"I already know. It's not for me."

"Don't tell me that, Rowan. Tell me yes."

"I can't, Don. I'm sorry."

"Come on."

"No."

Don slumped in his chair. He looked tired, tired of everything, and Petty could tell he'd been the man's last hope. After a few seconds of awkward silence, Don sighed deeply, struggled to his feet, and pulled on an ugly purple down jacket. "I've got to go," he said.

"Have another drink," Petty said.

"My daughter's holding dinner. Holidays are a big deal to her."

The two men shook hands.

"Be careful driving in the snow," Petty said.

"Yeah, yeah," Don said and shuffled off.

Petty returned to the bar and ordered a beer this time. The Packer game was kicking off. He stared at the screen, but his mind kept picking over the past and worrying about the future. Someone came up at one point and asked him the score, and he had no idea. Across the bar one of the homeless men clutched his head and rocked in his chair. "No, no, no," he muttered. It was more than Petty could bear this evening. He went downstairs and took a seat at an empty 6:5 single-deck blackjack table and proceeded to lose two hundred bucks in twenty minutes.

3

It was full dark by the time Petty left the Cal Neva. The snow had stopped, but his coat was still no match for the cold. Virginia Street was deserted, what with everyone watching the game or eating buffet turkey or throwing away their money in the casinos. The lights stained the wet sidewalk urgent red, electric blue, and acid yellow, and steam boiled out of various vents and grates.

He had tacos for dinner at a Mexican restaurant wedged between a failed tattoo parlor and a pawnshop closed for the holiday. The restaurant was crowded with families spread out over two and three tables, and Petty sensed that the waitress felt sorry for him because he was alone, the way she kept asking how everything was and refilling his water before he'd even reached the bottom of the glass. Her sympathy annoyed him.

After dinner he thought he'd go see the magician playing the showroom at Harrah's. Hokey card tricks, vanishing doves—maybe the guy'd even saw a hot chick in half. But when he checked the starting time on his phone, he found that the show was dark for the night. Okay. Fine. He'd head back to the Sands, then—drink himself jolly and play some Hold'Em. Thanks to TV and the Internet, every monkey who could fan cards thought he was a rounder these days, and Petty always got a kick out of schooling their asses.

Back on 4th he saw Tinafey from two blocks away, still working her spot. He started thinking about her long legs and naughty smile, the little gap between her front teeth through which you sometimes caught a flash of bright pink tongue. Another visit with her might be what he actually needed, this time let her do her thing. He hadn't been laid in two months, had been so busy scrambling he hadn't even thought about it, but now, suddenly, it was *all* he could think about. Tinafey looked up from her phone and grinned as he approached, and he found himself shivering more from anticipation than from the cold.

"About time," she said.

"You knew I'd be back, huh?"

"Of course. I hypnotized you."

"You said you had a room?"

"Right here," she said, indicating the motel behind her. "Ready for me to blow your mind?"

"I'm counting on it."

"I'd hold your hand, but mine's like ice. Come here."

Tinafey crooked her arm and snuggled up to Petty when he snagged it with his. They walked across the parking lot to a room on the ground floor. Tinafey unlocked the door, and they stepped inside.

The room smelled of skunky marijuana and some kind of "fresh" scented cleaning product. Bed, dresser, TV. A painting of an Indian slumped despondently over his horse hung on the wall, and the lamp on the nightstand created more problems than it solved, the shadows it threw turning the bedspread sinister and the mangy carpet into roadkill.

"Pardon the mess," Tinafey said. She plucked a red bra and thong off of the floor, tossed them into a wheeled suitcase on the dresser, and zipped the suitcase shut. She closed the pizza box next to the suitcase, too, and rearranged a couple of two-liter bottles of soda, a jug of wine, and a fifth of tequila. The Doritos and chocolate doughnuts she shoved into a drawer.

"You want a drink?" she said.

"Sure," Petty said.

She poured three fingers of Cuervo into a plastic cup and handed it to him. He sipped the stuff and wondered what he should do next. The worst part of being with a whore was figuring out how to get down to business. It was different every time. He was grateful when Tinafey took charge, guiding him to the bed and saying, "Go ahead and sit." She backed away and did a sexy little routine where she slowly opened her coat and let it slide off so he got a good look at her tight body in that halter top and those short shorts.

"It's gonna cost you two hundred," she said.

Petty pulled out his wallet, removed the bills, and held them out to her. She took the money and tucked it into the pocket of her shorts.

"You want to see these titties?" she said, running her hands up her sides to cup them.

"For starters," Petty said. He had to clear his throat first.

She helped him along like that. "You want me to take my clothes off now?" "You want me to take off your clothes?" "You want to lie back?" "You want me to suck on that dick?"

Petty answered yes to everything and ended up naked on the

bed, trying not to pop too soon as Tinafey worked magic with her mouth. He was thinking that this was going to be worth every penny when the door to the room swung open and a big black dude in an Atlanta Falcons jacket stepped inside. He rushed the bed, shoved Tinafey aside, and threw himself on top of Petty, wrapping his hands around his throat.

"Bo!" Tinafey yelled. "What the fuck you doin'?"

"What the fuck *you* doin'?" Bo yelled back.

Petty struggled against Bo's hold, tried to grab a finger to break it, but the bastard punched him in the face with a fist like a twenty-pound sledge and knocked the fight out of him.

"Who you think you are, fuckin' my wife?" Bo said. He moved up so that he was sitting on Petty's chest and squeezed Petty's windpipe even tighter. "I could kill you right now, you know that? I could kill you and get away with it."

Tinafey leaped onto Bo's back and pounded at him. He struck out with his elbow, catching her in the head and forcing her to retreat. He punched Petty again, in the ear this time. "What you gon' do to make things right?" he said. "What you gon' do?" He loosened his grip so that Petty could speak.

"There's two hundred dollars in my wallet," Petty said.

"Two hundred dollars?" Bo said. "If you caught me fuckin' your wife, would two hundred dollars do it for you?"

Tinafey reappeared, brandishing the jug of wine. She raised it with both hands, let out a roar, and brought the bottle down hard on the back of Bo's head. Bo released Petty and sat back, stunned. Tinafey hit him again. His eyes rolled, and a string of drool hung from his lower lip. He toppled over sideways.

"That's what you get, layin' hands on me!" Tinafey shouted.

Petty scrambled off the bed. He gathered his clothes and began to dress.

"You all right?" he asked Tinafey.

"That motherfucker can't hurt me," she said, but Petty could see she was shaking. Her wig had been knocked askew, and her right eye was swollen. She crossed her arms over her tits and stared at Bo, who lay motionless on the bed.

"Did I kill him?" she said.

Petty wondered the same thing. He bent over the body and peered into Bo's face. Bad breath still wheezed out of the bastard, and his eyeball twitched when Petty lifted the lid.

"He's alive," Petty said to Tinafey. "But you fucked him up pretty good." He went back to buttoning his shirt.

"I wish I *had* killed him," Tinafey said. "The motherfucker."

"Is he really your husband?"

"Used to be, but we been divorced for a while. He showed up here outta nowhere a couple days ago, talkin' 'bout he was gonna be my man again. I told him fuck that, I like bein' on my own, but he didn't want to hear it."

"So you let him come in and rob your tricks?"

"Are you blind?" Tinafey snapped. "Didn't I just bash his goddamn head in?"

"He had a key to the room."

Tinafey picked up her coat from the floor and wrapped it around herself. "I been lettin' him stay here," she said. "He doesn't have any money, no car, nothin'. I felt sorry for him. I shouldn't have, but I did. He's supposed to be leavin' tomorrow, said one of his bitches was wirin' him the money for a ticket back to Atlanta. That was probably a lie, though. He lies all the time."

Bo groaned and went back to snoring. Tinafey began to cry. "He's gonna kill me when he wakes up," she said.

Petty didn't want to be around when he came to, either. He put on his shoes and grabbed his coat.

"Look here," Tinafey continued. She pulled up the sleeve of her coat and leaned into the light. Petty saw four or five circular scars on the underside of her arm. "He did that with a cigarette the first time I left him, threatened to sew my pussy shut, too, and throw lye in my face."

"And you still let him stay here?" Petty said.

"I told you—I felt sorry for him," Tinafey said. "He swore he'd changed. 'I understand you don't want to start up with me again,' he said, 'but let me at least be your friend.'" She collapsed in the only chair in the room, sat there sniffling and shaking her head. "I'm not stupid," she said, "but I guess soft-hearted's almost the same thing."

Petty checked his pants for his wallet, his coat for his phone. Everything was where it was supposed to be. He walked to the door, then stopped short. Tinafey had probably saved his life by knocking Bo out. He couldn't leave her here to take a beating—or worse.

"Grab your stuff, and I'll get you a cab to another hotel," he said. "You can stay there until this asshole takes off or you figure out what you want to do next."

"I don't know," Tinafey moaned. "I don't know."

Petty knelt in front of her and made her look into his face. "*I* know," he said. "I know this fucker doesn't give a shit about you. I know you need to get the hell out of here. So put your clothes on, grab your stuff, and let's go."

She stared at him for few seconds, wiping at her nose with the backs of her hands, then made her decision.

One of the wheels on the suitcase was broken, so Petty ended up carrying it the two blocks to the Sands. Tinafey trotted along beside him in her stiletto heels, a duffel bag slung over her shoulder. A passing truck honked for no reason, and Petty ducked. The brawl in the room had put him on edge. He didn't even feel the cold anymore.

He and Tinafey hadn't spoken since fleeing the motel. He was irritated at her for leaving a hundred dollars on the dresser for Bo. The inexhaustible, irrational compassion of some women had always confounded him. What they should have done was roll Bo up in the bedspread and take turns stomping him black and blue.

He led Tinafey to the Sands main entrance. A taxi was parked at the curb. Petty told the driver to open the trunk. The guy popped it from the inside, couldn't be bothered to get out. Petty put the suitcase in, but Tinafey hesitated when he turned to her for the duffel.

"Where you sendin' me?" she said.

"A nice place out by the airport," he said. "Bo'll never find you there."

"You sure?"

"Not unless you call and tell him where you are, and you wouldn't do that, would you?"

Tinafey frowned at his sarcasm.

Two cowboys walked out of the hotel, both smoking big cigars. Tinafey waited until they passed before saying, "Can't I stay with you tonight?"

"What do you mean?"

"I still owe you a party."

"Don't worry about that."

"I promise I'll be on my way first thing in the morning." She touched his hand. "I'm scared."

And she was, Petty could tell. Looking into her eyes, he could see this wasn't a scam. Against his better judgment, he reached into the trunk and took out her suitcase. He felt a little noble; he felt a little doomed.

"What the hell," he said. "Couple of drinks, couple of laughs."

"That's right, baby," Tinafey cooed. "Coupla drinks, coupla laughs." She cuddled up to him as they passed through the double doors of the hotel and headed toward the casino, with its eternal promise of warmth and light and a future that could turn on a dime.

4

PETTY COULDN'T READ THE ROAD SIGNS IN THE DREAM. HE WAS frantically lost on an interstate he was certain he'd driven before. Jumbled letters and numbers flashed past, and glowing arrows pointed every which way. What a relief it was when he woke suddenly in his room at the Sands, lying in his bed instead of sweating behind the wheel of his car. Bright daylight burned at the edges of the blackout curtains drawn across the windows, and Tinafey slept silently, out of his reach now, her back to him, the sheet pulled taut around her.

It had taken them more than a couple of drinks to loosen up last night, to get to those laughs, but once there, they'd thrown themselves into having a good time with the zeal of people who knew how rare good times were. They danced some, gambled some, and ignored any worries that Bo might stumble upon them, hungry for payback.

"That man is so high right now he can't even crawl,"

Tinafey assured Petty. "He's on another planet in another universe."

They ended up in bed, Tinafey riding Petty like a bucking horse. He remembered every toss of her head, every bounce of her tits, and how her pussy gripped him like it'd never let go. When it was over she bent to kiss him, pressed her sweat-slick chest to his, and whispered, "Ooh, Daddy, you wore me *out*." He drifted off with a smile on his face.

He smiled again now as he watched her sleep. *I like this girl,* he thought. And she must like him, too, if she'd trusted him enough to stay the night. He considered waking her to see if she wanted coffee from the snack bar downstairs but decided to let her be.

He pulled on sweatpants and a hoodie and ran a brush through his hair. Before he left the room he put on his watch and pocketed his wallet and phone. A hooker in Vegas once snuck out with every dollar he had in the world, and as much as he dug Tinafey, he wasn't somebody who got burned twice.

The line at the snack bar stretched into the casino. Petty took his place at the end, the ceaseless chatter of the slots adding an extra helping of pain to his hangover. "Wheel! Of! Fortune!" one of them blared over waves of canned applause, while another broadcast the sound of coins clinking into a metal tray even though it paid off with a paper ticket that had to be redeemed by the cashier.

Two big women wearing Mardi Gras beads and cardboard tiaras preceded him in line. Their matching purple T-shirts commemorated Sarah's bachelorette party. One of them cradled a shivering Chihuahua. She kissed its head and baby-talked while it licked her face.

"What time did you all get to bed?" the dog lady asked her friend.

"I don't know," the other woman replied. "All's I remember is eating nachos around three."

"Did you win anything?"

"Don't ask."

"How much did you lose?"

"I said don't ask."

Petty fingered the spot on his cheek where one of Bo's punches had landed. It hurt so much he was surprised there wasn't a bruise. His phone went crazy. He pulled it out and saw that it was Avi calling. At 7:30 a.m. The morning after a holiday.

"You didn't send me any fish yesterday," Avi said.

"I knocked off early," Petty said.

"You decided that all by yourself?"

"Nobody's gonna talk to a salesman on Thanksgiving, with the family there and everything."

"What about people who don't have families?"

The women in front of Petty spotted another woman they knew and called to her across the casino. This upset the Chihuahua, which started barking.

"Where the fuck are you, the zoo?" Avi said.

"Yeah, the zoo," Petty said. "Dodging monkey shit."

"You ought to be working. It's what time already?"

Petty imagined Avi looking at his watch, trying to remember where Petty was, then calculating the time difference between Reno and Miami, not sure if it was two or three hours.

"Eight, nine," Avi continued. "It's almost eleven here. You ought to be on the phone."

Back in Jersey, when he was training Avi, Petty caught wind the kid was sleeping in a car and let him crash on his couch. He sprang for lunches so the dude didn't have to live off Tastykakes and McDonald's and had Carrie set an extra plate at dinner sometimes. None of this mattered to Avi now. He had his head so far up his own ass he couldn't see where he'd come from or where he was going. He'd been treating Petty like dirt ever since he'd started working for him, and Petty was fed up with it.

"Hey," Petty said. "Watch your tone. I'm not on any clock, and you're not paying for my time, so I'll get on the fucking phone when I want to get on the fucking phone."

"Hey, you," Avi said. "You're the one who called begging for work, sad-sacking it like 'Come on, man, I taught you this game, remember?'"

"That's not true?" Petty said. "I didn't teach you?"

"So what if it is?" Avi said. "I need people around me who want to work hard and make money. If you're looking to take it easy, try Walmart. I need you to be fired up. I need you to be amped about what we're doing."

"Fuck you. I've made you plenty of money."

"There's no such thing as plenty of money, and you're a perfect example. I don't ever want to be scrabbling for handouts like you are."

Scrabbling for handouts. That's how the dude saw him. That's how everybody saw him. Petty felt sick.

"I told you to watch your tone," he said.

"You don't like it, hit the road," Avi said.

"I'm taking today off," Petty said.

"You don't even hear me, do you?"

"The whole town can hear you. I'm just not listening."

"Yeah? Well, hear this: if tomorrow you don't send me five leads that pan out, you're done. And what I mean is, each lead better be good for at least five grand."

"I don't have any control over that. You're the one who does the squeezing."

"Tough!" Avi yelled. "Tough! Five fish worth five grand or find another charity."

Avi wasn't going to back down, he wasn't made that way, so Petty decided to drop the matter for now, before his own head exploded.

"I've got to go," he said.

"Yeah, you've got to go," Avi said. "You've got to go work that fucking phone."

The connection went dead. Petty found himself standing at the counter, the girl behind it giving him a strange look.

"What?" he said to her.

"Can I help you?" she asked for the third time.

"Two large coffees," he said. "And what else do you have? Doughnuts?"

It was clear to him now: the time had come to make a move. A big move. He'd been working the same old scams for twenty years, and the same old scams weren't getting him anywhere. And a fuckhead like Avi talking to him that way? Unacceptable. Unacceptable. Two seconds later he was on the phone again, waving the counter girl quiet when she asked about here or to go.

Tinafey was still asleep when he got back to the room, and it looked like she hadn't stirred the whole time he'd been gone. Gathering some clothes, he tiptoed into the bathroom to change.

He stared at himself in the mirror as he brushed his teeth. Guys he knew had broken overnight, gone from looking thirty to looking fifty so quickly that you wondered if they were sick. But he was hanging in there. And really, it wasn't your appearance that mattered most anyhow. He'd heard that people age in two ways, physically and mentally, and mentally he was still firing on all cylinders. Okay, maybe not this morning, with the hangover and all, but most days, bro, you better keep one hand on your wallet and the other on your wife, because he could talk his way into both.

It struck him that he was giving himself a pep talk, and he turned away from his reflection, ashamed of his insecurity. Pathetic.

Tinafey rolled over and squinted at him when he walked back into the room. Petty was glad to see that the swelling around her eye, from Bo elbowing her, had gone down.

"There's coffee if you want it," he said. "I can heat it in the microwave."

She yawned and scratched her head. Her real hair was cut short, close to the scalp. "What time is it?" she said.

"Eight," he said.

"And you're up already?"

"I have a meeting."

"When?"

"In half an hour. I'm picking my car up from the shop on the way. When I get back, we'll go to breakfast, and I'll drive you to the other hotel."

Tinafey sat up but kept herself covered with the sheet. "Can I take a shower before I go?" she said.

"Sure," Petty said.

"Ain't you sweet," Tinafey said. "Go ahead and gimme that coffee. I don't mind it cold."

Petty handed her the cup. "You know what?" he said. "You're as pretty now as you were last night."

"Ha!"

"Seriously."

Tinafey shook her head. She popped the lid off the coffee and took a sip. "You mind openin' the curtains?"

Petty walked over and drew them aside, and the room was flooded with pearly light. Outside, a thin veil of clouds scrimmed a bright blue sky, and the sun gleamed off the new snow blanketing the hills.

"I have to go," Petty said.

"Come here," Tinafey said. She pulled him down and kissed him on the lips. "For luck," she said.

"What makes you think I need luck?" Petty said.

"Everybody needs luck," Tinafey said.

Petty couldn't argue with that.

He took a cab to the garage that was putting a new alternator in his Mercedes, a silver 2010 E550. He'd bought the car brand new from a Russian "broker" for half sticker price, paid cash and hadn't asked any questions. There was now a dent in the passenger-side door and a small tear in the leather of the backseat, but the car had run fine until it died the other day. The repair cost him a grand, so he was down to four thousand in cash and a few thousand left on his credit cards.

The Starbucks on 5th looked like every other Starbucks in the world. That's why people liked them, Petty figured. No surprises. A couple of smokers braved the cold to sit on the patio out front, while inside the usual contingent of laptoppers pecked away at whatever it was they were always pecking away at. Don had staked out a table in the corner. A newspaper was spread out before him, and he squinted at it through a pair of reading glasses perched on the end of his nose. He wore another Tommy Bahama shirt and the same awful down jacket and sneakers.

"There he is," he said when Petty walked in, betraying his excitement by standing and extending his hand. Petty shook it, and the two men sat across from each other.

"Beautiful morning, huh?" Don said.

"Better than yesterday," Petty said.

"You want coffee?"

"I'm good."

Petty gestured at the newspaper. "What's happening in the world?"

"This?" Don said "This is just the local rag. I only read it for the crime roundup. Last week a real genius got caught in a chimney trying to rob a house. You read a paper?"

"Nah," Petty said. "I don't have time."

"Me, I have to have my coffee in the morning, and I have to have my newspaper," Don said. "That's what made you a grownup when I was a kid."

Petty cocked an ear to the speaker in the ceiling. Someone was singing "Jingle Bell Rock." The day after Thanksgiving, and the bullying had already begun. Christmas is coming, dumbshits. Spend, spend, spend.

"So you didn't sleep too well last night," Don said.

"What are you talking about?" Petty replied sharply. How did the old man know anything about last night?

"You called so early, I figure you must have had that two million on your mind," Don said.

Petty relaxed. "I admit I've been thinking about it," he said.

"Good."

"But I'm gonna need a lot more information before I consider going any farther."

"Truthfully," Don said, "I've told you everything I'm willing to without a deal in place."

"It's not enough," Petty said. "I need more."

Don took off his glasses and narrowed his eyes. "Like what?" he said.

"Like where are we talking about?" Petty said. "Is the money in New York? In Chicago? In fucking—where was it, North Carolina?"

"L.A.," Don said. "It's in L.A."

Where Sam was living now. Huh. Petty pushed this thought out of his head, didn't need it influencing him.

"And what else do you have?" he said to Don. "What specifics?"

"I've got the name of the guy holding the money and where he's living."

"Which you got from a junkie you met in prison."

"Which I *bought* from a junkie I met in prison."

"What'd you pay him?"

"That's my business."

"A hundred dollars? Fifty? A couple packs of Top Ramen?"

Don stuck his glasses in his shirt pocket and folded his newspaper. "What's it matter?" he said.

"It matters because you need to know what a thing is worth," Petty said.

"It's worth ten grand up front and ten percent of the take," Don said.

"What?"

"That's my cut. Ten grand and ten percent."

"There's no way I'm giving you ten grand up front. If I had ten grand, I wouldn't even be talking to you."

"That's the price."

"It's not gonna happen, so come up with something else."

Don paused and picked at the lip of his paper cup. "Make me an offer," he said.

Petty wanted to smile. When someone said, "Make me an

offer," you'd won. But his next move needed to be a bold one to ensure this. He took out his wallet and slid two dollar bills from it. "You know what a symbol is?" he asked Don.

"Of course," Don said. "Something that stands for something else."

"So this," Petty said, holding up the bills, "is symbolic payment to you for your information regarding the money. Two dollars against two hundred thousand." He set the money on the table.

Don snorted his disgust. "I don't know who you think you're talking to," he said.

"You asked me to make an offer, and that's what I'm doing," Petty said. "This"—he tapped the ones—"is all I'm willing to lay out in advance for what is, basically, a piece of prison-yard gossip. At the same time, I'm prepared to invest my own time and money going to L.A. to see if there's anything to your junkie's story. If I find the guy whose name you're gonna give me and the safe and the money and all that, and if I can figure out a way to get my hands on it, this"—he tapped the bills again—"is your guarantee of ten percent."

Don sank back into his chair. He gave Petty a wry smile. "That's a new one on me," he said.

"It's not a hustle, Don. I'm serious."

"You're gonna go down there, scope things out, get the money, and give me my cut?"

"That's the deal," Petty said. He knew his word was enough for Don. They were both honest men when honesty was required.

Don drummed his fingertips, then picked up the money and stuck it in his pocket. Another song was playing now—"Rudolph, the Red-Nosed Reindeer."

"This junkie," Petty said. "Is he gonna run his mouth to anyone else?"

"Not likely," Don said. "A week after they let me out, he got stabbed over a dope deal."

"Good," Petty said. It came out harsher than he meant it to, but maybe now was the time to be a little harsh.

Don sipped his coffee. "Did I ever tell you about the first con I ever ran?" he said.

"I don't think so," Petty said.

"I learned it from an old-time grifter. He called it the Smack. This Mexican I palled around with, Rudy Rodeo, and I used to pull it in the bars in El Paso and Juárez after I got back from Vietnam. How it went was, I'd strike up a conversation with some good ol' boy on a bender, some hick from the sticks, and get him talking about his army days or baseball or what a big shot he was back in Mayberry. 'Let me buy you a beer,' I'd say. 'Let me buy *you* one,' he'd say. We'd smoke a joint, blow some coke, and pretty soon we were the best of friends.

"Right about then Rudy'd show up, acting like a drunk spic. He'd muscle his way into the conversation, being as obnoxious as possible, flashing a roll and saying he'd sold a car and was gonna spend all the money he made off it fucking white women. He'd go on and on about them swallowing and taking it up the ass and loving Mexican cock until that good ol' boy was seeing red.

"That's when I'd suggest a game of coin matching. Nothing heavy, all in fun. We'd each put a quarter on the bar faceup or facedown and cover it with our hands. On the count of three, we'd reveal the coins. The player with the odd coin won, meaning if two of us had heads, for example, the guy who had tails took all three quarters. If all the quarters were set the same, the round was a push.

"This'd go on for a while, everyone winning some and losing some, then Rudy'd go to the pisser. While he was gone, I'd say to the good ol' boy, 'Let's teach this taco bender a lesson. You set your quarter to heads every time, I'll set mine to tails, and that way one of us'll always win. We'll split the take down the middle after the Mex leaves.'

"The game'd start up again when Rudy came back. After he lost four or five times in a row, he'd get frustrated. He'd say if we were real men, we should play for real money. How about five dollars a pop? The good ol' boy and I would hem and haw, but of course we eventually agreed. Rudy would lose a few more rounds and get *really* irate. 'Fuck this fucking kid stuff,' he'd say and drop his whole roll on the bar. One last round, he'd say, all or nothing, with him matching whatever bets we put up.

"I always had five hundred dollars that I'd say my rich uncle had just sent me for my birthday, and the good ol' boy, expecting to win, would go into his boot for his bank or run out to cash a check. We'd all lay down our bets—the most ever was a thousand bucks each—and show our coins. Of course either the good ol' boy or I would win, and Rudy would put on a real show, spitting and cussing and swearing the devil was on our side before finally stomping out of the bar.

"Then came the blowoff. I'd tell the good ol' boy we were getting funny looks from the other customers and get him to pass me his winnings. I'd put his money together with mine in an envelope, which I'd lick and seal right there in front of him. The deal was we'd go somewhere private to chop it up. 'And you can hold the money until we get there,' I'd say. As I was handing him the envelope, though, I'd spot a cop and shove it in my own pocket. After a minute or so I'd say, 'Wow, I was wrong. That dude isn't a cop,' and I'd give the good ol' boy *another* envelope, this one filled with newspaper. 'Wait here while I take a piss,' I'd say, and I'd slip out the back door with all the money and Rudy'd be waiting to drive me away."

Don slapped the table and laughed out loud when he finished the story.

"Can you believe I was ever that crazy?" he said. "I'm telling you, the rush we got, even if the score was just fifty bucks, man! And, in our minds, those lames *needed* to be taken off. We were teaching them a lesson."

"You can't cheat an honest man," Petty said.

"Oh, fuck that," Don said. "I can cheat anybody."

A woman came in with a parrot on her shoulder. Don asked the woman the bird's name and stood to pet it. The bird squawked, and Don pulled back in mock terror. Petty checked his watch. A schedule for the next couple of days was coming together in his head. He had a plan of his own now, a direction, a destination. It felt good.

"So," he said to Don. "The name? The address?"

5

THE CLOUDS HAD CLEARED BY THE TIME PETTY GOT BACK TO the Sands, and the sky arched overhead like a flawless blue dome, at the apex of which hung the weak winter sun, doing its best to burn away the previous night's snow. Petty didn't even bother to zip his coat for the walk across the parking lot. He dodged all the puddles rippling in the breeze, little mirrors that showed the cars, the casino, even a passing flock of birds.

Tinafey, freshly showered and in full makeup, was sitting on the edge of the bed watching QVC when he came in. She wore her blond wig, a pair of skintight jeans, and a sleeveless Rihanna concert T-shirt. The room smelled of soap and perfume and, again, pungent weed.

"Welcome, Barb from Kentucky," the saleswoman on TV crowed.

Tinafey stood to greet Petty. He noticed that her bags were already packed.

"Time for breakfast," he said.

"Scrambled eggs," she said. "Burnt bacon, biscuits, and gravy."

"You *are* from Memphis," he said.

Watching her put on her high heels turned him on all over again. In fact, every move she made got his blood going. He had to reach down and adjust his hard-on so it didn't show. He couldn't remember the last time he'd been that fired up by a woman.

They went down to the diner and took a booth that looked out onto the parking lot. Their waitress, a sixty-year-old dressed as a carhop, chewed her gum in time to the Buddy Holly song playing on the sound system.

"And what about you, handsome?" she said to Petty after taking Tinafey's order. He usually went light on breakfast—coffee and toast—but today he was ravenous. He asked for the Wolfman Jack, a coronary on a plate: pancakes, eggs, bacon, ham, sausage, and hash browns.

He caught Tinafey smiling at a little girl in a high chair pulled up to a booth near the entrance, a little black girl with her hair in braids. The girl's mother spooned oatmeal into her mouth while her father made gobble-gobble noises to encourage her to eat.

"She's cute," Petty said.

"Sure is," Tinafey said. She reached across the table and tickled the back of Petty's hand with a long red fingernail. "You got kids?"

"A daughter," Petty said. "She just turned twenty-one."

"You guys close?"

Nah, I managed to fuck that up, too, was the first answer that came to mind, but "Not really" is what Petty ended up saying. "I haven't talked to her in years. She doesn't want anything to do with me."

"Well, you're the daddy, so you got to make the first move to fix that," Tinafey said.

"Is that right?"

"Of course it is. Children don't bear the blame for anything. They didn't ask to be born."

"What about you?" Petty said.

"Me what?" Tinafey said.

"Do you have kids?"

"I can't," Tinafey said. "Something with my ovaries. But it's just as well. I don't think I'd have the patience." She sorted through the condiment bottles corralled at the end of the table. "They must have Tabasco," she said. "Everybody's got Tabasco."

Petty turned his coffee cup around so he could get at the handle. The last time he saw Sam she was fourteen. She'd been living with his mother for five years at that point. Their weekly phone calls had degenerated into him asking questions and her mumbling one-word answers, so he detoured through Tampa on his way to Miami and paid her a surprise visit. He did all the talking over burgers and cherry slushes at Sonic while she picked at her flip-flops and made faces into the mirror of a hot-pink compact. Every year since Carrie had run off, the two of them had taken a summer trip together, and that year he was looking at Cancún. What did she think of that? he asked her.

"Actually," she said, "I don't want to go anywhere with you."

"Oh, yeah?" Petty said.

"Yeah," Sam said. "And I don't even know why you're here now. Does it make you feel better about yourself or something?"

"You're my daughter," Petty said. "I want to see you as much as possible."

"Please," Sam said. "Pretending we're any kind of family, that we ever were, is such a lie, and I'm not gonna do that. I'm not gonna be a liar like you and like my mom."

So no Cancún. In fact, no trips at all after that. And the phone calls ended, too. Sam stopped taking them, so Petty stopped making them. He got by on updates from his mom and continued to send money to Sam through her until she told him that Sam wanted him to donate the cash to a cat rescue organization instead. Over the years he'd managed to convince himself he'd done the best he could by her—better than her mother, anyway. He'd never considered forcing the relationship, didn't feel he had the right, but he'd always hoped she'd reconsider things someday and at least give him a call.

"Is there a Jacuzzi at this new hotel?" Tinafey asked him.

"Probably," Petty said. "It's a nice place."

"I like a Jacuzzi," Tinafey said.

She started to say something else but froze, open-mouthed, and stared out the window.

"What's wrong?" Petty said, turning to see what had caused her to stall out.

"Bo," she said and slid low in the booth.

And there he was, hurrying down the sidewalk like he had somewhere to be. Petty watched him until he passed from sight, then said, "Okay, he's gone."

"I got to get out of here," Tinafey said.

"We'll leave right after we eat," Petty said.

"I mean *out* of here, farther than that hotel."

"You have any place in mind?"

"I'm gonna go back to Memphis for a while. I got family there, places to stay."

Petty guessed this was probably the smart thing for her to do, but he wasn't looking forward to saying good-bye. He hadn't met a woman like her in a long time. She was funny and sexy and knew what was what. He could relax around her, didn't have to lie about what he did and the circles he ran in. And she was nice. Genuinely nice. That was rare in his world. An idea came to him, a crazy idea, and he found himself sharing it with her before he'd thought it all the way through.

"Look," he said. "I'm leaving for L.A. this morning, driving down. Why don't you come along and keep me company? We'll get a hotel when we hit town, do some sightseeing, and you can fly to Memphis from there."

Tinafey closed one eye and looked at him askance.

"L.A.?" she said. "To do some sightseein'?"

"Yeah. Sure. Why not?" he said.

"You've known me not even a day, and you already want to take me on vacation?"

"It's not a vacation. I'm trying to help you put some distance between you and Bo. If you don't feel comfortable, all you have to say is no thanks."

"Does it seem like I can't take care of myself?"

"Not at all. I saw what you did to that asshole last night."

"That's right, and you best remember that."

They paused the conversation while the waitress delivered their food. She called them honey and darlin', and Petty wondered if her drawl was for real or a put-on for the customers.

"Are you sweet on me?" Tinafey said as soon as the waitress left. She stared at Petty while scraping grape jelly onto her toast.

"Maybe some," Petty said. "You're so cute it's hard not to be."

Tinafey scoffed at this. "That's a motherfuckin' hustler talkin' right there," she said. "How long's it take to drive to L.A.?"

"I'll get us there in eight hours."

"Your car ain't gonna break down in the middle of the desert, is it?"

"I just got it checked out. Everything's good."

"'Cause I don't want to be stuck out there with all those serial killers and shit."

Petty smiled and dug into his pancakes.

He called Avi from the car as he and Tinafey were on their way out of town, put the phone on speaker, and told him he could shove the fishing job up his ass. Avi started in with "You ungrateful fuck" and "After all I've done for you," but Petty cut him off, saying, "Hey! Hey! Remember Jersey? You'd still be living in that Corolla if it wasn't for me."

"Bullshit!" Avi said. "What I have I got through my own initiative, and you'll be calling back in a week, begging to shine my shoes."

"Don't hold your breath," Petty said. "I'll eat rocks and shit sand first."

Tinafey laughed out loud at this and bounced in her seat.

"Is someone listening in?" Avi roared. "Take me off speaker!"

"Fuck you," Petty said.

"You're a loser, Rowan. Nobody says it to your face, but they're all thinking it."

"Yeah, yeah, yeah."

Petty ended the call and tossed the phone onto the dash.

"A grown man actin' like that," Tinafey said.

"Avi?" Petty said. "He's not a man."

"I was talkin' about you," Tinafey said, then slapped his thigh to let him know she was joking.

Petty sat back and grinned at the high desert scrub rolling past outside. The tufts of yellow grass that poked through the melting snow looked like flickering flames. He always got excited when he hit the road. It signaled that something was about to happen. Maybe good, maybe bad, but something. And that rush of possibility took the sting out of any disappointments that had preceded it.

He was so busy enjoying the feeling that he didn't notice the truck, the mud-streaked Ford Explorer that had been following them ever since they'd left the Sands, the one that had been keeping a careful two cars between itself and the Mercedes as both vehicles sped down the highway.

6

Petty took the 395 south, a straight shot almost all the way down to L.A. The weather stayed nice, so he and Tinafey had clear views of the jagged, snow-capped Sierras to the west and the dusty desert ranges humped in the east.

They stopped at Mono Lake and walked out to see the tufas—tall, spindly rock formations that resembled ruined castles and broken bones—but a cold wind blowing off the water and swarms of small black flies sent them running back to the car after just a few minutes. They stopped again in Bishop, for gas and lunch at a Carl's Jr., and once more in Lone Pine, so Petty could show Tinafey Mount Whitney in the distance, crowned with wisps of cloud.

"The tallest mountain in the contiguous United States," he said.

"Contiguous?" Tinafey said.

"Not including Alaska and Hawaii."

"Okay."

"And over there"—Petty pointed east—"about a hundred miles away, is the lowest spot, Death Valley."

"You must have been good in school," Tinafey said.

"Not really," Petty said. "You never know what's gonna stick."

"The area of a rectangle is length times width," Tinafey said. "The area of a triangle is one-half base times height. The area of a circle is pi times the radius squared."

"Whoa!" Petty said.

"Don't ask me to explain any of it, though," Tinafey said.

She fell asleep as they approached Mojave, curled in her seat, and didn't wake up until Petty was getting off the freeway in Hollywood. The sun had set by then, and she blinked like a drowsy child at the lights, the traffic, the strolling crowds.

"Hey," she said. "We made it."

Petty consulted a hotel discount app and found a deal at the Loews Hollywood, two hundred bucks a night. He'd have looked for someplace cheaper if he'd been alone, but he'd promised Tinafey a nice time. The hotel wouldn't take cash, so he put it on one of his cards, crossing his fingers that there was enough space on it.

Their stark black-and-gray room on the tenth floor had a view across a freeway of the Hollywood sign propped against a chaparral-covered hill. Tinafey oohed and aahed and snapped a dozen too-dark photos. Petty crept up behind her and kissed her on the neck. She purred and stretched when he reached around to cup her tits through her T-shirt, then turned and forced him to walk backward until they both fell onto the bed. She undressed him, he undressed her, and they knocked the lamp off the nightstand going at it, left it on the floor until they finished.

Afterward, they showered and got ready to go to dinner.

"Nowhere too nice," Tinafey said. "I don't have anything fancy."

"You look great," Petty told her, and she did, in her tight jeans, silky red blouse, and black knee-high boots.

"You don't mind short hair on a girl?" she asked as she put the finishing touches on her lipstick.

"I like it on you. You've got the face for it."

They walked across a bustling open-air shopping mall to the Chinese theater and had a look at the movie-star footprints immortalized in concrete there. Costumed hustlers worked the crowd, posing for photos in exchange for tips. Superman, Darth Vader, a princess, a raggedy SpongeBob.

Tinafey wanted pictures with all of them, and Petty obliged. He shelled out a buck here, a buck there, pointed her phone, and said, "Smile!" Everything was cool until Edward Scissorhands demanded five dollars after previously agreeing to two. The guy got mouthy, and Petty leaned in close and whispered, "Don't make me knock you on your ass in front of all these kids." He gave the freak two singles and sent him on his way.

"Michael Jackson!" "Jackie Chan!" "Britney Spears!" Tinafey walked along Hollywood Boulevard and called out the names on the pink terrazzo stars sunk into the sidewalk. "Tom Selleck! I think I heard of him." "The Muppets!" "Chill Wills? Ha! Chill Wills? Who's that?"

Petty didn't recognize most of the names himself. He'd never been interested in movies, was always too busy. He'd taken Sam to see Disney stuff now and then, *Shrek* and *Nemo,* but he usually fell asleep as soon as the lights in the theater dimmed.

Still, this was his first time in Hollywood, and being in the thick of things was kind of exciting. The touts hawking bus tours to the stars' homes, the music blasting out of the tourist bars, the toy Academy Awards arrayed in souvenir-shop windows. He enjoyed a cheap thrill as much as anybody, and it was good to get out every once in a while and rub elbows with real people, somebody besides gamblers and hustlers.

There was a thing going on at one of the theaters, an event that involved limousines, a red carpet, and a cadre of photographers. Tinafey pulled Petty through the throng of onlookers until they reached the metal barrier that separated the public from the arriving celebrities. From there she scrutinized the stars as they slid out of shiny town cars and Escalades, gasping with excitement when she saw anyone she recognized.

"Angie! Angie!" she called to a sleek redhead in short shorts. "She's on that show, you know, with her sister." Petty didn't know, didn't care, but as long as Tinafey was enjoying herself, he was happy.

After a while the doors to the theater closed, the photographers lit cigarettes and packed up their cameras, and the crowd evaporated, off to the next thing.

"Okay, now I'm starving," Tinafey announced.

Petty spotted a sign up the block: MUSSO & FRANK GRILL, OLDEST IN HOLLYWOOD. He and Tinafey came off the street into a hushed, high-ceilinged room with a long counter on one side and old-fashioned wooden booths on the other. Petty liked what he saw: spotless white tablecloths, red-jacketed waiters. The smell of meat grilling and potatoes frying set off a primal rumble in his stomach.

The maître d' pointed them toward a bar in a second dining room, said he'd have a table shortly. A wizened gnome of a bartender smiled from behind thick glasses and asked what they'd like. Tinafey had a glass of wine, Petty Johnnie Black.

"This is nice," Tinafey said.

"Old-school," Petty said.

"Like you," Tinafey said.

"You from out of town?"

The guy asking was a short man with a barrel chest. He wore a bright yellow jacket over a sky-blue button-down, faded jeans, and canvas deck shoes with no socks. Somewhere north of sixty, he still had a full head of suspiciously black hair that was combed straight back and hung to his collar.

"Yes, sir," Tinafey said. "I'm from Memphis."

"Love Memphis," the man said. A couple of rings flashed on his fingers when he adjusted his tinted aviators and reached for his martini. "I was stationed at Fort Campbell in 1967 and used to ride the bus down there every time I got leave. Beale Street, man. Fucking wild. It was supposed to be off-limits to the military, but I didn't give a shit. Guys I knew got jumped, got robbed, but nothing bad ever happened to me."

"It's all cleaned up now," Tinafey said. "Mostly tourists."

"Everything's cleaned up now," the man said. "Everything's mostly tourists. Look outside this place. You used to be able to get into trouble out there, have some fun."

Petty felt like he'd seen the man before. If they were anywhere else, he'd think they'd played cards together. Here, though, he suspected it was something else.

"You ever been on TV?" Petty asked the guy.

He sat up straighter and showed his perfect teeth.

"Some," he said. "Quite a bit, actually."

"Like, name something I'd have seen you in."

"Oh, man, going back? *Gunsmoke, Rockford Files, Murder,*

She Wrote, Dr. Quinn. More recently, *Sons of Anarchy, Boardwalk Empire, CSI.* Features, too. Bruce Willis beat me up in *Die Harder.*"

"What's your name?" Petty said.

"Stanley Beckett." The guy held out his hand. "Call me Beck."

"Rowan Petty, and this is Tinafey."

"Tinafey?" Beck said.

"Like the woman on TV," Tinafey said.

"Yeah, but you're prettier," Beck said.

"Listen at you," Tinafey said.

Beck winked and sipped his martini.

"You guys taking in the sights?" he said.

"Sort of mixing business with pleasure," Petty said.

"That's smart," Beck said. "What do you do?"

"Commercial real estate," Petty said.

Beck looked past him to Tinafey. "And you?"

"I sing a little, dance," Tinafey said. "I always wanted to try actin'."

"You're in the right place," Beck said. "Maybe you'll get discovered while you're here."

"That doesn't really happen, does it?" Tinafey said.

Petty worked on his Scotch. He was thinking about how much dough a guy like Beck made. You heard the movies paid crazy money, but you heard a lot of shit that turned out not to be true. He couldn't tell anything from the dude's clothes except that he might be color blind. And people dressed down anyway. The real question was how smart he was with the cash he had. Petty had gotten over on doctors, lawyers, college professors, but never an actor. It'd be a challenge, bullshitting a professional bullshitter.

Even as he was thinking this, Petty scolded himself. Here the man was, nice as could be, telling Tinafey funny stories about the stars he'd worked with, and here he was, trying to come up with ways to rip him off. Sure, it was scary being down to, what, three grand and change now, but there was no need to panic yet, not with two million dollars possibly floating around out there.

Tinafey asked Beck for his autograph. Beck called to the bartender for a pen. *To my Memphis belle* he wrote on a napkin and scribbled an ornate signature.

The maître d' came by and said their table was ready. Beck stood when they did. "That's my cue to exit, too," he said. He reached into his back pocket, looked confused, then patted his jacket. "I don't believe it," he said. "I must have walked out of the house without my wallet."

"Don't worry about it," Petty said, still feeling guilty for sizing the guy up as a possible mark. "I'll get it."

"Hey," Beck said. "Thanks, amigo." He shook Petty's hand again and gave Tinafey a quick hug. "Manny," he called to the bartender on his way out. "This handsome devil is taking care of my tab."

Manny brought over Beck's bill and set it on the bar in front of Petty. Thirty-six bucks. Turned out the dude owed for three martinis, not just one. Petty chuckled to himself. The sly fucker had played him like a fiddle.

The maître d' led Petty and Tinafey to a booth with a view of the dining room: the wooden beams arching overhead, the old-fashioned coatracks and chandeliers, the fancy folk going at their steaks. Something about the acoustics muted the various conversations into a genteel murmur, and the wainscoting and yellowed wallpaper imbued the light with the warm caramel sheen of aged varnish. It was a place where old men felt young and young men felt wise.

Petty ordered a New York strip. Tinafey had spaghetti and meatballs. Everything was à la carte—the salad, the dressing, the asparagus—but Petty quit trying to add it up in his head and even had a port with dessert. He'd go back to worrying about money tomorrow; tonight would be a splurge.

7

T HE MASSIVE SANDSTORM ROLLING TOWARD BAGRAM AIRFIELD looked like a brick-red cloud aboil on the horizon. It added extra urgency to Staff Sergeant Armando Diaz's search for Keller. Get caught out in one of those bitches and you'd choke on moon dust and be sneezing black *mocos* for a week. Diaz ducked into the DFAC, but Keller wasn't chowing down on hot dogs and Tater Tots with the rest of the troops there.

"Yo, Jingle Man," someone called from one of the long cafeteria tables.

Diaz waved in the general direction of the voice and hurried back outside. *Jingle Man* because he was in charge of dealing with the jingle trucks, Afghan vehicles the army hired to transport supplies to its various bases, the theory being, why use American trucks and drivers when you could pay locals to run the gauntlet of IEDs and Taliban headhunters? *Jingle trucks* because the wildly painted semis, flatbeds, and tankers were festooned with chains that made a god-awful racket as they bumped along the country's rutted roads.

The hot wind scooted trash across the baseball diamond chalked in the dirt between the dining facility and the MWR building, snatched up Styrofoam cups and plastic bags, swirled them, then carried them over the razor-wire fence and ran off with them across the scrub.

Keller wasn't on the phone at Morale, Welfare, and Rec; wasn't on a computer. Diaz finally found him stretched out on a couch in the little theater, the only guy there, watching a DVD of *The Hangover*. He tapped him on the shoulder and jerked his thumb toward the exit.

They headed for one of the bunkers that dotted the base. The storm was about to break over them like a thousand-foot wave, and the weight of it tilted the world that way and wouldn't let you take your eyes off it. Day turned to dusk as the cloud blotted out the sun.

It was even darker inside the bunker, a long, narrow, windowless tomb constructed of sections of concrete blast wall reinforced with sandbags. Diaz and Keller stepped into it as the storm hit. The wind was so powerful, the walls shook, and sand from the joints pitter-pattered on the ground like hard rain.

These days you could be assured of privacy in the bunkers. There hadn't been a mortar or rocket attack—not even a false alarm—in months. The bad guys knew the troops were on their way out, so no sense wasting ordnance to try to take a couple of them down. This particular bunker was curtained with spiderwebs that Diaz and Keller had to sweep out of the way in order to get to the beat-up office chairs someone had requisitioned for the space. They plopped down in the chairs, and Keller lit a cigarette.

"Somebody'll smell that," Diaz said.

"In a fucking sandstorm?" Keller said. He took a deep drag and exhaled the smoke slowly. "How many days you got left?"

"I fly out Monday," Diaz said.

"Fuck you."

"What about you?"

"Another month."

Sergeant Daniel Keller was a big pimply hick from Maine, still as pale as the Pillsbury Doughboy even after three tours. He worked in a hangar prepping cargo for shipment back to the United States. With the drawdown in full swing again, they were going nonstop these days. Everything from computers and printers to microwaves and washing machines had to be crated, labeled, and loaded onto planes.

Keller was in for a quarter cut of Diaz's treasure. As Jingle Man, Diaz had been responsible for paying the Afghan truckers for their runs, drawing from a mountain of cash kept in a vault on base. He'd quickly spotted holes in the system and taken advantage of them. At the height of the scam, between the kickbacks he got from the trucking companies and the ghost shipments for which he paid himself, he'd been siphoning off a hundred grand a month.

He'd needed a way to get the money out of the country and back to the U.S., and that's where Keller came in. The two of them had previously been partners in another swindle, buying TVs, Blu-ray players, and game consoles at a discount at the PX and reselling them to local shop owners. When Diaz told Keller about his jingle truck idea, he was all in from the get-go. Diaz would pass the stolen money to him, and he'd stash it in legitimate shipments on their way to Fort Bragg. There, a buddy of his, for another quarter cut, retrieved the cash and sent it on to L.A.

Keller held out his hand and wiggled his fingers.

"Gimme gimme," he said.

Diaz passed him a bindle of heroin. He'd copped it from Izat, the dirty who ran the haji store on base. Izat peddled carpets, man dresses, and bootleg DVDs to the troops and did a side business in dope. Keller liked to get high but was too chickenshit to score on his own, so Diaz sometimes did him the favor with an eye toward keeping him happy.

Keller took out an Oakley sunglass case that held a syringe, a spoon, cotton balls, powdered vitamin C—everything he needed to fix—and set about cooking up a shot.

"So as soon as I get back," he said as he tapped junk into his spoon, "we'll have a big reunion."

"Chop up the take," Diaz said.

"We should do it in Vegas. I've never been there."

"That's cool with me," Diaz said. He rolled back and forth in his chair, pushing himself off the wall with his foot. Outside, the wind howled and the sand whispered.

"They got bitches there that can suck the chrome off a trailer hitch," Keller said. "Bitches with nuclear titties." He held his lighter under the spoon. The simmering dope gave off a sour smell. "I'm gonna buy a full-on purple pimp suit just to fuck with everyone," he said. "Just 'cause I'm rich enough. Big fucking hat with a feather and everything."

"You ain't that rich."

"Five hundred grand?" Keller said. "That's rich where I come from. And anyway, I'm gonna double my money while I'm there, playing baccarat." He dropped a bit of cotton into the dope and tied off with his neon-yellow PT belt.

"What the fuck do you know about baccarat?" Diaz said.

"I know all the rich Chinks play it," Keller said, massaging a big blue vein. "They know what's up."

Diaz held his breath as the needle slid into Keller's arm, held it until Keller depressed the plunger on the syringe.

"Whoa," Keller said when he loosened the belt and sat back in his chair. He said it like he was losing his balance. "Whoa." He blinked and shook his head. "This shit...."

"Give me the best stuff you got," Diaz had told Izat. "One hundred percent pure, no garbage." He'd paid triple for the dose.

Keller slumped, chin on chest. He was already on his way out, the uncut junk too much for him. He tried to raise a hand to his face, maybe to wipe the drool from his lips, but the hand stopped halfway, wavered, and dropped back into his lap. His breathing slowed. A couple of seconds later he fell out of the chair and lay unmoving on the ground.

Diaz bent over him and saw dust dancing around his nose and mouth. He sat back and listened to the storm for a while. When he checked again, Keller was dead. Gone to wherever stupid white boys from Maine go when they OD. *One down,* Diaz thought. He left the dude lying there and stepped out of the bunker and into the swirling sand, where the sun through the murk was a blood-red hole in the sky.

8

Petty woke at dawn, feeling like his mind had already been working for hours. He slipped out of bed without disturbing Tinafey and watched the sunlight creep up the Hollywood sign. He tried to make use of the quiet to plan a few moves ahead, but it was like attempting to draw a map from inside a tornado. Too many thoughts spinning too fast. And besides, everything that came next depended on what happened today. He brushed his teeth, got dressed, and went downstairs.

Guests starting early on long days of sightseeing mobbed the coffee counter in the lobby. A couple of Germans scrutinized Disneyland brochures, a Japanese family struggled to decipher the menu, and a tattooed Brit in a straw fedora jabbed at his phone and shouted, "Hello? Hello?" Petty wasn't in the mood to wait in line. He walked outside to search for another option.

The Boulevard by day looked hungover, woozy. Its bruises showed through its powder and rouge. The sidewalks were empty, the trash cans overflowing. Steel roll-up doors decorated with ugly paintings of the stars of black-and-white movies covered the storefronts, and a noisy flock of ravens that was perched on the art deco flourishes of an old building put Petty in mind of vultures waiting for a meal to drop.

He bought a foam cup of shitty coffee and a pack of gum at a convenience store across the street from the wax museum. The bus bench he sat on in front of the store had an ad on it for a bargain dentist. Some joker had blacked out the dentist's teeth with a Magic Marker and scrawled *666* on his forehead. Petty gave the first bum that asked a dollar but ignored the next two.

A tall bearded dude in a trucker cap and cowboy boots caught his attention. He was smoking a cigarette and leaning against a lamppost down the block. Petty at first thought he was one of the photo hustlers, supposed to be somebody from a movie, but his jeans and cowboy shirt weren't much of a costume. He had a weird feeling the guy was watching him and tried to catch him at it, turning away, then whipping back around. Sure enough, he found himself looking right into the dude's eyes for an awkward instant before the two of them broke it off.

The interaction made him uneasy. He got up from the bench and started back toward the hotel. He checked over his shoulder to see if the cowboy was following, but the guy stayed where he was, watching traffic roll past with a blank look on his face. So just some lunatic, then, a redneck on a bender, wigged out by all the sun and sparkle.

★   ★   ★

He made a lot of noise coming into the room, whistled and slammed the door, not wanting to startle Tinafey in the shower.

"I'm back!" he called out.

"I'll be just a second," she said.

He sat on the bed and turned the TV to the news. The water went off, and Tinafey came out wrapped in a towel.

"I've got some business to take care of today," Petty said.

"What happened to sightseein'?" Tinafey said.

"We'll get around to it, I promise."

Tinafey was disappointed but tried not to show it.

"So maybe I'll go swimmin' instead," she said. "They got a nice pool here."

Petty took two hundreds out of his wallet and held them out to her. "Buy yourself a new bathing suit," he said.

"I got my own money," she said.

"Take it," Petty said. "I might not have it to give next time."

Tinafey let him tuck the bills into her hand but remained standing in front of him.

"Are you really comin' back?" she said.

"Of course," Petty said. "And you'll still be here, right?"

"Do you want me to be?" she said.

Petty sat her on the bed beside him.

"Let's be straight with each other," he said.

"Why? You been lyin' so far?"

"I've only got a few thousand dollars to my name right now. I'm here chasing a score, but things might get tight before it happens. I like you a lot, and I'd like you to stick around, but whenever you want to go, let me know, and I'll put you on a plane to Memphis."

Tinafey leaned away from him and pulled her towel up higher.

"I won't whore for you," she said. "If that's what you're hopin', forget it."

"I'd never ask you to do that," Petty said.

"That's what you all say till your pockets are empty."

"I'm not a pimp, Tinafey," Petty said. "That's not my game."

Tinafey squinted into his eyes, looking for the truth, then said, "Nobody's waitin' on me in Memphis, so I might as well stay a little longer. I ain't even been to the beach yet."

"We'll do that."

"And Beverly Hills? Rodeo Drive?"

"Wherever you want."

"And if somebody asks, can I say I'm your girlfriend?"

Petty was taken aback by the question.

"Do you *want* to say you're my girlfriend?" he said.

"It'd make things easier," Tinafey said.

"Can I say I'm your boyfriend?"

Tinafey made a face. "That sounds stupid, doesn't it?" she said.

"Not to me," Petty said.

"Boyfriend," Tinafey said in a funny voice. *"Girlfriend."*

"You ever had a white boyfriend before?" Petty asked her.

"Once, in high school," she replied. "His daddy 'bout shit, though. Made him break up with me."

"That's Memphis for you."

"That's everywhere for you."

Petty played with a drop of water on her shoulder.

"You ever had a black girlfriend?" she said.

"Sure," Petty said.

"One you didn't pay for?"

The sound of sirens spiraled up from the street. Tinafey hurried to the window, and Petty joined her. They watched three fire trucks and an ambulance weave through traffic, lights flashing, horns braying. In the distance a pillar of black smoke rose into the sky like an angry fist.

"Someone's havin' a bad day," Tinafey said.

Petty stared at her reflection in the window. He wanted to kiss her but decided not to start something he didn't have time to finish.

"So," he'd said to Don the day before at Starbucks. "The name? The address?"

And that's when Don began to hem and haw. Turned out the only actual information he'd gotten from the junkie was that the dude holding the money was named Tony, that he lived in East L.A., and that his mom owned a store, Alma's Party Rentals, on Cesar Chavez Avenue. Petty googled the shop right there in Starbucks, confirmed that it existed, and let Don keep the two-dollar deposit. He'd already decided by then to say fuck you to Avi and get out of Reno. L.A. was kinda sorta on the way to Phoenix, where he was headed next, so what the hell. The couple hours he'd waste if the army money thing turned out to be a wild-goose chase were nothing compared to what the payoff would be if it panned out.

It took him twenty minutes to get from Hollywood to Boyle Heights. He sped along the 101 through downtown and across the concrete channel of the L.A. River, then exited onto surface streets in a scruffy Mexican neighborhood.

The party store sat in a block of old brick buildings from the thirties. Next to it on one side was a beauty salon offering *tintes, rayitos y facials,* on the other side was a mom-and-pop pharmacy. Petty parked in a loading zone across the street, in the shade of a giant ficus, the gnarled roots of which had buckled the sidewalk so badly that the displaced concrete slabs tripped old ladies shuffling home from the market. He watched the entrance to the party shop from the front seat of his car. In twenty minutes only one person, a girl pushing a stroller, went inside, leaving shortly afterward.

Petty started the Benz, drove around the corner to a spot where the car couldn't be seen from the shop, and parked again. After giving himself a once-over in the rearview mirror, he got out and walked back to the store.

The place sold everything you might need for a fiesta. This time of year it was full of Christmas stuff. Ornaments of every size and style, cheap fake trees, laughing Santas, and angels, angels, angels. There were also cases of off-brand soft drinks stacked against the wall and a display of cleaning products. Overhead, dusty piñatas swayed in a breeze whipped up by a fan above the door.

"Do you rent those bounce-house things?" Petty asked the woman behind the counter. She was around fifty, a bottle blonde with a mole on her cheek and orange-and-black tiger stripes painted on her long fingernails.

"I got a few," she replied, not returning Petty's smile.

She showed him pictures in a photo album of one that looked like a castle, one that looked like a birthday cake, and one that looked like a race car. Petty pretended to be interested, asking about prices and delivery and setup, then stopped suddenly and narrowed his eyes.

"You're not Tony's mom, are you?" he said.

The woman frowned, suspicious. "Why? Who are you?"

"My cousin went to school with Tony."

"At Garfield?"

"Garfield, yeah," Petty said. "That's crazy. I'm standing here talking to you and thinking, *This lady looks so familiar.* I met you a couple times."

"What's your cousin's name?" the woman said.

71

"José," Petty said. "He moved to Texas after he graduated. What about Tony? He still around?"

"He was in the Marines, but he's been back two years now," the woman said. "José what?"

"What?" Petty said.

"Your cousin."

"Garza. José Garza. Do you see Tony much?"

"Every day. He does my deliveries for me."

"He still driving that...that...what was it?"

"He never had a car," the woman said. "But they gave him a truck when he came back from Afghanistan." An alarm had gone off in her head, and she was now scrolling through her memory in earnest, trying to place Petty. "Where do you live?" she said. "Not around here."

"I'm in Hollywood," Petty said. "My girlfriend stays over here." He'd pushed it far enough. The woman was about to start in with harder questions. Pulling out his wallet, he asked how much of a deposit it'd take to reserve the race-car bounce house for the second Saturday in December. "Twenty dollars," the woman said. He gave her the money, and she pulled out a rental form.

"My girlfriend will call you with all that," he said. "It's for her kid."

"I got to put something down," the woman said. "What's *her* name?"

"Maria Rosales," Petty said. "She'll call you this afternoon."

The woman was flustered. First a friend of her son's she couldn't recall shows up out of nowhere, and now a deposit with no form. Petty made for the door before she could get her bearings.

"Good seeing you again," he said as he backed out of the store. "Tell Tony that Bill Miller said hello."

He hurried around the corner. The sun had turned his car into an oven while he was gone. He lowered the windows and drove aimlessly until he came to a taco stand, where he stopped for a chorizo-and-egg burrito.

An hour later he was back watching the shop, parked half a block away, across the street, slumped low in the driver's seat. Not a soul went into the store during the first hour, and only the UPS guy during the second. Petty listened to the radio for a while but shut it off before too long, worried about draining the battery. A stray dog trotted down the sidewalk, looking like it knew where it was going. For a while a police helicopter circled nearby. Petty watched it until it moved on, then made a game of clucking his tongue every time a car drove past.

He thought about Tinafey, wondered what she was doing, wondered how long she'd hang around now that she knew he was broke. He thought about Sam, his daughter. He couldn't believe it had been seven years since he'd seen her, five since they'd last talked on the phone. It was crazy how time got away from you. Maybe he'd give her a call while he was in town, ask his mom for her number.

His foot fell asleep, and he stepped out of the car to stretch his legs. While he was wiggling feeling back into his toes, a black F-150 drove up and parked in the loading zone in front of the party store. A short, sturdy Mexican kid in jeans and a white T-shirt got out. His gait was a little off as he walked into the store. There was a wobble there, a hitch.

Petty slid back into the Benz and started it up. He drove past the store, made a U-turn at the next corner, and parked again half a block behind the truck, facing in the same direction. The Ford's license plate caught his attention. There was a little blue wheelchair on it along with the letters *DV*. He got on the Internet and found out the *DV* stood for "disabled veteran."

73

Five minutes later the kid limped out of the shop and climbed back into the truck. Petty waited until he got moving before pulling away from the curb and slipping into traffic behind him. They spent the next hour touring the neighborhood. Petty cooled his heels outside a supermarket, a barber shop, and a Burger King. Their last stop was a two-story stucco apartment building on a noisy street lined with stucco apartment buildings. The kid turned into a driveway that led to a garage beneath the complex. He stuck a card into a slot, a steel gate rose with a sound like a clanking chain, and down he went, out of sight.

Petty circled the block twice before he found an open spot. The Mercedes stuck out among the banged-up, Bondo'd, beat-to-shit Nissans, minivans, and gardeners' pickups, but Petty was more worried about the trail going cold than about his car getting jacked. He opened the trunk and took out a yellow safety vest he kept there. He buttoned the vest over his black T-shirt and added a baseball cap and a clipboard. The costume came in handy when he was working real estate scams and needed to get access to properties he was planning to bid on without revealing his interest to a Realtor. He could pass as a meter reader in the getup—a cable installer, a delivery guy, whatever.

Most of the apartment complexes he passed on his way to the kid's building were barely holding together. Broken windows had been boarded over instead of replaced, bare wires dangled where light fixtures had been stolen, and graffiti climbed walls like ivy, as high as an asshole with a spray can could reach. Yet not everyone had given up. Here and there you saw pushback. A pot brimming with flowers, a well-tended shrine to the Virgin Mary, three shades of pink paint where someone had repeatedly covered the local gang's tags.

On this Saturday afternoon, it seemed that everyone who lived on the block was out and about. Children pumped scooters past Petty, volleyed soccer balls in dirt yards, and hollered from driveway to driveway. A group of women were gathered around a panel truck, out of the back of which a vendor peddled vegetables, tortillas, and bags of rice. A man squatted in the shade of a sagging carport to let a pit bull puppy lick the condensation off his can of Bud Light and cracked a joke that made his friends laugh.

Petty checked the directory for the kid's building, but most of the numbers didn't have names next to them. The steel security gate had been propped open with a cinder block, so he stepped inside for a look around.

Two stories of apartments ringed a central courtyard landscaped with palms and banana trees in lava-rock planters. It was a nice touch, but the bars on the windows put Petty in mind of a prison cell block. Petty figured the kid, being crippled, lived on the ground floor. He began a slow circuit of the courtyard, peering into the windows of apartments while pretending to inspect the plumbing. The curtains in 101 were drawn tight. Through the open door of 102 he saw an old man lying on a couch, watching TV. Nobody was in 103. A crib and an air mattress took up most of the living room, and a Jesus calendar hung on the refrigerator.

The kid was in 104. He came limping out of the bathroom, where he'd changed from jeans into cargo shorts. His right leg was a complicated metal-and-plastic prosthesis. Petty scanned the room and glimpsed a USMC flag and a sixty-inch TV, but no safe. He moved on before the kid noticed him. If he actually had the money stashed in the apartment, he'd be skittish, and Petty didn't want to spook him. Better to take things one step at a time. Now that he knew where the dude lived, he could put together a real plan.

A pair of *vatos* in a lowered Caddy slowed to stare at him as he was walking back to his car, mad-dogging the *pinche gabacho*. He ignored their glares, kept his eyes on the clipboard. The Benz was right where he'd left it, all four tires intact. He got in, started it up, and only then noticed that his T-shirt was soaked with sweat.

9

PETTY DROVE BACK TO HOLLYWOOD WITH THE SETTING SUN in his eyes. He squinted behind his shades until the fireball dropped below the horizon just as he reached the hotel. The orange glow left behind faded quickly, and night rushed in with bared teeth.

Petty crossed the lobby to the elevator with a smile on his face, feeling good. He'd tracked down Tony, found his apartment, and made all the right moves so far. And even if the rest of Don's story turned out to be bunk, at least he was out from under Avi's thumb and doing his own thing again.

Tinafey was lounging on the bed in a white bikini. She'd spent the day by the pool, and her skin radiated heat when Petty ran his hand up her leg.

"Eighty degrees in almost December," she said. "You believe that?"

He felt like jumping her bones right then, to burn off some

nervous energy, but he didn't want her to think she was only there to ball him whenever he got the urge. He took a quick shower, and the two of them walked over to the open-air mall next door at Hollywood and Highland.

"What's that supposed to be? Egypt?" Tinafey said, pointing up at the three-story arch engraved with winged monsters and the two enormous pillars topped with plaster elephants that towered over the plaza. Petty found a plaque that explained they were re-creations of a set from a silent movie about ancient Babylon. The plaza was already decorated for Christmas. A giant tree stood next to the fountain, Santa and his elves cavorted in window displays, and carols warbled out of hidden speakers.

And still the hordes of tourists were disappointed. Petty could see it in their eyes: they'd been had, and they knew it. They'd come expecting movie stars, palatial homes, and fancy cars and instead found themselves dragging their bored kids around another goddamn mall exactly like those they'd slogged through in Vegas and Orlando and Nashville.

A sweaty daddy carrying a sweaty baby bumped into Petty and didn't say "Excuse me," and his sweaty wife almost knocked Tinafey down in her haste to get to a booth where a girl was passing out free tickets to a game show. Petty took Tinafey's hand and started looking for somewhere to have dinner. The mob eventually spit them out in front of the Hard Rock Cafe. That'd do, they decided.

As soon as they sat down Petty wished they'd kept looking. The restaurant was too dark and too crowded, and he could barely hear Tinafey over the music. He felt like as much of a sucker as the tourists outside. He and Tinafey both had ribs, and Petty nursed a second Scotch afterward while she walked around looking at the memorabilia on display. Jim Morrison's leather pants, Eddie Van Halen's guitar, a drum set used by the guy in Metallica. She came back from the gift shop with two T-shirts, one for her and one for Petty.

They stood out front for a while and watched the Saturday night circus on Hollywood Boulevard. A drunk girl lay on the sidewalk by Michael Jackson's star and couldn't get up after her friend took her picture. Down the block, Spider-Man and Freddy Krueger went at it, shoving each other and swinging wildly.

"Kick his ass, Freddy!" Tinafey shouted, then clapped her hand over her mouth like she couldn't believe the words had come out of her.

"You want to get a drink?" Petty asked her.

"I'm sorta tired," she replied.

"Okay," he said.

"And they're showin' *Beauty Shop* on TV."

"So we'll go back."

They stopped at the store where Petty got his coffee that morning and bought Fritos, bean dip, and Diet Coke for the room.

Ten minutes into the movie Petty knew he wasn't going to make it through the whole thing. His mind kept wandering, and Tinafey, lying beside him on the bed, asked him twice to please stop shaking his foot; it felt like an earthquake. He got up and put on his coat and told her he was going out for a nightcap.

A raucous birthday party had taken over the bar in the lobby—a pack of young, stylish people dressed like all the young, stylish people you saw on TV. Petty kept going and ended up on the Boulevard again. He poked his head into a few places, but they were too loud and too crowded. So back to Musso & Frank. The same smiling gnome was tending bar, and he had Petty's Johnnie Black in front of him almost before he'd finished ordering it.

Petty turned at the sound of a familiar laugh: Beck, chatting up two women who were overdressed just enough to show they didn't get out much.

"This one's on him," Petty said to the bartender, pointing at his Scotch, then at Beck.

The bartender moved down to where Beck was regaling the ladies and whispered to him. Beck turned to Petty with a frozen smile, recognized him, and lifted his glass.

A few minutes later he swaggered over.

"We even now?" he said.

"Just about," Petty said.

"It was an honest mistake, you know. I lost count."

"It happens."

"Where's Memphis?"

"She had a hard day hanging out by the pool."

Beck finished his martini and called for another. He was drunk tonight, or deeper in his cups than he'd been last night, anyway, his ragged edges showing.

"You know anything about this place?" he said.

"What's to know?" Petty said.

"Charlie Chaplin came here, William Faulkner, Steve Mc-Queen."

And then it hit Petty where he'd seen Beck before, something that had been nagging at him since last night. "Hey," he said to him. "Say something in puppy."

Beck looked confused for a second, then it came to him. He smiled. "You remember that?"

It was a commercial for a fancy brand of dog food that ran on TV when Petty was a kid. A much younger Beck played a snooty fucker in a turtleneck and a beret. Leaving his apartment building, he said good morning to the doorman in Russian. Then you saw him in his office, talking on the phone in French. On his way home he chatted in Chinese with the grocery store guy and in Spanish with his cabdriver. Back in his apartment, he opened a can of the dog food, dumped it into a bowl for his cocker spaniel, turned to the camera, and said, "And I also speak fluent puppy."

"I must have seen that thing a thousand times," Petty said.

"Well, laugh all you want," Beck said. "But that spot paid for my first Corvette."

"I'm in the wrong business."

"You're a good-looking dude, got sort of a slick thing going on. You should give it a shot."

"I'm sure there's more to it than that," Petty said. "A lot of 'who you know, who you blow,' that kind of thing."

"Who you blow?" Beck said.

"You know what I mean."

"That I'm a faggot?"

"'Who you know, who you blow.' It's a figure of speech."

Beck's face reddened, and his chest swelled. The bartender brought over his martini. Beck downed half of it, set the glass on the bar, and squared off like he was preparing to throw a punch.

"Hey, man," Petty said. "Relax."

"Relax?" Beck said.

"I didn't mean to insult you."

"You called me a faggot."

"I did not."

"Yeah, you did."

Petty stood and balled his own fists, confused by Beck's sudden anger. Beck glared at him for a few tense seconds, breathing heavily through his nose. Then his face broke, and he burst out laughing.

"What the fuck?" Petty said.

"I was just playing around," Beck said.

"Seriously?" Petty said.

"Seriously," Beck said.

Petty gulped his Scotch. He wasn't used to being fucked with, and Beck had already gotten him twice, first with the drinks last night and now with this. Never again, though; never again.

Beck picked up his martini and used the napkin under it to wipe a tear from his eye.

"You should have seen your face," he said.

"Did you go to school for that?" Petty said.

"For what?"

"For what you just did."

"Acting?"

"Yeah."

"I took classes when I first got here from Milwaukee. Introduction to the Method, Acting for the Camera. But you know what really got me my first gig?"

"What?"

"Being able to take a punch. I was at this audition for two lines in a TV show, and it was down to me and two other hippies who looked just like me. The director said, 'Let's try the punch,' which was how the scene ended. A stuntman buddy had taught me how to fake a fight, so I was the only one who sold it, and that's how I got the part."

Petty thought about telling Beck how he'd fooled Tony's mom today and put on the show with the clipboard and safety vest, but then he remembered the two million dollars that might be in the kid's apartment and decided to keep his mouth shut.

"What are you doing right now?" Beck asked him.

"What's it look like?" he said.

"Finish your drink and let's get out of here."

"Where are we going?"

"Up to my place. It's right off Mulholland."

"Why would I want to go to your place?"

"To see my wife's Oscar."

"Your wife's got an Oscar?"

"And an Emmy, too," Beck said. "The family jewels. Come up and see them. I hate drinking alone."

Petty clutched the dash of Beck's Jaguar as the dude whipped out of the restaurant's parking lot and sped north toward the hills, away from the carnival on the Boulevard. Even though the night had turned cold, Beck put the top down, cranking the heater to compensate. Petty still wasn't sure why he'd agreed to accompany him. If anything, it'd be a story to tell—the time I ran around Hollywood with the "I speak puppy" guy.

They drove up a dark, narrow canyon lined with big houses that glowed like jack-o'-lanterns through the trees. At one point a deer bounded out of the underbrush and froze on the road in front of them. Petty braced for a crash, but Beck swerved around the animal without so much as tapping the brakes.

Higher and higher they climbed, until they popped out of the canyon and onto a road where each curve revealed a new vista of the endless orange grid of the city. The sprawl thrilled Petty. All those streets stringing together all those people. Somewhere down there was the one-legged Mexican kid and maybe the money. Somewhere down there was Tinafey, watching her movie. And somewhere down there was Sam, his daughter, unaware.

Beck swung into a driveway and stopped in front of an ornate wrought-iron gate.

"You want to wrangle that?" he said. "The thingy's burned out."

Petty got out of the car and swung open the gate. They proceeded up the driveway to a big Spanish-style hacienda with a tile roof and arched verandas. The inside of the house was dark, but spotlights in the yard lit up the exterior so that the place gleamed against the night. Beck drove past it and parked in the shadows in front of a second structure, a three-car garage in the same style as the house.

"This way," he said to Petty and motioned to stairs leading to an apartment above the garage. An owl hooted nearby. Petty turned to look for it in a silvery eucalyptus tree, then had to hurry to catch up to Beck.

"My wife and I split five years ago," Beck said, "but instead of divorcing me and having to give me half of everything, she offered me a deal where I live here free of charge and get an allowance for keeping my mouth shut. The queen bee, you see, likes to keep her private life private."

Beck continued his monologue as he unlocked the door of the apartment and walked through the tidy living room to the tidy kitchen and grabbed two Coors Lights out of the refrigerator.

"Is it degrading? Yeah. Do I feel like a fucking parasite? At times. But then I remind myself that they-who-have-not sponging off they-who-have is a tradition here. In fact this might be the only city in the world where 'estranged husband' is a legitimate job description."

He handed Petty one of the beers.

"At least it's a nice pad," Petty said.

"Kind of a comedown from the big house," Beck said. "But what are you gonna do? You close your eyes and hang on."

Petty sat on the couch in the living room, Beck in a worn recliner. There were lots of pictures of Beck and various movie stars on display, but the one that got Petty's attention was a big black-and-white photo of a younger Beck and his wife that hung on the wall. Petty recognized the woman but couldn't come up with her name. She and Beck were at a party. He was in a tux, she was wearing diamonds, and they looked happy. Petty used to have photos of him and Carrie looking happy, but one night after she left he tossed them all in the kitchen sink, soaked them with lighter fluid, and burned them to ash.

"So what do they teach you in acting class?" he asked Beck.

"The mysteries of the universe," Beck said.

"Is it like, 'Hey, look, a bear. Pretend to be scared'?"

"You've seen too many cartoons," Beck said.

He got up and grabbed a chair from the dining room and placed it in front of the TV.

"Lesson one," he said. "Sit here."

Petty humored him. Stood, walked over, and plopped in the chair.

"You're on stage," Beck said. "The curtain's rising; the play's about to begin. The scene is you sitting alone, silently, for three minutes. Go."

"What do I do?" Petty said.

"Whatever you want," Beck said.

"I don't want to do anything."

"Then don't."

Beck sat on the couch and stared at Petty. Petty shifted on the chair, uncomfortable under his gaze. The only time he'd been on stage before was as a kid, in a church Christmas pageant, when he'd played a shepherd and wore a bedsheet for a robe. He looked past Beck to the photo on the wall and concentrated on that. Beck and his wife. Melanie? Mary? He drank some beer. He crossed his legs. His stomach gurgled. His ears rang. That had to be three minutes. He glanced at his watch.

"Curtain," Beck said.

Petty stood quickly. "So I was supposed to learn something from that?" he said.

"Now you watch me," Beck said.

Petty took Beck's place on the couch, and Beck sat in the chair, back straight, hands on his knees. He stared past Petty with a blank look on his face. Gradually his expression changed, and it seemed to Petty that he was remembering something. Petty glanced over his shoulder to see what he was focused on. Maybe it was the photo, and he was thinking of better days. A sad smile came to his lips, and his chest rose and fell, a single deep breath, a sigh. The smile faded, and slowly, slowly, he bent forward, rested his forearms on his thighs, and stared at the floor. Then slowly, slowly, he sat up. His face was blank again, but now tears filled his eyes.

Petty blinked back tears of his own. He marveled at this as he would have marveled at a magic trick.

Beck dropped his head for a few seconds and came up smiling his real smile. "Stanislavsky's first rule," he said. "When you're on stage, you've always got to be acting, either inwardly or outwardly. If you're good, even if you're just sitting there, saying nothing, the audience'll be affected."

"That's some crazy shit," Petty said.

"It can *make* you crazy, that's for sure."

"What were you thinking about?"

Beck waved off the question. "What's important is what *you* were thinking about while you were watching," he said.

Petty gestured to a shelf full of DVDs. "Do you have anything you were in?"

"They're all crap," Beck said.

"Let's watch one."

"That's not why I asked you here."

"I know, but come on," Petty said.

Beck looked at him sideways. "You're trying to get me to break out the good booze, aren't you?" he said. He walked into the kitchen and came back with a chilled bottle of Absolut and two glasses.

The disk he put in was a movie from the nineties, something called *Hollywood & Vice,* two cops chasing a serial killer. "Shot for a buck and a half in beautiful downtown Toronto," Beck said. He played the older cop, Sergeant Blackburn, the married one, the good dad, the by-the-book dude always bickering with his partner, a nut job who wrecked cars and roughed up suspects. Petty had seen the same story a hundred times before, but Beck was pretty good in it.

In the first scene, he and his partner were about to bust up a bank robbery. It looked to be a suicide mission, and before they charged in, Beck as Blackburn slipped away to call his wife from a pay phone. You thought he was going to say something hokey to her like "I love you," but instead he asked normal questions like "What's for dinner?" and "What are the kids doing?" and you realized, mainly through Beck's acting, that what he really wanted was just to hear his wife's voice for what might be the last time.

The scene hooked Petty, and he would have paid more attention to the rest of the movie if Beck hadn't kept talking over it, pointing out who was an asshole and who was cool and telling a long story about an explosion going off at the wrong time and nearly killing an extra. After a scene in which Blackburn was forced to relinquish his badge and gun to his boss, Beck pressed Pause, went to a bookshelf, and came back with the actual badge and prop gun from the film.

"I took these when we wrapped," he said. "They owed me for making me use a Porta-Potty as a dressing room."

He settled down after that and stopped cracking jokes. By the time the movie ended he was asleep in the recliner, glass of vodka still in his hand. Petty decided not to wake him. He got up from the couch as quietly as he could and crept toward the front door. As he touched the knob, Beck let out a loud snore that froze him in his tracks. He waited for a second snore and a third before slipping outside.

The big house was still lit like a shrine. Petty walked past it and down to the gate, where he used his phone to find out where he was and call a cab. A mist had settled over the road, blurring the streetlights and dampening the pavement. Something moved in the distance. Petty shook off the vodka and squinted. Two spectral coyotes were headed right toward him, trotting side by side down the middle of the road. "Hey!" he shouted, trying to frighten them away, but they kept coming. Eyes. Teeth. Claws.

He opened the gate and stood behind it. The coyotes padded silently past, one of them shooting him a hateful yellow glare. "Git!" Petty shouted. The animal smirked and continued on its way. Petty stayed behind the gate until the taxi drove up and honked its horn.

10

Iт's Rowan," Petty said.

His mom had picked up the phone in the middle of her ancient answering machine's outgoing message and was now barking "Hello? Hello? Hello?" while her instructions to "leave your name and number" played in the background. She'd had a hip replaced a month ago and was still using a cane, which slowed her down some. When the message ended and the beep came, she shouted once more: "Hello!"

"It's Rowan," Petty said again.

"You scared me."

"How?"

"I must have dozed off."

Petty was surprised to hear this. Before the surgery, Joanne never took naps, was constantly out and about. Church stuff mostly. She belonged to a nondenominational congregation with a gay pastor. The church ran a homeless shelter, and

Joanne was in charge of collecting food for it, going from su-permarket to supermarket, restaurant to restaurant, asking for donations. If it wasn't the homeless, it was illegal immigrants or runaway teens or mothers in prison. She'd joined the church shortly after Sam moved out and had been devoting herself full-time to doing good since retiring three years ago. Petty couldn't help but suspect that someone somewhere down the line was making money off her selflessness, but hey—whatever made her happy.

Because she'd been through a lot. When she was growing up, her dad ran the house like it was a boot camp, and her mom let him. Lots of yelling, lots of hitting. Joanne was in sec-retarial school in Kansas City when she met Petty's dad at a bowling alley bar. He was on a hot streak, in the midst of a cross-country ramble on which his mission was to take down the biggest home game in every city he stopped in.

"I asked him if he was going to San Francisco" was how Joanne's story went. "It was 1972, and I really, really wanted to see San Francisco. He said, 'You want to go to San Francisco, I'm going to San Francisco,' and when he left town, I left with him."

They never made it to the West Coast. Petty's dad's luck ran out in Denver, where they ended up stuck for three months, liv-ing in a leaky yurt on a commune. This was the first in a string of broken promises, a string that culminated years later with Petty's dad abandoning Joanne and eight-year-old Rowan in Tampa. Joanne's early lessons in discipline kicked right in. Within a week she'd rented an apartment for the two of them, found a job at a real estate office, and arranged for a neighbor to watch Petty af-ter school. Then, seemingly without a moment's hesitation to get her bearings or a single spasm of self-pity, she set about giving Petty the stable home life he'd never had before.

A year passed, two, and they settled comfortably into a routine that consisted of work, school, and weekends at the beach. Even back then, though, Petty could read people, and when he looked at Joanne, he saw a woman holding her breath. She was nice looking, kept herself up, and men were always asking her to dinner or drinks, but she turned them all down, and Petty knew it was because she secretly hoped his dad would reappear.

Instead, five years after he split, she got a call informing her he'd been found dead in a Saint Louis motel room. Murdered, the cop said. Stabbed to death over a two-hundred-dollar gambling debt. Petty couldn't say what his mom learned from this disappointment, but he knew what he took away from it: that's what you get for hoping.

And then poor Joanne got screwed all over again, saw another dream go up in smoke, when Petty ended up being no better than his old man, blood winning out in spite of all her efforts to put him on a different path. So if it did her heart good to pass out ham sandwiches and tube socks to hobos, that was okay with him. She deserved whatever peace she could find.

"I'm in L.A. for a couple of days, and I want to get in touch with Sam," he said to her now on the phone.

"Oh," she said.

"Oh what?"

"I don't know if she'll be up for that."

"Why not?"

"She never has much nice to say about you."

"She talks about me?"

"No. But when she does, it's not nice."

Petty and Joanne still butted heads on occasion, especially when he detected judgment in her voice. But he didn't want to spar with her today. Not while he was sitting by a swank hotel pool in the dead of winter, watching a woman he was hot for float tits-up in the shallow end.

"Mom, just give me her number," he said.

"She might not want me to," Joanne said.

"I don't give a shit."

"Listen to yourself."

"She's my daughter. She's gonna have to endure a call from me whether she likes it or not."

"You really should," Joanne said. "You should listen to yourself sometime."

She set the landline down to search for her cell phone. Petty could hear music playing on her end. Joni Mitchell. She loved Joni Mitchell. The sun sparkling on the water made him blink. He adjusted his chair so that he was lying flat on his back. A small plane passed overheard, dragging a banner behind it, an ad for an energy drink.

"How have you been?" he said to Joanne after she'd given him Sam's number.

"Now my knee hurts, too," she said.

"So go to the doctor. And take something stronger than herbal supplements. Those things are complete bullshit."

"You know everything, don't you?"

"I just don't want to have to worry about you," Petty said. Tinafey waved at him. He waved back.

"How are *you* doing?" Joanne said.

"I'm fine. Everything's great."

"Are you gambling?"

"I'm working on a project."

"A project. I see. And what is it you do for a living these days?"

"Come on, Ma."

"Ha!" Joanne said. "Your dad could never answer that question, either."

Tinafey wanted pizza for lunch, so they walked to the mall's food court. Petty told her he had business to take care of and put her on a bus for a two-hour tour of movie stars' homes. His original plan for the afternoon had been to head back to East L.A. to do more reconnaissance on Tony. Instead he dialed Sam's number. He felt bad about fibbing to Tinafey, but the messiness between him and Sam was nothing she needed to be involved in. His call went to voice mail, but a few minutes later his phone rang.

"Who's this?" Sam said when Petty answered.

"Your dad," Petty said.

"Who?"

"Your dad."

"I heard you the first time. What do you want?"

"I'm in L.A. Let's get together."

"When?"

"Today. Right now, this evening, whenever."

"I'm busy today."

"Tomorrow, then."

"I'm busy tomorrow, too."

Petty smiled to himself as he stared out at the Hollywood sign from the window of his and Tinafey's room. Did this kid think she actually stood a chance against him?

"It'd mean a lot to me to see you, even if it's just for a few minutes," he said.

"Why?" Sam said.

"It's been seven years. We let it go too long. *I* let it go too long."

"I'm happy with the way things are. I don't want any... confusion."

93

"Confusion?"

"I'm trying to keep my life simple."

"That's great. That's smart. Simple is good. But all I'm asking for is ten minutes, a cup of coffee. We don't even have to talk. I just want to *see* you."

Sam paused, thinking this over. Petty smiled to himself again. The hook was set.

"I don't know why," Sam said. "After all this time."

"You said it right there," Petty replied. "Time. The years are starting to fly by. You remember about my dad, right, what happened to him?"

"How he died and all that, when you were a kid?"

"I hadn't talked to him for five years, and then, all of a sudden, he was gone. The guy was a bastard, but these last few years, you know what I find myself thinking about when I wake up in the middle of the night?"

"What?" Sam said.

"I find myself thinking, after all this time, that I wished I'd seen him one more time before he died," Petty said.

This wasn't true—he hated the man as much as he ever had—but when it came to closing, you had to be ruthless. He picked out a car on the freeway below, watched it climb toward the Cahuenga Pass.

"Jesus. Listen to you," Sam said.

"I'm serious," Petty said. "Regret, I guess you'd call it, right?"

"You're fucking shameless."

Echo Park was right off Sunset Boulevard around twenty minutes from the hotel. Its centerpiece was a small man-made lake that reflected the tall palm trees that surrounded it and the blank blue sky overhead. The spray from a fountain in the middle of the lake cooled the Mexican families circling in rented pedal boats.

Petty found the statue of the woman at the edge of the water where Sam had said to meet her, but Sam was nowhere in sight. A bench next to the statue looked out toward the skyscrapers of downtown. Petty sat there for a second, then stood again, his antsiness getting the best of him. He walked to the water and stared at the ducks muttering in the reeds. A woman with butterfly tattoos and pink hair pushed a stroller past. Her kid flung a pacifier that bounced to a stop between Petty's feet. He picked it up and handed it to the woman. She took it without acknowledgment, kept talking on her phone.

A tall girl in a knee-length skirt, a T-shirt, and a green army fatigue jacket appeared on the path that circled the lake. Sam. There was no mistaking her long, elegant neck and willowy frame, both inherited from her mother. Petty was shocked, though, at how pale she was. Dark circles ringed her eyes, and her lips were dry and cracked. He forced a smile as she approached. "It's you," he said.

"You sure about that?" Sam said.

They didn't hug. Sam pulled the black knit cap she wore lower over her greasy blond hair and rewrapped the scarf around her neck like she was hiding from someone.

"What do you really want?" she said. "Grandma isn't sick, is she?"

"I really wanted to see how you're doing," Petty said.

"I'm doing fine," Sam said.

"Great, so we're good for another seven years," Petty said. The joke fell flat. "Is there a place to get coffee around here?"

"There are ten places to get coffee around here," Sam said.

"I could use some. How about you?"

95

Sam hesitated. "I'll go with you," she said. "But don't try to daddy me."

"I don't even know what that means," Petty said.

"You're right, you don't," Sam said. "What was I thinking?"

They walked to a bookstore that had a café in back. It was full of kids who were probably living off their parents while playing in bands or studying art history. Part hippie, part punk—Petty couldn't figure it out. He ordered a coffee and persuaded Sam to let him pay for her green tea and vegan cookie. They sat at a table on the patio next to a bearded guy who alternated between staring into space and jabbing at the keys of his laptop.

Sam took off her jacket. The word *veritas* was tattooed on the inner biceps of her right arm.

"What's that?" Petty asked her.

"'Truth,' in Latin," she replied.

She'd been barely a teenager when he'd last visited her at Joanne's, awkward and excitable, one hand hiding the braces on her teeth, the other flailing like a wounded bird as she laid into him for asking how her grades were. It pained him to see her as she was now. Her fingers trembled when she raised her cup to her mouth, and her pretty blue eyes were as dull as a dead girl's. Petty knew a dope fiend when he saw one, but he couldn't bring himself to ask her what she was strung out on, wasn't sure he had the right.

"You like country?" he said instead, pointing at the photo of Willie Nelson on her shirt.

Sam pulled the shirt away from her torso and looked down at it like she was seeing it for the first time. "It was in the dollar bin at the thrift store," she said.

The dollar bin. Jesus Christ.

"Your grandma says you're studying to be a teacher," Petty said.

"Trying to," Sam said. "My scholarship—"

"Scholarship?" Petty said.

Sam shrugged. "I'm a good student," she said. "I've always been a good student."

"You didn't inherit that from me," Petty said with a little laugh.

Sam ignored this. "Yeah, so my scholarship covers tuition and books, but I've got to scrape together the money for everything else," she said. "Grandma sends a little now and then, and I waitress four nights a week."

"That must be tough, working and going to school at the same time."

"It's pure hell, but I'm used to it."

"I don't know," Petty said. "You look a little run-down."

Sam raised a warning hand. "No daddying."

Petty sat back and sipped his coffee. Talking to her was like trying to pet a porcupine.

"Want to hear something crazy I was thinking about earlier?" he said. "When I was your age, your mom and I had already been married two years, and you were already walking and talking."

Sam ignored him. She concentrated on pushing back her cuticles.

"We were living in New Jersey," Petty continued. "Remember that?"

"What the fuck were you doing?" Sam said.

"In Jersey?" Petty said. "It wasn't that bad."

"Having a kid so young," Sam said.

"Oh," Petty said. "That. Truthfully? Not a whole lot of thought went into it. We sort of took life as it came."

"So I was a mistake."

"A surprise, maybe, but not a mistake."

Sam went back to staring at her fingernails.

"Is that how you think of yourself?" Petty said. "As a mistake?"

"I used to," Sam said. "But I got over it."

"Good," Petty said.

"I got over everything you guys did to me."

She was laying it on a little thick. He'd done the best he could. For a year after Carrie ran off with Hug McCarthy, he'd tried to raise her on his own, like Joanne had raised him. They were living in Denver when Carrie left, but he moved them back to Vegas, where he had more connections. He got a job selling cars, dropped Sam at school every morning, and sat down to dinner with her every night. The whole time, though, he felt like a scientist being forced to run one of his rat's mazes for slivers of cheese. Frustration, humiliation, every shitty thing at once, ate away at his good intentions.

And Vegas. What was he thinking trying to go straight there, with easy money at every turn and suckers galore? He started gambling again after six months, then ran a deposit scam on a condo he found on Craigslist and made more in two weeks than he'd earned the whole time he'd been shilling for the local Ford dealer. Next he and a partner set up a pump-and-dump boiler room for a failing telecom start-up. It was the kind of thing where the feds might have come knocking any day, so that's when he decided to send Sam to live with his mom. Better that than her seeing him dragged off in cuffs. And he still believed it had been the right decision, no matter how Sam felt about it then or now. Of course he wasn't about to try to convince *her* of that.

"You ever hear from your mom?" he asked her.

"She showed up at Grandma's when I turned sixteen," Sam

said. "She'd bought me a car and, man, did it piss her off that I wouldn't take it."

"You should've taken it," Petty said. "She owed you."

"Yeah, right," Sam said. "It was probably stolen anyway. And the whole time she was there, Hug or Bug or whatever her husband's name is was staring at me like he wanted to kill me."

"He's that kind of guy," Petty said.

"And yet he was able to convince your wife to leave you," Sam said.

Petty couldn't tell if she was trying to be hurtful or funny, so he kept his mouth shut.

A kid with a stupid mustache mumbled "Hey" as he walked past.

"Hey," Sam mumbled back. She balled her napkin and spread it out again on the table. "So why are you in L.A.?" she said to Petty.

"Playing tourist," Petty said.

"Robbing tourists is more like it," Sam said. "What are you really up to?"

Her smugness finally got to Petty. He couldn't hold back any longer. "What are *you* really up to?" he said.

"What do you mean?"

"You look like shit."

"Wow. Thanks."

"I'm not stupid," Petty said. "I've been around dope and dopers longer than you've been alive."

"Dopers?" Sam said, mocking him.

"Cut the crap," Petty said. "You've obviously got a problem."

Sam's tight, angry smile quivered. She was suddenly struggling not to cry.

"Well, this has been great," she said. She stood and brushed cookie crumbs off her skirt.

"How about you sit down?" Petty said.

"How about no?" Sam said. "How about fuck you?"

She turned to leave.

"Let me help you," Petty said.

She whirled, ready to cut loose on him, but whatever she was about to say got tangled in a sob. She hurried out the door, pulling her scarf up to cover her mouth.

Petty lay down on the bed when he got back to the room and dozed off while Tinafey was telling him about her movie-star tour. He slept for two hours, the past few days finally catching up to him. He'd have been out even longer if Tinafey hadn't started making noise and bumping the bed every so often.

"I'm awake," he finally said.

"The parade's at five," she said.

The Hollywood Christmas Parade. Someone by the pool had told her about it. Floats and marching bands and movie stars, Santa Claus bringing up the rear. You'd have thought she'd had enough of the tourist grind after a day of taking pictures of Tom Cruise's mailbox and Madonna's driveway, but the girl was buzzing as she rattled off the list of celebrities scheduled to appear. She rushed Petty out of the shower and dragged him to the elevator, eager to stake out a prime viewing spot.

Spectators stood shoulder to shoulder on both sides of Hollywood Boulevard. Petty and Tinafey ended up with a foot of curb in front of Hooters, in between a Mexican family and a pack of drunk college students from UCSB. The stars smiled and waved from the backseats of shiny classic convertibles. Petty recognized Sulu from *Star Trek* and some of the kids from *The Brady Bunch*—old men and women now.

A marching band stomped to a halt in front of them and

honked out a brassy version of "Frosty the Snowman" while a troupe of girls in skimpy elf outfits twirled batons. Tinafey bounced in place and hummed along under her breath. Petty's gaze wandered over the crowd on the other side of the street and stopped on one particular face. It was the bearded cowboy in the trucker cap who'd been playing peekaboo with him yesterday morning, staring at him again. He saw Petty notice him and turned away.

A scuffle broke out among the college students. Someone called someone an asshole, someone pushed someone, and a girl screamed. The Mexicans got into it, shouting, "Hey, there's kids around! Be cool!" and doing some shoving of their own. A couple of cops stepped in and told everybody to take it easy. By the time things calmed down, the cowboy had disappeared, and Petty chalked up seeing him again to coincidence.

11

Raindrops bouncing off the windshield like a handful of gravel startled Petty out of a one-eyed catnap. He'd been parked in front of Tony's building all morning. After checking the garage and seeing no sign of the kid's truck, he'd spent the next couple of hours watching a strange woman across the street pace back and forth while dark clouds filled the sky.

The woman's well-worn track was a strip of bare dirt lying between the sidewalk and the curb. She was sixty or so, retarded in some way, a hunched figure with a jutting lower jaw and heavy-lidded eyes. Wearing baggy jeans and a *Nightmare Before Christmas* sweatshirt, she wobbled back and forth from driveway to driveway, back and forth, ignored by kids on their bikes, ignored by Jehovah's Witnesses going door-to-door, ignored by jumpy stray dogs. Petty had grown drowsy watching her and dozed off.

When the rain woke him, she was still there, still pacing,

undisturbed by the downpour. Another woman ran out of the apartment complex the strip of dirt fronted. She grabbed the pacing woman's arm and tried to steer her toward the building, but the pacing woman refused to change course. The second woman gave her an umbrella, forced her stubborn fingers to grasp the handle, then ran back inside. The pacing woman returned to her circuit, twenty steps one way, turn, twenty steps the other. The dust beneath her feet darkened and thickened into mud.

Just after noon the black F-150 turned into the apartment building driveway and descended into the garage. Petty stretched and thumbed a bit of crud from the corner of his eye. The storm had let up. Only a few fat drops pelted him when he went to the trunk for the yellow vest and clipboard. The objective for today was to enter Tony's apartment and look for a safe. If it turned out to be more than the fantasy of some junkie talking out of the side of his neck, Petty would move on to figuring how to lay his hands on the cash inside it.

He walked toward the building. Wind chimes tinkled somewhere, somehow louder than everything else. The runoff sluicing down the gutter slowed and pooled around a sluggish storm drain, the puddle spreading into the street so that cars plowing through it sent up sheets of spray that rose and fell in the gloom like great black wings flapping. A bloated earthworm writhed on the sidewalk. Petty wondered where it had come from. There was no grass for several blocks in either direction. Just concrete and chain link and stucco.

The rain picked up. Petty jogged the last fifty feet to the gate, which was again propped open. He stopped in the passage leading into the complex and glanced at the mailboxes, memorizing names. The water pouring off the second-floor walkway formed a beaded curtain that veiled the courtyard planters, and the sound of splashing echoed everywhere.

Petty moved around the complex, gradually working his way toward Tony's unit. In case anyone was watching, he paused often to examine faucets, bang pipes, and scribble notes on the form stuck to his clipboard. It was a heater repair estimate sheet. A contractor he used to play poker with had given him a stack of them. Even with all that, he still got to Tony's quicker than he meant to, was all of a sudden there, standing at the door with nothing left to do but knock.

"*Qué?*" a voice called out.

"Reliable Plumbing," Petty said.

Tony opened the door a few seconds later. He'd have been a nice-looking kid if not for the scar that snagged the outside corner of his left eye, causing it to droop, then continued down the side of his face to geek his mouth, too. Petty hadn't noticed the scar before or that the kid was missing a couple of fingers on his left hand.

"How's it going?" Petty said.

"Okay," Tony replied.

"Your neighbors"—Petty glanced at his clipboard—"the Salazars and Perezes. Their sinks are stopped up. Any problems here?"

"I don't think so," Tony said. "Let me check."

He limped into the tiny kitchen, which Petty could see into over the top of the breakfast bar that separated it from the living room. The kid turned on the faucet, verified that the water swirled down the drain, then disappeared into the bathroom. Petty inventoried the place: couch, chair, coffee table, TV, Xbox. No safe.

"They're all working fine," Tony said, walking out of the hallway.

"You mind if I come in and look around?" Petty said. "The main leach line for the building runs behind your unit, and rain can overload it. That might be what's causing your neighbors' problems. It'll only take me a minute to check."

"You're not gonna fuck anything up, are you?" the kid said.

"I'm gonna look for soft spots on the walls," Petty said. "Dampness. You don't want the pipe to bust and flood you out."

Petty played it cool when Tony waved him into the apartment. He'd long ago learned to hide the buzz that juiced him whenever he got over on a mark. He started in the kitchen, pressed on the drywall above the sink. No dirty dishes, and the counters wiped clean. The kid kept a tidy house.

Tony followed him to the bathroom and stood in the doorway while Petty continued his mock inspection. There was nowhere to stash a safe in there, but Petty looked around anyway. He opened the medicine cabinet and glanced inside long enough to note there was no makeup or tampons and only one toothbrush. One bottle of shampoo in the shower, too, so the kid likely lived alone.

Petty walked back out into the hall and turned toward the bedroom. Tony stopped him as he was about to open the door.

"Do you have to go in there?" he said.

"The pipe runs this way," Petty replied with a vague gesture. "It's just…"

Aha! Petty thought. The kid was hiding something.

"It's kind of a mess," Tony continued. "I just did my laundry."

"I've seen laundry before," Petty said.

Tony entered the bedroom first and bent awkwardly on his prosthesis to snatch a stack of underwear off the queen-size bed that filled most of the room. The bed was covered with freshly washed and folded jeans and T-shirts and bath towels. The only other furniture was a three-drawer dresser from Ikea, where the kid now stashed his skivvies, and a small bedside table with a lamp on it. No safe.

Petty opened the closet. A set of Marine Corps dress blues hung there, stored in a plastic dry-cleaner bag, and five pairs of sneakers were lined up neatly on the floor. Again, no safe. Petty shut the door without even pretending to check for a leak and walked back into the living room. There was nowhere else to look. Don's junkie had been full of shit, and this whole stopover in L.A. had turned out to be a waste of time and money.

"You're all good," he said to Tony. "No problems here."

"Nah, there's plenty of problems," Tony said as he followed Petty to the front door, his fake leg creaking. "Stuff breaks down, and the owner doesn't even give a shit."

Yeah, yeah, yeah, Petty thought. All he wanted right now was a double Scotch and a little TLC from Tinafey to help ease his disappointment.

"You like being a plumber?" the kid said.

"It's okay," Petty said.

The kid grinned, but the scar on his face messed it up. "See, I knew you'd say that," he said.

"Yeah? How?" Petty said.

"There's this money I can get for school, and I'm trying to figure out what I should study, so I ask everybody about their jobs. And you know what everybody says?"

"It's okay?"

"It's okay."

"You're asking them about work," Petty said. "What do you expect?"

"Yeah, man, I get that, but it's still sad," the kid said. "People should love what they do for a living."

"What do you love doing?" Petty said.

Tony grinned again. "Ah, man, I'm bad," he said. "I like drinking beer, playing video games, watching porn—"

"Try getting paid for that," Petty said.

"I feel you, I feel you," the kid said. "But seriously, my dad? He painted houses for twenty years before he died. Hated it. My mom? She owns a store? Hates it."

He scratched his scar with his disfigured hand but stopped when he realized Petty was watching. "I know what you're thinking," he said. "This dude can't be too choosy. And you're right. I'm all fucked up. I got one leg, one good hand, headaches. But I'm still not gonna take the first job someone'll give me. That's how I ended up in the Marines. That's how I ended up like this."

"What happened?" Petty asked.

"Afghanistan," Tony said. "Motherfuckin' Afghanistan."

"Well, good luck to you," Petty said. "With school and everything."

He opened the front door to leave but pulled up short. There on the threshold stood the cowboy he'd been seeing around Hollywood, the one with the beard and the trucker cap. Now the guy had a pistol in each hand, matching Smith & Wesson revolvers. He pressed the muzzle of one of the guns to Petty's forehead and forced him backwards into the apartment. The other gun he trained on Tony.

"Hands up, up, up," he said.

Petty's were already in the air, an instinctive response to having a gun shoved in his face. Tony lifted his. The cowboy patted Petty down, then did the same to Tony. When he finished, he said, "Both of you sit on the sofa."

Petty complied immediately, but Tony remained standing.

"What the fuck's going on?" he said.

"Come on now," the cowboy said. "It's the guy with the gun who asks the questions." He gestured at Tony's prosthesis. "You need help or can you manage?"

Tony lowered himself onto the couch.

"Let's get right to it," the cowboy said. "Where's the money?"

"I got forty bucks," Tony said. "Take it and get out of here."

"Forty bucks?" the cowboy said. "A blow job and a Snapple? Buddy, I'm after that big army money."

"Army money?" Tony said.

"Tell him, Rowan," the cowboy said.

Petty was shocked to hear his name. That meant this clown must be in cahoots with Don, the two of them working together to fuck him over. He didn't give the cowboy the pleasure of a reaction, though. All he said was, "I don't know what you're talking about."

The cowboy cocked the pistols. "Yeah, you do," he said. "Tell this boy why you're here."

Maybe the guy was crazy enough to shoot him, maybe not. Petty decided not to test him. He decided to do everything he could to increase his odds of getting out of the apartment alive.

"People are saying some soldiers smuggled a couple million dollars out of Afghanistan and that you're the guy holding it for them," he said to Tony.

"For real?" Tony said.

"For real," the cowboy said.

"I heard about it and decided to check the story out," Petty continued. "I followed you here from your mom's store on Saturday and came back today to look for the money."

"So tell this dude, then," Tony said. "Tell him there's no money."

"It's true," Petty said to the cowboy. "I didn't find anything."

A flash of lightning burned up all the shadows in the room. Thunder rattled the windows, and rain poured down outside. The cowboy glanced at the ceiling, nervous, and used the barrel of one of the revolvers to push his hat back on his head. "I think I'll check for myself," he said.

He herded Petty and Tony into the bathroom and shut them inside with a warning that he'd shoot through the door if he heard so much as a rustle. Petty leaned against the sink, and Tony stood in front of the tiny window, wavering between angry and afraid.

"Sorry about this," Petty said. "He must have been tailing me."

"Is he gonna kill me?" Tony said.

"What for?" Petty said.

Tony didn't reply. He scratched his scar with the nubs of his missing fingers.

They could hear the cowboy tossing the apartment, opening and slamming shut closets and cupboards, pulling out their contents and dropping it to the floor.

"Get your asses out here," he said when he finished, frustration souring his hokey drawl. He directed Petty and Tony back to the couch and stood in the middle of the room again with his guns. The floor was littered with high school yearbooks and VA paperwork.

"Listen, RoboCop," he said to Tony. "I don't like being fucked with."

"I'm not fucking with you," Tony said.

"Then tell me where the money is."

"There isn't any money."

"Let me call Don," Petty said. "That's who sent you, right?"

"Who?" the cowboy said.

"I'll call him and tell him the story was bullshit. He'll listen to me."

The cowboy laughed. "Man," he said. "Ain't nobody gonna listen to you."

It incensed Petty that Don had played him, but now wasn't the time to get hung up on settling the score. Right now he needed to get out of here. He pushed himself to his feet and started for the door.

"I'm leaving," he said.

The cowboy pointed one of the revolvers at his nose. "No, you're not," he said.

Petty paused with his hand on the knob.

"I've been thinking," the cowboy said. "If I had two million bucks, I wouldn't keep it in this shithole, either." He turned to Tony. "Your mama's store got a safe."

"No," Tony said.

"I don't believe you," the cowboy said. "She a hot tamale, your mama?"

"There's no money," Tony said. "No money anywhere."

"Seriously," Petty said. "Put the guns away, and I'm gonna call Don."

"What you're gonna do, Rowan, is get your ass in that kitchen and bring me the duct tape I saw under the sink," the cowboy said.

"Fuck that," Petty said. "This is between you and the kid."

The cowboy tightened his fingers around the triggers. "Get me the tape!" he said.

Petty went into the kitchen, grabbed the tape, and came back into the living room, all the while trying to brainstorm a way to get past the pistols.

"Tape RoboCop's hands," the cowboy said.

"You're fucking up big-time," Petty said.

"I'm getting tired of telling you shit twice," the cowboy said.

Petty bent over Tony and wrapped a couple of loops of

tape around his wrists, binding them together. The kid's breath stank, his mouth gone dry from fear. He was trembling like a drawn bowstring.

"Now hit him," the cowboy said.

"What?" Petty said.

"Haul off and belt him as hard as you can."

"No."

"Hard as you can. Right in his lying fucking face."

"I'm not doing that."

"Hit him, or I'll shoot *you*."

Petty stared at the cowboy, stared down the barrels of the revolvers, stared at the bullets nestled in the cylinders, then turned and popped Tony in the jaw.

"Fuck!" Tony yelled.

"Harder!" the cowboy said.

Petty reset and hit the kid again, so hard this time it hurt his knuckles. Tony tried to stand but couldn't without using his hands. A sound came from him, a rising hiss, like a safety valve about to blow.

"Stop crying and tell me where the money is," the cowboy said.

"Antonio Mendoza!" Tony shouted. "Corporal, United States Marine Corps, 573344076!"

The cowboy blinked, confused. "What?"

"Antonio Mendoza, Corporal, United States Marine Corps, 573344076!"

"His name, rank, and serial number," Petty said. "That's all he's giving you."

"Is that right?" the cowboy said.

He turned to Petty.

"Pull off that fake leg and beat him over the head with it."

"You're fucking crazy," Petty said.

The cowboy pointed both revolvers at Petty. "Take off that leg and beat him till I see blood."

Pow! A gun went off. *Pow! Pow!* Petty ducked, wondering where he'd been hit and waiting to feel the pain. The cowboy dropped his pistols and stood, stunned, in the middle of the room. His hands rose like a lover's to his chest, where three black holes suddenly gushed red. Another *Pow!* sent his hat flying. This bullet entered under his eye and blew off the back of his head. He dropped, and Petty turned to see a vision of smoking doom, Tony now pointing a Glock at him.

12

PETTY'S SURVIVAL INSTINCT KICKED IN. HE WAS TWO SECONDS from taking a bullet from a one-legged Mexican kid while a no-name stranger bled out at his feet. Time to do some fast talking.

"Hold up!" he shouted, thrusting his hands in the air.

"Don't move," Tony said.

"It's okay," Petty said. "I'm on your side. Everything's cool now. Everything's fine."

The gun in Tony's hand wavered the tiniest bit.

"It was self-defense," he said.

"Absolutely," Petty said.

"You're my witness."

"You were in fear for your life. He was gonna kill us both."

Tony lowered the gun. His mouth opened and closed like a fish dragged onto dry land as he stared at the dead cowboy. Petty edged toward the door. Rain was still coming down hard outside, buckets of ball bearings, and thunder roared again and shook the apartment in its jaws. So maybe, *maybe,* the neighbors hadn't heard the shots.

"Can you get this off me?" Tony said, talking about the tape, extending his hands.

Petty hesitated. All he had to do was twist the doorknob and step outside, and he'd be clear of this mess. But the kid looked so pitiful slumped on the couch, and the sneaker on his fake foot was suddenly the saddest thing Petty had ever seen. He walked over and tugged at the tape but couldn't get a decent grip on it with his fingers shaking like they were. He found a steak knife in the kitchen and used that to cut the kid free. He was at the door again when Tony called from the couch.

"Wait."

Petty turned, expecting to see the gun, but the kid was just sitting there, his hands in his lap.

"You gotta help me," he said.

"I can't help you," Petty said. "Call the cops."

"I can't."

"Why not?"

Tony hesitated.

"The money," he said.

"What about the money?"

Tony paused again, but Petty already knew what he was going to say.

"I've got it. Not here, but I've got it."

"Stop," Petty said.

"If you help me—" Tony continued.

"Stop," Petty said again. Someone was already lying dead on the floor, and Petty wasn't about to stick his head any further into the lion's mouth. He turned back to the door.

"Okay, go ahead and go," Tony said. "But if you do, I'll tell the cops you were trying to rob me, too. You'll be an accomplice or whatever they call it."

"You do that, and I'll tell them about the money," Petty said.

The kid's face fell. Fear had stripped years off him. He looked like a scared little boy.

"Come on, man," he said. "What do I do?"

"About this?" Petty said, gesturing at the dead cowboy.

Tony nodded.

"How the fuck should I know?" Petty said. "You're the killer. You're the Marine."

"Yeah, but with my leg and everything."

"Pull yourself together and *semper fi* this piece of shit."

"I need help."

"Not from me."

"I'll give you half my share of the money, two hundred and fifty thousand dollars."

"I don't want it."

"Please," Tony said. "I can't go to prison."

Petty's gut was still screaming *run,* but deep down he knew things would only get worse for him if he left the kid to handle this mess on his own, that somehow it would come back to haunt him. Fighting his natural instinct wasn't easy, though. It was as if he'd decided to battle a river, to stand suddenly against a strong, snatching current. He was nearly swept off his feet as he shuffled closer to the frightened kid and the cowboy's corpse.

"Get up," he said.

"You gonna help me?" Tony said.

"I'm gonna try," Petty said.

"Thanks," Tony said as he struggled to stand. "And we can go get the money afterward."

"I told you, I don't want it," Petty said.

"Why not?" Tony said.

"Because it looks to me like it'd be way more trouble than it's worth," Petty said. "Now, listen, do you have any plastic bags?"

Petty focused on the USMC flag hanging on the wall as he grabbed the cowboy's blood-soaked shirt and lifted so that Tony could slip a Hefty Ultra Flex over what was left of the dude's head. Not having the corpse's eyes staring at them would make the rest of it easier.

Next Petty sliced open some of the bags, spread them out on the floor, and duct-taped them together to form a makeshift shroud. He felt calmer now. He'd drawn up a mental punch list, and all he had to do was work his way down it, step by step. The kid had also settled once Petty started giving orders. The only time he bucked was when Petty told him to empty the cowboy's pockets.

"Me?" he said.

"What's wrong?" Petty said.

"I don't know if I can."

"Empty his fucking pockets!"

Tony grimaced and bent over the body. He rooted around in the cowboy's jeans and found a key ring, a phone, and extra rounds for the revolvers. They rolled the corpse on its side, and a back pocket yielded a wallet attached to a chain. Tony tossed the wallet onto the couch with the pistols and the other items.

"What we're gonna do now is lift him onto the bags," Petty said. "I'll get his shoulders, you get his feet."

"Roger that," Tony said, moving into position.

"One, two..."

They carried the body across the room, its ass almost dragging on the floor, and lowered it gently onto the shroud. Petty got busy with the tape and scissors again. He wrapped the shroud around the corpse, sealed the seam, and finished with loops of tape drawn tight at the neck, waist, and ankles. When he was done, the package looked like a sailor ready for burial at sea.

The blood that was puddled on the linoleum where the body had lain was already beginning to darken and dry. More blood was spattered on the wall. Luckily Tony was a clean freak. In the cupboard under the kitchen sink were bottles of Lysol and Mop & Glo and a pile of rags.

They set to work swabbing the gore. You couldn't be more thorough than Tony was. He used his fingernail to scrape out the crack between the baseboard and the floor and rinsed the mop again and again in the sink until the water drained clear. An hour later there wasn't a drop of blood anywhere.

"I need a beer," Tony said. He was in the kitchen, stowing the cleaning supplies. "You want a beer?"

"Sure," Petty said. He sat on the couch and closed his eyes, pushed out everything but the sound of the rain. Something poked his leg. He reached under his thigh and came up with Tony's Glock. He'd only held a gun once before, while target shooting with a friend. Even with earmuffs on he'd flinched whenever the pistol went off and missed the paper target nine times out of ten.

Tony stopped short when he came into the room and saw the gun in Petty's hand, looked nervous. Petty didn't let on how uncomfortable he was holding the pistol. He released the magazine—remembered how to do that—dropped it, and slid it back into place.

"Where'd this come from?" he asked Tony.

"I keep it under the cushions," Tony said. "You never know around here."

Petty set the gun on the couch beside him. Tony passed him

a Tecate and sat on the couch, too, leaving the gun lying between them.

Petty popped open his beer, picked up the dead man's wallet, and looked through it. A Texas driver's license identified
the cowboy as Greg Cherry. He didn't have a beard in the
photo, but it was him. He carried a Visa card, a Bank of
America debit card, players' club cards from a couple of Reno
casinos, and a Safeway rewards card. A thousand dollars in
hundreds and twenties was nestled in the main pocket of the
wallet; an ancient condom moldered in another.

One of the three keys on the ring was to a Ford. The
others, who knew? The phone was locked. Petty tried 1234
and ABCD as passwords, hoping to get lucky. He didn't.

Tony watched him with a blank expression, like this was TV
and not something he was living through.

"We've got to get rid of the body," Petty said.

"Right," Tony said.

"I'm not making an announcement, I'm asking for sugges-
tions. I'm not from around here."

"The mountains are close. They're always finding dead people there."

"How about someplace they won't find him?" Petty said.

"The desert?" Tony said.

Petty saw that he was going to be doing most of the thinking
tonight.

"All right, the desert," he said. "Anyplace in particular?"

"It's the desert," Tony said. "Shouldn't anywhere be good?"

Petty checked his watch: 3:00 p.m. Because of the storm,
it was already dark outside and would soon be darker. If they
left now, they'd be in the middle of nowhere by nightfall.
He pulled up a map on his phone and followed the 15 over
the Cajon Pass and past the sprawl of Victorville. Plenty of

dead ends out there and not many houses. He noted one possibility—a nameless spur off a dirt track called Sidewinder Road. It petered out on a flat behind a low hill that would hide them while they worked. But then how long would it take to dig the grave? An hour? Two?

Petty smelled something funny. A balky sewer line, he hoped, and not the corpse already going bad. The last of his beer tasted strange, too. He needed to call Tinafey. Cell signal was likely to be iffy where they were headed.

"Do you have a shovel?" he asked Tony.

"A shovel?" Tony said, like he'd never heard the word before. "No. Maybe the neighbors?"

"Right," Petty said. "Nothing weird about that if the cops come asking around later, some dude banging on your door in the middle of a storm and wanting to borrow a shovel."

"Oh," Tony said.

"Get dressed."

Petty put the cowboy's pistols, wallet, phone, and extra bullets in a Hefty bag.

"You should get rid of this, too," he said, holding up Tony's Glock.

"Yeah, fuck yeah, get rid of it," Tony said.

Petty wiped the gun down and dropped it in with the other stuff. He and Tony rolled the body up in a blanket, a fleece swap-meet number with Iron Man printed on it, as if that would be any less conspicuous than trash bags to anyone watching them carry the bundle out of the apartment and down the stairs to the garage. They had the rain for cover, at least, and the gloom. And then there was the fact that the people who lived in the neighborhood tended to ignore anything that smacked of trouble.

Tony's fake leg made him awkward descending the stairs, but he never asked Petty to slow down. The garage was already flooded with a foot of water, and more flowed down the driveway every second. Petty and Tony sloshed across the pond to Tony's F-150 and lowered the dead cowboy into the bed. Tony pulled a plastic tarp out of the truck's toolbox and covered the body with it, tucked it tight, then got in and started the engine. Petty settled into the passenger seat, his soaked Nikes leaking all over the floor mat.

The truck splashed to the driveway. The wake it created smacked the cinder-block walls. They climbed up and out into the last of the dripping daylight, pure gaudery, silver trees, silver streets, silver sky.

Halfway up the block Petty had Tony pull over. He aimed the cowboy's Ford key out the window and pressed the Unlock button. The taillights of an Explorer parked near the corner flashed.

"Boom!" Tony said.

Petty stepped out of the pickup and carefully squished his way to the Explorer, carrying the bag containing the cowboy's effects and Tony's gun. The rain had slowed to a sprinkle, but he still didn't trust the oily pavement, wouldn't risk a slip by hurrying. He climbed into the Explorer and slid the key into the ignition. Classical music blared when the truck started. Petty slapped the radio's Off button and gunned the engine, listening for trouble in the rev.

The Explorer smelled like restless nights and hungover mornings. The cowboy had been living out of the vehicle. The rear seats were down, and a sleeping bag was spread in the cargo bay. McDonald's cups here, Taco Bell wrappers there, and a pizza box on the floor. The ashtray was overflowing. Petty poked around in a duffel stashed under the passenger seat:

underwear and socks; a kit bag containing a toothbrush, deodorant, and a disposable razor; and a paperback book with a dragon on the cover. Nothing helpful. The center console and glove compartment were full of the usual junk.

He lowered the window and motioned for Tony to pull up.

"Where's the nearest Home Depot?" he asked him.

"Pretty close," Tony replied. The scar on his face flashed like more lightning in the watery dusk.

"I'll follow you."

The sloppy black streets took them past bus stops where the lucky huddled under umbrellas and plastic bags and the unlucky stood out in the rain bareheaded. A cop waved traffic through a chaotic intersection, every light blinking red, and in a neighborhood where the power had gone out, flashlight beams swept the walls and ceilings of darkened apartments like the search was on for someone.

Only the driver's-side wiper worked in the Explorer, but the storm was breaking up anyway. The blanket of clouds had unraveled in the west, revealing a patch of battered sky. At a long light Petty reached for a Christmas card that had fallen off the dash. On the front was a nativity scene—Mary, Joseph, baby Jesus—and inside was a note written in carefully looped cursive. Petty let the card drop without reading it. He didn't want to know any more about the cowboy than he already did.

A cricket chirped louder than the engine, louder than the lone wiper. Petty looked around for it before realizing that the sound was a ringtone. He reached into the bag for the cowboy's phone. The call was from the 305 area code. Miami, and Petty recognized Avi's number.

So Avi was in on the double cross, too. In fact he had to be the brains behind it. He'd never play second fiddle to anyone, much less a broken-down has-been like Don. Petty thought about answering. *How you doin', motherfucker?* But that would be stupid. That would give the man everything he needed to plow him under. Instead he opened his door at the next red, dropped the phone to the pavement, and stomped it to pieces.

When they got to Home Depot he sent Tony in to buy two shovels; let him be the one on the security cameras. The orange parking-lot lights sparked the drizzle into liquid fire that poured down on the handymen pushing carts piled high with plastic sheeting and roofing tar, on the day laborers in their driveway exile, on a fat security guard wearing soggy reindeer horns.

Petty adjusted the heater vents so that hot air blasted his wet shoes. He cleared his throat and called Tinafey.

"Hey, baby," he said.

"Where are you?"

"Still working. It looks like I won't be back until late."

"Uh-huh. And what am I supposed to do? I been locked up here all day, watchin' TV, watchin' it rain."

"Go out to dinner," Petty said. "Go to a movie." He shut one eye and looked at the world through a raindrop clinging to the windshield, everything turned upside down.

"I'm lonely," Tinafey said.

"You can't be lonely when someone's thinking about you," Petty said.

"Who's that? You? Well, I'm thinkin' about you, too."

"Good. I'll be back as soon as I can."

"You better be, 'cause it ain't like you're the only man on the face of the earth."

The rain began to beat down again with a hiss like radio static. Petty cracked his window so the windshield wouldn't fog, and the air that rushed in reeked of gasoline and scorched rubber. Driving a dead man's car. He was driving a dead man's car.

"Listen," he said to Tinafey. "I put some money in the room safe. I want you to have the combination."

"Why?" she said.

"In case."

"In case of what?"

"Get a pen or put it in your phone or something."

"Why you tryin' to scare me?"

"There's nothing to be scared of. You never know what might happen, that's all."

The sound of the TV in the background on Tinafey's end faded away. "What's goin' on?" she said.

"You ready?" he said.

"Don't ignore me," she said.

"The combination is 9229. Got it?"

"I said don't ignore me."

Petty was sweating from the effort of pushing around in his head all the different ways things could go wrong. He turned down the heater.

"If you don't hear from me by tomorrow night, take the money in the safe and go to Memphis," he said.

"So you're gonna order me around now, too?" Tinafey said.

"I'm sorry, baby," he said.

He ended the call. A rubber gorilla, a toy, hung from the rearview mirror. He punched it like he was hitting a speed bag, one fist, then the other, over and over, faster and faster, concentrating, not letting anything else in.

13

THE MOON EMERGED BRIGHT WHITE AND MERCILESS AS PETTY crested the Cajon Pass. The veil of clouds that previously concealed it had been torn to shreds by a bullying wind that rocked the cowboy's Explorer every time it gusted. Petty tightened his grip on the wheel and tapped the brakes to slow his descent into Victorville, which flickered like a bucket of embers strewn across the desert. He checked his rearview mirror for the lights of Tony's pickup, and there they were.

After racing through a kaleidoscope of fast-food joints and big-box stores, the two men found themselves again in the wilderness, what passed for civilization out here giving way to rushing darkness. Ten minutes out of town, Petty's phone prompted him that the exit for Sidewinder Road lay ahead. He put on his turn signal, slowed, and slid into the right-hand lane behind a big rig. Tony tucked in behind him.

They got off the freeway and crossed over it to pick up

Sidewinder, which devolved quickly from pavement to graded dirt. Petty slowed way down after bottoming out in a puddle that turned out to be deeper than it looked. The parched ground had already soaked up most of the day's rain, but water still stood in potholes and washes. The wind continued to buffet the truck, and tumbleweeds bounded across the road, flashing in the headlights like fleeing animals.

Motorcycle and ATV trails crisscrossed the surrounding hills, a delicate tracery under the moonlight. Petty, followed by Tony, drove until he came to the turnoff he'd noted on the map. It was a narrower, rougher road than the one they were on. They'd have to take it slow.

Thanks to the rain, there was little dust, so Tony was able to stay close as they bounced along the rutted track. The road ran along the base of the scarred hills, circling them to end in a wide, flat expanse of hardpan that served as a shooting range and a party spot for off-roaders. Broken beer bottles, empty shotgun shells, and other trash littered the site, and a ring of blackened stones formed a fire pit. Massive boulders, defaced by graffiti, hulked nearby. Petty had wanted to bury the cowboy in a less trafficked spot, but this would have to do. It was no night to go rattling around in search of somewhere better.

He pulled up to the fire pit. Tony did the same. It was colder than Petty had expected when he stepped out of the truck, dark-side-of-the-moon cold, and all he had on was a T-shirt, the safety vest, and a hoodie.

"Fuck!" Tony said. "I shoulda brought a coat."

Petty moved away from the vehicles and peered into the darkness. The cooling engines ticked, and the wind moaned whenever it ramped up to full strength. "Do you have a flashlight?" he asked Tony.

The kid passed him his keys, which had a tiny Maglite dangling from the ring. Petty twisted the light to turn it on and kicked his way toward open desert, probing for softer ground in which to do their digging. Hardpan gave way to sand at the edge of the gathering place, but Petty continued out into the scrub for some distance before calling for the shovels.

Tony carried them over his shoulder. "Here?" he said when he reached Petty.

"It's far enough away if we go deep."

"Roger that."

They dug in the dark, scooping a rough rectangle. It was frustrating at first. Sand rushed back into the hole every time Petty lifted out a load. A foot down, the soil was more compacted and began to hold the shape of the grave. The two men worked in silence except for the huffing of their breath, which plumed blue-white. When Petty's conscience nagged him in the quiet, asking, *What the fuck did you get yourself into?* he drowned it out by counting. One shovelful, two shovelfuls, three.

The cadence superseded time. One, two, three. One, two, three. A minute, an hour, a lifetime. Sand, wind, stars. The fugue was interrupted when Tony threw down his shovel and sat heavily on the edge of the grave.

"I gotta. Take. A break," he said, panting.

Petty stopped digging, too, cupped his hands on the rounded end of his shovel's handle and rested his chin on them. He felt a sting in his palm and discovered a blister, already torn. A polar gust chilled the sweat sliming his face and neck and arms, and he was cold again. He spit mud and cleared his nostrils of black snot. Tony lay back with a loud groan.

"We're down about, what, three feet?" he said.

"About that," Petty said.

"Does he deserve three more?"

It didn't matter what he deserved. What was important was that he stay buried.

Petty couldn't get his rhythm back when they resumed digging. Every second dragged, and every scoop was distinct, painful in its own way. Petty's hands hurt, his back, his shoulders. He got sloppy, whacking Tony with the blade of his shovel and dropping dirt. They decided to take turns in the hole, ten-minute shifts, so that whoever was digging would have room to maneuver.

During his breaks Petty sat on the mound humped around the grave and let his heart slow to normal. The one time he looked up at the stars, he felt like he was falling into them, so he kept his eyes on the ground.

The deeper they dug, the more difficult it was for Tony, with his prosthesis, to get in and out of the grave. Petty had to lie back and pull with all his weight to haul him onto the lip of the hole, then the kid would crawl the rest of the way out. When they got down to five feet, Petty started having trouble climbing out himself, even with the toeholds they'd chopped into the wall. They'd been digging for more than three hours. No critter, no matter how hungry, was going to work that hard to get at the body. Petty tossed a last scoop of dirt over his shoulder and announced, fuck it, they were finished.

They limped their way back to Tony's truck. The kid turned the heater on high. Petty could have sat there forever, warming his hands at the vent, but it was past midnight. There was no time to rest if they wanted to be gone by sunrise.

Tony pulled two bottles of water from behind the seat and passed one to Petty. Petty gulped it down.

"At least covering him'll be easier," Tony said. His face was smeared with dirt, his T-shirt black with it.

"Let's hope," Petty said. He ran his fingers along the dashboard. "Nice truck."

"They had a fund-raiser at my high school when I got back," Tony said. "Everyone pitched in."

"That was cool," Petty said.

"Yeah," Tony said, then his face crumpled. "But now I've fucking blown it."

"Trouble found you," Petty said. "It happens."

"What kind of advice is that?"

"Calm down," Petty said. "Keep it together."

"I am keeping it together."

"Good. Let's finish this."

They lifted the cowboy's wrapped corpse, already beginning to stiffen, from the back of Tony's truck. Petty thought he had the head, but for some stupid reason wanted to be sure. He reached down and felt an ear through the plastic and wished he hadn't been so curious. When they got to the grave they stood holding the body over it, unsure how to proceed.

"Drop it on three," Petty finally said.

"Drop it?" Tony said.

"One, two..."

The corpse hit bottom with a thud, and the moon showed it lying in the grave. It fit perfectly. Petty went back to the truck for the bag containing the guns and the wallet and threw that in the hole, too.

The filling went faster than the digging. Petty waited to check their progress until they'd been working for a while. By then the body had been covered by sand. Petty took this as the first step toward forgetting about it.

In a little more than an hour they were stomping on the grave a final time to pack the dirt. When that was done, they scattered rocks around the site and swept away their footprints. In the dark you could barely tell the ground had been disturbed. A couple of days of sun and scouring wind, and all traces of their dirty work would be obliterated.

Next on the agenda was getting rid of the cowboy's Explorer. Tony suggested they drop it at a chop shop run by a friend of his, but Petty pointed out it wouldn't be smart to involve anybody else. He also rejected the idea of torching the truck nearby, worried that a fire in the night would attract attention. They finally decided to ditch the Explorer at the Indian casino in San Bernardino. The casino was only a couple-mile detour on their way back to L.A., and Petty knew gamblers who lived out of their cars during weeklong binges at those places, so a vehicle sitting in the lot for an extended period of time wouldn't be out of the ordinary.

The casino was one of those designed to look more like a desert resort than another sad, smoky grind joint. The faux adobe building sported heavy wood beams, natural stone columns, and subdued signage. Petty backed the Explorer into a spot on the second floor of the parking structure and wiped down the steering wheel and dashboard with a T-shirt from the cowboy's duffel. When he was finished, he pulled the hood of his jacket over his head and jogged down a flight of stairs to a door that opened onto the driveway.

The pavement was still wet from the rain, and water murmured in the gutters and dripped from the trees. Tony was waiting two blocks away, parked on a dark side street. While he drove them back to the freeway, Petty reviewed his mental checklist. As far as he could figure, he'd done everything he could to cover his tracks. Now it was down to Tony. If the kid kept his mouth shut, they'd both be in the clear.

As they approached the on-ramp Tony turned into a Shell

station for gas. Petty told him to pay cash. After inserting the nozzle into the tank, the kid motioned for Petty to open his door.

"I'm so hungry I'm about to pass out," he said. He pointed to a Denny's across the street. "You want to get something to eat?"

Petty was bone-tired, but it was important he keep the kid happy. People who felt like they were alone often made selfish decisions, and Tony would be less likely to blow this if he thought Petty had his back.

So: "Sure," Petty said. "I could handle a Grand Slam."

They washed up in the restaurant's bathroom and got a booth by the window. Petty ordered egg whites and turkey bacon, and Tony asked for chicken-fried steak. Their waiter had a glass eye. At 3:00 a.m. there were only two other customers—an old man reading a newspaper at the counter and a woman doing something on her phone. Mexican music leaked into the dining room from the kitchen.

Tony poked at a blister on the web between his thumb and forefinger. His lips moved slightly, like he was whispering to himself.

"You okay?" Petty asked, stirring sugar into his coffee.

Tony reached for the sugar, too. "I'm fine," he said. "What's next?"

"Nothing," Petty said. "You go on with your life, I go on with mine, and we forget this ever happened."

"That's what I'm gonna do," the kid said. "I'm gonna go on with my life."

Petty sipped his coffee. He'd never tasted anything so good.

"Let me ask you something," he said to Tony. "How the fuck did you get into this?"

"It was my cousin," Tony said. "He called last year from

Afghanistan. I hadn't heard from him in forever, not even when I got wounded. 'How'd you like to make some money?' he said. 'You know what happened to me, right?' I said. 'That's why I picked you,' he said. 'Time for your payback.' That sounded good to me, so I didn't ask too many questions. Pretty soon after that FedEx started dropping off boxes of money every month or so."

"Next time, ask more questions," Petty said.

"There ain't gonna be no next time," Tony said. "When Mando gets back and I get my cut, I'm moving away."

"You don't like L.A.?"

"I been living here all my life, but after Afghanistan, I'm too jumpy. A car backfires, I have a heart attack."

"The V.A. has shrinks."

"Yeah. So?"

"Go see one. Maybe it'll help."

"I'm not crazy," Tony said with a dismissive wave of his hand. "I just don't like noise and shit. And all the fucking punks who think they're hard 'cause the *abuelitas* in the neighborhood are scared of them. I'd like to drop them into Helmand and see how badass they'd be. The fucking hajis'd cut their heads off and put it on YouTube."

The kid kicked Petty with his fake foot under the table and sloshed coffee over the rim of his cup when he lifted it to drink. He was getting worked up.

"You know what's weird, though?" he continued. "What happened to me wasn't even the hajis' fault. It was the Russians. The mine I stepped on was one of theirs from the eighties or whatever. Can you fucking believe it?"

"That's fucked up," Petty said.

"Yeah, but at least I still got my dick," Tony said. "A lot of dudes got their dicks blown off, their balls, their *assholes*."

The waiter delivered their food. Petty watched the kid tear into his breakfast. It was a shame what had happened to him over there, but he was nothing but trouble, and Petty knew the sooner he cut him loose, the better.

"So this is the last time we're gonna see each other," he said.

"You breaking up with me?" Tony said, mouth full of hash browns.

"I'm serious," Petty said. "But I need to tell you some things before I go."

"So tell me," the kid said.

"The guy who sent the cowboy, he might not give up."

"That Don dude you wanted to call?"

"It's not Don you have to worry about. It's another guy, a guy named Avi."

"What do you mean, worry?"

"I mean the cowboy was probably reporting to Avi, so Avi probably knows where you live, which means more assholes might show up on your doorstep, looking for the money."

"It's not there, though," Tony said. "It's somewhere else."

"Doesn't matter," Petty said. "They're gonna come to your place, and you're gonna have to deal with them."

"How?"

"You want my advice? Move out of your apartment."

"Where am I supposed to go?"

"I don't know," Petty said. "You've got to think for yourself from here on out."

"This is fucking crazy," Tony said.

"It gets crazier," Petty said. "Avi also knows about your mom's store, so she's in danger, too."

Tony brought his fist down on the table, made everything jump. "If he fucks with her, he's dead," he said.

"Have her close up for a while and take a vacation," Petty said. "That way Avi can't use her to find you."

"How am I gonna explain that?" Tony said. "She doesn't know anything about what's going on."

"Once again, you're gonna have to think for yourself," Petty said.

Tony ground his palms into his eyes. "Mando'll kill me if he finds out about this," he said.

"That your cousin?"

"He'll kill me if I fuck this up."

"So don't fuck it up. Get out of your apartment, get your mother out of her store, and lay low until Mando gets back."

Tony continued to shake his head. Plates clattered in the kitchen, and someone back there whistled. The man at the counter asked the waiter what time a certain bus made its first run of the day. The waiter didn't know.

"Hey," Petty said to Tony. "Look at me."

Tony's bloodshot eyes rose above the tips of his fingers.

"Man the fuck up," Petty said.

"Right," Tony said. "I have to. I just fucking have to."

Maybe things would work out for the kid. Petty doubted it, but at the same time he didn't wish anything bad on him.

They drove back to L.A. in silence, Petty getting lost in the tail-lights of the car in front of them on the freeway. Forty years of fighting gravity, and what did he have to show for it? A failed marriage, a daughter on dope, and a wallet full of maxed-out credit cards. Every time he managed to put together two pennies, he threw it away in a poker game. And now, to top it off, the biggest score he'd ever gotten close to had gone south, and he was an accessory to murder. He was sure somebody somewhere was having a good laugh at his expense.

But he still wasn't ready to give up on himself. He wasn't a quitter, never had been. You asked yourself the hard questions, the whos, whats, and whys, but you didn't let the answers drag you down. You took a hot shower, you got a good night's sleep, you figured out what had to be done, and you did it.

When they got to Tony's neighborhood, he had the kid drop him off a block from his car, didn't want him to see what he was driving.

"Good luck," he said as he slid out of the truck.

"You ever shoot anyone before?" Tony said out of nowhere.

"I told you, I don't mess with guns," Petty said.

"I shot some hajis in Afghanistan, but it was from far away," Tony said. "Today, though, that guy—" He paused and shook his head, looked like he was about to cry.

"Listen," Petty said. "It was him or you, right?"

"Right. He would have killed me if I didn't kill him," Tony said. "Killed you, too."

"So you did what you had to do," Petty said. "Simple as that."

"Him or me," Tony said.

"You or him," Petty said. He closed the door, eager to end the conversation and be on his way. "You're tired," he said. "Get some sleep."

He waited to walk to his Benz until the truck had turned the corner. He thought he'd feel better as soon as he got behind the wheel and even better when he reached the freeway and started putting some miles between him and Tony and the day's trouble, but when he got back to Hollywood there was still a stone where his heart should have been, and his throat was still clogged with mud. The look on the cowboy's face when he realized he'd been shot kept strobing behind his eyes, and the feel of the guy's ear through the plastic before they dumped him in the hole clung to his fingers. He took deep breaths as he cruised the empty predawn streets, flexed his jaw and rolled his shoulders, forcing himself to relax. *You did what you had to do,* he thought. The words circled in his head like a chant, a mantra. *You did what you had to do. What you had to do. What you had to do.*

14

PETTY PULLED A MASTERCARD WITH SOME ROOM ON IT OUT OF his wallet and passed it to the girl behind the counter at Gucci. His hand still hurt from last night's digging.

"For real?" Tinafey said.

"Merry early Christmas."

Tinafey hugged the gold leather purse to her chest. "It's too much, isn't it?" she said.

It was, but at least now Petty could be sure she wouldn't forget him when she left for Memphis, and that sliver of space in her memory was worth two grand.

They'd been walking up and down Rodeo Drive for the past hour, Tinafey getting off just saying the names of the stores they passed: Prada, Dior, Tiffany. She'd tried on shoes at Jimmy Choo and spritzed perfume at Chanel before they'd stopped at Gucci and she'd picked up the purse and said, "Isn't this gorgeous?"

"I'm gonna carry it out," she said to the salesgirl now.

The girl slid her old purse into a bag, and Tinafey kissed Petty on the cheek as they left the store.

"I wasn't askin' for it," she said. "I was showin' it to you."

"I know," he said. "But I wanted you to have it."

She kissed him again and held the purse out in front of her and chanted what sounded like a nursery rhyme: "Gucci, Gucci, Louis, Louis, Fendi, Fendi, Prada."

Petty smiled. He'd been feeling good ever since waking this morning and finding himself safe in bed at the hotel.

"Where do you want to go today?" he'd asked Tinafey over room-service breakfast, finally ready to do the sightseeing he'd promised her.

"How about Beverly Hills?" was her response.

Tinafey looked into a few more stores and had him take photos of her posing with her new purse in front of a palm tree and next to a Lamborghini parked at the curb. They sat down at a café that had tables outside and ordered coffee. Tinafey was hoping to see somebody famous, but most of the passersby were tourists.

"If you were Beyoncé, you wouldn't be hangin' around here anyway," Tinafey said. "When you're that big, you got people who do your shoppin' for you."

"You're probably right," Petty said.

"Or you come at night, after the store's closed. That's what Michael Jackson did."

"Yeah?"

"I wouldn't be like that, though. I'd want people to see me. I'd sign autographs, take pictures, be a nice person. I'd be grateful for my fans."

"I'm a fan of yours," Petty said. "What are you gonna do for me?"

"You're my number one fan," Tinafey said. "You get special treatment."

She reached under the table and gave his thigh a quick squeeze while grinning her gap-toothed grin, then sat back and said, "So what happened yesterday?"

"What do you mean?" Petty said, feeling like she'd set a trap for him.

"You come in at five in the morning covered with mud, all tore up, groanin' like an old man in the shower, and I'm not supposed to notice?"

"It's nothing you want to hear about."

"Meanin' it's nothin' you want to talk about."

"Right."

"Meanin' you don't trust me."

Petty shifted in his chair, uncomfortable. A skinny blonde passed by, walking a dog wearing a sweater. The sky was clear, the sun was out, but there was still a chill in the air, one you didn't notice until you were in the shade.

"I trust you fine," Petty said. "But this is one of those the-less-you-know-the-better deals."

"Oh," Tinafey said with mock seriousness. "One of those."

"Look," Petty said. "Why'd you come with me from Reno?"

"To have fun."

"Right. And that's what we're gonna do now."

"Are you in trouble?"

"I don't think so," Petty said. "Not anymore."

"And how long we got?"

"What do you mean?"

"Together. Here. How long we got?"

Petty had been trying to figure that out himself. If the cow-boy had been in regular contact with Avi, Avi probably knew

Petty was staying at the Loews and that he'd made contact with Tony. Eventually he was going to wonder what had happened to his man, and Petty didn't plan to be around if someone came asking questions. At the same time, it was important that he didn't look like he was running away, like he knew anything about the cowboy's disappearance.

"I'm leaving for Phoenix on Friday," he said to Tinafey. "That gives us three more days."

Tinafey tapped her long, red fingernails on the table and thought this over.

"Three days, huh?" she said. "Well, we best make the most of them."

Petty smiled at her response. If she'd asked for something else right then—another purse, a pair of shoes—he'd have knocked over the nearest bank to buy it for her.

"How'd I get so lucky?" he said.

"What do you mean?" Tinafey said.

"You're the hottest woman out here."

Tinafey smirked at this. "Ain't you smooth?" she said. "You must be pretty good at your hustle."

"I better be," Petty said. "I've been doing it long enough."

"Partin' fools and their money, huh?" Tinafey said.

Petty shrugged, like *You got it,* and reached over and covered one of her hands with his. "But this is no hustle," he said.

Tinafey scoffed again. "See, that's hustlers," she said. "They don't even know when they're hustlin'."

"You're not gonna show me any mercy, are you?" Petty said.

"It's all right, baby," Tinafey said. "We're all some kinda fucked up."

A homeless woman, a muttering crone layered in filthy sweaters, caught her attention. She called the woman over and gave her five dollars.

"Bless you," the woman said.

"Bless you, too," Tinafey said.

The woman continued on her way. Tinafey turned to Petty and wrinkled her nose.

"Did you smell that?" she said. "Oooooooweee!" She reached into her old purse for a bottle of Purell and squeezed some onto her hands. "Don't it break your heart?"

That night Petty called Don. The old man's betrayal, his plotting with Avi to send him to L.A. to look for the money and to take it from him if he found it, had enraged Petty. Under normal circumstances he'd have bitten off his own tongue rather than talk to the man again, but in order to create a cover story that would allow him to deny any involvement in the cowboy's disappearance, he had to report in, as he'd promised to do when he left Reno.

"Rowan, hey, how's it going?" Don said.

"Not good," Petty said. "Our little thing was a bust."

"What do you mean?"

"There's no money. I found the guy and got into his apartment and looked around, but there was nothing there."

"You're sure?" Don said.

"I'm sure," Petty said. "The trip was a total waste of my time."

Don paused, then said, "I'm sorry to hear that."

"Yeah, well, great," Petty said. "Your sorry and five bucks might buy me a beer."

"What are you gonna do now?"

"Something that'll make me some money. A buddy of mine's got a deal going in Denver. I might head out there."

"Well, good luck to you."

"Yeah, yeah, yeah."

"I mean it," Don said. "It was good seeing you again."

"Good seeing you, too," Petty said, choking on the words. "Take it easy."

He ended the call and hoped he'd never see either of them, Don or Avi, again.

The next morning he and Tinafey got directions from the hotel's concierge and drove to the Santa Monica Pier. The same tourists who'd been strolling Rodeo Drive the day before swarmed the pier today, but the beauty of the place made it easy to ignore them. The sky was once again a dreamy blue; the sea a crystalline purple that seemed to be lit from below. The swath of coastline on view stretched all the way from Malibu to the Palos Verdes Peninsula. Catalina Island, forty miles away, looked close enough to swim to.

Petty and Tinafey walked to the end of the pier. The massive wooden structure breathed under their feet, rising and falling with the swell. Fishermen lined the rails. They stared down at the water and slowly cranked their reels to get rid of the slack in their lines. Tinafey peeked into a few buckets. Nobody was having much luck. She told Petty a story about fishing with her grandfather, how he'd snag catfish by hand—hogging, he called it—groping blind in their hidey-holes and dragging them out.

A commotion erupted near the bait shop. An old Filipina, barely five feet tall, had hooked something big. Her family swarmed around her, shouting advice in Tagalog, but the woman slapped away all helping hands, determined to land her catch by herself.

She reeled in her line, and a baby tiger shark, two feet long, came into view. Tinafey gasped and clutched Petty's arm. The woman had the shark halfway to the rail, where a kid waited with a gaff, when it bit through the line. Down, down it dropped, back into the sea, sinking quickly from sight. A groan rose from the onlookers, and the woman hissed her disappointment and throttled her pole as if to punish it.

Tinafey wanted to ride the Ferris wheel, so they did, and the roller coaster, too. Petty warned her that the carnival games were rigged, but the barker at the basketball toss convinced her otherwise. Twenty dollars later she'd won a pink stuffed bear worth a buck and was delighted to have proved Petty wrong.

"'Don't play that,'" she said, imitating him, waving the bear in his face. "'That shit's a scam.'"

They went down to the beach and walked to the water's edge. What waves there were were small and sloppy, rising only a foot or so before making feeble dashes toward shore. Tinafey carried her shoes in one hand, the bear in the other. The gulls she chased squawked their annoyance and fled on bright orange legs.

It was warm enough for bathing suits, and looking at all the people stretched out on blankets and towels, you'd have thought it was the Fourth of July instead of the second day of December. A little boy and his dad braved the frigid water up to their knees, the boy shrieking like something wounded every time a wave swirled around them. Three high school girls in bikinis snapped photos of themselves after carefully adjusting their straps and smiles. An Indian woman wearing a sari poked at a knot of kelp with her bare foot and backed away in horror when a swarm of flies rose from it like a puff of black smoke.

"Let's sit a while," Tinafey said.

She picked a spot near the lifeguard station. Petty started to lay down his coat so she wouldn't get her dress sandy, but she said, "That's okay. I want to feel how warm it is." She leaned back on her elbows and turned her face to the sun.

"I'm gonna get freckles from this, you watch," she said.

"I feel like ice cream," Petty said. "You want anything?"

"I'll take a diet soda, if you're goin'."

He walked to a snack bar and waited in line behind a harried mom and the ten preteen boys she was chaperoning. One of the boys slugged another in the shoulder. The woman grabbed the first boy's arm and yanked hard.

"Chill out," the boy said.

"*You* chill out!" the woman yelled.

A girl passed by who resembled Sam, the Sam Petty remembered, not the ghost he'd met three days ago. He wondered how deep his daughter was into dope. Most of the coke fiends he knew straightened out after a while, mainly because they couldn't afford to keep going. The tweakers, too, but that shit took more of a toll, left guys sketchy for life. With alkies, it was fifty-fifty, but the math was simple: those who managed to quit lived, and those who couldn't died slowly and painfully.

Heroin addicts and pill poppers had the hardest time of it. Their poison fooled their bodies into thinking it was medicine. That's why ex-junkies always seemed so sad: the one thing they'd found that made them feel good would also eat them up.

It was Petty's turn to order. A soda for Tinafey and an ice cream sandwich for himself. The trash can at the end of the counter was overflowing. Yellow jackets hovered above it like military helicopters on a mission.

Tinafey was texting when Petty returned. It was none of his business, but still he wondered who it was. She stashed her phone in her purse when he sat beside her.

"Diet Pepsi's all they had," he said, passing her the cup.

"They're all the same," she said.

A pod of dolphins was making its way north beyond the

breakers. They launched themselves out of the water and arched through the air like targets in a shooting gallery, the sun glinting on their backs. Petty and Tinafey followed their progress up the coast until they finally lost them in the glare and the spray and the distance.

That night after they fucked Tinafey got up and went into the bathroom. Petty lay on his back, watching lights from outside skitter across the ceiling. He smelled weed and wondered why Tinafey thought she had to get high in secret. He didn't smoke himself, didn't like the way it separated his brain from his body, but he was fine with other people doing it. He was about to tell her to come out when her voice rose above the hum of the bathroom fan.

"Rowan," she said.

"Yeah?" Petty replied.

"Can you hear me?"

"Yeah."

"I'm gonna tell you somethin'."

Petty sat up and pulled the sheet to his waist.

"All right," he said.

"My real name's Yvonne."

"Yvonne. That's pretty."

"But I want you to keep callin' me Tinafey."

"Okay."

"And I'm thirty-three, not twenty-three."

"That's fine, too."

"It doesn't matter?"

"Of course not. Now, come out here."

"I will, but I don't want to talk about this when I do."

"We can talk about whatever you want."

"I don't want to talk about nothin'."

144

"Okay."

Tinafey returned to bed without a word. Wrapping her arms around Petty's neck, she buried her face in his shoulder. They lay like that a long while, breathing in sync, until Petty finally whispered, "You want to watch TV?" Tinafey nodded, and Petty put on a sitcom. Tinafey sat against the headboard and watched the stupid show with tears in her eyes, as intent on it as if it were news about the end of the world.

Later Petty dreamed about the cowboy. He and Tony were burying him in the desert, and the guy kept trying to climb out of the grave. Petty panicked and swung the shovel at him, hitting him in the head. The cowboy fell to the bottom of the hole but got right up again. Petty laid into him then, brought the shovel down sideways like an ax on the guy's head over and over until it split his skull and his brain sloshed out. And still he kept coming. Petty finally forced himself awake and lay there in the dark, tasting vomit.

15

PETTY FELT BETTER THE NEXT MORNING, AND WHATEVER HAD
been troubling Tinafey had passed, too. Petty heard her singing
in the bathroom, and she was as cheerful as ever at breakfast.
Their plan for the day was to drive to Disneyland.

"I know it's silly," Tinafey said. "But I always wanted to go
there."

They arrived at the front gate before the park opened. There
was already a line. The first thing Tinafey did when they got
inside was buy a Minnie Mouse hat from a shop on the old-
timey street of shops the park funneled everyone down after
loosening their wallets at the entrance. The hat had plastic ears
and a pink bow stapled to it, and Tinafey wore it in the photos
Petty took of her with Donald Duck and Goofy and a princess
dressed all in blue.

They went on the jungle boats, the Indiana Jones ride, and
the Haunted Mansion. Tinafey started conversations to pass

the time in the long lines, asking people where they were from and talking to kids about their favorite rides.

"You havin' fun?" she asked Petty every so often.

"Sure," he'd say. "What's next?" He'd vowed never to set foot in another theme park after a long, hot week with Sam in Orlando, but he didn't bring this up to Tinafey.

They had chicken nuggets and chili fries in an Old West saloon, then walked forever against the crowd to get to the Small World ride, which was at the top of Tinafey's list. The outside of the ride was a giant clock. It clicked and whirred every fifteen minutes during the hour they waited to get on. A band of toy soldiers appeared, and there'd be a parade of dolls dressed like leprechauns and geishas and flamenco dancers. More dolls danced and sang inside, herky-jerky cowboys and hula girls and Arabs on flying carpets, depending on what country your boat was supposed to be passing through.

Petty had a slight headache when it was over. He took some Midol Tinafey had in her purse before they set out for the Matterhorn.

"Then Star Wars," Tinafey said, consulting a map of the park. "My nephew said you got to."

Petty's phone vibrated in his pocket. It was his mom calling. He thought about letting her go to voice mail, but a bad feeling prompted him to take the call.

"Where are you?" Joanne said.

"Still in L.A.," Petty said. "Why?"

"Sam's in the hospital."

Petty motioned for Tinafey to hold up. He put a finger in his ear to block out the noise.

"The hospital?" he said.

"She passed out on a bus," Joanne said.

"Is she all right?"

The call was breaking up. Petty turned in a circle to see if he could snag a stronger signal. Then he realized that what he'd thought was static was actually Joanne crying.

"Is she all right?" he said again.

"I don't know," Joanne said. "But it can't be good. The paramedics had to come."

"What hospital?" he said. "I'll go right now."

"Someplace called Good Samaritan. The emergency room."

"I'll call as soon as I find out what happened."

Petty ended the call. Tinafey was watching him with a worried look.

"My daughter," he said and had to leave it at that when his voice suddenly choked off.

He came clean with Tinafey on their way back to L.A., told her that he'd met with Sam and suspected she was strung out on something, and now it appeared he'd been right. If Tinafey was upset he hadn't mentioned the meeting before, she didn't show it. He offered to drop her at the hotel, but she insisted he drive straight to the hospital, not wasting any time. He called Good Samaritan and was able to verify that Sam had been admitted to the ER. That was it, though. They wouldn't give him any more information over the phone.

The hospital was a modern complex at the edge of downtown. Mirrored windows in a sandstone facade. The girl manning the desk at the main entrance directed Petty to the emergency room. Tinafey told him to go on; she'd wait for him out front.

Petty's anxiety peaked as he approached the receptionist's window in the ER lobby. He was out of his element here, didn't know the rules or how to get around them. The woman behind the bulletproof glass didn't look up when he asked about Sam. She demanded ID, glanced at the driver's license he gave her, and told him to have a seat.

All the chairs were filled, so he stood against the wall. A lady judge scowling down from the TV shook a bony finger at the waiting room. At the girl trying to rock her crying baby quiet, at the Mexican with his hand wrapped in a bloody rag, at the fat woman in a wheelchair who moaned under her breath every few seconds, "Oh, God. Oh, God."

Petty couldn't keep still. His foot tapped, and his knee bounced. He took a couple of laps around the room and pretended to browse a rack of pamphlets on eating right and quitting smoking. A kid trying to knock loose a bag of Fritos punched the vending machine. The bang made everybody jump. Petty was suddenly certain that Sam had died. *That's why they won't let me see her,* he thought.

He was about to confront the receptionist, ask her what was taking so long, when a man in a white coat opened a door and called his name.

"You're Samantha Petty's father?" the guy asked, consulting a clipboard.

"Yes," Petty said.

"I'm Dr. Avakian," the guy said. He was short, with a shaved head, thick black eyebrows, and yellow teeth. Petty followed him into a small, cluttered office.

"So, okay," Dr. Avakian said. "The reason your daughter is here is that she had a seizure."

"From the drugs, right?" Petty said.

"What drugs?" Dr. Avakian said.

"I saw her a couple days ago, and she looked awful," Petty said. "I think she's on something."

Dr. Avakian checked his clipboard again. "We asked about drugs, and she indicated she didn't use any," he said.

149

"And her saying so is enough?" Petty said.

"We haven't seen any evidence that she wasn't telling the truth, and her blood work came back fine in that respect."

"Well, what, then? What caused the seizure?"

"That's what we're trying to find out. We're going to run some tests."

"What kind of tests?"

"For starters," Dr. Avakian said, "we're doing an MRI of her brain."

Her brain? Cold black water trickled down Petty's spine.

"Why?" he said.

"To look for anything out of the ordinary," Dr. Avakian said.

"Like what?"

"It could be any number of things."

"Stop it," Petty said. "Don't give me the runaround."

Dr. Avakian's face didn't change, but Petty could tell he was perturbed. His voice had an angry undertone when he said, "I know you're upset, but..."

Petty didn't back down. "Worst case," he said. "Tell me."

"It's much too early to talk about worst cases," Dr. Avakian said.

"Is it a tumor?"

"A tumor is one possibility."

"How long until you know for sure?"

"A few days," Dr. Avakian said. "We'll be keeping her here for observation until then."

Petty had to pause for a second. He stared at a photo on the wall. Half Dome in Yosemite. When he felt like he could talk again without stammering, he said, "Can I see her?"

"You can," Dr. Avakian said. "But only for a minute. She needs to rest."

Petty followed the doctor out into the ER, a ring of curtained cubicles surrounding a central nurses' station. They'd tried to soften the place with soothing colors and blond wood accents, but fear and pain and worry clung to everything like cigarette smoke in a cheap motel room. The fake Christmas tree, the pink scrubs, the poster of panda bears hugging: bullshit, bullshit, bullshit.

Dr. Avakian pulled aside the curtain of one of the cubicles. Sam lay there on a gurney, a blanket drawn up to her chin. Her eyes were closed, and thin blue veins fanned out over the lids. She looked even more frail than she had the other day. A bag of something dripped into her through an IV line, and some kind of monitor beeped quietly.

"Hey," Petty said.

Sam's eyes opened, and she gazed at him with no surprise, as if she'd expected to see him there.

"Hey," she replied.

Petty laid a hand on her shoulder. She let him.

"You doing okay?" he said.

"Yeah," she said. "I'm fine."

"What happened?"

"I don't know. I was on the bus going to work, and I woke up here."

"Grandma called, and I got here as fast as I could."

"She shouldn't have done that," Sam said.

"Yes, she should have," Petty said. "You should have called me yourself."

Sam frowned and took a deep breath that shook her whole body. She was acting tough, but Petty could see in her eyes how scared she was.

"What did he tell you?" she said, pointing with her chin at Dr. Avakian. "Quick. No bullshit."

"You had a seizure," Petty said. "They're trying to figure out why."

"What else?"

Petty glanced at Dr. Avakian.

"What else?" Sam said.

"Nothing else," Petty said. "They need to do tests." Sam made a face like she didn't believe him. He moved his hand to her forehead to push aside a strand of hair. She let him do that, too.

"Everything's going to be fine," he said. "They're gonna take good care of you."

Sam started to say something in response but instead bit her lip and turned away. A woman laughed out in the ER. A phone rang.

"Okay, Dad's got to go," Dr. Avakian said. "We're going to move you now, put you in a nice room."

Petty didn't want to leave, but at the same time he couldn't wait to get out. "I'll be back soon," he said. "Do you need anything?"

Sam shook her head without looking at him. A nurse bustled into the cubicle and said, "Time to draw more blood." Petty stepped away from the gurney, and the nurse pulled the curtain closed, shutting him out. Dr. Avakian walked him back to the ER lobby.

"I acted like an asshole earlier," Petty said. "I'm sorry."

"It's fine," Dr. Avakian said.

"It's just that I want you to keep me informed about what's going on. I want to be involved."

"I understand. Leave your number at the nurses' station."

Petty shook the doctor's hand like they were sealing a deal, but he wasn't sure the guy had heard a word he said. He felt like they'd been talking through a thick pane of glass. How many sick girls had he attended to already today? How many worried fathers had he dealt with? It was probably all a blur to him.

★   ★   ★

Tinafey was waiting on a bench outside. Petty told her everything was still up in the air and that meant a change of plans. He wouldn't be leaving for Phoenix tomorrow after all. Instead he'd move to a hotel closer to the hospital, closer to Sam.

"Even if she doesn't want me to, I'm staying," he said.

"She wants you to," Tinafey said.

"As for you, no problem," he said. "I'll drop you at the airport in the morning for your flight."

"It's okay," she said. "I'll get a taxi."

"What taxi? No taxi. I'll drive you."

"I don't want to be any trouble."

"You're no trouble."

Petty drove up Western Avenue to avoid the freeway at rush hour. All the signs for the stores and restaurants were in Korean. Petty had known a Korean once. All the dude talked about was golf.

Tinafey stared silently out the window, didn't even hum along with the radio like she usually did. Petty wished she would. Anything to take his mind off Sam.

"Even with all this shit going on, we should do something special," he said.

"Why?" Tinafey said.

"It's our last night together. We have to do it up right."

He pulled into a liquor store for Champagne and a bottle of Scotch. The Korean behind the register had a dent in his head, like someone had taken a chunk out of it with a hatchet. One of his eyes stared blindly off into space. He asked Petty for his ID.

"I'm older than you," Petty said.

"The police," the Korean said with a shrug. "ID, ID, all the time."

Back at the hotel, Petty sent Tinafey up to the room while he called his mom from the lobby. He filled her in on what the doctor had said and told her he'd be sticking around.

"I'm coming out, too," she said.

"With your hip all jacked up?" Petty said. "What are you talking about?"

"She needs her family."

"I'm her family."

"All of a sudden?" Joanne said.

Petty let her get away with that one.

"At least wait until they find out what's going on," he said. "It may turn out to be nothing."

"And you'll stay with her until it's sorted out?" Joanne said.

"Of course," Petty said.

"You know what I mean, right?" Joanne said. "I'm asking you not to run out on her again, like you did when you left her with me."

It made Petty angry to think that's how she saw it, how she saw him. "Mom..." he said, a warning, a plea.

"I'm trusting you," she said.

He ended the call before he lost his temper.

When he got back to the room, Tinafey popped the Champagne and poured it into water glasses. It was decent stuff, but all it did was fill Petty's chest with bubbles.

"What are we gonna toast to?" Tinafey said. "We got to toast to something."

"To you," Petty said.

"I'll drink to that," Tinafey said.

They tapped glasses.

It was too early for dinner, so they watched TV for a while.

Petty switched to Scotch, drinking it without ice because he was too lazy to walk down the hall to the machine. All the shows Tinafey put on had people screaming at each other, and she changed the channel whenever there was a commercial. Petty tuned it out. He concentrated on the details of the scam he was counting on to bring in a little quick cash.

Tomorrow he'd put a dozen phony listings for Maui condos on Airbnb, offering below-market weekly rates for places in Wailea and on Kaanapali Beach. The listings were already on his laptop from the last time he'd used them, complete with photos snatched from other sites. He'd ask anyone who bit to contact him by phone for more details, and he'd offer the people who called an even lower rate if they'd wire payment directly to him through MoneyGram. Crude as the swindle was, it usually brought in ten grand or so before someone complained and his accounts were deactivated. The only other thing he needed was a new burner to take the calls. He'd pick one up in the morning and be in business by noon.

Tinafey went into the bathroom to take a shower. Petty called Sam but got her voice mail. The hospital connected him to the phone in her room. That phone rang and rang until a nurse answered. She told him that Sam was asleep and would probably sleep through the night. He asked her to recommend a florist, then he made another call to order an arrangement of white roses and a teddy bear holding a stuffed heart to be delivered to Sam's room. He was about to get a bunch of balloons from another place when Tinafey, wrapped in a towel, came out of the bathroom.

"How old did you say this girl is?" she said.

"Twenty-one," Petty said.

"She don't want balloons."

"It's no big deal. It's the thought that counts."

"Yeah, well, you're not thinkin', you're drinkin'," Tinafey said. She sat next to Petty on the bed and took the phone out of his hand. "You need to eat somethin'."

She was right. Petty felt the booze when he stood, the floor tilting as he made his way to the bathroom. He scrubbed his face with cold water, combed his hair, and changed into a clean shirt.

Tinafey wanted Mexican food. There was a Cabo Wabo Cantina in the mall next to the hotel. As they walked over, a gust of paranoia rattled Petty's bones. He turned and looked over his shoulder. A big bald dude with tattoos on his arms was twenty feet behind him and Tinafey, keeping pace with them. Could Avi have sicced someone new on him already? Or maybe there'd been two of them from the start, the big guy and the cowboy.

"Hold up," Petty whispered to Tinafey. He took her arm and led her to a souvenir-shop window.

"What's wrong?" she said.

"We're shopping," Petty said.

Tinafey was sharp enough to figure out what was going on, or at least sharp enough to know to wait until later to ask more questions. The two of them pretended to be mesmerized by the sequined T-shirts and trucker caps on display in the window as the big man passed behind them. Petty kept an eye on him. He walked up to a woman carrying a baby and took the kid from her. The baby giggled, and the man held it out in front of him and made goofy faces at it. Petty relaxed when he saw this, chalking up his jitters to the long, stressful day.

"What was that about?" Tinafey said as they continued toward the restaurant.

"Nothing," Petty said. "I'm a little drunk, I guess."

He ordered a Coke with his burrito instead of a beer, didn't want Tinafey to remember him sloppy. She was subdued during dinner—no jokes, no movie-star gossip. Thrown off by his momentary freakout, Petty supposed, and disappointed at the way her trip to L.A. had ended, how heavy everything had gotten. He apologized and promised to make things up to her.

"You wait," he said. "I'm gonna show up in Memphis and drag you off to Miami for a week."

Tinafey didn't scoff at him, but she didn't smile, either. She chewed on the straw from her iced tea and gave him a look he couldn't decipher.

"What if I don't go to Memphis tomorrow?" she said.

The bartender was singing along to "Highway to Hell" as he poured shots for a couple from Houston. Petty wished the guy would shut up so he could concentrate.

"What do you mean?" he said to Tinafey.

"What if I stay with you a little longer?" she said.

This threw Petty, and his first instinct was to search for the angle in her offer.

"Why would you want to do that?" he said. "I'll be at the hospital most of the time, and when I'm not, I'll be working."

"I'll help you out."

"Help me how?"

"While you're taking care of your daughter, I'll take care of you."

"Is it that you've got cold feet about Memphis?" Petty said. "We can exchange the ticket if you'd rather go somewhere else."

"I'm fine with Memphis," Tinafey said. "Memphis is gonna be great. But right now you need a friend."

Petty sat back and stared at her. If she was playing him, he couldn't figure out for what.

"I'm almost broke," he said. "I'll be moving to a cheap motel, and there won't be any more fancy dinners. You don't want to hang around for that."

"I don't need fancy," Tinafey said. "And I've got money. Not much, but some. You don't have a wife comin', do you?"

"No, nothing like that," Petty said.

"Okay, then," Tinafey said.

The realization that she was sincere about helping him was more troubling to Petty than the possibility that she might have been conning him. A con had a motive. It was all about cash, and he was comfortable with that. Kindness was more complicated. It muddied the savage calculus that reduced every decision in his life to "Am I taking or being taken?" and the last thing he needed now were complications.

"Baby," he said. "That's super sweet of you, but I think it's best if you get on that plane tomorrow."

"Why?" Tinafey said.

"Any other time, I'd beg you to stay, but you don't need to be around this. It's not your problem."

"I said I want to help out."

"And I'm saying you've got to go."

"Why?"

"I told you, the fun's over."

Tinafey's eyes hardened into two dark stones.

"Tell me the real reason," she said.

"That is the real reason," Petty said.

"No it ain't. The real reason is 'cause I'm a whore."

Petty scoffed at her. "You don't believe that," he said.

"Don't tell me what I believe," she said. "You don't want me around because I'm a whore. You're worried about what your daughter would think."

"That's ridiculous."

"No, it ain't," Tinafey said. She stood quickly, near tears. "I'm going to the room."

Petty saw that he'd hurt her by refusing her offer, that it hadn't been made lightly, and that she was as afraid of what it signified as he was.

"Sit," he said.

"I heard enough."

"Sit. Please."

She perched lightly on the edge of her chair, ready to flee in an instant if she didn't like the next thing that came out of his mouth. And right then he knew: he couldn't do it. He couldn't send her away, even though it was the right move.

"You're a good person," Petty said. "I don't meet many good people. I guess I don't know how to act around them."

"What's that supposed to mean?" Tinafey said.

"I'd love it if you'd stay," Petty said.

"You changed your mind just like that?"

"I never wanted you to go. I just thought it'd be better for *you*."

Tinafey thought this over, then said, "Well, maybe I don't want to stay now. Maybe I see I had you wrong."

"This isn't something I can beg you for, baby," Petty said. "It has to be your choice."

A smile rippled across Tinafey's lips. "You could beg a little," she said.

"Please stay," Petty said.

Tinafey let him dangle for a few seconds, then said, "You came that close to blowin' this good thing you got. You know that?"

"I'll try to do better."

"It ain't that hard."

Petty took her hand. He kissed her cheek. He'd made his decision, and a key turned. A key turned, a door opened, and he found himself standing somewhere he'd never been before—him, a man who thought he'd been everywhere.

16

THE NEXT MORNING PETTY CHECKED OUT OF THE LOEWS AND drove to the City Center Motel, his and Tinafey's new home. Still a little spooked after their encounter with the bald guy the night before, he kept an eye on the rearview mirror. At one point he circled a block, made four lefts in a row, but no tail was revealed. By the time they reached the motel, he was convinced they weren't being followed.

The City Center was a two-story cinder-block heap with thin walls and stained carpet hunched in the shadow of downtown's high-rises. You could smell every other person who'd stayed in the room, and the swimming pool was empty except for six inches of black sludge. The weekly rate was cheap, though, and it was only a couple of blocks from the hospital.

Petty decided to visit Sam before posting the listings for the condos, and he asked Tinafey to come with him.

"Nah," she said. "You go on. I'll hang out here."

Petty didn't push it. He'd put her through enough already.

He walked to Good Samaritan. It was cold enough that he needed a jacket, but the sky was clear, only a few fuzzy clouds hovering above the distant mountains. His route took him down a street lined with brick tenements packed with Central American families. Everyone was at work at that hour, so the neighborhood was quiet. Two women sat talking on the steps of one of the buildings, surrounded by a flock of bouncing children. A scavenger fished for cans in a dumpster. An old man sprayed the sidewalk with a garden hose.

The girl at the main desk of the hospital printed out a badge for him and directed him to Sam's room, on the third floor. As far as hospitals went, this one wasn't bad. The walls were freshly painted, the floors gleamed, and the staff bustled about with whitened smiles and an abundance of institutional good cheer. The air smelled funny, a hint of something troubling sneaking past the filters and deodorizers, but other than that, the place was nice enough.

Sam's room held three beds. In the first was an old Asian woman as shrunken and wrinkled as one of those dolls carved from an apple. Her head lolled on her pillow, and her toothless mouth gaped. What life she had left in her was concentrated in her eyes, which were glued to a TV on the wall, some game show. The second bed was empty, stripped of sheets, the helpless, humiliated mattress exposed. Sam lay in the third bed. Her TV was on, too, but she was gazing out the window.

"See anything interesting?" Petty said.

"This bird," Sam replied. "It flaps, then glides; flaps, then glides. I think it's a hawk."

"There are hawks in L.A.?"

"There's everything in L.A."

"Did you have breakfast?"

"I ate the fruit and toast, but the eggs were scary."

"I'll sneak some McNuggets in later," Petty said. Sam had loved Chicken McNuggets when she was a kid.

"Make sure you get sweet-and-sour *and* honey mustard," she said, playing along by reciting her standard childhood request.

"I was going to come back last night, but they told me you were asleep," he said.

"Until they woke me up at five for my MRI," she said.

"Is that the machine they slide you into? The one that looks like a spaceship?"

"It's more like being tied up inside a garbage can while someone pounds on it with a hammer."

"I don't know if I could handle that. I get claustrophobic getting on a plane."

"They also shoot you up with this dye that puts a nasty taste in your mouth. I almost vomited."

"Did they tell you anything afterward?"

"Just that it'll take a day or so to analyze the scan," Sam said. "I'm stuck in here until then, I guess."

She had more color in her cheeks this morning, more energy. Petty noticed the flowers and bear he'd sent sitting on a shelf.

"So those made it," he said. "I didn't know what you'd like."

"The bear's cute," Sam said.

"Is there anything else I can get you?"

"I'm good. My friend Jessica's bringing my phone charger and makeup and stuff."

"That's nice of her."

"She's an orphan, like me. We take care of each other."

"You're not an orphan," Petty said patiently.

"You know what I mean," Sam said.

"I'll be around as long as you need me."

"I don't need you at all," Sam said. "If it makes you feel better about yourself to be here, cool, feel better about yourself, but I'm fine on my own."

She was twelve when she first turned on Petty and bit. He'd never gotten over the shock of it. And every time she'd lashed out since then had stung just as much.

"Just let me play daddy for a couple days, all right?" he said.

"Whatever," Sam said. "But don't push it."

A nurse stepped into the room. "How you doing, Mrs. Kong?" she called to the old woman in the other bed. Mrs. Kong didn't respond. The nurse checked the monitors the woman was hooked up to and said, "The doctor will be by shortly, okay?" Again, no response. Mrs. Kong continued to stare at the TV.

"She woke me up last night," Sam whispered to Petty. "Singing a Chinese song."

"I'll ask them to move you to a private room," Petty said.

"No," Sam said. "I'm fine here."

The nurse, a Filipina with an accent and a mole on her cheek, came over to Sam's bed. "How you doing?" she said. "You need water? Juice?"

"Nope. Nothing," Sam said.

"You got the best bed," the nurse said. "By the window."

"Lucky me."

"You want to take a shower? The doctor said it's okay."

"That'd be awesome."

Petty was glad to have an excuse to leave. He needed to get back to the motel and put up the condo listings.

"I'll be back this evening," he said.

"Don't worry about it," Sam said.

"It's no big deal," he said. "I'm staying at a motel two blocks away."

"Really?" Sam said.

"Yeah, so call if you need anything."

"Cool," Sam said, sounding like she meant it. It wasn't much, but Petty counted it as a victory.

A woman was waiting for him in the hall.

"Mr. Petty?" she said. "I'm from the hospital's business department. Could we talk?"

Diane was her name, Diane Rhee. Korean, chubby, bright blue contact lenses. Her office was on the first floor. Petty guessed that the framed photo of her and her baby and her husband on her desk was supposed to humanize her and put him at ease.

"How's your daughter?" she said.

"I haven't heard anything yet," he said.

"That's hard."

"It is."

Diane tapped at her keyboard and opened a file on her computer. She kept her eyes on it as she spoke.

"Dr. Avakian mentioned that you wanted to be kept up to date on matters regarding Samantha's care," she said.

"That's right," Petty said.

"Well, unfortunately, as difficult a time as it is for Samantha and you, there needs to be a discussion of the financial aspects of her stay here."

"What's to discuss?"

"Samantha doesn't have insurance, and she earns too much to be eligible for Medi-Cal."

"Which means?"

"She's what we call a self-pay patient and will be personally responsible for the cost of her treatment. We offer discounts on certain procedures to self-pays, but the costs can still be substantial. So in cases like this, we often transfer patients to County USC Medical Center, a public hospital. Costs are lower there, and they offer more assistance programs for low-income patients."

"What's that like, County USC?" Petty said.

"It's a very nice facility," Diane said.

"Seriously, or is it the ghetto hospital?"

"As I said, it's a nice facility."

"Would you send your kid there?"

Diane hesitated a little too long, and that was all the answer Petty needed.

"I want Sam to stay here," he said. "I'll pay whatever it takes and sign whatever you need me to sign."

"I appreciate your wanting to help your daughter," Diane said, "but legally she's the patient, and it's her financial status we take into account when deciding whether to move her."

"So I'll give her the money, and she can give it to you," Petty said.

"That wouldn't have any bearing on the transfer," Diane said. "It's frustrating, I know."

"Look," Petty said. He took out his wallet, pulled all the money out of it, close to four hundred dollars, and placed it on the desk. "This is for you," he said. "Keep her here, and there'll be more tomorrow."

Diane stared at the money, then stared at Petty.

"That's not how things work around here," she said.

"Yes, it is," Petty said. "That's how things work every-where."

Diane pursed her lips, exhaled loudly, and turned back to her computer.

"I'll see what I can do," she said.

Petty got up and started for the door.

"You forgot something," Diane said.

"No, I didn't," Petty said.

"Yes, you did," Diane said, pointing at the money on her desk without looking at it.

Petty reluctantly retrieved the cash. "Everything'll be paid, I swear," he said.

Diane ignored him. Petty shoved the money in his pocket and went to the door again. He stopped on the threshold.

"If you could get her a private room, that'd be great, too," he said. "The one she's in is really noisy."

Diane didn't respond, didn't even stop typing. Petty wondered if she'd heard him but didn't push it by asking.

And just like that, he was in over his head again. The condo hustle wasn't going to bring in the kind of money he needed now, but at least it was a start. He stopped at a phone store and bought the cheapest disposable they had and loaded it with minutes. The wi-fi at the motel was so slow that it took him most of the afternoon to put the listings on Airbnb. "Affordable Luxury on Maui." "Beautiful Condo Steps from the Beach." "Sun! Fun! Sand!" They looked great, completely legit, and he expected the burner to start ringing at any minute.

Tinafey watched TV with the sound down while he worked. She got restless after a while and went out for a walk. An hour later she came back with a turkey sandwich and a bag of chips for him, then went outside and sat on the walkway in a plastic chair.

Petty heard her through the door, talking to someone. Even though there was no way anybody could know where they were now, this still made him nervous. He peeked out the window and saw two people, a guy and a girl, sitting in front of the room next door. They were young, in their early twenties. The guy had a big, bushy beard, and the girl's hair was cut short and dyed a faded blue. Both were smoking cigarettes. They didn't look like anything to be worried about, so Petty kept working and did his best to ignore the occasional laughter.

The conversation was still going strong when he finished posting the final listing. He straightened his clothes and opened the door.

"There he is," Tinafey said. She'd moved her chair to join the couple in front of their room.

The guy held up a bottle. "Would you like some wine?" he said.

"It's good," Tinafey said, raising a plastic cup.

"Sure," Petty said. He walked over and stood against the railing.

"This here's Bernard and Patricia," Tinafey said. "They're from France. This is Rowan."

"I hope we did not disturb you," Bernard said. He handed Petty a cup and poured wine into it.

"Nah," Petty said. "Sounded like you guys were having fun." The wine was white and cold and tasted like peaches.

"Guess what?" Tinafey said. "They're goin' to Memphis."

"And Nashville and Clarksdale, too," Patricia said. "To the crossroads. Do you know this place?"

"I was in Nashville once," Petty said. Drinking there, in a bar on Broadway. Some shitkicker came in and yelled, "Listen up, bartender! Gimme beer for my horses, whiskey for my men, and a nigger for my daughter!" That's all Petty remembered about Nashville.

Patricia explained the crossroads to him, the spot where a famous blues musician supposedly struck a deal with the devil. "It is very famous," she said in her cute accent.

"Satan dances in an empty pocket," Petty said. "Ever heard that one?"

"We are not religious," Bernard said.

"It's not a Bible thing. It's something my buddy Mike Dooky used to say."

"Ahh," Bernard said. "Like when you say, 'The devil made me do it.'"

"Exactly," Petty said.

"Where else should we go on our trip?" Patricia said.

She and Bernard were driving cross-country, having a big adventure. Petty suggested the Grand Canyon, Vegas. "Don't miss Vegas," he said. Tinafey told them where to get the best ribs in Memphis.

The sun put on a show going down. The sky looked like it was on fire, bright orange flames, billows of purple smoke. Petty explained it was smog that created the gaudy colors, the sun shining through the poison. When the streetlights flickered to life, he stood to go. He wanted to look in on Sam before it was too late.

"Do you want to come along?" he asked Tinafey. "I'd like you to meet her."

They were back in the room by then. He was getting ready to leave, and Tinafey was sitting on the bed. She squinted at him and rocked her head from side to side.

"I'm kinda feelin' that wine," she said.

"You're all right," Petty said. "She's gonna love you."

"I'd have to change clothes and everything."

"I'll wait," Petty said.

Tinafey threw a pillow at him. "Why you bein' so insistent?" she said.

"You said you wanted to help me."

"Yeah, but how's me goin' with you now gonna do that?"

"Because you know how to talk to anyone," Petty said.

Tinafey scoffed at this. "Shee-it, boy, you're supposed to be the hustler," she said.

"I know," Petty said. "But whatever I've got doesn't work with Sam."

Tinafey wore a baggy gray sweater Petty hadn't seen before, one that hid her curves. He drove to the hospital this time, stopping at McDonald's on the way for ten chicken nuggets with both sweet-and-sour and honey mustard sauces.

Sam was listening to music on her phone when Petty and Tinafey entered her room.

"Back again?" she said.

"You're yelling," Petty said.

She took out her earbuds. "Sorry."

She didn't say anything about being transferred to another hospital, so maybe Diane had worked some magic. Her hair was brushed and pulled back, her eyes were bright, and she looked even healthier than she had in the morning.

"This is my friend Tinafey," Petty said.

"Hi, Tinafey," Sam said.

"Do you like Sam or Samantha?" Tinafey said.

"Sam's fine."

"How you doin', Sam?"

"Ready to get out of here."

"I hear that."

"I got you something," Petty said to Sam. He showed her the McDonald's bag.

"Oh, my God, I thought I smelled deliciousness," she said.

Petty handed her the food, and he and Tinafey pulled up chairs next to the bed. Mrs. Kong was asleep. Her snores alternated with the beeps of her machines.

"Did you hear anything new?" Petty said to Sam.

"Another doctor stopped by, my neurologist," Sam said. "But all she did was introduce herself and say hi. And Jessica brought me a care package."

She gestured at a basket sitting on the shelf next to Petty's flowers. It was full of Goldfish crackers, See's Candies, and trashy magazines.

"She's taking care of my cat," Sam continued. "I was worried about him."

"You have a cat?" Petty said.

"Sherman," Sam said. "Stinky Sherman."

She pulled up a photo on her phone and showed it to Petty and Tinafey. The cat was a calico with bright green eyes.

"I like cats," Tinafey said. "They don't suck up to you like dogs do. You feel special when they want to be with you."

"I'm the only one who can pet Sherman," Sam said. "He's very antisocial."

Tinafey kept Sam talking, as Petty had hoped she would. He stayed out of it, sat back and let the women get acquainted. Their conversation warmed the room, chasing away the hospital's clinical chill. They seemed to forget Petty was there, and he felt like he was eavesdropping as they swapped stories.

Sam asked Tinafey if she'd ever been married. Once, Tinafey said. To a maniac. And that was enough. There wasn't anything a woman needed from a man that was worth putting up with that kind of crazy. Sam revealed that she'd come close to getting married a year earlier, but the guy had dumped her for a girl in his band. The band was called the Grit Eaters. Sam called them the Shit Eaters. She laughed when she said this, the first time Petty had heard her laugh since they'd reunited. It gave him hope. She couldn't be that sick if she was laughing.

She laughed again when Tinafey told a story about her

grandmother, how when she was in the hospital the nurses kept catching her smoking in the bathroom and nipping from airplane bottles of rum she'd smuggled in.

"Ninety-two years old," Tinafey said. "Wasn't nobody gonna tell her what she could do."

"She's my new hero," Sam said. "I'm gonna be like her when I'm ninety-two."

"Flora Mae Miller," Tinafey said. "She ran a bar in Smokey City, and she'd give me two dollars every year on my birthday, tell me to buy myself a hamburger."

"I wish I had some rum right now," Sam said.

"Girl, me, too," Tinafey said. "I was so nervous about meetin' you."

"How come?"

"I told your daddy, 'She don't want strangers around while she's laid up in there. She's got enough aggravation with the doctors pokin' her every five minutes.'"

"That's true, but I'm glad you came," Sam said.

Petty let them go on until they ran out of steam. He'd planned to stay fifteen minutes, but an hour passed before he and Tinafey finally stood and stretched and made jokes about keeping Sam up too late. Tinafey moved to the bed and hugged Sam.

"You have a good night," she said.

Petty stepped up and hugged Sam, too.

"Thanks for the McNuggets," she said.

Tinafey took Petty's hand as they walked to the car. The evening had turned cold, and the traffic signals cycled red, yellow, green with icy clarity.

"I think you scored me some points back there," Petty said.

"She's a nice girl," Tinafey said. "No thanks to you, I bet, but she's a nice girl."

★   ★   ★

Bernard knocked on their door when they got back to the motel and asked if they wanted to go to dinner with him and Patricia at a restaurant in Chinatown their guidebook recommended.

"It's up to you," Petty said to Tinafey.

"Chinese sounds good," she said.

The Frenchies didn't have a car—they'd been riding buses everywhere—so Petty offered to drive.

The restaurant was a twenty-four-hour neon-sign dive that had seen better days, a dingy, low-ceilinged dining room filled with worn Formica tables topped with lazy Susans. Wood paneling and smoked mirrors straight out of the seventies covered the walls, and the red linoleum on the floor harked back to sometime even earlier. Two cops slurped wonton soup at one table, and a mariachi band ate silently at another, the silver trim on their costumes winking in the fluorescent light.

The waiter wore a black vest over a white dress shirt. He was difficult to understand around his accent. Petty and Tinafey and the Frenchies ordered more food than they could possibly eat and laughed at themselves when plate after plate piled up on the table. Fried shrimp and spareribs, egg foo yung and chicken chow mein, all of it shiny with grease.

As far as Bernard and Patricia knew, Petty sold time shares and Tinafey was a hostess at a Reno steak house. So it was pure coincidence that Bernard brought the dinner conversation around to scams. How it happened was, he bet Petty five dollars that he could take a quarter from under a napkin without touching the napkin. Petty had learned the trick when he was in first grade, but he humored the guy. Bernard put a quarter on the table and covered it with a napkin. After making a few hocus pocus passes over it, he reached under the table and came up with a coin.

It was another quarter, one he'd palmed, but they were supposed to believe it was the one he'd placed under the napkin. Petty feigned amazement and lifted the napkin at Bernard's invitation to verify that the quarter had indeed passed through the table. This revealed the original quarter still sitting there, but it also allowed Bernard to snatch it up without touching the napkin, as he'd promised.

"Voilà!" he said. "You owe me five dollars."

"Check him out," Tinafey said. "He got your ass."

Petty took a five out of his wallet.

"No," Bernard said. "This is not necessary."

"Come on," Petty said. "I made the bet."

He asked Bernard if he knew any more tricks. Yeah, sure, Bernard said. He could tie a knot in a napkin without letting go of the corners. He could fold a cigarette without breaking it. It was all kid stuff, frat-boy keg-party bullshit, but the dude apparently fancied himself some kind of sharper. Petty didn't say anything to burst his bubble. He just smiled and ordered another Tsingtao.

"Here's one for you," he said. "My dad and his buddies used to pull it. One of them would go into a store—a pharmacy, a locksmith, a dry cleaner's—and act all frantic, pretending he'd lost a watch, a special watch his grandpa had given him. He'd ask the clerk if he'd found it, maybe in the parking lot.

"'No,' the clerk would say. 'No watch.'

"'Well, if you do find it, there's a thousand-dollar reward,' my dad's friend would say, and he'd give the clerk his phone number so he could get in touch with him.

"An hour later my dad would go into the same store. 'Anybody lose a watch?' he'd say. 'I found one in the bushes.'

"'Hey,' the clerk would say. 'Some guy was just in here looking for that.' Then, more often than not, he'd start angling to get the reward for himself. He'd say, 'Why don't you leave the watch with me, and if the guy comes back, I'll return it to him?'

"'I don't know about that,' my dad would say. 'But check it out—it's a nice watch, and I'm hard up right now. How about if I sell it to you for five hundred dollars?'

"The watch my dad had was nothing but a twenty-dollar swap-meet special, but the clerk, thinking he was gonna get a thousand bucks for it, would say, 'Sounds like a good deal to me.'

"My dad would take off with the five hundred, the clerk would call the number my dad's buddy had given him, and whoever answered would say, 'Nobody by that name lives here.'"

"Aha!" Bernard said, delighted.

"But this must be illegal, no?" Patricia said.

"What it is is the clerk getting what was coming to him," Petty said. "He was trying to pull his own scam."

"Payback's a bitch," Bernard said. It sounded funny with his accent.

"Exactly," Petty said.

"I know this phrase from Tupac," Bernard said. "'Ballad of a Dead Soulja.'"

"Tupac?" Tinafey said. "Listen at you, talkin' about Tupac."

When it was time to pay, they agreed that Bernard would put the meal on his card and Petty would give him cash for his and Tinafey's share, which came to forty dollars. Petty took out two twenties and showed them to Bernard, then secretly swapped one of them out for a single before handing the money over. Bernard shoved the bills into his pocket without checking them again.

Hey, Frenchie, Petty thought. *Who's the sharper now?*

17

THE SHIPMENTS OF MONEY FROM BAGRAM ENTERED THE
United States at Fort Bragg's Pope Field, where master sergeant
Scott Lindstrom worked in the cargo warehouse. Alerted by
Keller, Lindstrom took charge of the containers the cash was
hidden in, surreptitiously removed the money, and snuck it off
base. He then sent it from North Carolina to Diaz's cousin in
Los Angeles.

Diaz had never met Lindstrom. He was a friend of Keller's,
someone Keller swore they could trust. And this turned out to
be true. The books had balanced perfectly in the end. Diaz had
had Tony check each package before locking it away, and every
dollar that passed through Lindstrom's hands on its way from
Afghanistan had made it to L.A. For his service, Lindstrom was
due a quarter share.

He didn't seem surprised when Diaz called out of the blue
and said he was in Fayetteville at a Holiday Inn near the base.

They kept the conversation vague, agreeing to rendezvous that evening at an Applebee's.

Diaz got there early and waited for Lindstrom at the bar. He ordered a beer but didn't drink it. The restaurant was crowded and noisy, with football on the TVs and a big birthday party spread over three tables pushed together. All the men at the party had shaved heads or high and tights. The place catered to soldiers from the base. Unit flags hung on the walls—Eighty-Second Airborne, the Sky Dragons, Special Forces—alongside photos of troops in uniform.

Lindstrom materialized out of thin air, like he was trying to sneak up on Diaz. The first thing Diaz noticed about him was his permanent smirk. All the other features on his pinched face swirled around it. The second thing Diaz noticed was how jacked the dude was. He was the same height as Diaz, but every muscle on his body put a strain on the flesh laid over it, and his neck looked like a tree trunk rooted to his torso. So it was funny when he spoke and his voice came out as high and squeaky as that of a kid whose balls hadn't dropped yet.

"You're the man, right?" he said.

"I guess I am," Diaz replied.

They didn't shake hands. Lindstrom moved his chair away from Diaz's, put some distance between them.

"You heard about Keller?" Diaz said. Neither had mentioned him during their phone call.

"Yeah," Lindstrom said.

"How fucked up is that?"

"Dude was a junkie," Lindstrom said. "I don't have any sympathy for junkies."

"We all got our problems," Diaz said.

"What's yours?" Lindstrom said.

"I'm getting out of the army after twelve years of shit shoveling," Diaz said. "I got no problems at all."

The bartender asked if Lindstrom wanted anything. He ordered tonic with lime. Diaz pretended to sip his beer. A country song came on, and the grunts at the birthday party sang along. Lindstrom watched them, his smirk more pronounced than ever.

"So you live in L.A.?" he said to Diaz.

"Used to," Diaz said warily.

"I'm only asking because that's where you had me send the packages."

"I didn't have you send them anywhere. That was Keller."

"Oh. Yeah. Right," Lindstrom said.

"What else did Keller tell you?" Diaz said.

Lindstrom shrugged. "Enough," he said.

"What's that mean?"

"Enough to make me comfortable doing business with someone I'd never met."

Diaz was uneasy. Lindstrom wouldn't even look him in the eye. Instead he kept flexing his forearm and watching the muscles and tendons there jump. Diaz had had to share more information than he'd wanted to in order to get Keller on board. Keller had evidently passed some of this info on to Lindstrom, and who knew who he'd talked to about it? It was too late to worry about that now, though.

"You here to deliver what's mine?" Lindstrom said.

"That's right," Diaz said.

"Outstanding."

Lindstrom waved the bartender over. "I'm getting a shot of Jack to celebrate," he said to Diaz. "Want one?"

"I'm good," Diaz said.

"I usually don't drink when I'm in training," Lindstrom said. "But fuck it. It's not every day you get your pot of gold."

"What are you training for?"

"The NPC All-Military's coming up. I've been dialing it in, doing doubles to get ready."

"Bodybuilding?"

"The real deal."

"A thong and all that?"

"Posing trunks. You wear them so the judges can see your glutes."

Lindstrom downed his shot and chased it with a sip of tonic. His arm was so big he could barely bend it at the elbow. "Every little thing counts," he said. "Like this." He pointed to an indentation in his biceps. "That's the baby's butt, the cut between the two heads. I've been working on it for weeks."

Diaz fingered the knife in his jacket pocket. He wished now he had a gun.

The birthday party got louder when the waitress delivered the cake. It had a picture of a girl in a bikini on it. A girl in a bikini shooting an M4. This earned another smirk from Lindstrom. Then the Panthers scored, which started a commotion at the other end of the restaurant. Lindstrom smirked at this, too. He was one of those guys, Diaz could tell, who thought the whole world was stupid but him.

"So where's my money?" Lindstrom said.

"You know Clark Park? The river trail?" Diaz said.

"Come on, bro. All the way out there?"

"You want me to give it to you here?"

"Works for me."

"Not for me. I don't like the idea of someone checking tapes and seeing me pass you a bag."

"Checking tapes?" Lindstrom said. "Who's gonna be checking tapes?"

"Hopefully nobody," Diaz said. "But I'm not gonna make it

easy for them if they do. This is a big score. I'm covering all the bases."

Lindstrom scoffed at this and stared at his forearm again. "I know the trail," he said.

So did Diaz. He'd scouted it the day before.

"Park at the nature center," he said. "A quarter mile down the trail is a bridge. Meet me there at midnight."

"Midnight?" Lindstrom said. "That's four hours from now."

"Midnight," Diaz said. "Got it?"

Lindstrom shook his head in annoyance. He ran a thick finger along a bunched blue vein on his wrist.

"I got it," he said.

Diaz dropped a five on the bar for the beer. "I'm splitting now," he said. "Hang tight for ten minutes."

"In case somebody checks the tapes," Lindstrom said, like it was the dumbest thing he'd ever heard.

Diaz headed for the door. A chill had settled over the town while he'd been in the restaurant. He'd parked at a Verizon store across the road rather than in the Applebee's lot, and he hugged himself as he hurried back to his rental. The sign at the Hyundai dealership flashed forty degrees, but it seemed colder. Diaz unlocked the car and got inside, then had to figure out how the heater worked. He had a heavier coat back in his room, a nice down parka, but he'd hate to mess it up doing what he was going to be doing later.

The trail at the park was actually a paved path, ten feet wide. It followed the west bank of the Cape Fear River, crossing a few creeks and a marsh. During the day it was crowded with joggers and bicyclists and dog walkers. When the gates closed at dusk, the deer came out, and raccoons raided the trash cans.

Diaz arrived an hour before he was supposed to meet Lindstrom and parked a couple blocks from the trailhead. He pulled on a pair of gloves, hopped a waist-high fence, and set out to scramble cross-country to the bridge. It was his mistrust of Lindstrom that kept him off the main trail. For all he knew the fucker was lying in wait there, ambush on his mind.

Bushwhacking turned out to be more difficult than Diaz had expected. In the dark, in the cold, through the mist rising from the black swirl of the river. The duffel bag stuffed with newspaper he was carrying didn't make the going any easier. He started in a stand of tall bare trees but soon found himself sliding down a steep slope that ended in a bog. He paused there to slap wet leaves from the seat of his jeans and get his bearings before continuing across the quagmire. Despite his best efforts to place each step carefully, he slipped a couple times and ended up ankle-deep in ooze that sucked at his feet like something hungry.

When he got close to the bridge, he scrambled up to the pavement, surprising a skunk. The skunk raised and fanned its tail, and Diaz almost tripped as he backed away. He moved as quickly as he could down the path. His shoes were caked with stinking mud, and his socks squished when he walked. Every twenty yards or so a dim light, low to the ground, illuminated the trail, but Diaz stuck to the shadows at the edge. The ghostly whinny of a screech owl made him reach for his knife; the bony scrape of branches stopped him in his tracks. He'd decided to go back to the hotel for his parka after all and was now sweating under it.

By the time he reached the bridge, the mist had thickened into a low, dense fog. He squatted, trying to peer through the murk. No sign of Lindstrom or anybody else. Still, he opened his knife and held it in front of him as he stepped onto the span. The twenty-foot wooden bridge hung above a deep, fast creek that tumbled down to the river. Diaz could hear the water but not see it. He'd wait on the far side. When Lindstrom approached from the nature center, he'd step out of the dark and show himself, walk out to meet him. *How you doing? This goddamn fog. Sorry about the rigmarole.* And then he'd kill him and have one more share of the money to himself.

The owl bleated again. Diaz squelched across the bridge and sat on a boulder to wait. He could barely make out where he'd come from. The world over there was turning to smoke, dissolving into nothing. He checked his watch: 11:30. Half an hour to go. By then, who knew? The fog might have swallowed the trail, swallowed the bridge, swallowed him. He was happy to have the parka now, zipped it all the way to his chin.

Just before midnight he heard footsteps on the pavement. If it was Lindstrom, he definitely wasn't trying for stealth. Diaz slipped the knife into his coat pocket and moved to the middle of the trail, duffel bag in hand. A figure solidified out of the soup. Lindstrom it was, wearing a green army field jacket and a black stocking cap. He stopped at the end of the bridge and stared at Diaz like he wasn't sure it was him. Diaz motioned him forward.

"Come and get it," he said.

They walked toward each other, boards creaking beneath them. When they were ten feet apart, they stopped. Diaz held out the duffel. Lindstrom didn't move to take it, kept his arms at his sides.

"What about Keller's share?" he said.

"What about it?" Diaz said.

"I should get a cut."

"You decided that?"

"It's what's right."

"I'm the one who put this together," Diaz said. "You were working for me."

"You couldn't have done it without me," Lindstrom said.

He was ready for a fight, fists clenched, neck tensed. He'd been ready for a fight since the restaurant. Diaz pretended to consider the guy's point.

"That's an extra hundred fifty, hundred sixty thousand," he said.

"One hundred sixty-six thousand and sixty-six dollars," Lindstrom said. "Give me just the thousands. You can keep the change."

His smirk widened briefly into a smile. Laughing at his own joke.

"Fair enough," Diaz said. "Do you want to take what I have here for now, or do you want to wait until I get it all together?"

"I'll take what you've got for now," Lindstrom said.

Diaz couldn't hear the creek anymore, couldn't feel the cold. His whole world was Lindstrom. He set the duffel down in the space between them and took two steps back with his hands in the air.

"All yours," he said.

Lindstrom kept his eyes on him as he moved forward and bent to the bag. He picked it up and couldn't resist, set it on the bridge railing and unzipped it. Diaz made his move when he turned away to look inside. He was on him in an instant with the knife.

He stabbed as hard and as fast as he could, aiming for the big man's chest. Something was wrong, though. Lindstrom didn't yell, didn't fall. The knife blade skidded off him like he was made of ice. He was wearing Kevlar under his jacket, a vest. He reached out for Diaz and caught him by the throat, lifting him in the air.

Diaz hung there for an instant, stunned, but snapped out of it when Lindstrom punched him in the head with his free hand. He slashed at the big man's arm, slicing through fabric to reach flesh. Lindstrom hissed in pain and dropped him. As soon as Diaz's feet hit wood, he sprang at Lindstrom again, blade held high. The bridge shuddered when he slammed into him and drove him back against the railing. The duffel fell into the creek and was carried away by the current.

Lindstrom threw his giant arms around Diaz and squeezed hard. The air whooshed out of Diaz's lungs, and he thought his spine would snap. He stabbed Lindstrom in the neck. The blade went in deep, and a jet of hot blood warmed Diaz's fingers even through his glove. Lindstrom's hold on him relaxed. His arms still encircled him, but all the strength had gone out of them.

Diaz stabbed him two more times in the neck, withdrew the blade, pulled it back, and buried it to the hilt in the guy's temple. Lindstrom's knees buckled, and he dropped to the bridge in a sitting position, his back against the rail, the knife sticking out of his head. Diaz backed away. Lindstrom's chest rose with a wheeze. One breath plumed out of him, another, then no more. His eyes stared at nothing. His blood was blacker than the night.

When his own breathing had slowed, Diaz pulled out the knife and tossed it off the bridge. He then tried to lift Lindstrom over the railing. No way; the guy was too heavy. There was enough space under the bottom rail, though. Diaz laid Lindstrom flat and used his feet to push him. It was a tight fit, but he managed to squeeze him through. The body splashed into the creek and sank immediately. There was so much blood on Diaz's gloves that he worried he'd cut himself during the fight. A quick check showed he was fine. As for the blood on the bridge, he couldn't do anything about that, so he headed out, back across the bog and up the hill to his car.

18

THERE WERE A FEW QUERIES ABOUT THE CONDOS WHEN PETTY woke early Saturday morning. He responded with the burner number, and the first call came at 8:00 a.m. He pulled on his sweats and stepped out onto the walkway to take it. The woman on the line was suspicious. She asked why there were no reviews for the unit she was interested in on Airbnb. Petty told her it was because this was the first time he'd listed it. And why, she asked, did he want her to wire the money to him instead of paying through the site? "I don't want to pay taxes," Petty said. "The less I have to deal with the IRS, the better." The woman said she'd think about it and call back. Petty doubted that, writing her off as a stroke, a waste of time.

He spent the rest of the morning replying to e-mails and answering the phone. Tinafey went out and came back with coffee and a bagel for him from the chintzy breakfast buffet the motel provided. He was so busy that he managed only two sips of the coffee before it got cold. By the time he was ready to turn off the burner and leave for the hospital, he thought he might have a couple of fish on the line, but he wouldn't know for sure until they sent their MoneyGram transaction numbers.

He asked Tinafey if she wanted to come with him again to check on Sam.

"You need to learn to talk to her on your own," she said.

"Fine," Petty said, "but she'll be disappointed not to see you. She likes you a lot more than she likes me."

"Maybe so," Tinafey said, "but she *loves* you."

He walked to Good Samaritan, down the street of tenements. It was the weekend, so the neighborhood was much livelier. More people hanging out, more music. The same women and kids were on the same stoop as last time. They passed around a plastic bag of pineapple chunks and a fork. A little girl skipped down the steps to block Petty's way. She stared up at him with a defiant pout until one of the women hissed her back to the group. A wreath strung with lights blinked in the window of an apartment; a cardboard Santa hung in another. Petty hadn't noticed them before. Christmas kept creeping up on him.

His phone rang. He took it out of his pocket and looked at it. Someone calling from Miami, but not Avi. This unnerved him. He let the call go to voice mail. Whoever it was didn't leave a message. Petty wondered who it could be but didn't press Call Back. If it was nothing, it was nothing; if it was trouble, no sense running toward it.

He heard a commotion in Sam's room as soon as he stepped off the elevator. Mrs. Kong's family was visiting. Old people, kids, babies. They'd lined up all the chairs in the room next to the woman's bed. She was asleep, but they carried on anyway, eating cookies from a pink bakery box and passing

186

around a photo album. The conversation was in Chinese, which sounded like stones clattering down a shallow stream. A Mexican woman lay in the middle bed now, a bandage wrapped around her throat. She ignored the party and stared at her TV, listening to it through headphones.

Sam was reading an astronomy textbook. She raised her hand and told Petty to hold on while she finished a paragraph. Her tone irked him, but he let it go.

After a minute or so she closed the book. She had big news to share: her friend Jessica had managed to get the two of them tickets to a concert that had been sold out for months.

"Have you heard of him?" she asked Petty about the guy who was playing.

"I don't follow music," he said.

She pulled up a song on her phone and insisted that Petty put in her earbuds, enthusiastic about hipping him to something she liked. It was electronic stuff, dance stuff, the shit they played in all the clubs in Vegas, the shit that made him feel old and out of it. He didn't tell Sam that. He kept his mouth shut and listened to the music while watching a cartoon on the TV, an orange elephant eating ice cream. When he felt enough time had passed, he handed the phone back.

"Sick, right?" Sam said.

"Sick," Petty said.

An argument broke out among Mrs. Kong's family about how to arrange all the flowers people had sent her on her single shelf. Granny had a boy set them up one way, but then a young woman jumped up and repositioned the baskets and vases.

"I really liked Tinafey," Sam said.

"She liked you, too," Petty said.

"How long have you guys been together?"

"Not long."

"Is she bad like you? Or good?"

"She's good," Petty said.

Sam's phone dinged. She picked it up, checked the screen, and started texting. Petty's first instinct was to be angry at how quickly her attention had shifted, but again he kept his cool. Nothing would change between them if he blew up every time she irritated him. He went back to watching the elephant.

"Sorry about that," Sam said when she finished. "I had to tell Jessica where to buy Sherman's food."

"Do you remember that cat in Cancun?" Petty said.

During one of their summer trips she'd made friends with a stray cat that hung around their hotel in Mexico. By the time they left, the mangy thing was eating out of her hand, and it tried to jump into the cab taking them to the airport. Petty knew he was treading on dangerous ground by bringing up the past, but some of the best times they'd had with each other had come during those trips. He was hoping she'd recall them as fondly as he did.

A smile spread across her face.

"I loved that cat," she said.

"What was its name?"

"Letty," Sam said. "They called it Letty."

"That was the same trip I got stung by a scorpion."

"On the beach. I remember."

"You couldn't stop laughing."

"Come on! You hopping around on one foot, yelling 'Fuck! Fuck! Fuck!' It was hilarious."

"My lips went numb. I thought I was a goner."

"You wanted somebody to pee on the bite. The guys from the hotel were cracking up."

"Hey, though," Petty said. "One hour later I was back on the beach."

"Because you saw me talking to a boy there," Sam said.

"That was the dad in me coming out," Petty said.

"What, for the first time?" Sam said.

Petty tried not to let her see that her jab had connected, but some flicker, some pulse, gave him away. Her mean grin softened.

"I'm kidding," she said.

"It's okay," he said. "I get it."

The silence that followed stretched into something awkward. They both focused on Mrs. Kong's family, watched them straighten her blanket and wipe her face with a damp cloth.

"I don't know anything about you," Sam finally said. "I mean the big things, yeah, but not much else."

"What do you want to know?" Petty said.

"Did you ever have any pets?"

"My mom had a dog, but it didn't like me, went crazy every time I got near it. After that I was always moving around too much to keep an animal."

"What's your favorite food?"

"I don't have one."

"What's your favorite color?"

"Don't have one of those, either."

"That's weird," Sam said.

"Why?" Petty said.

"Why wouldn't you have a favorite color?"

"I'm not picky. It makes things easier."

"It makes things weird," Sam said.

"What's *your* favorite color?" Petty said.

"Green."

"And your favorite food?"

"Cheese enchiladas."

They went on like that for a while, Petty asking what she

liked and she answering. He'd never remember all her preferences, wasn't even listening, really. What was important to him was that they were talking and she seemed to be enjoying herself. That was a step forward, an accomplishment, and he felt pretty good about it, like he'd pulled off something slick.

He went back to the motel and spent the afternoon replying to queries about the condos and answering calls. When he wasn't on the phone, he watched TV with Tinafey. She did a good job of hiding her boredom, but Petty noticed how quickly she said yes when he asked if she'd run out and get him something for lunch.

"Did you like your sandwich yesterday?" she asked as she changed out of the Hard Rock T-shirt she'd taken to lounging in and into a red tank top.

"A sandwich'll be fine," Petty said.

"Or they have salads," she said. "Like Caesar and spinach."

"You know what? A salad sounds better—spinach," he said and handed her forty dollars. "Get whatever you want, too."

As the door closed behind her, the thought flashed in his head that she wasn't coming back. She'd found a cockroach in the sink that morning, and the noise from the bus stop in front of the motel had kept her awake all night. He wouldn't blame her for rethinking sticking around. Her current situation was a step up from working the street, but a pretty girl like her could do better.

When she returned forty-five minutes later, saying the spinach salads looked nasty so she'd gotten him a Cobb instead, the intensity of his relief shocked him. He was more stuck on her than he'd thought. And while that wasn't a bad thing, it also wasn't entirely good, because he wasn't at his best right now, not by a long shot, and he wanted to be at his best for her.

He e-mailed and talked to twenty-three people over the course of the day. Five said they'd send money, and two actually e-mailed confirmation numbers: a woman from Toronto paid five hundred dollars for three nights on Napili Bay, and a man from Seattle transferred twelve hundred dollars for a week at a place in Lahaina. Petty sent them both bogus receipts. There was also another call from Miami, from the same number as before. Again Petty let it go to voice mail. Again no message.

Toward dusk Bernard and Patricia returned from a day of sightseeing. Tinafey was sitting out on the walkway, texting. Petty heard her greet the Frenchies and ask where they'd been. He had a grinder on the phone. The dude had spent twenty minutes trying to chisel down the price of a two-bedroom unit at the Eldorado in Kaanapali. Petty had offered it to him for two hundred dollars a night, and the guy had immediately countered with nine hundred for a week. After too much back-and-forth, Petty finally said he'd let him have it for eleven hundred.

"No deal," the dude said and ended the call.

Petty kicked himself for not accepting the first offer. What did it matter if he took the guy for nine hundred or eleven hundred? Every haggle didn't have to be life or death.

Tinafey came in and said the Frenchies were going to a jazz club in Little Tokyo and had invited them along.

"You go ahead," Petty said. "I'm gonna stay here until the calls die down, then run over and see Sam."

"You're a good daddy, stepping up like you are," Tinafey said.

"No, I'm not," Petty said. "I'm an asshole. I'm showing off to impress you."

"That was my other idea," Tinafey said.

Petty was back on the phone when she got into the shower

and still on when she got out. The bathroom was so small she had to step into the room to dry off. Petty lost track of what he was saying to the mark he was trying to reel in as he watched her put on her panties and choose a bra. She noticed he was watching and started teasing him. She arched her back and swayed her ass as she applied her mascara and turned to him and smiled as she slowly buttoned her blouse. The room heated up, the air turned swampy. Petty finally tossed the phone aside and charged her.

"No, no, no," she said, batting him away. "Uh-uh."

"What do you mean, 'Uh-uh'?" Petty said.

"You're gonna mess me all up."

"I'll be careful."

"I got them people waiting for me."

"I'll be quick, too."

"Get back," Tinafey said.

She sashayed out the door after letting him kiss her on the cheek. Some trick getting him all worked up like that and leaving him wanting more. She was as good at her hustle as he was at his.

He took a few more calls. The news came on the TV. Russia and China. Israel and North Korea. He couldn't have found China on a map if you'd held a gun to his head, much less Korea. He put on ESPN and dozed off watching college basketball.

The nap didn't last long. He fell right into another bad dream about the cowboy, bullets and blood and dirt, and came awake again feeling like he was going to be sick. He knew a guy who'd never gotten over the shit he saw in the army in Iraq, would start crying out of nowhere, punch brick walls. He hoped he didn't end up like that. He found a music channel on the TV and played it loud while he got ready to go out, singing along to the Rolling Stones, trying to clear his head.

★ ★ ★

The MoneyGram outlet was in a mini-mall on 6th Street. It shared a parking lot with a Laundromat, a *pupuseria,* and a water store. All the poor neighborhoods had stores that sold "filtered" water. The immigrants who crowded into the creaking boardinghouses and roachy apartments couldn't trust the tap water back in Honduras or wherever, and they didn't trust it here, either. This particular store also sold scratch-off lottery tickets, running two scams at once.

The *pupuseria* and Laundromat were hopping, everybody smiling, happy to be throwing around a little money on a Saturday night. Petty walked into the MoneyGram place and stood in line behind a kid in paint-spattered boots who was sending money to Guatemala and a skeevy white couple clearly strung out on something. They fidgeted repetitively, cycling through a sequence of tics: arm scratch, nose wipe, eye bulge, cough—two scarecrows in dumpster-dived jeans and T-shirts.

"You got the number?" the guy asked the girl.

"Shut the fuck up," the girl said.

"This even the right place?"

"Shut the fuck up."

The guy turned to Petty. "Bro, sir," he said. "Do you have five bucks to help us get to Oxnard?" His mouth moved twice as much as it needed to in order to form the words. He looked like someone in an old kung fu movie. Petty blamed him for the girl's being messed up. He couldn't help it; he had a daughter.

"Sorry," he said.

"Leave him alone," the girl said, grabbing the dude's sleeve and yanking him back to her side.

When it was their turn at the window, the girl *didn't* have the number. Luckily for Petty, they were too messed up to argue much. The clerk explained the problem, the girl said, "But we need the money," the clerk explained the problem again, and the girl said, "Fuck you," and she and the guy staggered out.

Petty stepped to the window and gave the clerk the confirmation numbers from Toronto and Seattle. The clerk gave him seventeen hundred dollars. He peeled off two hundreds and rolled the rest up and stuck it in his sock before leaving the office.

The woman at the *pupuseria* didn't understand when he asked if they had enchiladas—or pretended not to, anyway. There was a Mexican joint across the street, ENCHILADAS painted right on the sign. He ordered two cheese to go and sat down to wait. Three old men in cowboy hats were eating tacos and drinking beer at a table in front of the window. The music coming from the jukebox was so loud that the glass rattled whenever the tuba honked.

Petty reached down to check the money in his sock. His phone rang. The Miami number. *Enough,* he decided. A punch meant for you wasn't gonna miss because you closed your eyes. He walked outside to answer.

"Who's this?" he said.

It was a recording.

"The FBI estimates that there are three break-ins every minute and urges you to take steps to prevent this from happening to you. If you allow us to put a small sign in front of your house, we'll install an advanced security system at no cost to you."

Petty smiled, relieved. Steve Roberts used to run this scam out of Dallas. And Corey Brown, out of Atlanta. Both did pretty well with it. And now someone else was giving it a go. That's the way things went: a good con never died.

19

Petty heard voices coming from Sam's room. Surely Mrs. Kong's family wasn't still there. Maybe the doctor was with Sam, or a nurse, taking her temperature and blood pressure. He approached slowly and peeked in.

"Hey, Dad," Sam said with exaggerated enthusiasm. "Join the party."

Carrie—Petty's ex-wife, Sam's mother—smiled from a chair beside Sam's bed. It was a vague smile, a slippery smile, a smile that might have meant anything or nothing. Petty hadn't seen or spoken to Carrie in thirteen years. He'd made a couple of pathetic phone calls right after she walked out on him, but once he realized she was gone for good, she might as well have died. What little communication they'd had since then had been through his mom.

She looked about the same. She was a woman who kept herself up. That was one of the things Petty had liked about her.

The only sign of aging Petty noticed was a few lines on her brow that might eventually deepen into creases. She was still blond, still thin, still pretty but not quite beautiful. It was her eyes that had always prevented her from being a complete knockout. They were a nice shade of blue, but there was something hard about them, and about her mouth, too, something tough.

"Hello, Rowan," she said.

"Carrie," Petty said. "Hug."

Hug McCarthy, standing against the wall, arms crossed over his massive chest, nodded slightly. The man Carrie had taken off with still looked the same, too, like the biggest beach bum you'd ever seen. Six five, 250 pounds, all muscle. Still had the shaggy blond hair, the tan, the slow, stoned blink, still gave the impression he'd be more comfortable in board shorts and flip-flops than in the business-casual drag he wore, Polo shirts, pressed khakis, and loafers.

Petty had met him in New Jersey, their paths crossed again in Miami, and when he showed up in Vegas, he came on like an old friend. He took Petty and Carrie to dinner at the nicest restaurants on the Strip, helped build a deck on their town house, and played as a shill in Petty's crooked poker games, acting as muscle when necessary. Petty once saw him knock out a sore loser with a single punch and break another's finger like it was nothing.

In this respect he lived up to his reputation. Dark rumors circulated about how he made the money that paid for his Porsche, his courtside seats at Rebels games, and the high-roller luxury suites he lived in. Bodies buried in the desert, bodies sunk in the ocean; bodies chopped up and fed to pigs. You heard stories like those, and you definitely wanted to keep on the right side of old Hug.

Petty set the bag containing the enchiladas on Sam's table.

"What's this?" she said.

"Your favorite food," he said.

"I'm gonna get fat with you around."

"You sitting?" Petty said to Hug, motioning to an empty chair.

"Go ahead," Hug said with a drawl. Something-burg, South Carolina. Petty moved the chair next to Carrie's and sat down. *See how cool I am with this?* was the message he was sending. *See how relaxed?*

"Your mom called and let me know what was going on," Carrie said to him. "We got here as fast as we could."

"You didn't need to come," Sam said.

"Of course we did," Carrie said.

"You guys being here is only stressing me out."

"That's ridiculous."

"It makes me worry there's something really wrong with me. Why else would you show up?"

"Because we love you?" Carrie said.

"That's sweet," Sam said. She didn't mean it.

"Let's be nice," Carrie said. "We've been driving for forty-eight hours straight, and I'm feeling fragile."

"Sure, *Mom*," Sam said. "Whatever you want."

Petty enjoyed seeing Sam poke at Carrie. The bitch had it coming. Carrie had brought flowers. An elaborate arrangement of orchids sat on the table next to the enchiladas. The room stunk of them.

"Tell me about school," Carrie said. "How's that going?"

"School's fine," Sam said.

"I'm glad one of us got some brains. I actually thought about being a nurse, but your dad came along and you came along and things went a different way. Do you need a lot of math to be a nurse? I'm terrible at math."

"The job wouldn't have paid enough," Sam said. "You've got expensive tastes."

"I don't know about that," Carrie said.

"What about that ring?" Sam said, pointing at the diamonds on Carrie's finger.

"That's my wedding ring," Carrie said. "It's supposed to be flashy."

"See, that's the sort of wisdom I missed out on, not having you around," Sam said.

"Nice, now, be nice," Carrie said.

"You left me when I was eight years old and visited me once afterward. Was that nice?"

"You were better off without me," Carrie said.

Sam pointed at Petty. "That's what he said, too, when he left me with Grandma. 'You'll be better off without me.' So what are you two doing here now, then?"

"Don't they teach you manners in college?" Carrie said. She kept her voice calm, but Petty knew her well enough to recognize that she was close to losing her temper.

"If you think I'm gonna thank you for showing up, you're crazy," Sam said.

Carrie sighed long and loud. "Sweetie, I'm sorry you're not feeling well, but please quit being so shitty," she said.

"You're shitty," Sam said. "You've always been shitty. You're a shitty fucking person."

"Hey!" Hug roared, startling everyone. "Watch your mouth with your mother."

"She's not my mother," Sam screamed at him. "She's just the woman who had me. And you, you're nobody. What are you even doing here?"

Mrs. Kong was out cold, but the Mexican woman's finger was on the call button. Petty got up to go. Anything he said would only be fuel for the fire. He'd come back later, after things had calmed down.

"I'm heading to the cafeteria for coffee," he said.

"Hold on," Carrie said. She stood and grabbed her purse. "I'm going with you."

Petty wanted to say no, but no polite way to do it came to him, and he'd decided polite was how to play this.

Sam waved at all of them as they left the room. "Bye-bye," she said in a parody of cheerfulness. "Thanks for the flowers."

Hug took his coffee outside, in search of somewhere to smoke. Petty and Carrie stayed in the cafeteria. Petty let Carrie choose the table. She picked one next to the Christmas tree. The fake fir listed to one side, struggling under its burden of twinkle lights and ornaments. Each ornament had a name written on it in glitter. Miguel, René, Leilani. The LED star that topped the tree blinked on and off, on and off, like a warning signal at an intersection in the middle of nowhere.

Carrie stirred a packet of Equal into her coffee with a little red straw. That was something about her that had changed. She used to use three sugars.

"My mom didn't say anything to me about calling you," Petty said.

"I told her not to," Carrie said. "I knew you'd have a shit fit. But truthfully, now that I'm here, I don't even know why I came. I hate hospitals."

"Why did you?" Petty said. "Why did you come?"

"She's my daughter," Carrie said. "It sounded serious."

Petty sipped his coffee.

"Is she always like that? So pissed off?" Carrie said.

"I haven't seen her since she was fourteen," Petty said. "But she was pretty pissed then, too."

"It's no way to go through life."

"I don't know," Petty said. "I'm pissed most of the time, too. Aren't you?"

This wasn't what Carrie wanted to hear. She changed the subject.

"You just happened to be in town?"

"Just passing through," Petty said.

"That was lucky. It's nice you could be here for her."

"I don't know that I'm doing anything useful. It's mostly been sitting with her, keeping her company."

Carrie ran her fingers through her hair. She looked like she wished she had a mirror. Petty couldn't help noticing that the one button on her blouse that separated modest from sexy was undone, so that anyone who wanted could see her cleavage. They used to go toe-to-toe over things like that.

"She says you've got a girlfriend," Carrie said.

"I hope you guys had something more interesting to talk about than that," Petty said.

"A *black* girlfriend," Carrie said, making it sound scandalous.

Petty ignored her. An ornament had fallen off the tree and lay on top of the fake gifts piled underneath. Petty picked it up and hung it on an empty branch.

"Where did you come from that it took two days?" he said.

"Houston," Carrie said. "Hug's a security consultant there."

"Is that what they call it now?" Petty said.

"Why don't you ask him?" Carrie said.

Petty sat back and smiled at her.

"You two do make a cute couple," he said.

"It's been almost thirteen years," she said. "Don't tell me you still cry yourself to sleep every night."

"You're not funny," Petty said.

He stood and picked up his coffee. Warm air blew out of a

vent overhead and started the paper snowflakes hanging from the ceiling swinging.

"I'm sorry I couldn't be what you wanted," Carrie said.

"And what was that?" Petty said.

"The same thing most men want. Something they saw on TV or read about in a book. That wasn't gonna work for me."

"And Sam?" Petty said. "She didn't work for you, either?"

"I lasted eight years. That's good for someone who wasn't meant to be a mother in the first place."

"She deserved better than us," Petty said. "It's a miracle she turned out so well."

Carrie scoffed at this. "Kids are tough," she said. "My mom worked twelve-hour shifts at a cannery and waitressed on the weekends. I was lucky if I saw her an hour a day. From the time I was seven years old I had to cook for my brothers and clean the house."

"Yeah, but we were supposed to give Sam a better life than we had," Petty said.

"It *is* better," Carrie said. "She's going to college, going to concerts, going to parties. She's not stuck at home with a kid like I was."

Poor Carrie. Still and always poor, poor Carrie, who'd suffered more than anyone else ever. Petty had had enough of her for one night.

"How long are you going to be around?" he said.

"I don't know," she said. "Until we find out what's going on, I guess."

"Let's work it so we visit at different times."

"Man, you sure hold a grudge."

"It'll be easier on Sam. I'm going to sit with her now. You take the morning shift."

Carrie said something else mean, but Petty was already on

his way, waved at her over his shoulder. They fought all the time when they were married, and even after they'd made up he'd lie in bed next to her and worry that she'd snuck a knife out of the kitchen. She was scary like that then. Hell, she was scary like that now.

Sam was finishing the enchiladas when Petty got back to her room.

"These were *good*," she said.

Petty sat in one of the chairs. From the hallway came the sound of squeaking wheels and hushed voices. The evening bustle was in full swing. It was dinnertime, and visitors trying to find their relatives' rooms had to stand aside for food carts and dodge workers delivering trays. Doctors made their late rounds, and nurses distributed meds, asking patients their names and checking their wristbands before handing over the paper cups.

The Mexican woman in the bed next to Sam's asked the orderly if she could take a walk. The orderly, a burly Mexican kid with the Dodgers logo tattooed on his forearm, helped her get up, waited until she'd steadied herself, then led her out of the room and down the corridor.

Sam tried to push the table away from her bed, but it was stuck.

"You need help?" Petty said, leaning forward in his chair.

"I've got it," Sam said.

Petty sat back and let her wrestle with it on her own. When she'd moved the table to where she wanted it, she adjusted her pillows.

"I'm sorry I was such a bitch earlier," she said. "But it's ridiculous, her showing up here."

"I guess she's worried about you," Petty said.

"I guess she's fucking crazy," Sam said.

Petty didn't dispute this.

"I remember when I was six and she burned all your clothes," Sam said.

"I remember that, too," Petty said.

"She said she caught you cheating. I thought she meant at cards."

"I never cheated on her," Petty said, and it was true. "My dad cheated on my mom, and I saw what it did to her, and I swore I'd never do that to my wife."

"But she thought you did," Sam said.

"She was wrong," Petty said. "I might have been a bad husband in a hundred other ways, but I never cheated on her."

Sam chewed on this, deciding whether to believe him.

"Why did she leave then?" she said.

This was the great mystery of Petty's life, the question he still asked himself at 3:00 a.m. on sleepless nights. To this day he wasn't sure if Carrie had actually loved him for a time or had been playing him all along.

They were living in Denver when she took off. They'd moved there from Vegas and were renting a brand-new three-bedroom house with a view of the Rockies and driving brand-new cars. Petty was working a house-flopping scam with a crooked Realtor and appraiser. The Realtor would hook him up with "motivated sellers," homeowners under water on their mortgages and close to defaulting, and Petty would offer to help them get rid of the mortgages without ruining their credit and put a little cash in their pockets at the same time.

This was during the bubble, when the introductory rates on all the shitty variable mortgages the banks had issued were expiring, so there were plenty of motivated sellers. If a homeowner went for Petty's pitch, the Realtor and the appraiser would convince the bank holding the paper that the market value of the house was much lower than it actually was, and Petty would make an offer on the property based on this false valuation.

Nine times out of ten the bank would agree to a short sale, because settling for less would be cheaper for them than fore-closing. Once Petty was listed as owner of the house, he'd turn around and sell it for actual market value, pocketing the differ-ence between the short-sale price and the market price, that difference being anywhere from twenty to forty grand. The original homeowner and the appraiser each got 10 percent of this, and the Realtor was happy with her commissions from both sales. The bank got fucked over, but you know, fuck the bank.

Petty's plan had been to save enough money to buy some legit rental properties with an eye toward settling in Denver. Sam was eight years old, and they'd moved five times since she was born, either running from some kind of heat or chasing new swindles. He didn't want her to grow up like that, like he had.

Carrie seemed open to the idea of staying in town, too, had even been talking about a country club she wanted to join. But then one day she left Sam with a neighbor, e-mailed Petty to pick their little girl up there, and disappeared.

He managed to get hold of her a week later, paid one of her friends a hundred bucks for her new cell number. They talked twice before she changed the number again. That's when she told him she was with Hug. They'd had a fling in Vegas and been lusting after each other ever since. Petty asked her to re-turn for Sam's sake. The little girl had been crying since she left and jumped for the phone every time it rang.

"That's not going to happen," Carrie said.

"Was it really so awful being with us?" Petty said.

"Not awful, but not good, either," Carrie said. "Not *great*."

He'd had no direct contact with her since.

Some years later a rumor went around that she and Hug had been involved in a thing, guns and dope and bloody payback. She'd either done time or barely managed to avoid it, depending on who you talked to. Petty didn't care either way. He'd never forgive her for Sam's tears, and he'd never forgive her for making him a mark.

So why did she leave? Sam had asked. She stared at him from the bed, waiting for an answer.

"She said she was bored," Petty replied.

"Do you remember the poem I wrote back then?" Sam said. "'My mother ran away. Maybe she will stay. Or maybe she'll come home someday and take my pain away.'"

"Does it still hurt like that now?" Petty said.

"It made me tough," Sam said. "And that's good. I'm the one my friends come to when they're falling apart, all the girls who grew up in magic princess land."

"You wanted to be a princess, too," Petty said. "I bought you the dress."

"Yeah, well, you probably wanted to be a policeman, and look at you."

"A cop? No way. A fireman, maybe, but never a cop."

Sam laughed. "Look," she said, pulling a deck of cards out of her bag. "I had Jessica bring these."

She swung the table over, shuffled the cards, and had Petty pick one, memorize it, and place it on top of the deck.

"Does this ring a bell?" she said.

It was a trick Petty had shown her when she was a kid. She squared the deck, sneaking a peek at the bottom card as she did, and had Petty cut. Then she spread the cards out on the table faceup, looked for the former bottom card, and pointed to the card to the left of it, Petty's card.

"Sim sala bim," she said.

"What about the other trick?" Petty said. "The Seven Detectives."

"The Seven Detectives," she said in a funny voice and looked through the deck for the four kings, the setup for the trick.

"I can't believe you remember these," Petty said. "I can't even remember my own phone number."

Sam pulled the king of spades and froze. Her face went blank, like she was listening to a voice in her head. She began to tremble.

"What's wrong?" Petty said.

The trembling got worse. She dropped the cards, and her hands curled in at the wrists. Petty started to shake, too. He jumped up out of his chair.

"Sam?"

Her head flopped back onto the pillow, and her eyes rolled. The convulsions were so violent now that the bed squeaked their rhythm. Petty called for a nurse. Sam was making choking noises. Foam oozed from between her lips. Petty looked around for something to put in her mouth to keep her from biting her tongue. He grabbed the plastic fork from the enchilada tray, but his hands belonged to someone else; he couldn't keep hold of it.

"Nurse!" he yelled again. "Somebody get a nurse!" He was at the bottom of a dark pit, alone with the echo of his voice. He was in a crowded subway car with no room to draw a breath. He pried open Sam's clenched jaw and stuck his knuckle between her teeth. She chomped down hard, and he gritted his own teeth against the pain.

"Nurse!" he said again. "Nurse! Nurse! Nurse!"

20

T INAFEY SHOWED UP AROUND NINE. PETTY CALLED TO TELL her what happened, and she took a cab from the jazz club to the hospital. He decided to hold off on calling his mom until he heard something definite about Sam. All he knew now was that she'd been moved to intensive care. As for Carrie, he had no idea how to get in touch with her and didn't want to deal with her right now anyway.

He and Tinafey sat next to Sam's empty bed. Quiet had descended over the hospital, the fidgety quiet of a crowded place. Mrs. Kong and the Mexican woman were asleep. Petty counted the beeps of Mrs. Kong's machines to keep from going crazy.

"She's gonna be all right," Tinafey said out of nowhere, as if she'd read his mind. She took his hand and gave it a squeeze.

Dr. Avakian had a lousy poker face. Petty read him as soon as he walked into the room. Bad news. He asked to talk to Petty alone. Petty followed him out into the hall and down past the nurses' station. Avakian looked both ways before he spoke.

"Your daughter had another seizure," he said.

"I know. I was there," Petty said.

"It was a major one, but she's stable now."

"That's good, right?"

Dr. Avakian paused and exhaled forcefully. Petty caught a whiff of cigarette smoke on his breath. The doctor pinched the bridge of his nose and screwed his eyes shut.

"What I'm going to tell you next I'm not supposed to be telling you," he said.

"What do you mean?" Petty said.

"You're her father," Dr. Avakian said. "You should know."

"Thank you," Petty said.

Dr. Avakian opened his eyes. "The results of the MRI are in, and the neurologist will go over them with you tomorrow," he said. "But between you and me, it doesn't look good."

Petty stiffened like a soldier standing at attention, made his spine steel so he didn't slump to the floor.

"In what way?" he said.

"Without going into detail, there's a tumor," Dr. Avakian said. "A big one."

"Is she going to die?" Petty said.

"The neurologist will discuss the prognosis when you meet with her," Dr. Avakian said. "Why I'm speaking with you now is this. May I be candid?"

"Please do," Petty said.

"Your daughter is a self-pay patient, correct?"

"That's right. But it's not a problem. I'll cover everything."

"And how are you fixed for money?"

The question confused Petty. "I do okay," he said. "Why?"

"Treating a tumor like this is very expensive," Dr. Avakian

said. "You'll be able to negotiate the costs down, but still, an illness like this can break you if you're not prepared."

"How much are we talking about?" Petty said.

"A million dollars at least, and it could be much more, depending on how things go."

"Jesus," Petty said.

"That's why I'm giving you an early warning," Dr. Avakian said. "Father to father, I advise you to start gathering the funds now. I don't know what that means to you—selling stocks, selling property, borrowing from relatives—but start the process now."

"Jesus," Petty said again.

A fluorescent tube in the fixture above him had been flickering all through the conversation. He'd been able to ignore it before, but now it was all he could do not to reach up and smash it to bits.

Sam wouldn't be out of intensive care until morning, so Petty and Tinafey returned to the motel, where Petty spent a long night tossing and turning on the too-soft bed. Tinafey laid a comforting arm across his chest, but it felt like a strap yanked tight. He shrugged it off and rolled to the edge of the mattress. He knew what he had to do, but the city's noisy nocturnal simmer derailed his every attempt to come up with a way to do it. Helicopters hovered, brakes squealed, and sirens howled like madmen on fire. When he tried opening his eyes and concentrating on the ceiling, the calm, white expanse of stucco mocked his turmoil.

Somewhere near dawn, with daylight creeping in around the drapes, he dozed off. The anguished groan of a garbage truck hefting an overloaded dumpster woke him a couple minutes later, but the time away had been enough. The first step of a plan had tumbled into place.

He needed the army money, and to get it, he needed Tinafey's help. That meant telling her everything. About Avi and Don and the rumor that had brought him here. About Tony. About the dead cowboy. He laid it all out for her over coffee at the counter of an IHOP on the ground floor of a downtown office building. Ten seconds into his confession, she slipped on her sunglasses in order to hide her eyes from him. By the time he finished, she had a hand covering her mouth, too, so that he had no idea how his revelations had gone over. She sat silently for a long, tense moment, then sighed and reached for her cappuccino.

"Motherfuckin' hustlers," she said.

"It wasn't supposed to turn out like this," Petty said.

"When does it ever turn out like it's supposed to?" she said. She sipped her coffee and shook her head, disgusted.

The after-church crowd poured in, and the line of people waiting for tables stretched out the front door of the restaurant. Everybody in their Sunday best, everybody freshly sanctified. They talked excitedly about TV shows they liked and discount tickets to Universal Studios. The Korean guy at the host's station cracked bad jokes that kept them laughing.

"What kind of bagel can fly?" he asked a black woman in a fancy hat.

"I don't know. What kind?"

"A plain bagel."

"You were supposed to be in Memphis by now, and I was supposed to be in Phoenix," Petty said to Tinafey. "Both of us free and clear."

"But now what?" Tinafey said.

"I need that money to pay for Sam's treatment," Petty said. "And if the kid was telling the truth about having it, I'm gonna take it from him."

"You mean *steal* it from him," Tinafey said.

Petty shrugged.

"And what about the other motherfucker?" Tinafey said. "Avi. You said he might still be after the money, too, might have someone else looking for it, looking for *you*."

"If that's true, I've got to beat him to it," Petty said.

"What the fuck are you thinkin'?" Tinafey said. She leaned in and lowered her voice. "There's already one man dead here. You didn't kill him, but they can put you away for it just the same. Or maybe you'll end up out there in the desert, too, buried next to him."

"I'm going to get the money for Sam," Petty said. "After that, what happens happens."

"Oh, my God," Tinafey said. She put her hands over her ears. "Why are you even tellin' me all this?"

"I need your help," Petty said.

"And I need to get my ass up and walk out of here right now."

"Please, baby."

"What about your wife?" Tinafey said. "She's here. Get her to help you."

"I can't trust her," Petty said. "I can trust you."

"What's the best day to go to the beach?" the Korean said.

"Come on, now, what day?" a guy in a suit said, playing along.

"Sunday!"

Tinafey carved grooves into her foam cup with the tip of her thumbnail. She wouldn't look Petty in the eye.

"Baby...." she said.

"Make one phone call for me," Petty said.

"I know we're talkin' about your little girl and everything, but—"

"One call, and I'll give you ten grand and put you on a plane to Memphis this afternoon. I'm an asshole for asking, but I don't have anybody else."

"You don't understand."

"I do understand. It's not your problem, so why should you get mixed up in it? But I swear, nobody will ever know you had anything to do with it."

"You *don't* understand," Tinafey said. "It's not me I'm worried about." She gouged another groove into her cup, and another. "It's you."

The tumor was located on Sam's cerebrum. Petty asked Dr. Wilkes, Sam's neurologist, to spell that and wrote the word down so he didn't have to watch what happened to Sam's face while she digested the news. She was back in her room with Mrs. Kong and the Mexican woman. Carrie was there, too. Petty had dragged her number out of Sam and called her. It seemed like the right thing to do.

Dr. Wilkes was wearing heels. A white lab coat, a dark blue skirt, and turquoise pumps. The pumps irritated Petty. They hinted at frivolousness, at a life outside the hospital. He didn't want to think about her shopping. He wanted all her time to be spent helping Sam.

The first step was to operate, she said. In two days, on Tuesday, they'd go in and remove as much as of the tumor as they could without damaging the brain. Once they'd analyzed the tumor and determined what type they were dealing with, they'd be able to make a more accurate diagnosis and proceed with further treatment.

Dr. Wilkes breezed through this like she was reminding them of the rules to a game they'd all played before. Petty recognized the tactic. He used it in his phone scams to make marks feel stupid about asking questions, like his pitch was something they were already supposed to know. Sam, however, didn't fall for it.

"Is the tumor serious?" she said.

"All brain tumors are serious," Dr. Wilkes said. "But some are more serious than others." She had short gray hair and a forced smile. "We'll know exactly what we're dealing with after the surgery," she said.

"Brain surgery," Sam said.

"It sounds scary, I know. But your surgeon and everybody else involved are really, really good at what they do."

"Everybody who's going to cut my head open."

"Oh, my God, Sam," Carrie said with a look of horror. "Please."

"They'll be doing a craniotomy, which, yes, does involve temporarily removing a section of the skull," Dr. Wilkes said. "This will give them access to the brain and allow them to remove the tumor. The most interesting aspect is that you'll be awake during the entire procedure."

"Wait: what?" Sam said.

The color drained from her face, and Petty's own stomach lurched.

"You'll be guiding the surgeon, in a way," Dr. Wilkes said. "He'll stimulate areas of your brain and ask you if you feel it. Your responses will help him decide how much of the tumor it's safe to remove."

Sam slapped a hand over her mouth. "I think I'm gonna throw up," she said.

A nurse who'd been standing by stepped in with a plastic tray. Petty turned away while Sam vomited. The room's window was fogged over. He reached out and cleared a square of glass with the edge of his hand and watched the cars moving down in the street and the people going about their business. So we had all these fucking computers and lasers and miracle drugs, and it still came down to cutting a hole in someone's skull. Petty had always thought we were further along than that and now felt like he'd been sold a bill of goods.

Dr. Wilkes finished her lecture and left, and Petty held Sam's hand until she stopped crying. Carrie stood beside him but didn't touch her daughter, just kept saying, "It's okay, it's okay," while dabbing at her eyes with a blob of soggy Kleenex.

The nurse gave Sam a pill that made her drowsy. When her eyes closed, Petty gestured for Carrie to step out into the corridor.

"You've got to stay with her," he said.

"Why?" Carrie said. "Where are you going?"

"I have things to do," Petty said. "I'll be back this evening."

"She's asleep," Carrie said. "Wouldn't it be better if I came back later, too?"

"What if she wakes up?" Petty said. "You wouldn't want to be alone, would you?"

Carrie sighed loudly and went back into the room.

Back at the motel, Petty punched the number of Tony's mom's store into the burner. Tinafey stood beside him, chewing her thumbnail.

"Ready?" Petty said to her.

"Quit fuckin' around and let me do this," she said.

He handed her the phone. They'd rehearsed the call, so she knew exactly what to say.

Tony's mom's voice crackled over the speaker. "Party store."

Petty nodded at this first bit of good luck: Tony obviously hadn't taken his advice and gotten his mother out of harm's way.

"I got a message for Tony," Tinafey said.

"My Tony?" Tony's mom said.

"He has somethin' we want, and we're gonna get it, whatever we have to do," Tinafey said. "Pass that along to him. He'll know what you mean. Tell him we know where he lives and where you live and what happened at his apartment."

"Who is this?" Tony's mom said.

"Tell him to get what we want together," Tinafey said. "We'll call later with where to drop it."

"I don't understand what you're talking about."

Tinafey hung up and tossed the phone onto the bed.

"Now, why couldn't you do that yourself?" she said.

"The kid won't be expecting a woman to call," Petty said. "I've got to do whatever I can to keep him off balance. It'll make him easier to push around."

"Whatever," Tinafey said. She stuck her hand into her purse and came up with a joint. She lit it, took a hit, and sat at the room's little table.

"So where's my money?" she said around the smoke she exhaled.

"I have to give it to you in two installments," Petty said. He took a thousand dollars in hundreds out of his pocket and handed it to her. "There's a grand there, and I'll send the rest to Memphis."

"Installments?" Tinafey said. "This ain't fuckin' Kmart. This ain't fuckin' layaway. If that's how you're gonna do me, I want twenty thousand instead of ten."

She was angry at him for asking her to make the call and was going to punish him by grinding him for more money. Petty could understand that. He was being taxed for disappointing her.

"No problem," he said. "Twenty thousand."

"And you'll send it when you get it?" Tinafey said.

"That's right."

"And if you don't get it?"

"However this shakes out, one way or another, you'll get your money, I promise."

"In Memphis?"

"Wherever you are."

Tinafey took another hit off the joint and contemplated Petty through narrowed eyes. "So that's what you think of me, huh?" she said.

"What do you mean?" Petty said.

"As soon as shit goes bad, I'm gonna snatch what I can and run off."

"What I think is it's not your choice," Petty said. "I'm *telling* you you have to go. You said yourself, one man already died trying to get this money, and I'm not going to put you in danger."

"Shit," Tinafey said. "I been in danger my whole life."

"Maybe so," Petty said, "but you're going to Memphis on the next flight out."

Sparks flared in Tinafey's eyes. She drew her head back and glared down her nose at Petty.

"'Cause you say so?" she said.

"This time, yeah, 'cause I say so," Petty said.

"Is that what you'd do if things were turned around, cut out on me?"

"We're not arguing about this."

"You're right, we aren't," Tinafey said. "I'm gonna make it real easy for you: I don't want your money, and I'm not goin' anywhere."

"Baby..."

"Let me ask you somethin'," Tinafey said. "We haven't

known each other for too long, but do you think of me as a friend?"

"What are you talking about?" Petty said. "I fucking love you."

Tinafey's only reaction to this declaration was a slight curl at the corners of her mouth. She was too busy making her point to slow down.

"I don't run out on my friends when there's trouble," she said. "You might not get that 'cause you ain't never been with a ride-or-die bitch like me before."

Petty paused to catch up to himself and come up with a new tack.

"How about this?" he said. "Go to Memphis for a week. After I see how things play out, you can come back."

Tinafey licked her fingertips and pinched out the joint. "How about this?" she said. "I'm stayin', and I'll decide if and when I leave."

Petty could see he wasn't going to sway her. He was off his game after the bad news about Sam. His mind kept flashing back to it, and he kept losing his place in the present. The one thing he was certain of was that he had to work fast. The sooner he got to Tony, the better his odds of beating Avi to the money if he was still after it. And that meant he didn't have time to argue with Tinafey. She could stay for the time being, and when things slowed down, he'd persuade her to go.

He walked over and knelt in front of her. It was cold closer to the floor. The rinky-dink heater only warmed the top half of the room. He wrapped his arms around her calves. She sat back in the chair and looked down at him.

"I'm all talked out," he said. "If you want to stay, you can."

"I'm not tryin' to cause you trouble. I'm tryin' to be helpful," Tinafey said.

"I know," Petty said. He kissed her knees. She laid a hand on his head.

"You really love me?" she said.

"I really do," he said.

"That's sweet," she said. "I knew you were sweet."

"You're sweet, too," he said. "But hey, I have to go now."

"Oh, yeah? Well, fuck you, then."

"I'm sorry."

"I ain't even gonna ask where."

"I won't be long—an hour or so."

Petty stood and went to his bag for a clean shirt.

"There's money in the safe," he said. "Write down the combination."

"That shit again?" Tinafey said.

"Write it down."

He gave her the combination and walked into the bathroom and washed his face. He thought of Sam again but pushed it aside, blanked his expression, and checked his reflection in the mirror. It was a gift he'd always been thankful for, being able to hide what was going on inside his head. Even looking right into his eyes, nobody would have known how torn up he was.

21

Traffic on the 101 to East L.A. slowed, then stopped. If Petty had known his way around on the surface streets, he'd have exited the freeway, but he was worried about getting lost, so he stuck to his original route. The cause of the slowdown turned out to be a refrigerator lying on its back like a big white turtle in the middle lane. It had fallen off a truck that kept going. The sludgy river of cars parted to flow around the refrigerator and came back together on the other side. The people in the minivan in front of Petty stuck their phones out their windows to take photos.

Petty was behind the wheel of a Mazda SUV he'd rented downtown. He'd called a cab to take him there, left his Mercedes at the motel. He was being cautious in case Avi had new eyes on Tony's apartment, doing everything he could think of to avoid picking up a new tail.

He parked a few blocks from Tony's building. The neighborhood kids were at war in the street, soaking one another with giant squirt guns. The wet asphalt gleamed like spilled mercury, and the kids' shouts bounced like Ping-Pong balls between the dumpy apartment complexes. It had been a cool day, and it was getting cooler as the sun went down, but the kids charged about in T-shirts and shorts like it was the middle of summer. Petty passed a couple of combatants who'd dropped out of the battle and now shivered under beach towels, their lips blue, their teeth chattering.

As he walked toward Tony's building he scanned the vehicles parked along the curb for lookouts. He hoped anyone keeping watch would be distracted by the water fight and the other residents on the street, exchanging Sunday-evening gossip and walking boisterous dogs. The gate to Tony's building was propped open, as it had been both other times Petty had visited. This time Petty dragged the cinder block inside and pulled the gate shut behind him.

If everything was going according to his timeline, Tony's mom had by now told Tony about the call from Tinafey. A couple of things could have happened after that. One possibility was that the kid had panicked and gone into hiding, maybe even taking his mom with him. In which case Petty was screwed, because he had no way of tracking him down. What he was counting on, however, and what seemed more likely from what he knew about Tony, was that instead of fleeing he was cowering in his apartment, paralyzed by fear and indecision.

Petty approached the door slowly. The living-room blinds were closed. A toddler circled the courtyard on a toy motorcycle, watched over by an old woman sweeping the walkway in front of her unit. Petty knocked on Tony's door and got no response. He checked the blinds for movement. Nothing. He knocked again, louder.

"Tony," he said. "It's me."

He backed up so Tony could see him through the peephole. A few seconds later he heard a muffled voice from inside. He pressed his ear to the door.

"Tony?" he said.

"What do you want?" Tony said again, louder this time.

"I got a phone call," Petty said.

"From who?" Tony said.

"You know."

"I don't know nothing."

"Look, man, we're fucked," Petty said. "We need to talk."

After a long pause, the dead bolt clicked, and the door opened wide enough that Petty could see one of Tony's eyes and the muzzle of the sawed-off shotgun he was holding.

"You alone?" Tony said.

"Of course I'm alone," Petty said.

Tony moved aside, and Petty slipped past him into the apartment. The kid locked the door and wheeled on Petty with the shotgun.

"Lift your shirt and turn around," he said.

Petty pulled his shirt up to his chest and spun in a slow circle. He had a flash of the cowboy lying dead on the floor. The sooner he got the gun out of the kid's hands, the better.

"Sit on the couch," Tony said.

Petty nodded at the sawed-off. "Where'd you get that?" he said.

"I got homeys," Tony said.

"Well, you don't need it with me," Petty said.

Tony kept the gun pointed at him but let the barrel dip a bit.

"What did they say when they called?" Petty asked.

"It was a woman," Tony replied. "She said they know what happened with that asshole, and they know about the money."

"They don't know about the money, that you actually have it, unless you told them yourself," Petty said. "They're bluffing."

"It's that Avi, right?"

"Yep."

"What did they say to you?"

"They said if I didn't convince you to give them the money, they'd tell the cops about the dead guy. Which'd be bad for me but worse for you."

"Fuck!" Tony said.

"Seriously, could you get rid of that thing?" Petty said, gesturing at the sawed-off.

"Relax," Tony said. "It's not even loaded." He carried the gun to the breakfast bar and moved aside a few empty beer cans to set it down.

"I came to see what you're gonna do," Petty said.

Tony covered his face with his hands. "I don't know," he said.

"Well, figure it out, because my next move depends on yours."

"I been sitting here all day trying to figure it out."

"Let's go over your options."

"What options?"

"One: you give Avi the money," Petty said. "The end."

"And Mando and his crew take me out," Tony said.

"Two: you don't give Avi the money. You disappear like I told you to and take your mom with you."

"For how long?" Tony said.

"I don't know," Petty said. "Maybe a long time. Avi's a persistent motherfucker."

"My mom won't go for that," Tony said. He opened the refrigerator and got himself a Tecate. "She has a boyfriend and shit, my brother and sisters, their kids."

"Then there's option three," Petty said. "You fight back. You do what you have to to scare Avi off."

"How?" Tony said. "I don't know nothing about him."

"Yeah, but I do," Petty said. "He's a bad guy, but not as bad as he thinks he is, and what we're gonna do, me and you, is give him so much grief that he says, 'Fuck the money; it's not worth it.'"

Tony eyed Petty suspiciously.

"Why would you help me now when you wouldn't a couple days ago?" he said.

"Peace of mind," Petty said. "I don't want Avi holding anything over my head."

"Me, neither," Tony said. "I don't want him holding anything over me, either."

"And the half share you offered me earlier."

"Huh?"

"If this works out, I want the money you said you'd give me the other day. From your cut."

Tony rubbed the scar on his cheek with his mangled hand and stared at Petty like he was a puzzle he was trying to solve.

"What's your plan?" he finally said.

Bam! Something hit the door, hard. Tony pivoted on his fake leg and reached for the shotgun. Petty jumped off the couch and raced to the peephole. Nobody was there. *Bam!* Petty shifted his gaze downward. The little boy outside backed up his motorcycle and ran it into the door again. *Bam!*

Petty opened the door. The kid was startled almost to tears by the scowl on his face. He abandoned his toy and ran to the old woman. She slapped him on the head and called out to Petty, *"Lo siento, señor!"*

Petty closed the door and turned to Tony. He had no idea

if anyone was watching the apartment, but in order for his scheme to work, he had to make Tony believe there was.

"We need to get out of here," he said. "Do you have any other guns? Some with bullets in them, maybe?"

Tony made a face, didn't appreciate the joke. "We can get shells anywhere," he said.

"Okay, later," Petty said. "Right now, pack a bag. Underwear, toothbrush. You're going away for a while."

"Where to?" Tony said.

"Just do what I say," Petty said. "While you're standing here who-ing and what-ing and why-ing, more of Avi's stooges might be sneaking up on us. Grab your shit, and let's go."

Things were moving too fast for Tony. He scratched his scar and sipped some beer.

"Why would I go with you?" he said.

"If you don't, you might as well give Avi the money right now," Petty said. "Or call the cops and turn yourself in. That's another option. Although I don't know how safe you'd be in prison."

Tony flicked the pull tab on his beer a couple times, then said, "I'll kill you if you try and fuck me over."

"That's how it usually goes," Petty said.

"I'm not kidding."

"And I'm not gonna fuck you over."

Tony looked like he was going to keep arguing but then thought better of it. He headed for the bedroom.

"We can't go out the gate," Petty said. "Is there a back way?"

Tony led Petty to a door that opened onto a dead-end alley. Weeds had forced their way up through the asphalt like bony fingers, and gang graffiti slithered over cinder-block walls. The two of them hurried down the passage past crippled shopping carts and gory mattresses, past a discarded washing machine and a bum wearing a scrap of shag carpet as a coat.

They emerged near Petty's rental car and scrambled inside. Tony scrunched in his seat and pulled the hood of his jacket over his head like he was worried somebody might see him. Good. He was on the hook. Petty kept an eye on the rearview mirror as he drove to the freeway, made sure nobody was tailing them.

"Avi's gonna regret messing with us," Petty said. "We're gonna come down on him hard."

"How?" Tony said.

"First things first," Petty said. "Where's the money?"

Tony considered the question, then said, "A couple places. Hidden real good."

"Where?" Petty said.

Tony didn't respond, just sank deeper in his seat and pulled his hood tighter around his face.

"I'm trying to help you," Petty said. "But for me to do that, you're gonna have to trust me."

"Trust you?" Tony said. "I don't even know you."

"I don't know you, either," Petty said. "But that's the boat we're in. We've both got our dicks hanging out."

Tony clammed up again, sat there scratching his scar. It was time to get his attention, jack up his paranoia.

"Look out the back window," Petty said.

"Why?" Tony said.

"I think somebody's following us."

They had just crossed the L.A. River, headed west on the 101. The downtown skyline was silhouetted against the sunset. Petty twisted the steering wheel and swerved across two lanes of traffic to take the next exit.

"What the fuck?" Tony said, grabbing the dash.

Petty squealed into the parking lot of a Denny's and slammed on the brakes.

"Anybody there?" he said to Tony.

"Nobody."

"Good," Petty said. "Now where's the money?"

Tony hesitated for a second, then said, "Some of it's at my mom's store."

"Okay."

"And the rest's at my uncle's house, Mando's dad's, in his garage."

Petty nodded, thinking fast.

"Good," he said. "Good. But before we go after Avi, it should all be stashed somewhere safe."

"It's safe where it is," Tony said.

"I'm sure, but you're gonna want it all in one place now, not scattered all over. One secure place, locked up, under your control."

"So, what? We have to go get it all and move it?"

"Right," Petty said. "Let's start with what's at the store."

"My mom doesn't even know it's there," Tony said. "And I don't want her mixed up in this."

Petty was fine with that. They couldn't use the woman to carry the money out anyway, because there was still a possibility that the place was being watched. For the same reason, he couldn't send Tony to get the cash or go himself or even use Tinafey. They'd all be on Avi's radar. So, somebody else then.

He was still plotting when they pulled into the Holiday Lodge, where he'd booked Tony a room. The motel was a few blocks from where he and Tinafey were staying but far enough away that they wouldn't run into the kid on the street. Petty would keep Tony here until he got his hands on the money, keep him locked down, keep him scared.

"Why are we stopping?" Tony said.

"This is your hideout," Petty said.

"My hideout?"

"You need someplace to stay while we figure everything out."

"It's kinda ghetto."

"It's low-key," Petty said. "That's what you want."

The place did look like something that had curled up on the corner because it couldn't go any farther. The clerk took money and handed out keys from behind a sheet of cloudy bulletproof Plexiglas, and Tony's second-floor room had a view of the parking lot with its padlocked dumpsters and potholes filled with broken glass. The room itself smelled vaguely of shit. Shit dipped in pine-scented deodorizer. The bedspreads looked like clown vomit, and the TV remote was bolted to the nightstand.

Tony set his duffel on the dresser, unzipped it, and took out the shotgun.

"Keep that out of sight," Petty said.

Tony stowed the gun in the top dresser drawer and peeked into the bathroom.

"You sit on the head, and your knees are banging against the door," he said.

"It'll be three or four days at most," Petty said. "Then you can go home."

"Are you staying here, too?"

"Close by."

"Where?"

"Look, there's some stuff I'm gonna have to keep you in the dark about, okay? But it's for your own good."

"How's that?"

"If this thing goes south, it'll be the less you know the better."

"How's it gonna go south?"

Petty was tired of the kid's questions and tired of coming up with answers.

"It's not," he said. "Everything's gonna go smoothly. I'm just being extra careful. That's what you want in a partner, right?"

"I guess so," Tony said.

Petty led him out onto the walkway. The door to one of the first-floor rooms was open, and a Mexican polka oom-pahed from a radio inside. A shirtless *vato* slouched on the threshold, beer in one hand, cigar in the other, and flexed his tattoos.

"What do you need?" Petty said to Tony. "Food? Beer? There's a hamburger joint around the corner. I'll get you whatever you want."

"Why can't I go myself?" Tony said.

"Because you're the mastermind of this thing," Petty said. "The dude with the keys to the kingdom. Avi's goons are gonna be looking for you, so you have to lay low, stay outta sight. We're going to the mattresses."

"The what?" Tony said.

"It's an old Mafia saying. It means we're getting ready to go to war."

Tony raised his ruined hand.

"I already been to war," he said.

"This won't be that," Petty said. "I promise."

He went out and picked up a sandwich from Subway, a case of beer, and some Doritos, Gatorade, and Pop-Tarts. Enough crap to hold Tony until the next day. After dropping off the supplies, he drove to the hospital.

A ball of ice formed in his chest when he walked into Sam's room and found her bed stripped. He hurried to the nurses' station, where he confronted the prissy Latino on duty.

"Where's my daughter?"

"Please calm down, sir," the nurse said, very calm himself. "What's your daughter's name?"

"Samantha Petty," Petty said. "Room 314. Her bed's empty."

The guy pecked at his keyboard. "P-e..." he said.

"P-e-t-t-y," Petty said. "Come on, man."

The nurse raised a warning finger. "Sir..."

Petty swallowed hard. The ice didn't budge. Its chill spread to his arms, his legs.

The nurse squinted at his monitor. "She's been moved to another room," he said.

The dude was stalling now, dragging things out in order to punish Petty for snapping, but Petty didn't take the bait. "Which room?" he said, keeping his voice calm.

"Room 352," the nurse said.

"Where's that?"

"Down the hall."

Petty charged off in the direction the nurse pointed.

Room 352 was private—small but private. Petty silently thanked Diane Rhee. Sam was watching TV in the dark.

"*Here* you are," Petty said.

"Oh, shit," Sam said. "I meant to text you."

Petty glanced around the room. "This is nice," he said.

"It's definitely quieter," Sam said.

She looked younger in the flicker of the television. When the light played across her face, Petty glimpsed the little girl he remembered, and his heart was tossed by a rogue wave of grief. Without worrying about how Sam would react, he reached out and laid a hand on her shoulder.

"How are you doing?" he said.

"They have to shave my head," Sam said. "For the surgery."

"It'll grow back."

"Yeah, but I'll have a scar."

"Under your hair?" Petty said. "Who's gonna know?"

Sam made a face. Petty's responses seemed to irritate her. This frustrated him. He wanted to say the right things, especially tonight, with the surgery looming. He wanted to put her at ease.

She pushed a button to lower the head of her bed.

"I don't know why I'm so tired when all I do is lay here all day," she said.

"Go to sleep," Petty said. "I'll sit a while."

"I don't think so," Sam said.

"Why?"

"That'd be so awkward, you watching me sleep."

"I watched you sleep all the time when you were a baby."

"You did?"

In the apartment in Jersey where he and Carrie were living when she was born. He'd put her on the bed beside him and marvel at the rise and fall of her breath, the fairy flutter of her eyelids, and those long, quiet, numinous afternoons were some of the sweetest he'd ever known.

Sam finally agreed to let him stay, too exhausted to put up more of a fight. She lay back on her pillow and closed her eyes. The door to the room had been pulled almost shut, and all the lights were off except a dim one above the bed, so it was just the two of them again, in their own glow. Petty sat there until Sam's breathing settled into the rhythm of sleep. He kissed his fingers when he got up to go and touched them to her forehead. A smile flitted across her lips.

When he walked out of the hospital he was surprised to see Hug smoking a cigarette on the sidewalk in front of the parking structure. His pulse spiked at the sight of him. One night after Carrie split he was mouthing off in a bar, talking tough about tracking her and Hug down and beating the piss out of Hug with a crowbar. This got a laugh out of the dude he was drinking with, then a no-shit warning: *Don't even think about it.*

"He's got a swamp in Louisiana," the dude said. "Sometimes he kills you before throwing you in the quicksand, but sometimes he likes to watch you suffer as you go down. When you get the urge to do something stupid, picture that."

Petty had to pass by Hug to get to his car. He walked toward him without hesitation because that's what you did with mean dogs, didn't let them see that you were scared. Hug ignored him until they were practically face-to-face, then blew out a cloud of smoke and said, "Howdy, Rowan."

"Is Carrie here?" Petty said. He hadn't seen her on his way out.

"She lost her phone in there this morning, and she's trying to find it," Hug said.

"Bummer," Petty said without slowing his pace. "Have a good night."

Hug took a step sideways to block his path, a brick wall out of nowhere. It was difficult to tell how massive he was until you got right next to him. He blotted out the light from the rising moon. His hands dangled from his wrists like Easter hams.

"I want you to know I don't have anything against you," he said.

"Great," Petty said.

"But I imagine you've got a few things you'd like to say to me."

"Is that what you imagine?"

Hug flicked his cigarette away. It hit the curb and exploded in a shower of sparks.

"Don't do that," he said. "Don't repeat what I say like a smart-ass."

Petty backed up, stepped out of the guy's shadow, and looked him in the eye.

"Well, if we're being honest..." he said.

"We are," Hug said.

"If we're being honest, I hate your fucking guts."

Hug chuckled. "See, I knew that," he said.

"So how about you don't do *that?*" Petty said. "Ask questions you know the answers to."

"I get a kick out of it, knowing you don't have the balls to get back at me."

"Now you're just trying to hurt my feelings."

"That's the difference between me and you: I don't have any feelings you could hurt."

"That must be what Carrie liked about you."

Hug pulled a tube of breath freshener from his pocket and squirted it into his mouth.

"Get it all out," he said. "This is your big chance."

"I'm just saying she's got a mean streak, too, so you guys were perfect for each other."

"She's sorry how it went down with you and her. She'd never tell you, but she is."

"Her and I don't matter. It's what she did to Sam that I hope eats at her."

"You dumped Sam, too, on your mom. Does that eat at you?"

"At least I tried to stay in her life," Petty said. "Carrie never called, never sent a card."

Hug's laugh sounded like a snake hissing.

"She was busy," he said.

"Must have been," Petty said. "So fuck you both."

He stepped around the big man and made for the stairs that led to the second floor of the parking structure.

"You're not as smart as you think," Hug called after him. "You never have been."

Petty kept walking, expecting a bullet in the back of his head all the way until the door to the stairwell closed behind him.

22

AT TEN THE NEXT MORNING, BERNARD AND PATRICIA PARKED
Petty's rented Mazda in front of Tony's mom's store.

"You should've let me come by myself," Bernard said, his
eyes on the front door.

"We're a team," Patricia said.

They got out of the car. Up the block, a man in a uniform
was talking to a man wearing a hard hat and reflective vest,
part of a crew gathered around a storm drain. Bernard froze on
the sidewalk in front of the store, watching the men but pretending he wasn't. His nerves were raw. Too much coffee this
morning on top of too much bourbon last night. The man in
the uniform waved to the man in the hard hat and entered a
bank. Wells Fargo. Ahh. He was a security guard, not a cop.

"I need a cigarette," Patricia said. She pulled out a pack of
American Spirits and pinched one free.

"Now?" Bernard said.

Patricia ignored him. She lit the cigarette, took a long drag, and tilted her head back to blow the smoke up into the air. She did this two more times, quickly, then dropped the cigarette to the sidewalk and ground it out with the toe of her black Converse.

"Okay," she said in tough-girl English. "Let's do this."

They were sitting on the walkway in front of their room the previous evening, drinking wine and posting photos from their day at Venice Beach, when Petty strolled over with a bottle of Jack Daniel's. It was their last night in town. They planned to get up early the next morning, rent a car, and drive to Death Valley.

Petty insisted they have some whiskey. An American tradition between friends parting ways, he said. He filled their cups. Bernard grimaced after his first sip and cleared his throat.

"It is very strong," he said.

"You'll get used to it," Petty said.

"Where is Tinafey?" Patricia said.

Tinafey was sulking in the room. Petty's plans for Bernard and Patricia hadn't sat right with her.

"Why you mixin' them up in this?" she said.

"Because I don't have anybody else," Petty said.

"It isn't fair. They won't even know what they're gettin' into."

"They'll be fine, I promise."

"Fuck it," Tinafey said. "I'll do it."

"I already told you," Petty said. "That won't work. If anyone's watching the store, you'll lead them right to us. They don't know the Frenchies."

Tinafey huffed her disgust and crossed her arms across her chest. Petty reached out to touch her, but she pulled away.

235

"Keep your hands off me," she said. "And God forbid anything happens to those kids."

Out on the walkway, Petty refilled Bernard's cup.

"Tinafey's not feeling so good," he said to Patricia. "Hey, Bernard, do you play poker?"

"Of course," Bernard said. "Texas Hold'em."

"When you get to Memphis, there's a great game in the back room of a bar called Sully's. It's a bunch of muppets most nights, but if you know how to play that kind of table, you could clean up. A friend of mine walked away with two Rolexes and a diamond ring. That's how crazy it got. If you're interested, I can make a call."

"Sounds good," Bernard said.

"We don't have money for poker," Patricia said.

"There's always money for poker," Petty said. "Here's another Memphis story. A guy got into it with this dude named Wild Bill at a club there, and Wild Bill pulled a straight razor. He took a swipe at the guy's throat, and the guy laughed and said, 'You missed.' 'Oh, yeah?' Wild Bill said. 'Wait till you shake your head.'"

Bernard sat there with a confused smile. Patricia said something to him in French, and his face brightened.

"Ahh," he said. "It is a joke. Okay."

They drank more bourbon and watched a scrawny feral cat lead three scrawny kittens across the deck of the empty pool and into an oleander bush.

"What kind of car are you guys renting?" Petty said.

"Something small," Bernard said. "Something cheap."

"You should get a convertible," Petty said. "Do it right."

"A convertible is very expensive," Bernard said. "Plus the petrol."

"How about this?" Petty said. "What if I told you I had a

way for you to make enough money in an hour to be able to afford any car you want? Enough and then some. Enough to pay for your whole trip."

And then he poured more Jack.

"Good morning," Tony's mom said when Bernard and Patricia entered the store. "Can I help you?" She'd been expecting them, after a call from Tony: "Mom, listen. I'll explain later."

"We would like to buy piñatas," Patricia said.

Tony's mom gestured at the papier-mâché-and-crepe burros and Minions and Spider-Men hanging overhead. "Pick whichever you want," she said.

Bernard and Patricia pretended to shop, pointing out this zebra and that Winnie-the-Pooh, working their way to the rear of the store, as they'd been instructed. There hung three dusty, faded clown heads, all tagged with Post-its on which someone had written SOLD.

"We will take these," Bernard said.

Tony's mom came back with a broomstick that had a metal hook screwed to one end. She used the hook to lift the piñatas one by one off the pipe they'd been dangling from.

When Bernard and Patricia woke that morning, Patricia tried to get Bernard to back out of the job Petty had talked them into the night before.

"Tell him we were drunk," she said. "Tell him we changed our minds. What can he do?"

"Maybe something bad," Bernard said. "I think he's a criminal."

"Why did you say yes then?"

"You were there. You said yes, too. He made it sound like nothing."

Patricia flopped back onto the bed and pulled the blanket over her face.

"You always go too far," she said.

Later, when they were getting ready to leave, Bernard came out of the bathroom with his hair slicked back, not his normal style.

"Do I look like a gangster?" he asked Patricia.

"You're not a gangster, you're a postman," she replied.

"No," he said. "Today I'm a gangster."

Tony's mother took the fifty dollars Petty had given Bernard and Patricia and handed them five in change. She didn't have a cash register, just a lockbox.

"Have a nice day," she said.

Bernard and Patricia carried the piñatas out of the store. Big white clouds pressed down on them. The traffic signal across the street winked knowingly. It was like slogging through mud in someone else's shoes to get to the car, like walking on another planet. Patricia smelled smoke, burning rubber. If something bad was going to happen, it would happen now.

Bernard's hand shook as he stuck the key in the ignition. The clouds, the traffic light, then a jackhammer, loud as a machine gun. The workers up the block. Patricia lit another cigarette.

"Not in the car," Bernard said. "I think it's illegal."

"I don't care," Patricia said. "I'm a gangster."

Bernard pulled away from the curb laughing. He made the left his phone told him to, then the right. Patricia was laughing, too, by the time they reached the freeway. She threw her arms around Bernard and kissed him on the cheek, then lowered her window and screamed into the wind: "Fuuuuuuuck!"

★ ★ ★

The Frenchies were waiting out on the walkway. The three piñatas they'd brought sat on the bed. Tinafey stood against the dresser, tapping her foot. She was still mad at Petty for sending Bernard and Patricia to the shop.

Petty picked up one of the clown heads. There was a hole in the back where the candy was supposed to go. Petty stuck his hand into the hole and came out with a banded stack of hundreds. His heart hammered as he flipped through the bills. Ten thousand dollars. He reached into the hole again. Another stack. And another. And another. Tinafey's eyes widened.

"Oh, hell, no," she said.

Petty pulled twenty stacks out of the first clown. Two hundred grand. He'd never seen so much cash before, never *smelled* so much cash. He'd half expected this would turn out to be a bust, that Tony was either lying or crazy. But no: there it was.

Before going any further, he grabbed one of the stacks and stepped outside to pay off Bernard and Patricia. Bernard tried to act like it was no big deal but revealed how flustered he was when he couldn't figure out where to put the money. He tried to slip the stack into his pocket, but his jeans were too tight. Patricia took the bundle from him and put it in her bag. Eager to get out of town, they headed for the stairs, wheeled suitcases click-clacking behind them.

"Get the convertible!" Petty called.

Back in the room he emptied the other two piñatas and stacked all the money on the table. Six hundred and forty thousand dollars.

"Check that out," he said to Tinafey.

"Pretty proud of yourself, ain't you?" Tinafey said.

Petty shrugged. "I did what I had to do," he said. "But it *is* a big fucking score."

Tinafey sat on the bed and picked up one of the bundles of bills.

"Don't it make you nervous, though?" she said. "It makes me nervous."

Petty's burner rang, someone calling about one of the condos.

"It's booked for the rest of the year," Petty said.

He grabbed his laptop and went to work taking down the listings. He could leave that penny-ante grind behind for good now.

An hour later he drove to a Public Storage facility near MacArthur Park and put down a month's rent on a three-by-three locker. He bought a cardboard box from the woman on duty in the lobby, stacked all but twenty thousand of the money in it, and deposited the box in the locker. His next stop was a Rite Aid, where he bought a padlock. He opened the package, threw away the lock, but kept the keys.

He went to Tony's motel. As soon as the kid answered his knock, he said, "Think fast," and tossed a stack of hundreds at him. The kid managed to catch it, even though, judging by the empties on the nightstand, he'd been guzzling beer since breakfast.

"Is my mom okay?" he said.

"She's fine," Petty said. "Everything went great."

"Where's the rest of the money?"

Petty reached into his pocket for one of the padlock keys. He handed it to Tony.

"I got you a locker at a storage place," he said. "That's your key to it."

"What storage place? Where?"

"SoCal Self Storage in Hollywood," Petty said, naming a place he'd looked up earlier, in case the kid asked. "The money's in locker 376. Write it down. We'll leave it there until this is all sorted out. It's as good as a bank, twenty-four-hour security and everything."

"*We'll* leave it there?" Tony said. He sat on the bed, lifted his prosthetic onto the mattress, and slid back so that he was leaning against the headboard. "It's *my* money, you know."

"Yeah. And?" Petty said.

"And don't forget it," Tony said.

"You know I'm not the guy trying to take the money from you, right?" Petty said. "You know I'm the guy trying to help you keep it."

Tony picked up the Tecate he'd been nursing and had a swig. He stared at Petty like he was sizing him up all over again, like he thought his gaze would break him. The heater came on, noisy, the fan clattering against something. Petty decided to shift gears.

"Tell you what," he said. "You're the boss. I'm working for you. If you don't trust me, give me my two hundred and fifty grand right now and let me get the fuck out of here."

Tony continued to stare at him, his jaw clenching and un-clenching rhythmically.

"Just so we're straight, though," Petty continued, "if that's your choice, we're no longer partners, and I'm no longer oblig-ated to you. If Avi—the cops, whoever—come down on me, I'll tell them whatever I have to in order to save my own ass."

"Oh, yeah?" Tony said. "Well, what if I tell them you were there when that dude got shot and that you helped me bury him? That that whole thing and this whole thing were your ideas?"

"So then what? Both of us are fucked?" Petty said. "Doesn't

it seem like there's a better way to go, one where we both come out all right?"

Tony looked away. He shook his head in frustration.

"I don't even know your name," he said. "Ronald? Ronan? That's what the cowboy called you."

"Rowan," Petty said. "My name's Rowan."

"What kind of name is that?"

"It was my dad's dad's name. It's old."

"Old man Rowan," Tony said. He scoffed at this and reached for a fresh beer.

"Listen," Petty said. "We're on our way. Everything's going good. Let's make sure your money's safe and then show Avi he can't fuck with us."

"How exactly are we gonna do that?" Tony said. "Tell me."

Petty had a lie ready.

"I've known Avi for close to twenty years," he said. "I used to work for him in Chicago, which is where he still lives. I know where his office is, I know where his house is, I know where he eats lunch and where his kids go to school. What we're gonna do is take this thing right to his doorstep."

"We're going to Chicago?" Tony said.

"That's right," Petty said.

"Like on an airplane?"

"We're gonna get right in Avi's face. We're gonna stick a gun in his mouth and tell him enough is enough."

Tony thought this over. He picked up the stack of hundreds and slapped the bills against his palm a few times.

"It's cold up there, ain't it?" he said.

"Where? Chicago?" Petty said. "Colder than shit."

"I'll need to get a coat."

"We'll set you up," Petty said. "But first, tell me about your uncle's place. Where's the money hidden? What's the layout?"

★   ★   ★

Tinafey went with him again to visit Sam that evening. The surgery was scheduled for eight the next morning, and Sam was a little out of it. There was a slight but noticeable lag between Petty's questions and her responses and a sleepy drawl in her voice when she did answer. Petty wondered if they'd given her a pill to keep her calm.

"Grandma called," she said, like she was recalling something from the distant past.

"I talked to her, too," Petty said. "She really wishes she could be here."

"I'm glad she's not."

"Why?"

"I don't want people to see me like this. It's bad enough you and my mother are here."

"You look fine," Petty said. He turned to Tinafey. "Doesn't she?"

"Sure," Tinafey said. "But still, I bet it's hard bein' in here. You've got to smile and laugh for the people comin' to see you when you don't feel like smilin' at all."

"You don't have to entertain me," Petty said to Sam. "I'm fine sitting here."

"I know," Sam said. "Watching me sleep."

A nurse came in to check on her, to see if she needed anything. She asked for ice water.

"They didn't give me any dinner," she said to Petty and Tinafey. "They want my stomach empty for the operation. Which doesn't make any sense. They're cutting my head open, not my belly."

Petty thought he should ask if she was scared, but he didn't want to upset her with stupid questions. Of course she was scared. He was glad when Tinafey took over the conversation. She picked up a gossip magazine and soon had Sam talking about the Kardashians and *The Bachelorette*. Sam was laughing when they got up to go fifteen minutes later.

Petty stood next to the bed and held her hand, which was more bones than flesh. "Try to sleep," he said. "I'll be here early, before they take you in."

"You don't have to come," Sam said.

"I know," Petty said. "But I'm going to."

Tinafey took his arm as they walked down the long white corridor and rode the elevator and stepped through the automatic doors into the cold, rackety night.

"You're good with her," he said. "Way better than me."

"It's different," Tinafey said. "You're her daddy."

"You know what she was upset about yesterday? The scar from the surgery."

"And what'd you say to that?"

"A scar nobody'll see? I told her it was silly."

"To you, maybe, but not to her."

"I was trying to make her feel better."

"Is that right?" Tinafey said. "Well, if you want to do that, next time she tells you she's upset about somethin', don't tell her it's nothin'."

Petty stepped off the curb. A flash in the gutter caught his eye. A candy wrapper. Sloppy. Everything was sloppy. Sam, Carrie and Hug, Tony, Tinafey. He was tending ten fires at once, beating back the flames with his bare hands and praying the wind didn't gust.

He dropped right off to sleep when they got back to the room but woke an hour later from another nightmare about the cowboy. He felt like he'd run around the block a couple times and couldn't catch his breath.

Tinafey was sitting up in bed, staring at him.

"What's wrong?" she said.

"Nothing," he said.

"You sure were moanin' and groanin' like it was somethin'."

"A bad dream."

"About what?"

"That guy who got killed."

A train whistle hooted in the rail yard by the river, rode the breeze all that way to make Petty shiver. Tinafey lay back down and scooted over until she was right next to him.

"One time, a lotta years ago, I was partyin' with some friends," she said. "Someone had a motel room, some dope dealer we knew, and we all went over there to get high. Weed, crack, tar, the brother hooked everybody up. It went on and on. First it was midnight, then it was three in the mornin', and then all of a sudden the sun was comin' up. I was high as shit, feelin' no pain. My boyfriend at the time was there, my girl-friend, and we was dancin' and talkin' and jokin' around.

"Then we hear, 'Oh, fuck!' and some motherfucker came runnin' out the bathroom and kept on goin' out the front door. There was a girl layin' on the bathroom floor, not breathin', not movin', OD'd on somethin'. My heart was tellin' me, 'Help that girl. Do somethin'. Call someone.' But my brain was tellin' me, 'You're goin' to jail, bitch, they catch you here.' So when everybody up and left, pushin' each other out the way to get out the door, I ran with 'em, ran and didn't look back.

"I heard later they had trouble figurin' out who the girl was because someone stole her purse on the way out. That's the kind of cold-blooded motherfuckers there is in this world. Se-riously. She laid in the morgue for a week before her family knew she was dead.

"And you know what? I still dream about it. I see the bathroom, I see the girl, I see me doin' nothin', and I wake up cryin'. That's my punishment, and it's gonna be my punishment for the rest of my life. Whenever I get to thinkin' too much of myself, I'm gonna have one of those dreams and remember what I really am."

The train whistle wailed again. Petty wrapped his arms around Tinafey. She was as stiff and cold as an iron bar.

"You'll be all right," she said. "You won't never be the same, but you'll be okay."

23

Petty went to the hospital alone the next morning. Carrie was going to be there, so he told Tinafey it would be better if she didn't come along. Tinafey was fine with that, said she wasn't in the mood for any drama.

Petty walked to Good Samaritan. The streets already had traffic on them at seven. The homeless had broken camp, and flocks of ragged pigeons were on the wing, wheeling against a mass of dark clouds rolling in from the north. Petty watched the clouds swallow the sun as he waited for a slow-moving bus to pass.

The hospital revved up early, too. There were breakfasts to be delivered and piss jugs to be emptied. Sam was sitting up in bed with an IV in her arm. The surgeon who'd be removing the tumor was there, explaining to her what would happen in the operating room. Petty waved at him to keep talking as he crept in and took a seat.

The description of the procedure was similar to the one the neurologist had given them. Sam nodded along, stoic this time. When the surgeon asked if she had any questions, she said no.

"This is my dad," she said, gesturing at Petty.

"How about you, Dad?" the surgeon said. "Questions?"

Petty couldn't think of any.

"I'll see you in about an hour, then," the surgeon said to Sam. He looked like he was twelve years old.

When he had gone, Petty got up and stood next to Sam's bed. Sam grimaced and rubbed her forehead.

"I want this to be over with," she said. "I want them to cut the fucking thing out so I can go home to my cat."

"Soon," Petty said.

"I asked the neurologist if I'd be the same afterward, like if there was a chance they could damage something, and you know what she said? 'We're very careful.' What's that? That's not a yes. That's not a no."

"There are probably rules about what they can say—laws."

"And what if I have to have chemo or radiation?" Sam said. "That'll screw up my job, my school."

Her hand slid down so that it covered her eyes. She started to cry.

"Don't worry about that," Petty said. "We'll work it out."

"Who? You?" Sam said. "You're gonna work it out? Or my mother? Give me a fucking break."

She cried a little more. Petty stayed quiet, let her get it all out. When she finally calmed down, she pinched the bridge of her nose like she was trying to squeeze off her tears.

"I'm sorry," she said. "I'm being a baby."

"You want to see a baby?" Petty said. He took out his wallet and pulled a photo from it. It was Sam at three years old, wearing a *Sesame Street* T-shirt, her face screwed up like she was about to wail.

Sam smiled at the photo. "What am I doing?" she said.

"Look in your hand there." Petty pointed. "That's a lemon. You grabbed it off the table and bit into it, and I got a picture."

"Oh, my God," Sam said. She coughed out a throaty laugh. "Do you have any more?"

"That's it," Petty said.

"That's the only picture you have of me?"

"It's the only one I carry around," Petty said. "It makes me smile every time I look at it."

Sam handed the photo back to him. "You're crazy," she said.

Carrie swept in, coat billowing, purse bouncing, a frazzled cyclone that set everything spinning.

"I'm late, I know," she said. "We're staying all the way out in Santa Monica."

"You didn't miss anything," Sam said.

"I know, but I wanted to be here," Carrie said. She slipped in beside Petty to stand at Sam's bedside. Her pushiness annoyed him. He moved away and sat in one of the chairs.

"You've been crying," Carrie said to Sam. "Oh, no. Why?"

Sam started to pop off with something mean but thought better of it. "I'm just tired," she said. "How's Santa Monica?"

Carrie was in the middle of a story about how she'd scored a free night at her hotel because the kitchen had gotten a room-service order wrong when two orderlies came for Sam. They seemed to be in a hurry as they transferred her to a gurney and rearranged her IV bag, and their urgency triggered a spasm of panic in Petty.

"Hugs and kisses, family," one of the orderlies said. "Hugs and kisses."

Petty stepped over to the gurney. Sam's face was drawn, her

eyes jumpy. Petty bent to kiss her on the cheek. He was surprised when she wrapped her arms around him.

"I love you," he whispered in her ear.

"I love you, too," she said.

He stood in the corridor and watched her on the gurney until the elevator doors closed on it.

"She's a tough cookie," Carrie said.

Petty ignored her. He stepped back into Sam's room and sat again, needed a minute to recharge.

"How long are you planning on hanging around here today?" Carrie said.

"Until she gets out of surgery," Petty said.

"Really?" Carrie said. "The whole time?"

"You do what you want," Petty said.

Carrie sighed and glanced at her watch. "What I want is coffee," she said.

Six hours later Petty was sitting in a small waiting room near where the operation was taking place. A nurse had promised that the surgeon would stop in and give him an update after the procedure. He'd spent the morning shuttling between the waiting room and the cafeteria, trying to avoid Carrie. She and Hug had kept their distance. The table they set up housekeeping at in the cafeteria was as far from his as they could get, and Carrie hadn't said a word to him when she occasionally poked her head into the waiting room. The one time he'd ventured outside for fresh air, Hug was smoking across the street, but the big man acted like he hadn't seen him.

Petty stared up at a TV on the wall. A family had been gathered here earlier, Korean, anxious for updates about a relative, but they'd disappeared when Petty came back from a trip to the restroom. The TV was tuned to a news channel, and Petty watched the same ten seconds of footage of a plane crash in Russia he'd been watching all day: a slow pan over smoking wreckage, a soldier pointing at a suitcase lying in a snowy field, a woman crying in an airport.

Sam's surgeon stepped through the door. Petty scrambled to his feet.

"She's out of surgery, and everything went fine," the surgeon said. "We removed as much of the tumor as we could, and now we'll have it analyzed to see what we're dealing with."

"How long will that take?" Petty said.

"A couple of days," the surgeon said. "She'll spend tonight in the ICU. You can look in on her there, if you make it quick."

A few minutes later a nurse buzzed Petty into a dimly lit cave filled with the sounds of chirping monitors and hissing ventilators. Patients' vital signs flashed like stock prices on an array of screens above the nurses' station. Sam lay on a bed in an alcove partitioned off from the rest of the room by a curtain. Her eyes were closed, and her head was wrapped in bandages.

"She's pretty sleepy," the nurse said. "She's been through a lot."

Petty touched Sam's hand. She showed no outward reaction, but when he moved his fingers over hers, a reading on the monitor next to her bed jumped from fifty to fifty-two. Petty took this as a message from a long way off that she knew he was there.

He left the hospital without seeing Carrie again, had no idea if she and Hug were still around. Back at the motel he ate a sandwich Tinafey had waiting for him, called his mom to fill her in on Sam's condition, then lay down on the bed.

"Come here," he said to Tinafey.

She got in behind him, her chest to his back, and curved

her body to his. With her fingers swirling lightly in his hair, he was asleep in no time.

Beck was in his usual spot at Musso & Frank. The place was dead, so he was telling jokes to the bartender, and the bartender was a good enough bartender, a smart enough bartender, to pretend he hadn't heard them before.

"So she goes, 'Oh, shit, I left my baby on the bus!'"

"On the bus. Ha!"

Beck was wearing a black polo shirt and a tweed golf cap. He feigned shock when he saw Petty and Tinafey come in, then smiled and waved.

"Memphis," he said. "Looking good, girl."

Tinafey sat beside him; Petty stayed standing.

"So you two are still in town," Beck said.

"Things keep coming up," Petty said.

"Well, if you've got to be stuck somewhere, this isn't so terrible. What are we drinking?"

Petty ordered Scotch, Tinafey had red wine, and Beck got himself another martini. He was tipsy, and Petty was glad to see it. Only two tables in the restaurant had diners at them. The waiters and busboys were gathered at the end of the bar. They talked among themselves, one guy showing another something on his phone.

Beck kidded with Tinafey about her saying last time that she wanted to be an actress. Petty hadn't planned to bring her along tonight, but while he was getting ready she decided she wanted to come, saying she needed to get away from the motel for a while. Petty gave in quickly, thinking a pretty girl might be just the thing to grease the skids with Beck. He even hinted that he wouldn't mind if she flirted with the guy a bit, played up to him some.

"How many auditions have you booked?" Beck said to her. "I bet you've got agents stopping you on the street."

"Not exactly," Tinafey said. "You need to hook me up with your friends."

"All my friends are perverts," Beck said.

"I can handle perverts," Tinafey said.

"Maybe so," Beck said. "But I don't want any trouble with this guy." He squeezed Petty's shoulder. "Did he tell you I'm giving him acting lessons?"

"You gotta teach me, too," Tinafey said. "I'm better than him."

"Better looking, that's for sure," Beck said.

The drinks arrived. Petty took a sip of his and said, "I'm glad we bumped into you. I've got something to ask you."

"Go on," Beck said.

"I was wondering how much you get for a part."

"That depends," Beck said. "Is it a feature? TV? A commercial? A day's work or a week's? How big's the part? The union's got different rates for everything."

"A day," Petty said. "A couple hours."

"Did somebody offer you something?"

"No," Petty said. "I'm offering you something."

"Sorry," Beck said. "I don't do porn. Anymore." He chuckled at his own joke and bit into one of the olives from his drink. "Better watch out for this dude," he said to Tinafey out of the corner of his mouth.

"A couple of hours," Petty said again. "How much?"

"You're making a film?" Beck said.

"Two hours of your time. Give me a figure."

Beck chewed on his toothpick and thought this over.

"A thousand bucks," he finally said.

"I'll give you ten thousand," Petty said.

Beck took the toothpick out of his mouth.

"Great," he said. "But what the hell are you up to?"

A pack of barhoppers all wearing the same T-shirt swept in off the Boulevard and bellied up two deep to order drinks. Petty didn't want to have to yell over them to be heard.

"Not here," he said to Beck. "Let's go to your place."

Petty and Tinafey followed Beck's Jag up into the hills. One of Beck's taillights was out. Petty made a mental note to tell him about it. Tinafey marveled at the houses they passed—the castle, the casbah, the glass box ablaze. The views at the top knocked her out. She gasped at every glittering expanse and begged Petty to pull over so she could take a picture.

"Later," he said. "On the way down."

The gate to the property had been fixed since last time and opened on its own. They parked between the main house and Beck's apartment above the garage. Beck had hung a scraggly string of Christmas lights on his deck, tiny bulbs that twinkled in the cold, clear night. He led them up the stairs. He had a slight limp Petty hadn't noticed before. It made sense; the guy was older than he looked.

"The queen bee's still out of town," he said over his shoulder, "so we can howl at the moon if we feel like it."

"Howl at the moon," Tinafey said. "You're so crazy."

"Good crazy, though," Beck said. "Good crazy, right?"

While he was in the kitchen fetching drinks, Tinafey gawked at the photo of him and his ex-wife on the wall. "Hold on," she said. "You were married to Mimi Bird?"

"For ten—uhh...*very special* years," Beck said.

"And she lives in that house out there?"

"When she's around."

"Oh. My. God," Tinafey said. "I love Mimi Bird." She circled the living room, examining the other photos. "Is this Morgan Freeman?" she called out.

"Nice guy," Beck said. He came back into the room and handed Tinafey a glass of wine and Petty a beer. He'd poured himself a tumbler of Stoli. "A very sweet man."

They got down to business, seated at the dining-room table under a low-hanging lamp that pinned their shadows to the floor. Petty first sketched out, without going into detail, what he wanted Beck to do, just to see if he'd be up for it.

"You'll go to a house and pick up a couple of bags," he said. "Bags of money that have been hidden in the garage."

"Bags of money the guy who owns the house doesn't know are there," Beck said.

"That's right," Petty said.

"How am I supposed to get on the property?" Beck said. "You said the owner never leaves."

"You'll pretend to be a cop," Petty said.

"Pretend to be a cop?" Beck said.

Petty got up and grabbed the *Hollywood & Vice* prop gun and badge off the bookshelf and brought them back to the table.

"'Knock, knock,'" he said. "'Detective Blackburn, LAPD.' Just like in the movie. The only difference is, there's no camera."

"The only difference is, this is for real," Beck said.

They'd work up a story, Petty explained, write it out like a script if Beck wanted, go over it until it was perfect. Something that would throw a scare into Tony's uncle and make him eager to cooperate.

"It doesn't have to be too elaborate," Petty said. "A cop with a badge and a gun showing up at his door'll be enough. He's not gonna question that, look for trouble."

Beck wanted more information. Whose house was it?

Whose money? Why couldn't Petty pick it up himself? Petty used the same dodge he'd used with Tony: the less you know, the better. What sealed the deal was Petty dropping five grand on the table up front. When Beck reached out to touch the bills, Petty knew he had him.

"And just so you know," Petty said, "you're the good guy in this thing."

"Don't tell me that," Beck said. "Good guys are boring."

They celebrated coming to an agreement with another round of drinks. Tinafey asked Beck about acting lessons, wanted to know if you needed a high school diploma to take them.

"High school?" Beck said. "I barely made it out of sixth grade. If actors had to be book smart, Hollywood would dry up and blow away."

"Show her something," Petty said. "Like you did me."

"Nah," Beck said. "Some other time."

He didn't mean it; he just wanted to be asked twice.

"Come on," Petty said.

"Show me," Tinafey said. She reached out and squeezed Beck's leg, giving him her biggest smile.

"Oh, all right," Beck said. "A little somethin' somethin'."

He carried a chair into the living room and had Tinafey sit in it. Petty moved to the couch to watch.

"The first thing you have to learn to do is relax," Beck said. "You can't act if you're tensed up. That's like trying to do math in your head while lifting a piano. Seven times forty-three—you can't do it. In the same way, when your muscles are tense, your emotions can't get through, and you won't be able to communicate them to an audience."

Beck stood next to Tinafey and put a finger to each of her temples. "These are two of your major stress points," he said.

"When there's tension here, you unconsciously wrinkle your forehead, and you don't want that. You want to be in complete control of everything your face does. So relax these spots. Let all the tension flow out of them."

He moved a finger to the bridge of her nose, between her eyes. "Here's another problem spot. If there's tension here, you'll blink too much and put a furrow right where I'm pressing. To relax this one, all you have to do is close your eyes halfway, like you're about to fall asleep. Hold that while letting all the tension flow out of the area."

He then placed his fingers on either side of Tinafey's nose and dragged them down past her mouth to her chin. "These muscles are a real problem," he said. "They control the mouth, so they're always ready to go to work, which means they're always tense. Do this..." He let his face go slack so that his cheeks sagged and his mouth hung open. He looked like a drunk roused from a nap on the bar. Tinafey followed his lead.

"Let the skin dangle," Beck said. "Pretend there are no muscles in there at all."

Tinafey giggled. She tried to stop herself but couldn't.

"That's fine," Beck said. "Go ahead and laugh. Laughing releases tension, too."

"I did good, right?" Tinafey said.

"You did great," Beck said. "Of course, that's only the basics. In class you learn to relax your whole body. Back, shoulders, arms, wrists, hands, fingers."

"And then what?"

"Then you learn to control all those parts, to use them."

"Show me more."

"That's enough for now."

"Why you keep makin' me beg?"

"It's better that way."

"Come on, baby, show me something else."

"Okay," Beck said. "One more quick thing."

He walked back to the table and got the holster and badge. He buckled the holster over his shirt and stuck the badge on his belt. Tinafey sat next to Petty on the couch. He put his arm around her, but she didn't even notice, focused as she was on Beck.

Beck closed his eyes and took a few deep breaths. His spine straightened, and his shoulders went back. He opened his eyes and knocked on an imaginary door.

Someone answered, and Beck started talking nonsense. "Goo goo" and "Ga ga." He greeted the person who opened the door, introduced himself, and explained why he was there, all in baby talk. Petty could follow it, though, by watching Beck's facial expressions and gestures. He knew exactly what the dude was doing: acting out the visit to Tony's uncle, rehearsing how it might go.

The performance lasted a few minutes. Beck coaxed, Beck threatened, Beck cajoled, then he stepped across the imaginary threshold, patting Tony's uncle on the back as he did so. Tinafey clapped when he turned to them and bowed to signal that the show was over.

"That's a Strasberg exercise," he said. "You take something from your life or a scene from a play and act it out in gibberish. It divorces your actions from the words you're saying and the clichéd movements attached to those words."

"That was great," Tinafey said. She held out her arm. "I got bumps watchin' you."

"Hey!" Beck said. "That's the best review I've had in years."

He and Tinafey got to talking about one of his movies, and Petty knew it could continue all night—the stories, the drinking. Any other time, that would have been fine, but he needed Beck to be in shape for tomorrow. Tinafey groaned when he said they should get going.

"Hold on," Beck said. "Let me take you to see the queen bee's Oscar."

Petty saw the excitement on Tinafey's face and resigned himself to spending a few more minutes in Beck's thrall. Beck sloshed more Stoli into his glass while laying down the rules for the excursion. No touching, no wandering off, no pictures.

"The wrong person sees your selfie, and I'm on the street," he said.

Petty and Tinafey followed him down the stairs and across the yard to the main house. Their trail was visible even in the darkness, marked by where their feet had knocked the early dew off the grass. The imposing wooden front door of the house was crisscrossed with wrought-iron straps. Beck told them the door had come from a church in Mexico and had cost twenty thousand dollars. He told them his wife called the house El Casa de Sueños, the House of Dreams.

Tinafey clutched Petty's arm and shivered. It felt like they were breaking into the place. Beck squinted, trying to find the right key on his ring. He had to put down his drink and get eye level with the dead bolt to slip it in.

As soon as the door opened he hurried to the blinking alarm panel and entered the code to disarm it. He turned on a light in the two-story entryway. A wide staircase curved up to the second floor. Somber seascapes, all in frothy gold frames, lined the walls.

"She collects storms," Beck said, gesturing at the paintings.

He led them into the living room. Heavy wooden furniture, Saltillo tile floors, Navajo rugs. A massive fireplace gaped like an open mouth, and an array of awards gleamed on its mantel, a special bank of lights shining down on them. Gold statuettes, crystal obelisks, engraved plaques. In the center was the Oscar.

They approached it like it was baby Jesus in the manger. Petty almost stopped Beck when he reached for it, worried the man was drunk enough to do something stupid. But so what if he did? It was his house. Had been, anyway.

ACADEMY AWARD

TO

MIMI BIRD

BEST PERFORMANCE BY AN

ACTRESS IN A SUPPORTING ROLE

"UNCIVIL WAR"

2002

Beck read the tag screwed to the base out loud and handed the statuette to Tinafey. She gazed at it for a few seconds, then acted like she was going to put it in her purse.

"Hey, now," Beck said.

"What?" Tinafey said, feigning innocence. She lifted the statuette to her lips and kissed it. "That's gotta be good luck," she said.

Beck showed them Mimi's Emmy, too, and a medal from President Bush. He told them she was a Republican but didn't want anyone to know. He said she argued out loud with her dead mother when she was blotto and only showered once a week if she could get away with it. He wanted to take them upstairs to see her closet, claimed it was bigger than the house he'd grown up in, but Petty told him no, some other time, they had to go.

"You're right," Beck said. "It's a closet. Fucking shoes, fucking dresses. I'm too sensitive, I know."

He walked them out to the car and asked if either of them had a cigarette. Petty told him to get some sleep.

"I've got pills for that," Beck said. "Soon as you split."

They left him standing in the driveway, staring up at the big house. It was lit by the spotlights in the yard, like it was someplace where something important had happened. Petty wondered if it bothered Beck to live in its shadow, if he ever dreamed of watching it burn.

He dropped Tinafey at the motel and went by the hospital. It was late, after visiting hours, but the ICU nurse bent the rules and let him in to see Sam, who was still asleep in her alcove. He stood over her bed and listened to her breathe, like he had when she was a baby. The whisper of her tiny lungs was the first thing that had ever taken him out of his own head. Until then he'd half believed the world disappeared each night when he went to sleep and was re-created every morning upon his awakening—that his was the only mind that mattered. The realization that Sam was as alive as he was, as actual, doubled the size of his universe in an instant, but truth be told, nothing changed for him. What was bent didn't straighten, what was iced over didn't thaw. In fact the only thing the revelation did was give him someone else to fail, and fail her he had.

That night he tossed and turned for hours, dozing off and waking up every fifteen minutes. This time tomorrow he'd have the rest of the money. This time tomorrow he'd be rid of Tony for good. He couldn't tell if it was worry or excitement that wouldn't let him sleep. He gave up the struggle at dawn, lay in bed trying to get his bearings. The chair, his watch, Tinafey beside him, in a ball under the sheet. One pale rivulet of daylight streamed in through the gap between the curtains and flowed across the floor. He felt no more rested than when he'd lain down the night before. His knee popped when he stood. A muscle in his neck ached. He pulled on his sweats and staggered out onto the walkway, already texting Beck, the day already heavy upon him even before the sun had shown its face.

24

NOTHING HAD CHANGED IN THE FIVE YEARS SINCE DIAZ HAD last driven down Soto Street, during a Christmas leave. Carnitas Michoacan, with the giant burger and plastic T. rex on its roof, Pioneer Chicken, Ramirez Liquor. A new apartment building had gone up, but that was about it. Same corner market where he bought Lunchables and chili mango lollipops when he was a kid, same middle school, same storefront church. He couldn't wait to get his money and get the fuck out again. Between here and Afghanistan, he felt like he'd been living in the ghetto his whole life.

He hadn't told anybody in his family he was coming. Not his dad, not his brothers and sisters, not Tony. He'd ridden the bus from North Carolina. Two and a half days. His joints were still vibrating, and he could still smell the body odor of the kid claiming to be a chef who sat next to him from Dallas to Los

Angeles and kept trying to sell him sips from a fifth of Smirnoff he was nursing. "Dollar a pop!"

Arriving in L.A. late at night, he'd checked into a room in a downtown flophouse. Cash only, shared bathroom. He stripped the bed to the bottom sheet, rolled up his hoodie for a pillow, and slept in his clothes.

Someone pounding on a wall and screaming for help woke him at dawn. He peeked out his door and saw a security guard standing in front of a room down the hall.

"What's up?" he said.

"Nothin'," the guard said.

When things quieted, Diaz tiptoed to the shower and washed off the grime of the trip. Someone had left behind a bar of soap and a bottle of shampoo. The soap, no way, but he figured the shampoo was safe. He grabbed breakfast at McDonald's and took the subway to the Budget car rental kiosk at Union Station.

Everybody was on the way to work in the old neighborhood. The 7-Eleven was full of gardeners and painters and plumbers picking up coffee and Gatorade. The ladies in line at the Starbucks drive-through put on their makeup in their rearview mirrors and called their kids to make sure they'd gotten off to school. *And me, I'm up to no good,* Diaz thought. It made him feel like a spy.

He didn't have to worry that Tony would be leaving for a job. The kid had been on the government tit since getting his leg blown off. And Creeper, the dude he was going to see first, was another *vato* who wasn't blowing through stop signs in order to clock in on time anywhere.

Creeper ran his hustles out of an apartment in Ramona Gardens, a Boyle Heights housing project hard by the 10 freeway. He was a *veterano* in Big Hazard, the gang that claimed the

Gardens as their territory. Diaz had never lived in the proj-
ects and had never joined a gang, but he and Creeper had
teamed up when they were kids to rob houses and steal cars.
Los Thrill Killers they called themselves, like they were a band.
They'd exchanged sporadic texts since then, and, thinking that
someone with Creeper's connections might be useful during
his visit to L.A., Diaz had written his old homey a month ago
to say whassup and tell him he'd be in town soon. *Fall by whenever,* Creeper wrote back.

The Gardens had been built in 1940, and not much had
been done to it since. Every turn Diaz took led him deeper
into the maze of two-story brick buildings, all painted the
same depressing shade of tan. Surrounded by dead grass, they
looked like army barracks, but with bars on every window.

If you had to be a stranger here, 9:00 a.m. was the best time.
The streets were practically deserted. An old lady hobbling
along, two teenage moms pushing strollers. Not a gangster in
sight. The peewees were at school, jacking their classmates'
phones, and OGs like Creeper didn't stir before two or three in
the afternoon. Diaz pulled up in front of his old partner's unit
and got out of the Ford Escape he'd rented. A squirrel tugging
at something stuck to the sidewalk waited until the last instant
to move out of his way.

A twelve-foot sound wall stood between the Gardens and
the freeway, but it didn't help much. Diaz could still hear the
traffic, the rattle and whine of the tail end of the morning rush
hour. He knocked three times at Creeper's door before a pock-
marked *chola* yanked it open and glared at him through the
steel security screen.

"Is Carlos around?" he said, using Creeper's real name.

"Who the fuck are you?" the *chola* said. The baby on her
hip burst into tears.

"Tell him it's Mando Diaz."

The *chola*'s eyebrows, tattooed way up on her forehead, made her look perpetually skeptical. She had a diamond stud in her upper lip—a Marilyn, they called it. The baby pulled at her T-shirt, exposing a black bra strap. She slapped the kid's hand and carried him off into the darkness. Diaz smelled weed and dirty diapers.

After a muffled argument, Creeper materialized out of the gloom, shirtless and bleary. It had been more than ten years since Diaz had last seen him. He'd gotten fat. His face looked the same, but his head had doubled in size around it.

"What the fuck, holmes?" he said.

"You sleeping?" Diaz said.

"It's barely nine o'clock."

"I can come back later."

Creeper yawned and scratched his big belly. It was covered with a tattoo of a Big Hazard *placa*.

"You get up this early in the army?" he said.

"This is lunchtime in the army," Diaz said. He put his mouth close to the screen and lowered his voice. "I need to talk to you about something."

"What?" Creeper said.

"Getting hold of a *cuete*."

Creeper didn't flinch. Creeper never flinched. He drew his head back real slow to look Diaz up and down.

"Damn, *ese*," he said. "Nice to see you again, too."

He gave Diaz a choice. He could take the .22 he had hidden in a Pampers box in the bedroom or wait a couple hours for someone to bring by something bigger. After fifteen minutes of the baby crying, the *chola* glaring, and Creeper's bullshit gangster swagger, Diaz was ready to move on. He paid a hundred dollars for the .22 and lied about stopping by again before he left town.

He parked across the street from Tony's place around ten. Someone had stuck a brick in the gate, so he got into the courtyard without having to buzz. An old man in coveralls was hacking with a machete at a banana tree in one of the planters, and the sound bounced off the stucco walls. Fresh jet contrails crisscrossed the square of sky overhead. A fat orange cat stared up at them, ears twitching.

The old man nodded hello. Diaz nodded back. He went to Tony's apartment and knocked at the door. No answer. He moved to the window and tried to peer inside, but the blinds were shut. A voice in his head said, *Kick the door down.* Instead he called to the old man, asked in Spanish if he knew where Tony was.

"I don't live here," the old man said. "I don't know any-thing." He started swinging his machete again.

Diaz went back out to the street. He walked down the driveway to the parking garage under the building and peered through the gate. Tony's truck was there, the one they gave him when he came back with one leg. The kid had sent him a photo. Diaz felt a rush of panic, a need for answers right now. He couldn't return to the apartment, though, without looking suspicious. And maybe the kid was just at the corner store.

He went back to his rental car, got in, and moved it to a spot with a clear view of the driveway and the front gate. The watching and waiting nearly killed him. He sat nodding his head to nothing, like a bus-bench loco. Every slamming door made him jump, and he tensed whenever a car drove by. At one point he found himself holding the .22, unconsciously dropping and reinserting the magazine over and over right there in the car, where anybody walking by could see.

In two hours the only people who entered or left Tony's building were the *viejo* with the machete, who drove off in a battered pickup, and the mail lady. When a passing police cruiser slowed so the cops inside could look him over, Diaz decided it was time to go.

His dad had been living alone since his mom died, six years earlier. One of Diaz's brothers had stayed with him for a while, but the old man drove him away with his drinking and temper tantrums. The few times Diaz had called since the funeral, his dad had responded to his questions with grunts and one-word answers. Diaz's sisters had filled him in on what was going on: the old man didn't work anymore or go out much. The house was falling down around his ears, but he ignored the leaky roof and rotting floorboards and spent most of his time on the couch, beer in hand, staring at the ceiling. No cable, no computer, no cell phone. He pissed in empty milk jugs instead of getting up and walking to the bathroom.

The front yard of the little three-bedroom rancher was nothing but dirt. Diaz could remember when there was a thick, green lawn, playing football on it. Now it was strewn with bloated trash bags and old tires. A motorcycle frame poked out of a mound of dead leaves like a crime coming to light.

Diaz stepped over the brittle yellow newspapers and faded junk mail piled on the porch. The front door was ajar. He pushed it open. The inside of the house was as cluttered as the yard, unsteady stacks and overflowing boxes everywhere. An ancient doo-wop song, a whisper from the radio, swirled the dust in the air.

"Dad?" Diaz called out.

His father's head popped up over the back of the couch.

"Yeah?"

His hair and mustache had gone all the way white since Diaz had last seen him. The stubble on his chin, too. He hadn't shaved in a while.

"It's Mando," Diaz said.

"Mando?" the old man said like he didn't believe him.

"What the hell are you doing in the dark?" Diaz said.

"Taking a nap. What's your problem?"

"No problem."

"Good. You want a beer?"

They drank the Bud Lights sitting side by side on the couch because all the chairs were covered with junk. A two-inch crack in one of the walls zigzagged from floor to ceiling, exposing the lath behind the plaster, and tendrils of ivy had wormed their way in through a broken window to cling to the china hutch and twine around a lamp.

"You should clean this place up," Diaz said.

"It's fine," the old man said.

"It's like a crazy lady's house on TV."

"I don't have a TV. TV's for *pendejos*."

Something rustled in the kitchen, going through the trash piled there, the pizza boxes and KFC buckets. Diaz stomped on the floor, and the sound stopped. The Rays sang softly on the radio about two silhouettes on the shade.

"I don't have money to fix stuff anyway," Diaz's dad continued. "I been laid up because of my back. Disability's nothing."

"What's wrong with your back?" Diaz said.

"Hanging drywall since I was fourteen is what's wrong with it. I should've joined the service like you. Three hots and a cot plus a steady paycheck. But we had Hector junior and Lupe by the time I was eighteen, and I couldn't leave your mother alone with them."

"What if Mom could see you now?" Diaz said. "What would she think about how you keep her house?"

The old man made a face. "Don't be stupid," he said. "I thought you were in Afghanistan. They finally kick you out?"

"The war's over," Diaz said.

"Ha! Those fucking animals? They been fighting since the Bible. That war's not over."

"We're out of it, anyway," Diaz said. "Mostly."

"Hip hip hooray! God bless America!"

Diaz noticed something moving on the coffee table. Ants.

"I need you to do me a favor," he said to his dad.

"Yeah?" his dad said. "And what are you gonna do for me?"

There was a knock at the front door. Loud, like whoever it was meant business.

"Who's that?" Diaz said.

"Kobe Bryant," the old man said. "How the hell am I supposed to know?" He pushed himself up off the couch and walked stiff-legged across the living room to answer. The knocking came again before he got there.

"Hold on!" he yelled.

He opened the door. A white man in a sport coat and tie stood on the porch. His hair was greased back, and he had on sunglasses.

"Mr. Diaz?" he said.

"Yeah," the old man said.

"Detective Blackburn, with the Gang and Narcotics Division." The guy flashed a badge. "I'm afraid we've got a situation here."

A cop. Diaz tightened up. He wiggled the .22 out of his pocket and slipped it between the cushions of the couch but kept his finger on the trigger.

"What's that, a situation?" the old man said.

"The local bangers have been stashing drugs on your property."

"What? I'm here all the time, and I ain't seen nothin' like that."

"There's a garage out back, correct?"

"Yeah."

"Well, in that garage right now is two kilos of cocaine."

"Bullshit," the old man said. He seemed like he was about to close the door.

"I'm serious," the cop said. "What they're up to, these knuckleheads, is they hide their dope on someone else's property so we don't find it when we search their houses."

"But I don't know no gangsters," Diaz's dad said. "I'm too old for that shit."

"That's why they picked you," the cop said. "Why would we even think to look for dope here?"

"That's right, why?" Diaz's dad said.

"I'm saying we wouldn't," the cop said.

"That's right," Diaz's dad said, either playing dumb or being dumb.

The cop hadn't noticed Diaz yet, and Diaz sunk low on the couch to make sure he didn't.

"I'm here to ask your permission—" the cop began.

"Go ahead and get it if it's there," Diaz's dad said. "I don't want nothing to do with no cocaine."

"So I have your permission?"

"Sí, yeah, take it. The fucking thing's unlocked."

The cop thanked Diaz's dad for his cooperation and headed for the garage. The old man closed the door and came back to the couch. He picked his beer up off the floor and said, "You hear that?"

"He should have a search warrant," Diaz said.

"Yeah?" the old man said.

"Something."

"You can go tell him," the old man said. "I don't fuck with cops."

Diaz put the gun back in his pocket and got up and walked into the kitchen. Whatever had been digging in the garbage earlier fled at his approach. He heard its claws scrabbling on the warped linoleum. He went to the window above the sink, the one that looked out onto the detached garage slumped at the end of the driveway. The sink was full of dirty dishes. Diaz breathed through his mouth as he watched the cop lift the garage door.

As cluttered as the house was, the garage was worse, stuffed to the rafters with old paint cans, greasy car parts, and boxes of Christmas decorations. The cop knew right where to go, though. He moved aside a tamale pot and a sleeping bag, reached into the newly exposed hollow, and pulled out two 99 Cents Only store bags. He glanced inside the bags, backed out of the garage, and closed the door.

The guy's dirty. It hit Diaz all of a sudden. Cops didn't work alone like that. A snitch had told him about the dope, and now he was going to steal it and sell it himself. Diaz fingered the gun, pictured himself walking out there and taking the bags off the dude, teaching him a lesson. But then he remembered the two million dollars waiting for him. One more hurdle, and it was all his.

The cop didn't come back to the house. He walked right out to the street with the bags, got into a Mazda SUV with Enterprise Rent-A-Car plate frames, and drove away. Diaz swatted at one of the flies buzzing around the sink.

"Bring me another beer," his dad called from the living room.

Diaz grabbed a can out of the thirty-pack in the filthy re-frigerator and took it in to the old man.

"I need you to call Tia Maria," Diaz said.

"Por qué?" the old man said.

"I need to get hold of Tony. But don't tell her I'm here. Say you want to talk to him."

"I'm not gonna do that," the old man said. "I don't play those kind of games."

Diaz took the .22 out of his pocket. He held no grudges against his dad—didn't give a shit about him, really—and had never intended to involve him in this thing. But it had hap-pened, and now he had to deal with it. Collateral damage is what it was. The price of victory. *You're gonna make that call,* he thought. *And then you're gonna die.*

25

Pᴇᴛᴛʏ ᴅʀᴏᴠᴇ Bᴇᴄᴋ's Jᴀɢ ᴛᴏ ᴛʜᴇ Rɪᴛᴇ Aɪᴅ ᴘᴀʀᴋɪɴɢ ʟᴏᴛ ᴡʜᴇʀᴇ they were set to meet. The car was a nice ride but a little too flashy. Petty found himself constantly checking the rearview mirror for tails, nervous again. Beck pulled up in the Mazda, and Petty watched to make sure nobody was following him, either. Beck handed over the bags from the garage. He had a big grin on his face.

"That was too easy," he said. "I didn't even get to use my command voice."

"It was supposed to be easy," Petty said.

"I was hoping for more of a thrill."

Petty paid him off, five thousand dollars wrapped in a McDonald's sack, and gave him the keys to the Jag.

"Good doing business with you," he said.

Beck slid into his car. "See you at Musso's?" he said.

"Don't hold your breath," Petty said.

He waited until Beck had driven away to check the bags. Something was off; they seemed light. Back at the motel he counted the money twice to be sure, spread it out on the bed, and had Tinafey count it, too. Seven hundred thousand. If the total take was really two million, they were still short seven hundred thousand. Had Beck swiped it? He wasn't the type. Tony's uncle, then?

Petty drove to Public Storage and deposited everything except a single stack of hundreds in the locker. He then went to the motel where he'd stashed Tony. The same shirtless *vato* was standing in the same doorway. He nodded at Petty as Petty climbed the stairs to Tony's room.

"I gotta get out of here," Tony said as soon as he opened the door. "I can't be locked up anymore."

"We've got a problem," Petty said.

"What?" Tony said. Petty tossed the stack of hundreds onto the bed. Tony merely glanced at it.

"That's from the garage," Petty said. "But there was only seven hundred grand there."

"Yeah?" Tony said.

"Seven hundred plus the money from your mom's store only adds up to about one point three million," Petty said. "You said the total was two."

"Did I?" Tony said.

The kid was fucking with him. He'd spent too much time alone in the room, had too much time to put things together, take them apart, and put them together again in different ways, and had come to the conclusion that something wasn't quite right.

"Were you mistaken about how much there was?" Petty said.

"Maybe you were mistaken," Tony said.

"You said two million."

"You said a lot of shit, too."

Petty knew the safe play would be to cut the kid loose right now and be satisfied with the cash he had. But if there was more money out there, if that's what Tony was hinting at, he had to do everything he could to get it, to take down the whole pot and set Sam up for life. If there was more money out there, no way was this chump getting over on him.

"So we're through, is that it?" he said. "The partnership's done?"

"I want to know what's going on," Tony said.

"What's going on?" Petty said. "I thought what was going on was that we were following the plan. Get the money, go after Avi."

"Avi," Tony said dismissively. "I think you're hyping this Avi too much. I ain't even sure he's for real."

"Okay," Petty said. "Who do you think put the cowboy on my tail?"

"According to you, Avi," Tony said. "But how do I know?"

"You think I'm making stuff up?"

"I don't know what you're doing."

Petty charged the bed and grabbed Tony's T-shirt. He yanked him up and dragged him to the window. "Look at room 2 downstairs," he said.

Tony parted the curtains and put his eye to the gap.

"What do you see?" Petty said.

"Some *vato*," Tony said.

"No shirt, out front?"

"Yeah."

"He's been there every time I've come by."

"So?" Tony said. "He's staying here, too."

"So," Petty said. "Avi sends someone to talk to him, says, 'Hey, do me a favor for a hundred bucks. While you're out here mad-dogging the parking lot, keep an eye on room 26.'"

Tony laughed. "That dude's name is Tito," he said. "I went down and bummed a smoke off him last night."

"You went outside?" Petty said. "After we agreed you wouldn't?"

"He ain't watching nobody," Tony said. He pushed past Petty on his way back to the bed. "Homey can't even see straight half the time."

Petty kept his face blank. The kid had called his bluff. Fine. If he got up from the table now, he'd still walk away a winner. But he couldn't resist playing one more hand.

"All right, then," he said. "You've obviously got your own plan now, so let's go get the money, and I'll take my cut and be on my way."

Tony didn't reply. He sat on the bed and fiddled with his fake leg.

"Hurry the fuck up," Petty said. "I don't want to be here when Avi comes for your ass."

Again Tony failed to respond. He pulled off the prosthesis and examined its socket. Petty had never seen his stump before. It made him feel sorry for the kid, but not sorry enough to let up on him.

"Fine," he said, going to the door. "You've got your key. I'll go by myself and pick up my share."

Tony spoke up as Petty twisted the knob.

"This whole thing is too weird," he said.

"Tell me about it," Petty said. "I've never been in a shit storm like this, either."

"Nobody's watching me," Tony said.

"Maybe, maybe not," Petty said. "But do you want to take

that chance? Gamble with the money? With your life? With your mom's life?"

"You're paranoid, and you're making me paranoid."

"What's wrong with being careful just in case? It's one more day. We leave for Chicago tomorrow."

"Tomorrow?"

"I've already got the tickets, and after we go there and talk to Avi, we'll know what's what, and we'll both be in the clear."

Tony grabbed a beer off the nightstand and gulped half of it. After a long silence, he said, "There's one more bag."

"Okay," Petty said.

"I wanted to have something left in case anything happened with the first two."

"Makes sense," Petty said. "You want to get it now, make sure it's safe before we go to Chicago?"

"I guess so," Tony said. "But I have to go with you this time."

"Why?" Petty said. "I know you think it's all in my head, but what if someone *is* watching? We don't want you near the money right now."

"You'll never find it on your own," Tony said.

"Try me."

"You won't."

Petty had hoped that when he walked out of the room this time, he'd never have to see the kid again—had been looking forward to it, in fact. He decided not to push any harder, though. Tony was barely on the hook as it was, and he didn't want to risk his chance at the rest of the money.

"Okay, then," he said. "I guess that means I have to come up with a way to get you out of here without anybody catching on."

Tony grinned, unable to hide his delight at forcing Petty to bend to his will. "So get to work," he said. "Sharpen your pencil or whatever."

Petty left the room a few minutes later. He walked downstairs, got into the Mazda, and drove away. Tony came down soon after. "Go talk to your buddy the *vato* and ask where the closest liquor store is," Petty had instructed him. "That way, in case he's reporting to Avi, he'll think you're just going for cigarettes and won't get suspicious." Tony did as he'd been told, and the *vato* said there was a store on the next block, toward Alvarado. Tony started in that direction but made a quick turn up a side street as soon as he was out of the *vato*'s sight. Petty was waiting for him there in the car.

"Where to?" he said.

"Lincoln Park," Tony said.

The park was in East L.A. Tony talked a mile a minute during the drive over, happy to be away from the motel. He talked about the Clippers, he talked about a girl he'd hooked up with in Oceanside when he was at Camp Pendleton, he talked about everything but what they were in the middle of. That was fine with Petty. He was tired of improvising, tired of tap dancing.

"You like Takis?" Tony said as they exited the 10 at Mission and drove past hundreds of shipping containers lined up side by side in a dusty lot.

"What's Takis?" Petty said.

"They're chips, like Doritos. There's Guacamole flavor, Fuego, Nitro. I like Nitro best."

"Never heard of them."

"What about tostilocos?"

"Nope."

"That's when they cut open a bag of Tostitos and put jicama

in it and cucumber and pig skin and peanuts and hot sauce and lime."

"Now you're fucking with me."

"It's good, man. You get you some tostilocos and a beer, you're all set."

The park consisted of scruffy grass ringing a small lake. Palm trees, picnic tables, duck shit. Petty found a space in front of the senior center, where a blast of salsa music signaled the start of the 12:30 Zumba class. He and Tony got out of the car and walked to the lake, then halfway around it. They could still hear the music.

"We fished here when I was a kid," Tony said. "I caught a fifteen-pound carp once. Know what I used for bait?"

"Tostilocos?" Petty said.

"Corn out of a can," Tony said. "Carps love it."

The day had started out cold and never heated up. The sun was nothing but a bright smear in the hazy sky. Petty stuck his hands in the pockets of his jeans to warm them. Tony slowed and looked over his shoulder when they came to a concrete drainpipe, like he was worried about someone following them. The only people nearby were a trio of winos sharing a bench and a bottle and a few kids in the skate park, filming one another doing tricks.

"We getting close?" Petty said.

"We're here," Tony said. He gestured at the lake with his chin.

"In the water?" Petty said.

"Under it."

A mat of thick green algae covered the lake's surface here, studded with sodden trash that had been trapped against the drain's grate. Petty couldn't see the water, much less anything beneath it.

"I hid it at night, when nobody was around," Tony said. "I didn't think I'd be coming back for it during the day." He glanced at the winos again and stepped to the water's edge, where he knelt awkwardly.

"You need help?" Petty said.

"I got it."

The kid stuck his hand into the lake and swept aside the algae. He sank his arm to the elbow and came up holding a yellow nylon rope that had been tied to a metal ring on the drain. "This is where we used to stash beer," he said. "My friend stole it from a store he worked at."

After checking on the winos once more, Tony hauled in the rope hand over hand. A black plastic trash bag appeared, the other end of the rope tied to its drawstring. Petty's heart beat faster. Tony pulled at the algae clinging to the bag and dropped the fistfuls of goo back into the lake. When he lifted the bag onto the shore, dirty water streamed out of it.

"I put a hole in it, so it wouldn't be too heavy," he said.

He opened the bag. The money was wrapped in more trash bags and duct tape. Tony patted the bundles proudly. "Check it out," he said. "Nice and dry."

Petty felt like letting out a victory whoop. He helped Tony to his feet. This time they both looked around to see if anybody was watching—but, no, not the winos, not the skaters—and headed back to the car, Tony carrying the bag.

"You didn't eat them, did you?" Petty said.

"Eat what?" Tony said.

"The fish you caught in there. You didn't eat them."

"Nah," Tony said. "We threw them back. Except once this kid Adam bit the head off a crappie, showing off. He shot his girlfriend's dad a few years later. He was fucking crazy."

Traffic turned stop-and-go near the 101-110 interchange.

Petty was trapped in the sludge with no exit nearby, no bailout. Trying to find a reason for the jam, he tuned in a news station on the radio, one that advertised "traffic on the fives." The slowdown had something to do with a demonstration downtown. A cop had shot and killed a black kid. The LAPD had cleared the cop, and people were pissed. Protesters had gathered on an overpass, where they chanted slogans and unfurled banners. Drivers on the freeway below were slowing to gawk, causing a mile-long backup.

When Petty and Tony finally reached the bridge, Tony pulled out his phone to take a photo of the scene. He hissed in disgust when he discovered the phone's battery was dead, then lowered his window and stuck out his head.

"Fuck the police!" he yelled. The protesters whooped in response.

"Come on, man," Petty said.

"Come on what?" Tony said. "That's fucked up what they did."

"What would be fucked up would be to get pulled over right now," Petty said.

Tony frowned, and the anger and mistrust he'd displayed earlier in the motel room returned.

"Nah, you're just racist," he said.

"My girlfriend's black," Petty said.

"'Cause you fuck 'em don't mean you like 'em."

"Let's change the subject."

"You probably hate Mexicans, too."

Petty held his tongue. Ten more minutes and he'd be rid of the kid. They rode in silence, both staring out the windshield. After a while Tony began to fidget, tapping his foot and nodding his head like he was listening to music. He was building up to something. Petty kept his own face blank, his body still.

They were driving down 3rd, not four blocks from the motel, when Tony spoke up.

"What now?" he said.

He knew what now—they'd discussed it in the room before leaving for the park—but Petty explained it once again.

"I'll drop you back at the motel, make sure nobody's following me, and put the money in the locker," he said. "Tomorrow morning at ten we fly to Chicago from LAX. When we get there, we'll pick up guns from a guy I know and go see Avi."

"What if he tells you to fuck off?"

"He's no hard-ass," Petty said. "He's got a wife, kids, plays tennis every Wednesday morning. He's not gonna get himself killed over two million dollars. Two million dollars is nothing these days."

"Yeah, but what if he thinks it's you that's soft? What if he won't back down? You gonna shoot him? For two hundred and fifty thousand dollars? If two million's nothing, what's two hundred and fifty thousand?"

"It won't come to that," Petty said.

"You don't know."

"I do know. I've known this asshole for twenty years. It won't come to that."

Tony scratched furiously at the scar on his face. He sensed that something wasn't right but couldn't figure out what to do about it. Silence returned as they waited through a long red light. The protesters had set fire to a palm tree, the radio said. They'd marched down and blocked the freeway.

"I need beer," Tony said.

Fine. Anything he wanted. Petty pulled into the parking lot of a liquor store, a brick bunker with barred windows and a broken plastic sign.

"A bottle of tequila, too," Tony said. "And three microwave burritos. Ramona's if they got 'em, beef and potato."

"You want me to heat them up?" Petty said.

"I'll nuke them at the motel."

The old Korean lady behind the counter shouted *"Buenos días"* when Petty entered the store. The aisles were so narrow he had to turn sideways to get back to the beer cooler. A little of everything crowded the shelves, from rice cookers to tube socks. Petty grabbed a twelve-pack of Tecate and the burritos. The old lady had trouble understanding his request for Patrón.

"Whiskey?"

"No, tequila. Patrón."

Petty pointed at the bottle and kept pointing until she figured it out. He also bought five scratch-off lottery tickets, thought they might keep Tony occupied during their last minutes together. He handed them to him when he got back to the car, but the kid dropped the tickets into the bag without looking at them.

"So ten tomorrow?" he said.

"I'll pick you up at seven," Petty said.

"Give me my ticket now."

"I don't have it with me. I'll print it out and bring it with your dinner tonight, if you want."

Tony didn't reply.

"Is that what you want?" Petty said.

"Yeah," Tony said. "Bring it."

Petty turned onto a side street a block from the Holiday Lodge. All that was left now was the blowoff, getting the kid out of the car. He'd throw him out if he had to but would rather it went easy.

"I'm gonna drop you here," he said.

"Ain't nobody watching the motel," Tony said.

"Humor me," Petty said. "What do you want for dinner?"

Tony didn't answer for a while, just sat there chewing his tongue. Finally he said, "Whopper combo with large fries."

He took his time opening the door. Petty got ready. Two hard kicks would be enough to push him out. He exited on his own, though, reaching back in for the liquor-store bag, then slamming the door shut. He bent to look at Petty through the open window.

"When will you be back?" he said.

"Eight or so," Petty said.

Tony nodded, trying to think of another question, but what he really wanted to say spilled out: "Don't fuck me over."

"Don't worry," Petty said. "Everything's cool." But the kid knew it wasn't. Petty could see it in his eyes. It didn't matter. Tony had no way of getting in touch with him, no idea where he was staying, and when he drove away, he'd be disappearing from the face of the kid's planet, blasting off with two million free-and-clear dollars.

He watched in the rearview mirror as Tony limped toward the motel. He hoped the kid would find a way out of the mess he was going to be in when his cousin and his crew showed up for their money, but if he didn't, whatever happened was his own fault. He'd crossed a line when he agreed to hold the money. He'd stepped out of the village and into the jungle, where every tree hid a tiger and where, if you weren't smart enough or quick enough, you were going to get clawed, get bit, get eaten up.

26

W HEN DIAZ'S DAD CALLED TONY'S MOM, SHE SAID SHE HADN'T heard from Tony in a week and thought he was in Ensenada. This sounded like bullshit to Diaz, like she was covering for her son. Diaz had been uneasy ever since his visit to Tony's apartment, and getting the runaround put him even more on edge.

His old bedroom was as cluttered as the rest of the house, filled with more junk his dad had hoarded. Diaz set the stacks of old *Playboy* magazines that covered his childhood bed on the floor and lay on the bare mattress. He'd shared the room with his two brothers, Carlos and Hector. They both had wives now, kids, problems.

On a shelf next to the bed were some of the model cars the three of them had built. Diaz picked up a '49 Mercury coupe and turned it over in his hands while he contemplated his next move. One option was to return to Tony's apartment, break in, and see what he could see. Another option was to go to the kid's mom's store and pistol-whip the truth out of her about where he was. Diaz set the Merc down and grabbed a Camaro. He lifted the hood to examine the engine.

The house phone rang. Diaz jumped up and hurried down the hall to his parents' bedroom. The receiver was in its dock on the nightstand, surrounded by empty beer cans. Diaz picked it up and checked the display. Unknown caller. He pushed the Talk button and said hello.

"Tío?" a voice said.

"Who's this?" Diaz said.

"Tony. Who's this?"

"It's me, bro. Mando."

"No fucking way," Tony said. "You're here?"

"I'm here," Diaz said.

"Is that why your dad called my mom? I barely got the message now. I forgot to charge my phone."

"She said you were in Mexico."

There was a long pause. The kid was deciding whether to lie, Diaz knew. He opened a wooden box on the dresser and fingered the costume jewelry inside, took out a red rhinestone rose he remembered his mom wearing to church, pinned to her black dress.

"Things are kind of fucked up," Tony finally said.

"What do you mean?" Diaz said.

"I mean it's good you're back."

Diaz pulled his rental car into the parking lot of the motel, a toxic waste dump off Alvarado, where Tony had said to meet him. He wondered what the kid was up to at a crack den like this. Nothing good, that's for sure. Some *cholo*, some tweaker, flew out of a room on the ground floor and directed him to an empty space like he was the lot attendant. Diaz ignored him and backed into a spot close to the office. He took the .22 from the glove compartment and put it in his jacket pocket before getting out of the car.

"Five bucks, *ese,* I'll watch your car for you," the *cholo* said. "Wash the windows, too."

"No, thanks," Diaz said. "I'll be watching it myself."

"Why?" the *cholo* said, aggrieved, as if Diaz had insulted him. "I ain't gonna fuck with it."

Diaz climbed the stairs without replying.

"I ain't gonna fuck with it," the *cholo* said again, shouting this time.

"Be cool, *ese,*" Diaz said.

The *cholo* bugged his eyes and puffed his chest. "*You* be cool," he said and turned and went back into his room.

Diaz knocked at Tony's door. His other hand was on the gun. Tony answered right away, threw open the door and said, "Homey! Whassup?"

They clasped hands and leaned in for a quick bump, chest to chest. Diaz hadn't seen his cousin since the kid had been wounded. The fake leg, the missing fingers, the scar on his face. They fucked him up real good. He checked the room over Tony's shoulder, made sure he was alone.

Tony was nervous, his smile all clenched teeth, beads of sweat quivering on his forehead. He tried to get Diaz to sit but wouldn't sit himself. He offered beer, he offered tequila. Diaz accepted a Tecate to put the kid at ease. Tony passed him a warm one from a box on the floor and took a gulp off the can he'd been working on. The walls of the room heaved like the ribs of a cornered animal, and a story spilled out.

Diaz struggled to make sense of the flood of words. Other people knew about the money. A phony plumber had showed up looking for it, and a guy with guns. Tony shot that dude, and he and the plumber, Rowan, buried him in the desert. Then came a threatening phone call, and Tony had decided to take the money from its original hiding places, one of which was Diaz's dad's garage, and put it in a storage locker. Rowan had arranged for the locker and given Tony a key, then bought him a ticket to Chicago, where they were supposed to be going tomorrow to confront the dude who was after the money. But now the kid had a feeling that was bullshit, that Rowan was up to something shady.

By the end of the tale, Diaz's head was ringing like he'd been hit with a bottle, but he was certain of one thing: Tony had blown it. He'd been hustled hard-core, thoroughly clowned. And that cop this morning—there was no coke; he'd come to the house for the money. Diaz didn't let his anger get the best of him, though, didn't go off.

"What makes you think Rowan's sketchy?" he said to Tony.

"I don't know," Tony said. "Just a vibe I got. But look, check this out." He grabbed something off the dresser and handed it to Diaz. It was a cardboard parking pass for the City Center Motel, on 6th Street. "I snatched that out of his car today when he wasn't looking, so now I know where he's staying."

He was proud of himself and stood there waiting for Diaz to be proud of him, too, like the parking pass changed everything that came before it. Diaz didn't say anything, and his silence deflated the kid.

"Okay, I screwed up," he said. "But we can fix it."

Diaz wished he could sit a while and analyze every element of the clusterfuck, but there wasn't time. He needed to pick one problem, the most pressing, and solve it. And that problem was, obviously, getting his hands on his money.

"When did Rowan say he'd be back?" he said to Tony.

"He's supposed to be bringing me dinner at eight," Tony said, brightening at the possibility that someone else was going to be doing the thinking.

Diaz looked at his watch. It was 6:00 p.m. "Give me the key to the locker," he said.

Tony took the key out of his pocket and handed it over. "What are you gonna do?" he said.

"What you should have done a while ago," Diaz said.

He drove to SoCal Self Storage on Hollywood Boulevard and took the elevator to the third floor. He walked down the aisle, looking for locker 376. There was no lock on it when he found it. He opened it and looked inside. Empty.

Tony was watching a basketball game on TV when he got back to the room. Diaz felt like shooting the stupid motherfucker right then and there but again managed to keep his temper under control.

"You sure that was the place?" he said.

Tony took out his phone to show him what he'd typed into it. "SoCal Self Storage, number 376," he said.

"There was nothing there," Diaz said.

"Fuck!" Tony said. He threw his beer can across the room. "I knew that fucker was up to something." He dropped his head into his hands. "I'm sorry, Mando."

Diaz let him suffer some, then said, "It's seven already. We might as well wait and see if he shows up."

"And if he don't?" Tony said.

"We'll go from there."

"We'll find him and smoke his ass."

"We'll take care of it."

This seemed to settle things for Tony, and he went back

to watching the game. Diaz had questions for him but didn't want to freak him out, so he slipped his queries regarding the money and what had happened to it into the small talk that followed.

Tony was reluctant to revisit the tale. When Diaz asked him to repeat what happened the day he shot the dude who showed up at his apartment looking for the cash, he had to drag the details out of him. He couldn't tell if this was because the kid was drunk or because he was stonewalling.

"So the second guy, the one with the guns, he knew Rowan?" Diaz said.

"Not really," Tony said without looking away from the TV. "But they knew the same people."

"Like this Avi, the guy in Chicago you were supposedly going to see?"

"Definitely him."

"Could Rowan have been working with the second guy?"

"Bro, we shot him."

"*You* shot him," Diaz said. "Could be they were playing you together, and you fucked up their hustle."

"Could be," Tony said. "But what's it matter now? Now it's real simple: Rowan's got the money, and we want it."

The kid raised the volume on the TV, and Diaz gave up trying to pump him for information. Tony was right: the situation was simple, and things were going to be very quick and very dirty from here on out. Diaz sat at the room's table and pretended to watch the game, pretended to be interested in the player stats Tony shared, pretended to enjoy the kid's slurred reminiscences.

"I remember going to see you play ball when you were in high school," Tony said. "You had mad skills. And then we'd go to King Cole for pizza."

"The Chicano special," Diaz said. "What was it again? Chorizo, ham,…"

"Chorizo, ham, and jalapeños. That shit was good."

"It's still there? They didn't tear it down?"

"Still there, bro, still old-school."

As eight o'clock approached, the chatter died out. Tony began to fidget, got up to piss twice. His nervousness made Diaz nervous. They both sat knotted from head to toe, staring at the TV. It got dark, and nobody turned on a light. It got cold, and nobody switched on the heater. Eight ten. Eight fifteen.

Tony bent suddenly and reached under the bed. He came up with a shotgun, which he pointed at Diaz. Diaz almost pulled his own gun, almost lost his cool, but instead raised his hands into the air.

"He's not coming," Tony said.

"Don't look like it," Diaz said.

"Like I said before, I know I fucked up, but I'll do whatever it takes to make things right."

"I know you will."

"You strapped?"

Diaz reached slowly into his pocket and used his thumb and forefinger to lift the .22 out and show it to Tony.

"He had me convinced people were watching me," the kid said. "He said they were gonna hurt my mom. I was scared to stick my head out the door."

"Sounds like some kind of pro," Diaz said.

"You're gonna need me to point him out to you and everything. He's fucking tricky."

"Not trickier than us, right?"

"No way, man, no way."

"He fucked with the wrong people this time."

"The wrong fucking people," Tony said. He lowered the shotgun a bit. "So you forgive me?"

"We're family, bro," Diaz said. "That's why I brought you into this in the first place. I trusted you."

Tony squinted at him, trying to read him, then set the shotgun on the bed.

"Sorry. I had to make sure we were cool," he said.

Diaz tilted his head at the .22. "Can I put this away?"

"Go ahead," Tony said. He picked up his beer. "Truthfully, mine's not even loaded."

Diaz returned the pistol to his pocket. He picked up his beer and took things back to where they were before.

"You still go to El Tepeyac?" he said.

"Fuck, yeah," Tony said. "Manuel died a couple years ago, but it's still good."

"I dreamed about their burritos one night in Afghanistan."

"They were on TV and shit. *Man v. Food.* The joint is, like, famous now."

Diaz sipped his beer.

"You ready to get the hell out of here?" he said.

"You don't even know," Tony said.

Diaz watched *Wheel of Fortune* while his cousin packed up his clothes and the booze. He knew the answer to the puzzle before any of the contestants: birthday boy. Tony turned on a light, trying to find a missing sock, and the sudden brightness startled Diaz. He'd grown accustomed to the dark.

"Here," Tony said. He tossed him two bundles of hundred-dollar bills. "That's some of the money, at least."

Diaz flipped through the stacks, but it didn't make him happy; it made him even angrier. A perfect plan ruined, and him having to scramble to get back what was his.

293

★   ★   ★

They stopped at Taco Bell for burritos and ate them on their way to the City Center Motel. Diaz parked around the corner. The pass Tony had swiped had a room number on it, 23. Tony thought they should charge up there, break the door down, and take the money. Diaz told him to slow his roll, they needed to check things out first.

Since Rowan knew Tony, Diaz had the kid wait in the car while he walked back to the motel. He went upstairs and strolled past room 23. The room was dark, its curtains drawn, and there was no sign in the parking lot of the Mazda Tony said the guy was driving, probably the same Mazda the fake cop had used. This worried Diaz. If Rowan had already split with the money, there was a good chance he'd get away with it, as he and Tony had no more clues to his where-abouts.

Diaz walked into the office, a stuffy little room with two folding chairs and a rack of tourist pamphlets. There was no-body at the check-in desk, so he knocked on the bulletproof glass. A woman in a sari with a red dot on her forehead came out of the back room carrying a plastic bowl of rice and a fork.

"I'm looking for some friends in room 23," Diaz said. "They didn't check out, did they?"

The woman set down her bowl and consulted a computer. "No," she said. "They're still here. One more night."

Tony was watching a video on his phone when Diaz re-turned to the car to grab his jacket.

"They're out right now," Diaz said. "I'm gonna wait for them to get back. Chill here, and I'll come for you when I need you."

"Roger that," Tony said.

Diaz walked back to the motel and sat on the bench at the bus stop next to the driveway. From there he could see anyone going into or out of the parking lot. He scrunched down in his jacket, made himself small.

It was 9:00 p.m., and traffic on 7th Street had let up. A woman approached pulling a cart filled with folded laundry. She took a seat at the other end of the bench. A bus arrived, loud and bright, and the woman got on. The night seemed colder and darker when the bus drove away.

There was a poster advertising a movie on the shelter covering the bench. Diaz read the names on it a hundred times. At 9:30 a red Honda turned into the driveway of the motel. Diaz stood and peeked over the low cinder-block wall separating the parking lot from the sidewalk. A Chinese woman and two children got out of the car and went into a room on the first floor. Diaz returned to the bench and the poster. Music by Henry Jackman. Art direction by Ryan Meinerding. Two kids skateboarded past. One of them yelled, "Boo!" The shout echoed down the empty street.

Around 10:15 a silver Mercedes entered the lot. Diaz went to the wall again, ducking so only his head showed. A white guy and a black chick slid out of the Benz. They went up the stairs holding hands. The girl said something that made the dude laugh. Diaz got a feeling. He pulled out his phone. When the couple stopped in front of room 23, under the light, he zoomed the camera in and took a photo before the guy unlocked the door and he and the girl stepped inside.

Diaz watched the room for another half hour until the glow behind the curtains went out. He then crept into the parking lot and took pictures of the Mercedes and its license plate.

When he returned to the car, Tony was asleep, his seat reclined all the way back. The sound of the doors unlocking startled him awake, and he blinked and gulped like something newly thrust into the world. Diaz showed him the photo of the man and woman.

"That's him—Rowan," Tony said.

"And the girl?" Diaz said.

"Must be his girlfriend. He told me she was black."

Diaz started the car.

"We going to get them?" Tony said. He coughed and spit out the window.

"Not yet," Diaz said.

"But we got them cornered."

"They're down for a few hours, and I want to make a plan. We're gonna get one shot at them, so we need to have our shit together."

"We should both have guns," Tony said. "Do you have an extra? Or shells for the shotty?"

"Don't worry. I'll hook you up," Diaz said.

Tony thought it'd be best if he went up to the room alone first and talked his way inside with a story about finding the parking pass in the bag with the tequila and beer. After a few minutes Diaz would come up, and Tony would let him into the room. If the money was there, they'd take it. If it was somewhere else, they'd go with Rowan to get it.

"Are we gonna kill them afterward?" he asked. They were on the 4th Street bridge, headed east. Below, warehouses and railroad tracks crowded both sides of the river's concrete channel, shadowy and sinister in the septic glow of orange streetlights. A train rolled through the desolation, picking up speed, heading out.

"Would that be a problem for you?" Diaz said.

"Whatever you need me to do, I'm down," Tony said, but Diaz could tell he was just mouthing the words.

"I don't think it'll get that hairy," he said.

"Me, neither," Tony said, relieved. He sat back and scratched his scar, then leaned across to look at the car's instrument panel. Diaz smelled sweat on him, and stale beer.

"You know what side the gas tank is on in this car?" the kid said.

"The gas tank?" Diaz said.

"Where you put the gas, the hole."

"Nah, man. It was full when I rented it."

"Check this out," Tony said. He pointed to the gas icon on the dash, the one that looked like a pump. "See the arrow next to that? That's what side you fill up on."

"No shit?" Diaz said.

"No shit."

"I never noticed that before."

"I saw it on YouTube," Tony said. "Now you'll never be that fool pulling in and out at the gas station, trying to get it right."

When they got to Diaz's dad's house, the kid insisted on taking Diaz into the garage and showing him where the money had been hidden—on a shelf, behind some junk.

"A good spot, right?" he said.

Diaz was wondering who the fake cop had been who'd picked up the cash. It wasn't Rowan, so how many other people were involved in the scam?

"Is your dad home?" Tony said as they walked across the yard to the house.

"He's in Laughlin," Diaz said. "He's got a girlfriend there."

Tony kicked one of the newspapers lying on the porch. "My

mom's worried about him," he said. "She thinks he drinks too much."

"He's fine," Diaz said. "He's getting old, that's all."

Tony had his duffel, and Diaz was carrying the bag containing the booze. Unlocking the front door took both hands, so he set the bag down. Tony rubbed the stump of his leg where it fit into the prosthesis.

"That thing hurt?" Diaz asked him.

"All the time," Tony said.

They stepped into the dining room, and Diaz turned on a light, a bare bulb on the ceiling.

"Can you believe this?" Tony said, gesturing at the garbage piled everywhere. "I tripped out when I came to hide the money. Your mom used to vacuum every day. She'd make us take off our shoes before we came in."

"There's cold beer in the fridge," Diaz said. "Go get us a couple."

Tony looked for somewhere to put down his duffel, finally setting it on the back of the couch. He started for the kitchen but got distracted by an old computer on the dining-room table.

"Hey," he said. "This might actually be worth something. Dudes collect shit like this." He moved on to a box of eight-track tapes, pulled one out and looked it over. "These, too," he said. "Your old man's gonna end up richer than both of us."

"Beer, beer, beer," Diaz chanted, waving him on.

Tony dropped the tape back into the box. When he reached the kitchen door, Diaz sprang across the dining room and shoved him the last few feet through it. The kid stumbled and almost fell.

"What the fuck?" he said and squinted at something lying

on the floor, struggled to make it out in the greasy darkness. It was a body. Diaz's dad, facedown on the linoleum. Tony began to turn around, began to say something else, but Diaz had the .22 pointed at the back of his head. The first shot dropped him to his good knee, the second sprawled him on top of the corpse. Diaz was pretty certain he was dead but bent down and put one more round into him to make sure.

27

Pₑₜₜᵧ SLID THE BAG CONTAINING THE MONEY PULLED FROM THE lake into the locker with the other cash and paused for a second, just a second, to admire all of it, his big score. He then drove to the rental car office and turned in the Mazda. The risky business was completed, so he felt safe using his Benz again. The cabdriver who took him back to the motel had a thick Russian accent. He'd been in the United States for less than a year. Petty asked him how he liked it so far.

"Work, sleep," the driver said with a weary shrug. "Work, sleep."

Another epic sunset bloomed overhead, cold fire burning away the last of the chilly day. Tinafey scrambled off the bed when Petty came into the room and wrapped herself around him like he'd been gone for a month. He hugged her tightly and breathed in her scent: peach shampoo, coconut from the lotion she rubbed on herself after showering, and a hint of cannabis funk. The blend was still new to him, still turned him on.

"Everything went okay?" she said.

"Everything went fine," he said.

"You get away with it?"

"I'm pretty sure I did."

"Thank God," Tinafey said.

She let Petty go and sat hard on the bed, put her face in her hands and breathed deeply. It took Petty a few seconds to figure out she was crying.

"Hey," he said. "What's wrong?"

"Nothin'," she said. "It's just my mind's been racin' for days."

Petty sat beside her. "It's all over now," he said. "You can relax."

"I guess I ain't cut out for this shit."

"I'll never put you through anything like it again."

"I mean it," Tinafey said.

Petty lifted his shirt to wipe the tears from her face. She slapped his hand away and used her own T-shirt.

"I look a mess," she said.

"No, you don't," he said. "You look great."

"There you go, lyin' again already."

"I'm not lying."

"Motherfuckin' hustlers," Tinafey said.

While she was cleaning up in the bathroom, Petty called the hospital for an update on Sam. She'd been moved out of intensive care and was back in her room. Good news. Petty poured himself a Scotch.

"Let's go out tonight," he said to Tinafey. "Celebrate."

Tinafey slinked out of the bathroom wearing only panties and a pushup bra. She paused, hands on cocked hips, so Petty could get a good look at her, then sashayed toward him with a naughty smile.

"Celebrate?" she said. She grabbed his head and pulled it into her cleavage. "I'll show you about celebratin'."

Petty was sitting on the bed. Tinafey pushed him onto his back and climbed on top of him. With her hands on his shoulders, she ground her pelvis into his. His hard-on was trapped at a painful angle in his jeans.

"I feel that," she whispered in his ear.

He reached down and undid his belt. Tinafey tugged at his zipper.

"You want me to take these off you?" she said.

"Yes, please," Petty said.

Working together, they got rid of the jeans and his shoes. Tinafey slipped off her panties and lay on top of him again. She reached down and grabbed his cock.

"Can I ride this?" she said. "Can I buck on it awhile?"

Petty nodded, and she guided him into her pussy.

Full dark had settled by the time they collapsed, exhausted, onto the tangle of sheets. Their bodies cooled quickly, sweat chilling into icy webs on their backs and legs. Tinafey went from pushing Petty away, saying, "Leave me be; I'm burnin' up," to snuggling against him. He grabbed the blanket off the floor and spread it over the two of them. They lay there as long as they could, drowsing in a gentle eddy, until the cold forced them to get up and drove them to hot showers and warm clothes.

Petty was shaving when Tinafey announced that she wanted to go bowling.

"Bowling?" he said.

"I'm real good," Tinafey said.

"You don't want to go to a club? A movie?"

"You scared of gettin' whupped by a female?"

"Don't let your mouth write a check your ass can't cash."

"Okay, now you done asked for it," Tinafey said. "Get ready to lose some of them fat stacks you just hustled."

They stopped at the hospital first for a quick visit with Sam. She looked up from her chemistry book and smiled wanly when they walked into the room.

"I can still read," she said.

"Were you worried about that?" Petty said.

"I was worried about everything. Hi, Tinafey."

"Hey, girl," Tinafey said. "You're lookin' good."

Sam touched the bandages wrapped around her head. "I look like Aladdin," she said.

She was pleasant but spacey, still a little out of it. Petty was just glad to see her awake again and talking.

"Here's something else I can still do," she said. She held up her hand and quickly touched each of her fingers to her thumb.

"I ain't even had surgery, and I still can't do that," Tinafey said.

"How about this?" Sam said. "Pat your head and rub your stomach at the same time."

"Seriously, now," Petty said. "Take it easy."

Sam made a face at him and proceeded to lightly tap her head while rubbing her stomach.

"You're gonna pop a stitch," Petty said.

"Come on, Tinafey," Sam said.

The two of them patted and rubbed and chanted in unison, "Here we go, here we go." They started in on Petty, wanted him to try, too. He resisted briefly but then joined in, let them have their fun. They laughed so hard watching him try to keep up that an orderly gave them a dirty look around the door.

*   *   *

The nearest bowling alley was in the complex of restaurants and bars next to Staples Center. It was a tourist trap with a kitschy space-age theme that charged seventy-five an hour for a lane and fifteen bucks for a Manhattan. A DJ played booming hip-hop, and the customers stacked two deep at the bar danced in place and mouthed the words to the songs.

Half the lanes had been reserved for a Christmas party, and while Petty waited for the attendant to bring his and Tinafey's shoes, he watched a guy dressed as Santa roll a strike. The crack and clatter of the pins made him flinch, and he felt a headache coming on.

Tinafey, on the other hand, was enjoying herself immensely. She made a big production of choosing her ball, hefted three or four before settling on a bright orange one that blazed like a comet as it rolled down the blacklighted lane. She was as good as she had claimed to be. Her approach and delivery were smooth and graceful, arms and legs moving in perfect sync, and when she released the ball, her follow-through was perfect.

Petty had never been any good at bowling, had never cared enough to get any good. His mom's girlfriends bowled, slobs bowled, *cops* bowled. He rolled gutter ball after gutter ball, which delighted Tinafey.

"You need them to put up the kiddie rails?" she said.

He acted like he was interested when she gave him tips—kept his wrist straight as she instructed, took four steps to the foul line, aimed for the second arrow from the edge of the lane—but really he was counting the minutes until their time ran out. He threw one strike toward the end of their last game, sent the pins flying. Tinafey pointed at him with both index fingers, wiggled her butt, and sang along to the song blasting out of the speakers—"That's the Way," by KC and the Sunshine Band. Petty clasped his hands and shook them over his shoulders like an old-time boxer.

"Sorry I wasn't much of a challenge for you," he said later, after they'd turned in their shoes and found an empty sofa in the bar.

"Didn't matter," Tinafey said. "You wouldn't put up any money anyway."

"I might have, but you blew it," Petty said. "If you want to hustle someone, don't show how good you are right off the bat. Lose a few games first."

"Shit, baby," Tinafey said. "If I was lookin' to hustle you, you'd have been hustled. Believe that."

A waitress came over, and they ordered wings and chili fries. Tinafey told Petty about how she got kicked off her high school bowling team for smoking weed.

"And shopliftin'," she said. "A pair of shoes I didn't even need. And wouldn't you know it? The team made the state championship that year. I coulda gone to Nashville, coulda stayed in a hotel, gotten a trophy. Instead I spent four weekends pickin' up trash on the side of the highway."

"Fuck it," Petty said. "I'll buy you a trophy."

"Yeah?" Tinafey said. "And what else?"

"Whatever you want. And we're moving out of that shithole. They've got a Marriott right here. It's close enough to the hospital."

"Then what?"

"Then what what?"

"What next?"

"We wait and see what happens with Sam. We hope for good news."

"Ain't gonna be nothin' but good news from now on," Tinafey said.

"About time," Petty said.

"Good news, good luck, everything."

The DJ played the Jackson 5 version of "Santa Claus Is Comin' to Town." Tinafey sang along for a while, then said, "I want a Christmas tree."

"Sure," Petty said.

"And I'm gonna get Sam one, too, a little one for her room."

The wings came, the fries, another round of drinks. Petty and Tinafey ate it all up. Petty began to worry about Sam again as they walked through the cavernous parking lot to the car, wondering what the doctors would find when they analyzed the tumor. He batted away the troubling thoughts, but they continued to buzz in the background during the drive back to the hotel.

"What you thinkin' about?" Tinafey said.

"Nothing," Petty said.

"Nothin'," Tinafey said, imitating him.

"It's been a long day," Petty said. "I'm beat."

They pulled into the parking lot and lucked into a spot right under their room. Petty took Tinafey's hand as they walked up the stairs. It was ice cold. He lifted it to his lips and blew warm breath on her fingers.

Diaz had to piss, but now that the sun was up, he couldn't duck behind the bus shelter to do it. There were people all over the street and cars everywhere, and the last thing he needed was to get popped for urinating in public. He reluctantly left the bench and hurried around the corner, where he found an alley, a narrow walkway between two tenements. He sidled into it and unbuttoned his jeans. Steam rose as he cut loose—the morning was that cold.

He checked on the Mercedes when he returned to the bus stop, peered over the wall into the motel's parking lot. Still there. And no activity in the vicinity of room 23. It was a couple minutes after eight. He'd been at the stop since one, came right back after taking care of Tony. After twenty-four hours without sleep, his eyeballs felt like they'd been rolled in sand. He wished he had a can of Red Bull or a few go pills to get his heart pumping.

He sat on the bench and stared down at his shoes. He put his hand in his pocket and, for the hundredth time, hefted the .22. An old man and an old woman dressed for church sat next to him. The woman asked him in Spanish if this was the bus to Compton. Diaz said he didn't know and pointed out a map posted on the wall of the shelter.

The man walked to the map and squinted up at it. He traced the bus's route with a finger and called to his wife, "This is it."

The woman was peeling an orange, dropping the peels to the ground. "Take this," she said to the man and made him come over and get a piece of the fruit.

By the time the bus arrived, ten people were waiting for it. Diaz moved away from the crowd in order to maintain a clear view of the motel. He stood against the parking-lot wall until the bus departed, then sat on the bench again.

A pigeon swooped down on the orange peels. Diaz lifted his foot to scare it off but ended up letting it be so he had something to watch besides traffic. The bird had only one eye and couldn't decide whether to keep it on Diaz or the peels. It was a nervous wreck, swiveling its head back and forth between them.

The sound of a door opening turned Diaz around. His hand

went to his gun when he saw Rowan. *Easy,* he said to himself. *Easy.* He adjusted his stance so that he wasn't facing the motel, pretended to be looking in another direction. Rowan left room 23 and headed for the stairs. The dude was alone, meaning his girl was still inside. He jogged down the steps like a man in a hurry.

Diaz's plan had been to wait for Rowan to come outside and confront him in the parking lot, stick the gun in his ear and ask where the money was. He started toward him but then stopped, reconsidering. Say the dude had his own gun. Tony hadn't mentioned one, but that didn't mean anything. Or say he didn't have a gun but fought back anyway. Every crackhead holed up in the motel would be watching, and one of them was bound to call 911.

A better idea came to Diaz. He walked past the driveway and continued a short distance down the block, stopping in the shadow of a telephone pole. The Mercedes pulled out of the lot and turned right onto 7th. Diaz waited until the car was out of sight and returned to the motel.

He prepared himself as he climbed the stairs, turned his blood into kerosene, his muscles into barbed wire. He knocked hard on the door to room 23, making it sound urgent, but the girl still took her time before calling out, "What do you want?"

She had her eye to the peephole, Diaz knew. He imagined he could feel her heart pounding through the door.

"You know a guy named Rowan?" he said. "Drives a silver Mercedes?"

"Why?" the girl said.

"Someone ran a light and T-boned his car," Diaz said. "He's hurt bad and asked me to come get you."

"Just now?" the girl said.

"Barely a minute ago," Diaz said. "It doesn't look good."

He heard the girl scrabbling at the dead bolt, heard it pop, and waited, tensed, for the door to open. When it did, he slammed his shoulder into it, forcing his way into the room. The girl, startled, backpedaled until she tripped and fell onto the bed. Diaz kicked the door shut and held the gun high so the girl could see it.

"Stay down," he said.

The girl was sitting on the edge of the mattress, feet on the floor, leaning back on her elbows. She had short hair and big tits and wore a Hard Rock Hollywood T-shirt and nothing else.

"Don't shoot me," she said. "I'm not gonna do nothin'." She sounded scared but nowhere near panicking.

"Where's my money?" Diaz said.

"Your what?" the girl said.

Diaz stepped to her and put the muzzle of the gun between her eyes. "We're not gonna fuck around like that," he said.

The girl pointed with her chin at a small safe on the top shelf of the closet. "In there," she said.

"Open it," Diaz said.

The girl was going to say she didn't know the combination, but after peering again down the barrel of the .22, she got up, walked over, and punched some numbers into the keypad. The safe blinked and beeped, and she opened the door and stepped aside.

"Back to the bed," Diaz said. "Facedown with your arms out."

"You gonna kill me?" the girl said.

"All I want is my money," Diaz said.

He waited until the girl had stretched out on the rumpled sheets to grab the cash in the safe. It was nothing, half a ten-thousand-dollar bundle.

"Where's the rest?" he said to the girl.

"That's all there is," she replied.

"Bullshit!" Diaz said. He whirled around the room, opening drawers and emptying suitcases onto the floor, but uncovered no more money. He stood over the girl and pressed the gun to the base of her spine.

"I'll put the first round here," he said. "You'll suffer."

"That's all the money I know about," the girl said.

"There's more," Diaz said. "Lots more."

"Rowan must have put it somewhere, then."

"Where's Rowan now?"

"I don't know. I was sleepin' when he left."

"When will he be back?"

"I don't know."

Whether she was lying or telling the truth, Diaz had to make a decision. He could sit tight until Rowan returned, or he could force the guy to come to him. He looked around the room. It was no place for a showdown. No cover, paper-thin walls, too many witnesses.

"Put some clothes on," he said to the girl.

He kept the gun on her while she pulled on a pair of jeans and slipped her feet into flip-flops. Then, taking a length of rope he'd scrounged up in his dad's garage from the pocket of his jacket, he had her put her hands together. She didn't struggle as he wrapped the rope around her wrists.

"Where's your coat?" he said. "You got a coat?"

"On the chair," she said.

He picked up the pink hoodie lying there and draped it over her hands.

"And your phone?"

"Charging by the sink."

He took it and the charger and put them in his pocket.

"We're gonna walk out of here like best friends," he said. "If you play along, you got nothing to worry about. If you make trouble..." He put the gun to the back of her head.

"I ain't gonna make trouble," the girl said.

Diaz peeked between the curtains before opening the door. He threw his arm around the girl's neck and guided her down the stairs. His other hand was in the pocket of his jacket, tapping the barrel of the gun against her hip. Once they were out of the motel's parking lot, he steered her up the sidewalk toward his car. She came along easily, but he could feel her trembling. Good. He wanted her scared.

A lunatic dressed in rags was swinging a golf club against a light pole again and again, like a man doing a job. The crack, crack, crack of it jabbed at Diaz like a dentist's probe, every impact making him twitch. Before he could stop himself, he yelled at the guy, "Cut that shit out."

"Fuck you!" the guy yelled back and kept right on swinging.

28

Tinafey woke up craving pancakes. Petty went out to McDonald's to get her some. The line for the drive-through stretched down the block, so he parked and walked inside. While waiting to order he flipped through the credit cards in his wallet, trying to recall which ones had enough space to accommodate the cost of a room at the Marriott. He smiled to think that he wouldn't have to worry about things like this anymore after making deposits into a couple of his accounts.

Mexican families filled the tables in the dining room. On his way out Petty stepped over two kids playing on the floor and almost tripped on a toy car. It was a damp, cold morning, and the upper floors of the downtown office buildings disappeared into the milky sky that hung low over the city. Petty had to wait for yet another family to pile out of a minivan before he could get into his car. He had just set the pancakes on

the passenger seat and slid his coffee into the holder in the center console when his phone rang. It was Tinafey calling.

"Hey, baby," he said.

"Listen up, motherfucker," a man's voice growled. "I want
my money back, all of it."

Petty froze, heart, lungs, brain. He felt like he was folding in
on himself.

"Who's this?" he said.

"Don't be a fucking idiot," the man said. "I've got your girlfriend, and I'll put a bullet in her head if you don't do exactly
what I tell you. That's who this is."

"Let me talk to her," Petty said.

There was a rustle on the other end, then Tinafey said, "He
busted in right after you left."

"Are you okay?"

"I'm fine."

"Don't worry about anything."

"That's what I told her." It was the guy again. "I said, 'Your
boyfriend isn't gonna let you die.' She didn't look like she believed me, though."

Petty closed his eyes and concentrated. "I'm gonna give you
the money, no problem, so why don't you let her go?" he said.

"You think I'm stupid?" the guy said.

"No," Petty said. "I think this is between you and me. Cut
the girl loose, and we'll go get the money together. I'll meet
you wherever you want."

"That's not gonna happen," the guy said. "How it's gonna
go is, you're gonna get the money yourself and wait for me to
call. Understand?"

"Is this Mando, Tony's cousin?"

"It's whoever you want it to be. Just do what I say."

The tire shop across the street had one of those inflatable

dancing tube men out front, bright green. Petty watched it flail and tried not to think of Tinafey anxious, Tinafey frightened, Tinafey with a gun on her.

"I'll get the money," he said.

"There you go," the guy said.

"It'll take me an hour or so."

"That's fine, as long as there's no funny shit. It'd be no big thing for me to wax this bitch and leave her in a dumpster. No big thing at all."

"There won't be any funny shit."

"Good," the guy said and ended the call.

Petty dropped his phone. He rocked in his seat, faster and faster, then exploded, hammering the dash with his fist. He was panting when he finally ran out of steam. He felt like he'd been kicked in the chest, like all his ribs had been broken.

Crazy schemes flitted through his head, but all of them would have put Tinafey in more danger. The job had been jinxed from the start. He'd been making things up as he went along, squeaking by on dumb luck, and now the whole jerry-rigged mess had come tumbling down around his ears.

He drove to the storage facility in a daze, nearly ran a red light. The girl behind the counter in the lobby let him borrow a cart, and he pushed it into the elevator and rode up to the fourth floor. He was alone in the corridor, and it felt like a tomb. The stillness, the heavy silence. The cart had a sticky wheel and kept wanting to veer left. Petty wrestled it to the locker.

He took one last look at the money after opening the door. The plan he'd had for it seemed ridiculous now. He'd been fooling himself to think he could take care of Sam. He couldn't even take care of himself. One by one he lifted out the cash:

the bags from the lake, the bags that had been hidden in Tony's uncle's garage, the box containing the money from the piñatas. He piled them all onto the cart and slammed the locker shut. The sound echoed in the corridor like a gunshot.

Downstairs, he hesitated in the lobby. Now that Tinafey's life depended on the money, he was nervous about wheeling it down the street. He waited until the sidewalk cleared for a block in both directions before pushing the cart out to the Mercedes. He popped the trunk and quickly transferred the cash, not relaxing until it was locked up again.

Back behind the wheel, he couldn't think of what to do next. His hand hurt from pounding the dash, and he wondered if he'd busted something. He reached for the coffee in the console. It had gone cold, but he gulped some anyway. He opened the pancakes, smeared syrup on them, and managed to get one down. A fire truck came screaming past so close that it rocked the car. He decided it was smarter to keep moving than to sit in one place.

He drove aimlessly around MacArthur Park, Lafayette Park, Koreatown. West on Wilshire to Vermont, east on 6th to Alvarado. He couldn't follow the news on the radio, kept losing the thread of the stories, so he hit Scan and cycled through the stations twice before stopping on one playing classical music. It turned out to be Christmas songs, though. Fuck that. He shut off the radio and drank the rest of the coffee.

Without really meaning to, he ended up in front of the City Center Motel. He cruised past once, eyeing his and Tinafey's room, then made a U-turn at the next intersection, came back, and pulled into the parking lot. He was fairly certain the guy holding Tinafey was long gone but exercised caution just the same. He kept both hands visible as he slid out of the car and walked slowly to the stairs. At the bottom he paused and called out "Hello?" and got no response. He called again at the door, knocked, and again nothing.

He inserted the key card into the lock and pushed the door open when the light turned green. The room was empty. This was a disappointment. He'd half hoped to find Tinafey waiting for him. The room looked like it had been thoroughly searched. Empty drawers gaped at him, and Tinafey's bags had been dumped onto the floor. Petty stepped over piles of clothes and went to the safe. The cash it had held was gone.

He checked his phone. No call yet. He decided to move the money from the car into the room, thinking it'd be safer. It took him three trips to carry it all up. He slid the box and bags under the bed and rearranged the spread to cover them.

He turned on the TV and put on a poker tournament, tried to lose himself in the ebb and flow of cards shuffled and dealt, folded and mucked. One thought kept getting in the way—that he should visit Sam before things went any further. With so much dirty money changing hands, a hundred things could go wrong, the worst of which would mean he'd never see her again. His plan to pay her medical bills having turned to shit, the least he could do was say good-bye in case he disappeared forever.

He needed a shower, but a clean shirt and deodorant would have to do. He made sure the DO NOT DISTURB sign was hanging on the doorknob and checked the lock three times before leaving the room. Downstairs in the office, he paid the Indian guy who managed the motel for another night, not knowing if he'd be back before checkout at noon. The manager offered him a deal if he'd pony up for two more nights in advance, but Petty said no. One way or another, he'd be out of this dump today.

★   ★   ★

It was ten thirty when he got to the hospital. The elevator doors opened on Sam's floor, and Petty was shocked to see her standing there in the corridor.

"What are you doing?" he said.

"Walking," Sam said. "The doctor wants me on my feet."

Sam was accompanied by a tiny Filipina orderly whose main function was to push the IV pole and keep the tube that ran from the bag to Sam's arm free of kinks.

"Is this normal after one of these surgeries?" Petty asked the orderly.

"Sure, very normal," the orderly said.

"Take it easy," Petty said to Sam. "Baby steps."

He walked with them as they did another lap around the floor.

"Has the doctor been by?" he asked Sam.

"Not yet," Sam said.

"How do you feel?"

"Better than before. I'd been having headaches for the last month, like so bad they made me cry."

"And you didn't get a checkup?"

"I thought it was hangovers."

Petty made a sour face, and Sam grinned. "I'm fucking with you," she said.

When they got back to the room, Petty checked his phone again while the orderly helped Sam into bed. He'd told the guy he'd need an hour to pick up the money, and that was two hours ago. He wondered if he ought to call Tinafey's phone and let it be known he was ready to make the exchange instead of waiting to hear something.

"Hey," Sam said. Her exclamation brought Petty back to the room, back to the moment. She held out her phone. "Someone wants to say hi."

Petty took the phone and looked at the screen, at a photo of Sherman lying on his back in a pile of wrapping paper.

"Jessica says he misses me," Sam said.

"You'll be home soon," Petty said.

He handed the phone back, and Sam scrolled in search of other photos of Sherman. She showed him a few more, and he did his best to appear interested. The cat drinking from a faucet, the cat staring out a window. Sam suddenly remembered something. "I need you to do me a favor," she said, and asked Petty to pass her her bag. She pulled a black Sharpie out of it.

"Draw an eye on my bandage," she said.

"A what?" Petty said.

"An eye. A third eye. Like the third-eye chakra."

"I don't know what that means," Petty said.

Sam showed him a picture on her phone, a painting of a bald guy with a glowing eye in the middle of his forehead. "It's a Hindu thing," she said.

"You better get someone else," Petty said. "I can't draw for shit."

"It's easy," Sam said. "An eye. You can do it."

Petty reluctantly did as she'd requested, inking a very basic eye onto the dressing covering her head.

"That's as good as it's gonna get," he said when he finished.

Sam used her phone's camera to check his work. "Awesome," she said. She lifted her arm so that her tattoo, VERITAS, was also in the shot and took a selfie.

"The nurses are gonna freak," Petty said.

"They'll think I can read their minds," Sam said.

Carrie entered the room carrying a white paper bag and a Starbucks cup.

"Read whose mind?" she said.

Sam turned to face her. "Repeat after me," she said in

318

a deep, portentous voice. "I envision and create beauty and goodness in everything I do."

"That's creepy," Carrie said, noticing the eye. "Why do you want to be creepy?"

Sam laughed and took another photo of herself.

"I brought doughnuts," Carrie said. She set the bag on the bedside table. "You can have one, too," she said to Petty.

"I'm on my way out," Petty said.

"Take it with you."

"No, thanks."

Petty stepped to the bed to say good-bye to Sam. He'd pre-pared a short speech, something she'd maybe remember if this turned out to be the last time they saw each other, but now, with Carrie there, he lost his nerve.

"See you later," he said.

"Okay," Sam said.

"Call me if you hear anything."

"I will."

Petty touched Sam's shoulder, made sure she was paying at-tention. "I'm so proud of how you're handling this," he said, barely getting it out.

"What's wrong?" Sam said.

"Nothing," Petty said. "I think I'm getting a cold."

He turned and left the room without saying good-bye to Carrie. Everything was going to be fine, he told himself. He'd meet the guy, give him the money, get Tinafey back, and return to the hospital and good news about the tumor. Every-thing was going to be fine.

"Rowan!"

Carrie had followed him out and was trailing after him as he hurried to the elevator. He stopped and waited for her to catch up.

"Are you all right?" she said.

"I'm fine," he replied.

"No, you're not," she said. "I was married to you for almost ten years. I can tell when you're lying."

They'd been a good team in the beginning, the two of them against the world. Petty had liked that feeling, had enjoyed having a partner, but his contentment made him careless. He'd let his guard down, and to this day he was still ashamed to say that he never saw her betrayal coming, that it knocked the wind out of him and took him to his knees. He'd never forgive her for that, but he also couldn't help recalling the good times, both of them so young there for a minute, so happy, so *one*.

"I'm up against something," he said.

"What?" Carrie said.

"Let's just say I bit off more than I could chew."

"That's not like you."

"Tell me about it."

They moved aside to let a gurney pass. The old man strapped to it grimaced at the ceiling, showing yellow horse teeth.

"Almost there, boss," the orderly pushing him along said.

Carrie grimaced, too, then said to Petty, "You'll work it out."

"Sure," Petty said. "But if I don't, promise me you'll see Sam through this."

"Stop being dramatic."

"I mean it. You have to stay with her as long as she needs you."

"I'm not going anywhere, and neither are you."

"And don't bad-mouth me too much. I'm already on thin ice."

"Please," Carrie said. "I'm the one she's barely tolerating."

"So work your magic," Petty said. "You used to be able to convince anybody of anything."

"I know," Carrie said. "But something changed. Now I have a hard time even convincing myself."

Petty believed this was the first true thing that had come out of her mouth since she'd shown up in L.A.

"You make me nervous, talking like that," he said. "Next thing you know, you'll get religion."

"Fuck that," Carrie said.

"There. That's the Carrie I remember."

"Lil' Evil, right?" Carrie said. Lil' Evil was a nickname Petty had given her back in Jersey, something he got from a gang tag he saw on a wall.

"Lil' Motherfuckin' Evil," he said.

He pushed the call button for the elevator.

"I hope everything works out for you," Carrie said.

"Me, too," Petty said.

"And if it doesn't, it's been nice knowing you."

"Tell Hug to fuck off for me."

"I will."

The elevator arrived, and Petty stepped inside. As soon as the doors closed, he checked his phone. No calls had sneaked past him. He couldn't think of anything else to do but go back to the motel and wait for instructions from the guy holding Tinafey. He considered calling his mom, but she knew him well enough that she'd figure out something was wrong no matter how much happy talking he did, and there was no reason to upset her, because everything was going to be fine.

He drove back to the motel and climbed the stairs to the room. Again he imagined Tinafey waiting for him when he opened the door, having miraculously escaped her captor, and again he was disappointed. The room was freezing. He turned the heater up and kept his coat on, but none of it helped. He sat at the table, staring out the window at the parking lot, the empty swimming pool, and the dead white sky, and shivered all the way down to his bones.

Diaz brought Tinafey a glass of water and, because her hands were still tied, held it while she drank. That was her name, Tinafey. From Memphis. Diaz had been making conversation with her in order to put her at ease, but she wouldn't be so calm if she knew the truth, that she and her boyfriend were both as good as dead.

She finished drinking and sat back on the couch in the living room of Diaz's dad's house. Diaz asked if she wanted anything else.

"There's an apple," he said. "And some crackers."

"I don't want nothin' but to get out of here," Tinafey said. She glanced around the room, wrinkling her nose at the dust and clutter. Diaz imagined it must look pretty creepy in the grim light that forced its way through the filthy windows, like the killer's lair in a movie or someplace haunted. Which was pretty on the mark either way, considering the two dead bodies he'd had to step over in the kitchen to get to the sink.

His dad was already starting to smell. He'd noticed it while getting the water. The odor hadn't congealed into a stink yet, but there was definitely a primal must in the air that tickled the back of your throat and raised the hair on your arms. Maybe Tinafey smelled it, too, and that's why she kept fidgeting like she couldn't get comfortable.

Diaz turned up the radio. Tinafey wouldn't choose a station, so he left it on the oldies his dad had listened to. The Delfonics were on now: "La La Means I Love You." Diaz remembered whispering the lyrics during a slow dance in junior high, his sweaty hands cupping his date's ass.

Two in the afternoon. Three more hours until dark. Diaz had held off contacting Rowan, his thought being he'd keep the guy on edge, keep him worried about his girl, so that when Diaz finally did call, he'd be eager to turn over the money in order to get her back. Now, though, he began to wonder if he was putting too much pressure on the dude, pressure that might drive him to the cops or somebody else for help. Maybe touching base wouldn't be a bad thing after all.

He picked up Tinafey's phone and sent Rowan a text.

Got it?

Got it came back seconds later, the dude obviously waiting for word about what was going on.

Further instructions soon, Diaz texted. There. That should hold the guy for another couple hours.

The place Diaz had picked for their meeting was in the warehouse district, down by the river. The area was deserted after dark, a graveyard given over to scavenging rats and wild dogs. Trains rattled past occasionally, but the intersection where the rendezvous would take place was out of sight of any tracks. The perfect spot to get rid of a couple of low-life thieves.

He cleared a pile of newspapers off a chair and took a seat facing the couch.

"This freak you out?" he said to Tinafey, nodding at the gun in his hand.

"I don't know," she said. "You gonna use it on me?"

"Not if you behave yourself."

"You got me tied up. How'm I gonna misbehave?"

"You bitches always got something up your sleeves."

"Uh-uh," Tinafey said. "You don't know me well enough to be calling me a bitch."

Diaz wasn't in the mood to play games with her. They listened to the radio, and Diaz ran through things in his head, how it would go from here on out. He'd tell Petty to be by the river at six, but he'd show up early and cruise the neighborhood, keeping an eye out for anything suspicious. He'd park in one place for a while, then move to another spot, then another. If someone was planning an ambush, this might spook them into jumping the gun. Assuming everything checked out okay, at six he'd roll up to the corner where Rowan was supposed to meet him. He'd use his dad's truck, make Rowan put the money in the shell. When he had it all in there, *bang*. Then the girl. *Bang*. Leave them where they fell.

But what if his dad wouldn't lend him the truck? He was still pissed about the Toyota. Diaz had totaled it after taking it without asking when he was fifteen, and the old man was on him about it all the time, calling him irresponsible. Diaz's head snapped back so hard he bit his tongue. He'd dozed off, his lack of sleep catching up to him as soon as he stopped moving. Just as he was coming to, he thought he saw Tinafey get up off the couch and step toward him. He blinked himself to full wakefulness, and it was true; the girl was on her feet. He pointed the gun at her.

"What are you doing?" he said.

"Stretchin' my legs," she said.

"Well, sit the fuck down," he said. "And don't move again without my say-so."

"Yes, sir," she said, trying to be cute about it. She gestured with her bound hands at a framed piece of needlepoint hanging on the wall and asked, "What's that say?" It was something that had been there forever, something Diaz's mom had made. *Donde hay amor en el corazón, hay alegría en el hogar.*

"When there's love in the heart, there's happiness in the house," Diaz said.

"*Amor*—that's 'love,' right?" Tinafey said.

"Right," Diaz said.

"I wanna learn Spanish," Tinafey said. "It sounds so pretty."

"You know *amor*," Diaz said. "That's a good start."

"And *hola* and *adiós*," Tinafey said. "*Por favor. Gracias.* I went to Mexico once, to Cabo San Lucas."

"Cabo's nice," Diaz said. A little more small talk. Fine. It'd help keep him awake. "What else do you know?" he said.

"*Feliz Navidad*," Tinafey said. "That's 'Merry Christmas.'"

"Try this: *Dame dos margaritas.*"

"*Dame dos margaritas.*"

"That's 'Give me'—*Dame*—'two margaritas.'"

"*Dame dos margaritas,*" Tinafey said. "Teach me somethin' else."

"*La cuenta, por favor,*" Diaz said. "'The check, please,' like in a restaurant."

"*La cuenta, por favor,*" Tinafey said.

They went back and forth like that. Every so often Diaz would quiz the girl on phrases he'd taught her earlier, and she always got them right. He remembered seeing a can of coffee in the kitchen cupboard and a coffee machine on the counter and decided to make a pot. He stepped in a puddle of blood while filling the basket, and his shoes left prints on the linoleum. He thought about cleaning up the mess, but why, when the last part of his plan was burning down the house?

29

THE CALL CAME AT FIVE. PETTY WAS LYING ON THE BED, EYES closed but wide awake, listening to the blood roar through his veins like a secret underground river. When his phone rang he sat up, instantly alert.

"Be at the corner of Mission Road and Artemus Street at six," the guy said. "You and the money and that's it. I'm watching the corner right now, and if I get a bad feeling, I'll pull out, and your girl will die."

"How will I spot you?" Petty said.

"I'll blink my headlights three times."

Petty was standing now, pacing the room. He felt like he was full of helium, like his feet were barely touching the floor.

"Let me talk to Tinafey," he said.

"Hello?" Tinafey said.

"Say something so I know it's you."

"You still gonna get me that trophy?"

"The biggest one you ever saw."

"Six o'clock. Mission and Artemus," the guy said.

Petty pulled up a map on his phone. With traffic, the meeting place was twenty minutes away. He dragged the money out from under the bed and carried it down to the Mercedes. When everything was locked in the trunk, he got in the car and sat behind the wheel. He decided to wait a bit before taking off. He didn't want to be early to the meeting, and he didn't want to be late.

He zipped his coat and flipped up the collar. It was going to be another cold night, coldest of the year, the weatherman had said. Frost warnings across the region. The motel manager was sweeping the parking lot in shorts, a T-shirt, and flip-flops. What fucking part of India was he from that he could take the chill like that?

At five thirty-five Petty started the car. The phone directions took him on the 110 to the 101 to Mission Road. He made good time and arrived at the exit five minutes early. Instead of turning right like he was supposed to, he went left and passed under the freeway to park in front of a restaurant-supply store on the other side. The store was closed, and there were no other vehicles in the lot. He kept the Mercedes running.

One minute passed. Two. He checked his watch every thirty seconds. At exactly five fifty-nine he pulled out of the lot, took a right on Mission, and drove back under the freeway. Continuing south, he passed a sprawling public housing complex, a recycling center, and a cluster of small factories locked behind razor-wire fences and steel security gates.

Most of the streetlights weren't working, which left entire blocks swathed in darkness. Petty drove slowly, juddering over railroad tracks and steering around bottomless potholes. A pair of headlights appeared in his rearview mirror, but they'd disappeared by the time he reached Artemus. He pulled to the side of the road. Artemus dead-ended into a warehouse at Mission, and the three-way intersection was deserted.

A faint mist hung in the air, enough to blur the edges of the buildings and halo the orange sodium-vapor lights. Petty lowered his window and shut off the engine. The harsh stutter of a Jake-braking semi drifted over from the freeway. Closer, a train horn bleated. Petty squinted into the mist and detected movement. A truck solidified out of the night, an older Ford pickup with its lights off, running dark. It came to a stop in a patch of shadow on the opposite corner, facing Petty's Mercedes. Its high beams flashed three times.

Petty stepped out of the car with his hands up.

"Nice and slow," a voice called from the truck.

"Tinafey?" Petty called back.

A light went on in the cab of the pickup. Petty saw Tinafey sitting on the passenger side. The driver, a Mexican, was holding a gun to her head. The light went out. Petty walked back to the trunk of the Benz, opened it, and lifted out the box containing the money from the piñatas. He carried it to the middle of the intersection and paused there.

The Mexican got out of the truck.

"Bring it here and put it in back," he said.

Petty walked the rest of the way across the intersection, the Mexican tracking him with his pistol. The door to the shell was unlocked. Petty opened it and set the box in the bed of the truck. The Mexican kept the gun on him as he returned to the Mercedes.

"It'll take me two more trips," Petty said to him.

"Hurry it up," the Mexican said.

Petty's ears were cold, but sweat trickled down his back. He could see his breath when the light hit it. For his next load he chose the shopping bags that came from the garage, carried them by their handles. He glanced into the truck as he passed by and caught another glimpse of Tinafey. He put the bags into the shell and went back to the Mercedes as fast as he could without running.

He reached into the trunk and took out the last package, the trash bag Tony had hauled from the lake. He shut the trunk and was about to hustle to the pickup when he spotted someone approaching down Artemus, someone walking quickly but keeping to the shadows. Black pants, black coat, black ski mask, black sawed-off shotgun. Adrenaline surged through Petty's wiring. He dropped the money and sprinted for the pickup.

The Mexican hadn't yet noticed the intruder. He aimed his pistol at Petty and shouted, "Hold it, motherfucker!"

The mystery man stepped into the intersection, into a smear of orange light. He pointed the shotgun at the Mexican and roared, "Drop your weapon!"

The Mexican swung his gun toward the intruder. Petty ducked and wrapped his arms around his head as he passed between the men. Both fired at once. Petty hit the ground, rolled, and kept going.

The blast from the shotgun shattered the pickup's windshield. Pellets whizzed through the air. The Mexican crouched behind his open door in time and was unhurt, but his rounds all missed their mark. The mystery man jacked another shell into the chamber of the sawed-off.

Petty reached the truck. He yanked open the passenger door, nauseated with dread. Tinafey had slid off her seat and lay curled on the floor of the cab. Her hands were tied, and she was covered with shards of glass. Petty's heart started again when she looked up at him.

"About fuckin' time," she said.

The Mexican, still huddled behind his door, glanced their way. Rage twisted his mouth, and he pointed his gun at them, but Tinafey kicked his forearm as he pulled the trigger. The bullet punched a hole in the roof of the cab. The intruder fired again, and Petty dove on top of Tinafey as pellets buzzed around them like a swarm of angry insects, burrowing into vinyl and plastic. His left hand burned where one grazed him.

The Mexican had been hit, too. One side of his face was dotted with bloody freckles. He turned his gun on the mystery man and popped off more rounds. Petty backed out of the cab, and Tinafey scrabbled after him. They crouched and ran to the rear of the truck, putting steel between them and the gunfight.

The shotgun boomed again, like a giant stomping his foot. Petty heard the Mexican grunt. He lowered himself to the ground and peered under the truck, watched the dude drop to the pavement.

"Show yourself, Rowan!" the intruder shouted, and Petty recognized the voice.

"Hug!" he said. "What the fuck is this?"

Hug McCarthy approached the pickup cautiously, shotgun first. "A robbery," he said from behind his ski mask. "Come out with your hands up."

Petty helped Tinafey to her feet, and they side stepped slowly into the open.

Hug went wide to come around the open driver's-side door, kept the shotgun ready. The Mexican lay sprawled on his back on the damp pavement. His eyes were closed, and Petty couldn't tell if he was breathing. One arm extended out from his side, the other was twisted behind his back. Hug moved in, lowering the sawed-off until it was pointing at the guy's head.

"Turn over," Hug said to him.

The Mexican didn't respond, gave no evidence of having even heard the command.

"Hey, shitheel, turn over," Hug said again. By now he was standing above the dude. He prodded him with the toe of his boot. The Mexican rolled suddenly onto his side and brought the arm he'd been lying on straight up, the gun clutched in his fist. He fired twice before Hug could react. Both rounds slammed into Hug's chin, tore through his brain, and rocketed out the top of his head, accompanied by geysers of black blood.

Hug dropped the shotgun but stayed on his feet. He stumbled backwards into the intersection before crumpling. The Mexican jumped up, ran to where Hug was sitting like a man staring into a campfire, and pumped another bullet into him. He bent and pulled off the ski mask.

"Who is this?" he yelled to Petty.

"His name's Hug McCarthy," Petty said.

"And you guys were gonna rip me off?"

"Man, I have no idea what he was doing here."

The Mexican pondered this, then pointed his gun at Petty.

"Get the rest of the money," he said, jerking his head toward the last bag, the one Petty had dropped near the Mercedes.

Petty considered making a run for it but couldn't figure out how to communicate this to Tinafey, so instead he started for the car. He heard an engine rev and saw a pair of headlights zooming up Artemus. The Mexican faced the lights, too. A Range Rover popped out of the darkness and bore down on both of them. Petty ran back toward the pickup and Tinafey. The Mexican panicked and took off in the opposite direction, north on Mission. He fired wildly at the Range Rover as he fled. The Range Rover squealed around the corner and slammed into him before he'd gone fifty feet, mowed him down and rolled over him.

Brake lights flared as the vehicle came to a stop. The Mexican was lying on his side, moaning and thrashing about. The driver of the Range Rover got out, walked back to stand over him, and pointed a gun. Two shots boomed, and the Mexican went limp. The shooter then hurried to Hug's body. It was Carrie. She knelt, wrapped her arms around Hug, and cradled him against her.

Petty walked over. Carrie's eyes were closed, and she was humming a song into Hug's ear. Petty took the gun from her. She didn't resist.

"What's going on?" he said.

Carrie shook her head. She couldn't or wouldn't talk.

Petty tapped the back of her head with the barrel of the pistol. "Carrie," he said. "What's going on?"

She sniffed hard and cleared her throat but kept her eyes shut while she spoke.

"We got a call from Avi a few days ago," she said. "Hug did a job for him a while back. He wanted to know where you were and what you were doing. I said I hadn't heard from you in years. 'If you do, give me a shout,' he said. 'I'll make it worth your while.' The very next day your mom called about Sam and about you being out here, and I let him know."

She glanced up at Petty. He saw tears on her cheeks. "I'm sorry," she said, "but we were in a deep, dark fucking hole, and this was our only way out. Avi told us about the money he was after and said we could keep a third of whatever we got. That sounded good to us. That sounded like a lifesaver."

She sat back and wiped her face with her palms.

"We hauled ass out here," she continued. "Found you at the hospital. Hug wanted to beat it out of you, where the money was, or if there even *was* any money, but I said, 'Why push it?' We knew where you'd be. We could take it slow. He tailed you some, enough to find out where you were staying and that you were definitely up to no good, but we held off until this morning, when you told me something was wrong. I let Hug know, and we went back to watching you, stuck to you all day." She gazed down at the corpse in her arms. "And now here we are," she said.

Petty was still shaken from the firefight, felt it in his hands, his feet. He was angry at himself, too, for not noticing that Hug had been following him, for getting played once again. Right now, though, he had to keep moving. With all the shooting, someone surely must have called the cops.

He left Carrie sitting with Hug and ran to pick up the money he'd dropped in the street. After returning it to the trunk of the Mercedes, he hurried back to the pickup, where Tinafey was waiting, and untied her wrists.

"You all right?" he said.

"What the fuck you think?" she said as she rubbed the feeling back into her hands.

"Can you help me out?"

"Gimme your coat," she said with a shiver.

Petty took off his jacket and passed it to her. She put it on and followed him to the bed of the truck. He gave her the bags, and he carried the box. They jogged to the Mercedes and put the money in the trunk. Before slamming the lid, Petty reached into one of the bags and pulled out a stack of hundreds.

"Get in," he said to Tinafey. "I'll be right back."

He walked over to Carrie.

"Here," he said and gave her the cash.

"What's this?" she said.

"All you're gonna get. Be grateful for it."

"So you won, huh?"

"If I was you, I'd hit the road."

"Help me get Hug into the car."

"He's dead."

"Help me get him into the car."

The fewer corpses in the street, the better, Petty decided. He hooked Hug under the arms, and Carrie took his feet. They half carried, half dragged him to the Range Rover and wrestled him into the backseat. Carrie's hands were covered with blood. She wiped them on her jeans and walked around and got behind the wheel. Petty spoke to her through the open window.

"Drive as far as you can before daylight," he said. "Then get rid of the body and the car and lay low for a while."

"What about Sam?" Carrie said.

"I'll see to her."

Carrie started the car and flipped down the visor to check her face in the mirror on the back of it. She scratched at a speck of blood on her lip.

"I can do this," she said to her reflection.

"Sure you can," Petty said.

She drove off down Mission toward the freeway. Petty took one more look around the intersection—the pickup, the dead man. Wanting to leave the area as clean as possible, he ran over and scooped up the guy's pistol and Hug's shotgun and threw them onto the backseat of the Mercedes. As soon as he had a chance, he'd bury them so deep nobody would ever find them.

"Hear those sirens?" Tinafey said when he climbed into the car.

"I hear them," he said. He made a U-turn. The freeway was only a few blocks away.

"This is some fucked-up shit," Tinafey said.

"We're gonna be fine," Petty said, because what else was he going to say?

They got to the on-ramp without seeing a cop, merged onto the 101, and joined the stream of cars heading west. Petty's pulse slowed a bit, and the ringing in his ears faded. He reached over and squeezed Tinafey's hand and was glad when she squeezed back. Her head was turned to look out the rear window, to see if anyone was following.

Petty's phone rang. It was sitting on the dash. He was busy negotiating the transition to the 110 and couldn't get to it.

"Can you check who that is?" he said to Tinafey.

She picked up the phone and held it out so he could see the screen.

"It's the hospital," she said.

30

Papa Smurf's used-car lot, Best Auto Sales, was north of downtown Houston, across the street from a Walmart Supercenter. Petty parked in front of the office, a mobile home set on a cinder-block foundation. The red, white, and blue pennants strung overhead snapped like firecrackers in the cold wind. Two salespeople, a black man and a white woman, hunched over cigarettes on the lee side of the single-wide. They nodded and said "Howdy" as Petty climbed the stairs to the office and went inside.

Papa's real name was Chris Peters. He got his nickname from his side business. Actually, it was his main business, the car lot merely serving as a front for his real source of income, money laundering. Launderers were sometimes called Smurfs, after the cartoon characters, and the means by which they legitimized illegitimate funds was known as Smurfing. As far as Petty could determine, this was because the army of day laborers and dope fiends required to scrub any significant amount of cash had reminded someone of the busy blue elves.

The reception area of Best was furnished with a water cooler and a few chairs. A Texas state flag hung on one wall, posters of luxury cars on another. A little Christmas tree blinked in the corner, and the receptionist's desk had been draped with red and green garlands. The receptionist picked up the phone to let Papa know Petty had arrived and went back to reading her *Enquirer*.

Papa came out and shook Petty's hand. He was a fat man who wore chili-pepper-patterned suspenders over Brooks Brothers button-downs and alligator-skin cowboy boots with pressed khakis. A fringe of bright red hair ringed his otherwise bald head, and he waxed the ends of his handlebar mustache into two tight curls.

"Rowan, old buddy, always a pleasure to see ya," he said with an amiable drawl.

"Nice to see you, too," Petty said.

They'd done business in the past, but nothing involving anywhere near the amount of cash they'd be talking about today. Papa led Petty down the hall to his office and told him to have a seat. More Texas crap covered the walls, and a Stetson hung from a set of mounted bull horns. Papa dropped into a big chair behind a big desk and leaned so far back it seemed he might tip over.

"What can I do you for?" he said.

"I've got some money I want to send overseas," Petty said.

"How much?"

"Close to two million."

Papa tried to play it off, but Petty could tell he'd surprised the man when he sat upright and began fiddling with a pen lying on the desk, rolling it between his fingers like a baton twirler. He wanted to ask Petty where he'd gotten so much money, but that was against the rules, so he settled for, "How hot is it?"

"Getting colder by the day," Petty said.

"You know the deal, how it goes," Papa said.

Petty said he did, but Papa still went through the steps. Petty would give him the cash, and he'd divide it among his Smurfs. These Smurfs, over the course of a few months, would make a series of deposits into some of the hundreds of accounts Papa controlled at various banks across the country. All the deposits would be in amounts of less than ten thousand dollars so that the banks wouldn't be required to report them to the IRS.

The money would then be gradually wire-transferred to a bank in China, a country with lax reporting laws and one not likely to cooperate with American authorities of any stripe. Petty would be provided with ATM and credit cards giving him access to his funds in the Chinese bank, minus the 30 percent Papa took for his services.

Petty's eyes wandered while Papa explained all this. He looked at the cowboy hat hanging from the horns, looked at the bronze sculpture of a bronc rider sitting on the desk and the old-fashioned adding machine next to it. His gaze lighted on a framed photo of a younger Papa—full head of hair, no mustache—hugging a little redheaded freckle-faced girl who had the same smile he did. Petty stared at the picture, testing himself. For a second he thought his grief had eased some, gone from being a raw, oozing sore to a dull throb he could manage. But not yet. A flood of acid tears stung his eyes, and the cold, black snake lurking inside him coiled tighter around his heart.

She had another seizure. All alone in the darkest dark. The doctors did what they could, which was exactly nothing. The tumor had turned out to be a bad one, the worst, a glioblastoma. "Picture an octopus," Dr. Wilkes said. They'd been able to remove its body, but the tentacles remained, and Sam had had another seizure, and it killed her.

That's what they called to tell Petty the night of the shootout. "We have bad news." At first he thought he was going to lose it. Surely there had to be a limit to how much a man could deal with at one time.

"Pull over," Tinafey kept saying. "Let me drive."

But instead of breaking down, he shifted into problem-solving mode, and his thinking was as clear as ever.

"I'll drop you at the hotel," he said to Tinafey.

"I'm goin' with you," she said.

"It's not your problem."

"Go to your daughter. Now."

Sam's body still lay on a gurney in intensive care. An orderly drew back the sheet so Petty could see her. It wasn't her, though, not anymore. Petty didn't know what had made Sam Sam, but whatever it was was gone. He reached out and touched the cold clay that remained.

Tinafey was standing beside him. "She looks peaceful," she said.

Petty took her word for it. He couldn't bring himself to look at Sam's face. Watching her sleep all those years ago, a baby sighing and stretching in a patch of sunlight, he'd never imagined that one day he'd see her dead. He felt alone again, like he'd felt before she was born. It hadn't been a good feeling then, and it wasn't a good feeling now.

A woman took him to an office. She apologized all the way there. "It's a terrible time for this, but there are documents that have to be signed." Petty scribbled his signature on the papers she put in front of him without bothering to read them. The woman asked what he wanted to do with the body. "We have a list of funeral homes," she said.

Petty picked one at random and called from the cafeteria. The man who answered acted sympathetic at first but quickly launched into a sales pitch. You couldn't get colder than that, Petty thought, but on the other hand, what a perfect time to pick someone's pocket. They settled on fifteen hundred bucks all in—transport, cremation, and a box for the ashes.

Petty called his mom next. She took the news hard. All the years Petty had been roaming the country, chasing down scores, she and Sam had been close, each the only family the other had had. It was rough listening to her go to pieces. Petty had never heard her weep like that, not even when she found out his dad had been killed. He felt like he might weep, too, but no, not there in the fucking cafeteria, in front of the bored girl at the cash register and the orderly eating a burrito and the janitor mopping the floor. Joanne said she was flying out, hip surgery or no hip surgery. Petty told her that wasn't necessary. He'd bring Sam to her.

He thought the police might appear at the hospital or be waiting at the motel when he and Tinafey returned after midnight, but nobody leaped out of the shadows to slap handcuffs on him. They stayed at the motel just long enough to pack their bags, then Petty drove to the Marriott at Staples Center and checked them into a room on the sixteenth floor that had a view all the way to the ocean. He got dizzy looking out at it and had to sit on the bed. "I'm probably just hungry," he told Tinafey. He ordered food from room service but fell asleep before his burger arrived.

He spent the next three days in bed, drifting somewhere between asleep and awake, between alive and dead, unable to muster the strength to swim to shore. Every breath was an effort. He couldn't bear to be touched, couldn't string words into sentences. He only cried once. A knife to the chest, a clutch of strangled sobs, and a few fiery tears that gave him no relief. It wasn't any kind of grief he'd ever heard of.

On the second day he put on the news to see if they were saying anything about the shoot-out. There was a story on an investigation into a body found shot to death on an East L.A. street, that of a recently discharged army sergeant, Armando Diaz, and the subsequent discovery of two more corpses in a house in Boyle Heights, one of them being Diaz's father, Hector Diaz, the other his cousin Antonio Mendoza, age twenty-one. Speculation was that all the killings were connected to the drug trade. Petty turned off the TV and had Tinafey pour two bottles of minibar Scotch into a glass. He tossed back the drink and felt sick for an hour afterward. All night long he thought he heard cops out in the hall.

On the morning of the fourth day, he sat straight up out of a dream weird with numbers and was suddenly wildly alert. He rolled to the edge of the mattress, stood, and felt the floor level and steady beneath his feet. The worst seemed to have passed.

"You okay?" Tinafey said.

"Okay enough," he said, which was all he'd ever been anyway.

He put on his clothes, went down to breakfast, and came up with a plan.

Papa pulled one side of his mustache, straightening the curl. When he let go, it sprang back into place. He was asking for an exact amount. Petty blinked his eyes clear and got back to business. He gave Papa the figure, and Papa punched it into the adding machine and yanked the handle. He tore off the strip of paper that showed how much money Petty was entrusting him with, what his cut would be, and how much Petty would have left afterward.

"Your receipt, suh," he said, passing the tape across the desk with a flourish.

Petty glanced at the numbers and stuck the tape in his pocket. This was all the ink there'd be between them. Papa stood and tucked in his shirt. He opened the top drawer of the desk, took out a pistol, and slipped it into his waistband at the small of his back. Petty followed him through the reception area and back out to where his car was parked. He was now driving a white 2014 BMW 320i, having traded in the Benz in Arizona.

Papa called over the salesman Petty had seen on his way in. The salesman drew a gun from an ankle holster and stood guard while Petty and Papa took the money out of the trunk of the Beamer. Petty had managed to fit it all into three large duffel bags, so it only took them one trip to carry it into the mobile home. They stashed the bags in a safe in Papa's office.

"I'll move it to Fort Knox this afternoon," Papa said. "That's my other facility, the one where you get shot if you get within a hundred feet."

They shook hands good-bye.

"You doin' anything special for Christmas?" Papa said.

"Not really," Petty said, knowing Papa was only asking to be nice.

Petty headed out. He drove two hours to Lake Charles, where he checked into a room at the Isle of Capri Casino. He'd been stopping at casinos every night this trip, using them to do his own laundering of some of the hundred grand he'd held onto. He locked most of the money and Sam's ashes in the room before going down to the hotel's restaurant and having the blackened redfish special and a margarita for dinner.

The casino was housed in a paddle-wheel riverboat permanently docked on the lake next to the hotel. Petty cashed in five grand at the cage, took it all in hundred-dollar chips. He played an hour of blackjack at a twenty-five-dollar table, switched to craps until that went cold, then moved on to roulette, where it was just him, the croupier, and a deeply tanned old woman in big sunglasses who blew the smoke from her cigarettes out of the corner of her mouth.

He was down about a hundred dollars at the end of the night. He returned to the cage, cashed in his remaining chips, and asked for the money in a check. The next morning he deposited the check into one of his bank accounts. If anybody ever asked where the money had come from, he'd say he'd had a good run at the tables, and the check would serve as proof. It was the same routine the next night in the poker room at the Pensacola dog track, only there he walked away a winner, up four hundred.

Petty helped his mom out of the BMW at Pass-a-Grille Beach. She steadied herself with her cane before setting off across the parking lot. She was wearing a tropical print dress and a crown of little white flowers. They were at the end of the peninsula, where the beach was nearly deserted. A lone jogger and an old couple walking hand in hand were the only people in sight. A fat orange sun hovered an inch above the horizon. It was important to Joanne that they pour Sam's ashes into the ocean right as it set, and she hobbled as fast as she could over the sand toward the whispering waves.

Petty walked beside her, carrying the box containing the ashes and a bouquet of marigolds.

"Slow down," he said. "We've got time."

The sun touched the sea as they reached the shoreline. Petty opened the box and the plastic bag inside and passed the box to Joanne.

"Do you pray?" Joanne said.

"No," Petty said. "But you go ahead."

Joanne bowed her head and addressed Sam directly, telling her how much she loved her and how much she'd miss her. "Your dad's here with me," she said, "and he loves and misses you, too, but we're both happy you're at peace now, at rest, bathed in God's healing light."

Petty watched the sun go down while his mom spoke, watched it collapse into its reflection until all that remained was a white-hot horizon and single pink cloud floating in a purple sky. The sea murmured comfortingly, so vast, so calm.

"In the midst of life, we are in death," his mom said. She had kicked off her flip-flops and waded into the water until it reached her knees. She tipped the box and poured out the ashes. "Earth to earth, ashes to ashes, dust to dust, in sure and certain hope of the Resurrection."

The breeze caught the ashes and wafted them out to sea. Petty tossed the marigolds after them, and he and Joanne walked up the beach to dry sand and sat on a dune until daylight faded and the first stars appeared. A squadron of pelicans flew past, all in a line, hurrying home. Another bird, this one unseen, skirled and was answered. The air cooled quickly. Petty was conscious of the warmth of Joanne's arm against his. She had a sweater in the car. He asked if she wanted him to get it.

"No," she said. "It's time to go."

They had dinner at the Don CeSar Hotel, a pink Spanish-style castle that had towered over Saint Pete Beach since 1928. They sat in front of a floor-to-ceiling aquarium teeming with candy-colored tropical fish. It was Christmas Eve, and lots of families had gathered at the restaurant. The kids were unsure at first how to act in their dress-up clothes but soon got comfortable enough to chase one another under the tables and yell, "Hey! Hey!" at the moray eels and octopuses in the fish tanks.

Joanne tried to get Petty to split the grouper with her.

"I'll never be able to finish it on my own," she said.

"Take the leftovers home and feed them to your cat," Petty said.

"No, no. I'll just have a salad, then."

"If you want the grouper, get the grouper," Petty said. "My treat."

"Ha!" Joanne said. "So you're in the money these days."

"I've got enough to pay for your fish," Petty said.

They went back to Joanne's condo afterward. She made Irish coffees and kept apologizing for not having a Christmas tree. Petty had planned to check into a hotel, but Joanne insisted he stay with her. He slept in Sam's old room, in her old bed, and stared at her Foo Fighters and Gwen Stefani posters. He'd worried this might be too much for him, but he held up fine.

The next day, Christmas, he and Joanne went to a movie that he forgot as soon as it was over and then to a Chinese restaurant. He stayed another night with her and got back on the road.

Avi showed up at his office bright and early on the morning of December 29. Petty had been staking out the place for most of the past two days but had begun to worry that the guy might have moved his base of operations, even though Golden Triangle Mining was listed on the building's directory and there was still a sign for the company on the door to suite 304. The building was up toward Aventura, a new three-story stucco box with retro deco lines. The other tenants were

mostly connected to the medical field: doctors, physical thera-
pists, a dental clinic.

Avi lived in a gated community in Coral Gables, and the
boiler room for Golden Triangle was in an industrial park
near the airport. Avi didn't spend much time there. The
lowlifes who worked the phones disgusted him. He ran the
scam from the office, he and a secretary, a new girl every
couple of months, depending on when Avi got tired of banging the old one.

Petty, parked at the edge of the lot, watched him pull
up in his yellow Porsche Cayman and go into the building,
yammering into his phone the whole way. When the door
closed behind him, Petty reached under his seat for the
gun Carrie had used in the shoot-out and stuck it into the
pocket of his coat. He was supremely calm as he got out
of the car. He could have been walking into the supermarket when he entered the building, went to the elevator, and
pushed the Up button. He could have been taking out the
trash. He'd rehearsed what was coming next, gone over it
again and again. He'd even acted out the scene in baby talk,
like Beck had that night.

The third floor was deserted. Golden Triangle was at the
end of the corridor. It pissed Petty off that Avi had left the
door to the office unlocked, that he was so certain he was
safe from blowback. Petty stepped into the suite with his gun
drawn. Avi's secretary wasn't at her desk, had the week off,
Petty guessed, for the holidays. Avi's office door was open, and
Petty could see him standing with his back to him, looking out
the window, still on the phone.

Petty crossed the reception area and walked into the office.
Avi glimpsed Petty's reflection in the window and turned to
look over his shoulder. His eyes widened when he noticed the

gun, but that was it. He was thicker now than the last time Petty had seen him, on the road to fat. A scattering of plugs dotted the expanse of pink skin between his receding hairline and brow.

"I've got to go," he said into his phone and ended the call.

"Keep your hands where I can see them," Petty said.

"This is about L.A., isn't it?" Avi said. He tried a smile. "I'm in big trouble, right?"

"On your knees," Petty said.

"Seriously?" Avi said.

"Now," Petty said.

Avi dropped to his knees.

"Whatever this is, we can work it out," he said.

"Tell me about the money," Petty said. "The army money, from the beginning."

"The beginning?" Avi said.

Petty put the gun to his head. Avi wet his lips and swallowed hard.

"Don called me with his crazy story," he said. "You were in Reno, so I told him, 'What the hell, let's see if Rowan'll bite.' The plan was, if the money turned out to be real, we'd take it off you and split it fifty-fifty."

"And you actually thought you could get over on me like that?" Petty said.

"What I thought was that if that money was really there, you'd be the guy who'd be able to get it. Which is a compliment, right?"

"You were using me. That's no compliment."

"We use people for a living, Rowan. We do what we have to to get what we want."

"Finish the story," Petty said.

"I had a guy tail you to L.A.," Avi continued. "He was supposed to keep an eye on you and take the money if you found it, but all of a sudden he stopped calling in. I should've dropped the whole thing right then, but I'm a nut. I started really, really wanting that money, and I started really, really wanting to fuck you over."

Avi's phone rang.

"Leave it," Petty said.

Avi squirmed and grimaced, uncomfortable, waiting for the phone to quiet.

"My knees are trashed," he said. "Can I sit?"

"No," Petty said.

"Can you at least put the gun away?"

"No. Go on."

"I called Carrie to try to track you down," Avi said. "She called back and said you were in L.A. and that she and Hug were going there, too, something about Sam being in the hospital. We cut a deal, and that's the last I heard. So really, it's me who should be asking what the fuck is going on."

Still holding the gun on Avi, Petty tapped at his phone. Avi's phone beeped.

"Check your messages," Petty said.

Avi opened the text from Petty. Four photos: Avi's wife and kids at Whole Foods, at Chuck E. Cheese's, at the beach, and in the front yard of Avi's house. Petty had followed them for a couple of hours the day before.

"My family?" Avi said. "How dare you?"

Petty smacked him with the gun.

"Don't talk to me about family," he said.

Avi's bravado disappeared. He crumpled to the floor like a deflated balloon.

"Please, Rowan," he said.

"Facedown," Petty said.

Avi stretched out and buried his nose in the carpet. Petty pressed the gun to the back of his head.

"Here's what's going to happen," he said. "I'm leaving, and the minute I walk out, I don't exist anymore. Forget my name, forget my face, and forget about the money. If I ever suspect you're dogging me again, even if it's just a funny feeling and goose bumps, I'll be back, and if I come back, your whole life goes up in flames. Are we clear?"

"My whole life in flames," Avi said.

"Same goes for Don. If I ever see him again, I'll skin him alive with my teeth."

"I'll tell him."

Petty backed toward the door.

"You'd have done the same," Avi said.

"What?" Petty said.

"I'm sorry for trying to get over on you, but you'd have done exactly the same thing."

"No," Petty said. "No, I wouldn't have."

"Okay, okay," Avi said. "But just between you and me and the Staten Island ferry, did you find the money?"

"I don't know what you're talking about," Petty said.

He closed the office door, closed the door to the suite, and took the stairs at a run.

The two Mexican soldiers standing in the lobby of the Grand Solmar resort looked Petty over as he passed by on his way to the restaurant. They were just kids, but mean kids carrying machine guns and wearing shiny combat boots. Petty kept a nonchalant grin on his face even though alarms blared inside him.

Ever since leaving L.A. he'd been checking online daily for more news about Tony and his cousin, but nothing had shown up. He'd relaxed a bit when he had no problem flying from Miami to Cabo San Lucas, but it was going to be a long time before he stopped imagining cops lurking everywhere and panicking at the sight of a uniform.

The soldiers waved good-bye to one of the bellmen and left the lobby through the front door. Petty walked out the back and passed by one of the resort's infinity pools, where rich, tanned guests lounged on chaises and in cabanas and nursed tropical cocktails. A blond girl in a tiny black bikini swayed to chill music oozing out of hidden speakers, and a big buff dude rubbed sunscreen on the chest of another big buff dude.

The open-air restaurant was tucked under a circular thatched roof, the poles and palm fronds of which framed post-card views of an endless beach, a sparkling sea, and a pale blue sky. Petty took off his sunglasses and scanned the dining room. The restaurant host appeared, his smile as white as his guayabera.

"One for lunch?" he said.

"I'm meeting someone," Petty replied.

He spotted Tinafey at a table overlooking the ocean and crossed the restaurant to join her. She wrapped her arms around his neck and pulled him down for a kiss.

"You made it," she said.

"You, too," Petty said.

He hadn't seen her since L.A., since he'd put her on a plane to Memphis and set out for Florida. The plan had been to meet here for New Year's if everything worked out. Every day he'd worried there'd be a glitch, but now here she was next to him, and he never wanted to be away from her again.

The waiter came over to take his drink order.

"What'd you get?" he said to Tinafey.

"This here's a piña colada," she said. "It's delicious."

"I'll have one of those," Petty said to the waiter. He reached across the table with both hands and twined his fingers in Tinafey's. She looked great, her dark, dark eyes, those sexy lips, her nails painted bright red. She wore a gauzy wrap over a pink bikini and had a flower in her hair.

"I missed you," Petty said.

"I missed you, too," Tinafey said.

They watched two workers who were putting up decorations for the New Year's Eve party. There would be a band, Champagne, a countdown. One of the men hit his thumb and dropped his hammer. The other man laughed so hard that he let go of the ladder and doubled over.

"You take care of your business?" Tinafey said.

"I did," Petty said.

"And how you doin' otherwise?" Tinafey said. She was talking about Sam.

"It comes out of nowhere sometimes, knocks me on my ass," Petty said. "But I'm doing all right."

"And the bad dreams?"

"Less and less. What about you? How are you doing?"

Tinafey shrugged. "Nobody in the world knows where I am," she said. "I disappeared."

"Same here," Petty said.

"It's interestin'. It's excitin'."

Petty sat back and took in the view. Perfect waves slammed into the sand not fifty yards away, but swimming was prohibited because of the treacherous currents, which could drag a man under in seconds. Luckily, swimming was the last thing on his mind.

"You want to lay in the sun for a while after lunch, then go to the room? Or go to the room, then lay in the sun?" Tinafey said.

"Guess," Petty said.

He felt Tinafey's bare foot in his lap.

"I'm guessin' the room," she said.

"Tinafey, Tinafey, Tinafey," he said. "You read my mind."

She took her toes out of his crotch and had a sip of her drink.

"Yvonne," she said.

"What?" Petty said.

"Call me Yvonne."

"Okay," Petty said. He knew this was a big deal, her letting him use her real name, but he also knew it would embarrass her if he called attention to it, so he played it cool.

"You could be a model, you know that?" he said.

"Shit, son, that line is tired as hell," Yvonne said. "You're gonna have to do better than that."

The waiter delivered Petty's drink. He lifted the glass for a toast.

"To us," he said.

"And to everybody else," Yvonne said.

Sure, Petty thought. *Why not?* To everybody else. To Sam and Joanne, to Beck and the French kids, to poor Tony and the cowboy, who got caught in the middle, to Hug and Carrie, and—you know what? What the hell—to Don and even fucking Avi, to the lucky and the unlucky, the swindlers and the swindled, the living and the dead. To everybody.

Acknowledgments

Thank you to my team: Henry Dunow, Sylvie Rabineau, Jill Gillett, and Peter Dealbert. Thank you to Asya Muchnick and everyone at Mulholland Books. And thank you to Bryan "Breezy" Petty for the inspiration.

About the Author

Richard Lange is the author of the story collections *Dead Boys* and *Sweet Nothing* and the novels *This Wicked World* and *Angel Baby*. He is the recipient of a Guggenheim Fellowship, the International Association of Crime Writers' Hammett Prize, a Dagger Award from the Crime Writers' Association, and a Rosenthal Family Foundation Award from the American Academy of Arts and Letters. He lives in Los Angeles.

You've turned the last page.

But it doesn't have to end there . . .

If you're looking for more first-class, action-packed, nail-biting suspense, join us at **Facebook.com/ MulhollandUncovered** for news, competitions, and behind-the-scenes access to Mulholland Books.

For regular updates about our books and authors as well as what's going on in the world of crime and thrillers, follow us on **Twitter@MulhollandUK**.

There are many more twists to come.

MULHOLLAND:
You never know what's coming around the curve.